*It's a cold, cold winter in North Dakota when the Rough Riders come to roost...*

Washington Stewart used to be James Singleton, a drug dealing murderer now in the witness protection program. As Singleton he was shot in the face by a mobster (*Eddie's World*, 2001) and now is playing ball with the FBI as Stewart. Instead of a life sentence, he's given a new identity and another chance. If he helps the Feds sting a Las Vegas heroin connection running through Missouri and North Dakota, he'll keep his new life, courtesy of Uncle Sam.

But Stewart has his own plans, made with an air force colonel looking to get rid of his wandering wife. The colonel stumbled upon bundles of smuggled Afghani heroin and he sets up a scheme of his own to cash in. But he needs Stewart's help to do it, who still has a score to settle with the man who disfigured him for life. No problem, Stewart thinks, but before he can dodge the FBI, he has to deal with one of the NYPD detectives who came after him when he was Singleton. There's too much money, too much crime, and too much murder for anything to work out quite like anyone thinks it will.

## Charlie Stella Bibliography

Eddie's World (December, 2001, Carroll & Graf)
Jimmy Bench-Press (December, 2002, Carroll & Graf)
Charlie Opera (December, 2003, Carroll & Graf)
Cheapskates (March, 2005, Carroll & Graf)
Shakedown (June, 2006, Pegasus)
Mafiya (January, 2008, Pegasus)
Johnny Porno (April, 2010, Stark House)
Rough Riders (July, 2012, Stark House)

# ROUGH RIDERS
## BY CHARLIE STELLA

STARK
HOUSE

**Stark House Press • Eureka California**

ROUGH RIDERS

Published by Stark House Press
4720 Herron Road
Eureka, CA 95503, USA
griffinskye3@sbcglobal.net
www.starkhousepress.com

ISBN: 1-933586-39-7
ISBN-13: 978-1-933586-39-7

Cover design by David Terrenoire
Additional design and text layout by Mark Shepard, SHEPGRAPHICS.COM
Proofreading by Rick Ollerman
Director, Author Rights Agency: Svetlana Pironko

The publisher would like to add his thanks Rick Ollerman for all his work on
this project.

PUBLISHER'S NOTE

First Stark House Press Edition: July 2012

0 9 8 7 6 5 4 3 2 1

## Dedication

Amici:

Way back in the 8th grade, when I was attending St. Jude's Catholic School in Canarsie, I was a chubby, pimply-faced kid without much confidence, especially around girls. One day, I think when a few of us skipped school and headed to Neponsit Beach in Brooklyn to pre-celebrate our upcoming graduation, after tossing a football around and getting bored, most of the guys paired up with their girlfriends and walked their separate ways. It was awkward and embarrassing. I was the kid who didn't have a girlfriend. Then, out of nowhere, the most attractive girl in our class (she was actually very beautiful) suddenly took my hand and led me down to the water. It was all she did, take my hand and walk with me; a gesture of kindness I have never forgotten to this day (nor ever will). Her name was Karen Scanlon. I used to deliver the Long Island Press to her house. Her family was among the best tippers I had. Her younger brother and I used to toss footballs around for a while until I went off to high school. It was during high school everyone seemed to go their own way. Such is life.

I learned a few years after returning from college in North Dakota that Karen had tragically died in a car accident. I had always wanted to thank her for that day she took my hand and walked with me. Recently I was telling my wife the above story and we both decided that this book should be dedicated to Karen and the beautiful memory she left me. I can only hope her family, should they ever see this, or read this book, doesn't think this dedication anything less than a sincere return gesture of kindness. This is just a crime novel and Karen's memory deserves so much more than anything I can ever offer.

With that in mind, for Karen Scanlon.

## Acknowledgments

Rough Riders was first written about ten years ago as a sequel to my first crime novel, *Eddie's World*. Much of it takes place in the great state of North Dakota, where I originally attended college on a football scholarship. More importantly, it was where I met Dave Gresham, an English professor who turned me on to both education and writing and probably saved me from my incredible and relentless ability to screw up my life. Minot University was called Minot State College back in the day and although I and some of my New York teammates found our way into more trouble than one might imagine possible, it was a great place for a few city kids to attend college. It certainly made a huge difference in my life.

So, thanks to my fellow New York teammates: big Jim LaCugna (a.k.a., *The Fonz* and my roommate), Louis Rubio, Gary Barton, Gary Ohriner and Kerry McIntyre. We were the legendary New Yorkers; always in trouble (*Animal House* had nothing on us), but we always appreciated and mostly enjoyed our time there.

Thanks also to Chuck Kramer, the best linebacker I ever played with and an all American who led the nation in tackles his senior season. Chuck could hit like a freight train and often did. He was also one of the nicest guys you'll ever meet. He kept us employed up there hauling furniture around, I think to help keep us out of trouble.

Professional thanks, as always, to Peter Skutches, my first editor on the original *Rough Riders*. Because I turned down an offer from my original publisher long ago, I had to do some catch-up writing on the novel for its 2012 publication with Stark House Press. Some of the rewriting was fun, some of it very tough and time consuming, but it's always great to have help and I had quite a bit. A personal thanks to author, Ben Whitmer (*Pike*), for introducing me to Mr. Ward Churchill. Mr. Churchill provided some important fact checking on Native American references and also helped with the editing of this novel. Author and editor, Merle Drown (*The Suburbs of Heaven*), did the follow-up final editing, of which there was quite a bit because of all that was added and replaced since the original manuscript was written ten years ago. And Rick Ollerman, the Stark House eye, for his careful overseeing of this project.

Thanks to my agent, Svetlana Pironko.

Thanks to Jim (Doc) Nyland for his help with the guns yet again.

Thanks to David Terrenoire for the cover design. Please visit Dave's website at undercoverpublishing.com.

And thanks, of course, to my wife, Ann Marie, for pretty much everything that's been good in my life since we first met.

> *in te, vivo ravviso il sogno* (if I could see you in a dream)
> *ch'io vorrei sempre sognar* (I'd dream forever!)
> *O Soave Fanciulla, La Boheme*

And Rigoletto, our wonder dog.

# ROUGH RIDERS

## BY CHARLIE STELLA

## Part I

## Chapter 1
## Port Washington, New York; Billings/Miles City, Montana

Detective Dexter Greene looked both ways on Port Washington Boulevard, squinted at his former partner and said, "Isn't this the same neighborhood—"

"Eddie Senta, yeah," Alex Pavlik said. "About six blocks back the other way."

Greene took in the boulevard a few seconds. "And here we are all over again."

Ten years earlier there had been a hostage situation involving a Russian mobster, a federal informant in the witness protection program and a man Pavlik had suspected of killing three people during a Manhattan office burglary. Shots had been fired. The Russian had been killed, a fifteen year old boy had been wounded and the federal witness had been shot through an eye. It was Pavlik's last case working homicide with his former partner.

Today Greene was there as a favor in case there was trouble with the local police.

Pavlik motioned toward the two police cruisers blocking a gas station parking area twenty yards ahead. A tall man wearing a jogging suit and New York Jets sweatshirt was being handcuffed by one policeman while another stood guard, his weapon drawn.

"That clown there is filing false insurance claims and banging a personal trainer and some other woman from a local gym," Pavlik said. "He stopped for gas, and I was stupid enough to approach him with a deal that would keep him from going to jail and maybe save his marriage."

Greene spotted the welt under the tall man's right eye. "That guy there? The one you hit?"

"I didn't hit him," Pavlik said. "He got that from the locals. I put him in a half nelson is all I did. He took a swing at one of the uniforms and got tagged by the one with the gun."

Hot from the mild winter weather, Greene removed his sports coat and squinted toward the man in handcuffs. "This the guy I moonlighted on last week? The one from Great Neck? What he get, a haircut?"

"Crew cut it looks like," Pavlik said. "He's supposed to be out on disability. Ran a local marathon two weeks ago. Dumbass used his name, was in all the papers. Filed for permanent disability two months ago. He's from Great Neck but one of his girlfriends lives here in Port Wash."

"Marathons, the gym and two girlfriends, he should get some kind of medal."

"I tried to talk the dumb bastard into dropping the insurance claim, which was all they were looking for, the insurance company, but he had to take a swing at me. I calmed his ass down fast enough, but then he took a swing at one of the cops. There's nothing I can do for him now."

A sergeant with the Port Washington police approached. Greene showed his badge and introduced himself. The two men walked back toward the police cruisers.

Pavlik let out a long breath of frustration as he watched his former partner with the sergeant. Nine years into a forced retirement and here he was chasing insurance frauds, runaways, and cheating spouses. Although this job had been easy enough, less than two weeks of actual labor, he found the work boring. He wasn't sure how much longer he could stay with it. The alternative, what many of his fellow NYPD retirees were doing, working security in Manhattan office buildings, seemed even more mundane.

Pavlik missed real police work; the frustrating pursuit of justice and the rare rewards it sometime yielded. Working private investigations had become tough on his ego. He'd already had enough of it before having to duck a wild punch this morning.

Greene was on his way back, alone now. Pavlik waited for the verdict without expression.

"You're off the hook here," Greene said. "So long as you're willing to support what you said you saw from the knucklehead they cuffed."

"In case he files a complaint," Pavlik said.

"Which he probably won't now they cuffed him," Greene said. "They're gonna take him back to their station and explain it to him. He has half a brain, he'll take it on the chin and they'll let him walk. You got him fooling around on his wife, I suspect he'll drop his phony insurance claim as well."

"I hate this shit," Pavlik said.

"Be grateful you have it. I know I am. Between you and Russo working this private stuff my moonlighting career is what's paying my nut. And now I have a wedding to look forward to, so don't be hanging up your 'gone fishing' sign yet."

"How are the girls?" Pavlik asked.

"Expensive."

Pavlik smiled. "Seriously," he said.

"The one getting married or the one dating? Take your pick."

"Okay, I get it," Pavlik said. "But speaking of fishing, you ever go?"

"Not with a gun to my head," Greene said. "I don't like water or boats. I want fish I go to the Red Lobster. Why?"

"Aelish wants me to take her."

"Why?"

"It's an Irish thing. She used to go all the time when she was a kid she says. She went a few weeks ago with a cousin off one of the charters in Sheepshead Bay. Came home with a fish the size of a small kid. A cod she said it was. We got enough in the freezer to feed a small country."

"You've never done it, don't start now," Greene said. "Not this time of the year anyway. It might be warm here now, today, but it won't be on the water. Weather changes like that on the water." He snapped his fingers for emphasis. "Put it off until spring, maybe she'll forget."

Pavlik motioned toward the uniforms. The cop that had hit the man in cuffs waved. Pavlik acknowledged him with a nod.

"Well, at least you've got a friend here now," Greene said. "In case you're caught speeding or something."

"Just what I always wanted," Pavlik said, "another one like you."

Greene said, "Who said I was your friend?"

□ □ □

Washington Stewart pulled up alongside a white station wagon with North Dakota plates and lit a Marlboro. He'd made the eight hour overnight drive from Lake Sakakawea, North Dakota, to Billings, Montana, to catch up with Colonel Robert Schmidt. The colonel was also a medical doctor and had contracted to have his wife killed more than three months ago. Right then, watching the fool go through a series of stretching exercises outside in the freezing cold, all Stewart wanted to do was sleep. He had one other appointment before he could put his head to pillow, but it wasn't for another hour. It wouldn't be too bad if he could kill the hour inside the warmth of his Dodge Ram, he was thinking, but he knew he'd fall asleep within minutes if he didn't step outside and let the frigid air wake him up.

The temperature outside had yet to climb above five degrees. He kept the heat running high while Schmidt, dressed in heavy sweats, gloves, and a wool hat, stretched his quadriceps doing full lunges while holding small dumbbells in each hand.

"Man's a lunatic," Stewart said, then yawned long and loud. A strong gust of wind shook the Dodge Ram enough to keep Stewart from closing his eyes. When he looked at Schmidt again, he saw the colonel had spotted him and was waving.

Stewart buttoned up his jacket, pulled on his gloves, donned a wool hat, then adjusted his plastic face mask in the rearview mirror before stepping out into the cold. He moved quickly across the parking lot as a second wind gust moved him a few feet to his right. Stewart dipped a shoulder into the wind and fought his way through it. He smirked as the colonel went through his stretching routine as if he were on a beach somewhere, not a care in the world.

"You couldn't find a warmer place to do this?" Stewart called out.

Schmidt let go of the dumbbells and squatted down with his hands out to his sides. He held the position a moment before coming back up, stretching his arms out straight, then squatting again. They were outside a fence surrounding the Billings Central Catholic High School track. The track teams, both men and women, were warming up inside the oval. The runners wore heavy sweats with hoods.

Stewart jammed his gloved hands deep inside the pockets of his winter coat as he approached Schmidt from behind. The colonel was bent at the waist in mid-stretch when he acknowledged an upside-down Stewart.

"You're out of your element here," Schmidt said. "Brothers don't like the cold much, do you?"

"This one don't," Stewart said.

"Does that mask stick to your skin? That has to be painful if it does."

Stewart had a thick scar running from his left collarbone up his neck to his chin. He wore a black plastic face mask that covered a missing eye and disfigured cheek. He unconsciously adjusted the mask.

"Ever trick or treat with that thing?" Schmidt said.

"See that," Stewart said. "You a comedian, too. Doctor and a comedian."

Schmidt straightened up. A thin man with rough features, he had short, dirty-blond hair and blue eyes. At sixty-one he had remained in good physical condition.

Stewart pointed to the local high school logo, a ram's head, on the front of Schmidt's wool hat. "You a fan?"

"My wife went to this school. I thought it would be nice if I picked up a few things and brought them back as presents."

"Except she be dead when you get there."

Schmidt extended both arms straight ahead and performed a slow deep knee bend. "It's the thought that counts," he said on the way back up.

Both men watched two girls run sprints around the near curve in the track.

"They should be doing that inside," Stewart said.

"At least it's sunny," Schmidt said. "Be ten degrees colder the sun wasn't out."

Stewart waited for the colonel's full attention. "You up here, I have to assume our product is back at the base."

Schmidt stretched his arms one at a time behind his neck. "Something goes down, I'm not there, I'm not involved," he said.

"Something I might've done?"

"Something anybody might've done."

"Somebody I might've tipped off?"

"You're the man with two identities."

Stewart removed his face mask enough for Schmidt to see the disfigured cheek. He said, "Two identities, huh? You think that make a difference with this face?"

Washington Stewart was also James Singleton. His name had been changed when he reentered the witness protection program seventeen months earlier. Stewart, as Singleton, had been working undercover in the program when he was nearly killed during his first attempt to flee the country ten years ago.

Schmidt looked away from Stewart's face to watch another pair of girls run sprints.

"When you get in?" he asked.

Stewart replaced the face mask. "This morning."

"I'd like to make sure everything is kosher before I return."

"This a pilot brought it in?"

"You really need to know?"

"I need to know when to pick it up."

"After a certain situation is resolved," Schmidt said.

Schmidt had contracted Stewart to kill his wife in exchange for a split on Afghanistan heroin. Several months ago an Air Force combat pilot returned with several duffel bags loaded with the uncut heroin. Storing duffel bags in a grounded HH-60G Pave Hawk helicopter was the first stage of the pilot's plan to move the product off the base, but he was killed in a car accident. Schmidt found the duffel bags by accident, saw what they contained and removed them without incident.

Schmidt and Stewart planned to leave the country together in a week.

Now Schmidt pointed to the station wagon in the parking lot adjacent to the athletic fields. "There's a bag in the trunk with the explosives," he said. "You can trigger them from a remote site or set them by timer. There's enough incendiary action to turn most armored cars into a briquette. The trunk is open. Just lift the latch."

Stewart said, "Your wife leave yet?"

"Sometime today probably. She'll stop to pick up a few things on the way."

"She let people know she's going away?"

"I'm sure she's told her friends."

"And she told you she's going to Canada, right?"

"She told everybody she's going to Canada. But she's not. She's going to Mohall to fuck her new boyfriend."

"Except the man don't exist."

"She doesn't know that."

"You sure?"

"I have her on tape. She's all excited about meeting Private Lester Gooden."

Private Lester Gooden was an Internet phantom Stewart had created to lure the doctor's promiscuous wife into an extramarital tryst.

Schmidt handed Stewart a single key on a ring. "Mohall is about ten miles from the Canadian border. She rented the trailer last week. Paid cash. The last one on the lot."

"I guess we in business," Stewart said.

Schmidt bent at the waist to touch his toes. He spoke with his head tucked. "Your sponsor set a date yet?"

"No, but it's close. I can tell 'cause the man is getting antsy. Trying to keep tabs all of a sudden."

Schmidt glanced around the area. "He keeping tabs now?"

Stewart smirked under the mask. "I know what I'm doing," he said. "He in Missouri."

Stewart was working a sting for federal agents. He hoped to use the situation as a diversion for his second attempt to escape the country. Schmidt's Air Force connections were an integral part of the plan.

"And my wife?" Schmidt asked. "That tonight or tomorrow?"

"You really need to know?"

Schmidt rubbed himself through his sweatpants. "It excites me."

There it was, the man acting weird again.

"You do that shit, I don't know you're kidding or not."

Schmidt stopped rubbing himself. "Have you been baiting her?"

"Intimately."

"Tape it?" asked Schmidt, before he closed his eyes and took a long, deep breath. "I like listening when she's flirting on the phone."

The doctor's body language unnerved Stewart. "That get you off, listening like that?"

Schmidt answered without opening his eyes. "Sometimes."

"What about the other times?"

"I don't get jealous, if that's what you mean."

"Except you want me to whack her."

"Because she's dishonest," Schmidt said, opening his eyes now. "Because she did things behind my back. Because she's a cheater."

"She's excess baggage you won't need once we out the country. That's reason enough."

Schmidt closed his eyes again. "I get off when she lies to me," he said. "If you want to know the truth, it's what turns me on."

"That's more than I need to know."

"I like catching her without letting her know," Schmidt said. "I like it when she thinks she's outsmarting me." Then he opened his eyes and said, "Gives me wood."

The man was a psycho, Stewart thought. "Seriously," he said, "not my business."

Schmidt was eyeballing Stewart then. He said, "So long as I have those tapes, I'll never need another woman."

Stewart held both hands up as he stepped back. "You need to pull the plug here. You weirdin' now."

"Next time don't ask."

□ □ □

Stewart had checked into a Miles City motel room after the two-hour, twenty minute drive from Billings. When the man he was waiting for arrived with a bag of food from McDonald's, Stewart was in the middle of confirming his phantom date with Michelle Schmidt on his laptop. Roger Daltry stood inside the motel room doorway in silence.

"You waiting for a tip, you gonna grow a beard first," Stewart told him.

Daltry was a short black man with bad acne scars. He was wrapped in several layers of clothing under a heavy, double-X hooded United States Air Force sweatshirt. He set the bag of fast food on the small table and pulled off his gloves and wool hat.

Stewart had set the laptop on the bed. He was on his knees facing it, waiting for a reply from Mrs. Schmidt.

"You get mine without cheese?" he asked.

"Two with and two without," Daltry said before pulling off the sweatshirt.

"You get the milk shake?"

"Got it."

"Vanilla?"

"Vanilla."

Stewart turned to Daltry. "You checked, or you just took what they gave you? They do that sometime, give you whatever they got. Strawberry, for instance. I don't like strawberry."

Daltry checked the bag with the shakes and pulled out two chocolate. "Shit," he said.

"See what I'm saying?"

"You want, I can go back."

Stewart glanced at the laptop screen and saw there was a message.

"Hold it," he said.

*'Can't wait,'* the Internet message read.

"That's what you think," Stewart said. He powered off the laptop, stood up from the floor and then grabbed his cigarettes from the night table.

"You want me to go back?" Daltry asked again.

"Huh? No, I can deal with chocolate. Give it here."

Daltry handed Stewart the shake. Stewart set it on the night table.

"Thing is..." he said, taking a seat on the bed, "you'll wanna be more careful when you get to New York. You go to take a man out, you can't fuck up like with the shake."

Daltry peeled off another layer of clothes, sat at the small table near the door and unwrapped one of his burgers.

"For one thing, the man is no slouch," Stewart said. He pulled a cigarette from the pack. "He can handle himself. You get there, you get right to it. Go from the airport to the address and get it done. Make sure."

"I'm bringing somebody," Daltry said. He took his first bite from the burger. "Indian dude," he said while chewing. "Big sucker."

Stewart lit the cigarette. "For backup or to do the job?" he asked. "There's a difference."

Daltry shrugged.

Stewart pointed a finger and said, "See, that's what bothers me about motherfuckers. Too laid-back about it all. Don't think things out. Walk into a McDonald's and order shakes from some kid just breakin' his or her first pimples, got bullshit on their mind and you let them give you what they think you ordered. They don't check and you don't check. I order vanilla, you bring back chocolate. You see what I'm saying?"

"I said I'd go back, you want," Daltry said.

"You did, didn't you?"

Daltry shrugged again.

Stewart opened the night table drawer next to the bed and pulled out a Glock 9mm. He pointed it at Daltry's face.

"I tell you what," he said, "the next time you shrug something off, I'll blow a fuckin' hole in your head. How's that?"

Daltry froze mid-chew.

Stewart held the pose another long moment before setting the Glock on the end of the bed closest to Daltry. He said, "You get to the airport in Newark, you gonna have time to kill before the work. Don't spend it in some bar drinking. Stay focused. Bring whoever the fuck you wanna bring, but you kill Eddie Senta and his skinny ass wife and you don't make no mistakes. Understand?"

Daltry nodded.

"Say it," Stewart said.

"I kill Eddie Senta and his wife and I don't make mistakes," Daltry said.

"What time you leave?"

"Twelve-thirty. Two stops on the way. Supposed to be in Newark seven-thirty. You said it be a couple hours to Long Island."

"If you don't get lost."

"We figure before midnight. We flyin' back from LaGuardia, but that's the next morning. It's not far from Port Washington, the airport. 'Least not on the map. We take care of business, drive someplace close to LaGuardia, take a cab and start back. Should be in Bismarck tomorrow night, the morning after."

"I hope you know not to use your name," Stewart said. "Robert Daltrey too easy to remember. Singer for a rock group back in the sixties, *The Who*. People see a black man with the same name, they'll remember. Make sure your Indian don't use it, your real name."

"I wish I got half the bitches that white boy got. He the one killed himself, right?"

"That's Morrison you thinking of and nobody knows he killed himself or not. Daltry with *The Who*, I said. He still around. Morrison, Jim Morrison, he the dead one. He was *The Doors*."

Daltry looked confused. "Whatever," he said. "I bet they both got themselves boo coo pussy."

Stewart looked at Daltry a long moment.

"What?" Daltry said.

"Ask me, the dead one was half a fag," Stewart said.

"One with *The Who*?"

Stewart's eyebrows furrowed. "The fuck is wrong with you?" he said. "I just said Daltrey with *The Who*."

Daltry started to shrug, remembered not to and nodded instead.

Stewart sighed. The dumbasses he had to work with, he was thinking. "Change we can believe in, huh?" he said.

Daltry smiled. "That our boy, Obama," he said with sudden enthusiasm. "Our brother from another mother."

"A white mother, dumbass."

"Huh?"

Stewart rolled his eyes. "You remember the apple pie?"

Daltry pulled two apple pies from another bag. "Right here," he said with a smile.

Stewart frowned again.

"What?" Daltry asked.

Stewart said, "I told you cheese Danish."

## Chapter 2
## Queens/Port Washington, New York

"You do realize the old man didn't have to ask," Joe Sharpetti Jr. said. "Especially now he's away again. These are his good graces I'm conveying here."

"I appreciate the good graces," Eddie Senta said, "and no offense, but I'm still pissed off at your father."

They were having dinner in a connected restaurant on Cross Bay Boulevard in Queens. They were given a private booth in the back with windows facing the water. Sharpetti was the son of Eddie's former street rabbi with the Vignieri crime family. He was there to make a final offer to Eddie to return to work for the beleaguered crew. Eddie wasn't interested. He picked at the spicy fried *calamari* and sautéed *scungilli* while the wiseguy continued his pitch.

"Yeah, pop said you might be upset," Sharpetti said. "And he wishes he never did it, that thing you're pissed off about. Was one of the two people did the job gave him up. The prick even showed the feds where they buried your friend and some other MIAs."

"Bad karma," Eddie said.

"Huh?"

"When shit comes back to bite you in the ass."

Sharpetti looked confused. "Whatever," he said. "I asked him for names to run this offshore thing and he mentioned you, but then he warned me you probably wouldn't be interested. I asked him was it worth meeting and he said, yeah, sure, why not, you never know."

"And here we are."

"Except you're turning us down a third time."

Eddie set his fork down. "Look, I'm forty-eight years old," he said. "I've been legit the last nine years. I'm used to it now. And I still read the papers enough to see your thing is bad news. Why your father is in jail at seventy-two instead of home playing with his grandkids."

Sharpetti sat back with both arms out. "This another mob is dead speech I gotta here? I hear it from my wife a dozen times a day."

"Maybe you should listen to her."

"Yeah, right. The hell else I'm gonna do?"

Eddie picked up his fork and speared a *calamari* ring. "You obviously didn't listen to your father," he said. "I'm sure he didn't want this for you."

"No, he didn't," Sharpetti said. "And he mentioned that too about you. How you wore a couple different hats. But I'm not a computer guy. All I know is the streets. I don't have the luxury of changing careers now, not with the way things are. I'm too busy trying to hold shit together."

Eddie wiped his mouth with a napkin. "Look, don't get me wrong. I'm probably more boring than not, but there is something to having piece of mind. Coming home nights knowing I don't owe favors to people I can't trust. There's something to that."

Sharpetti took offense. "You saying you can't trust me?"

"Kid, I don't even know you. I trusted your father and so did he trust me. But like I said, I read the papers. I doubt it'll be long before the mob has its own reality show. Your thing right now, it's a train wreck."

Sharpetti's eyebrows furrowed. "The old man said you didn't use a filter."

"I mean no offense," Eddie said, "but you gotta admit, a lot more guys are making deals than holding their water. Christ, even the bosses flip now. How the hell you supposed to maintain order with that going on? You gotta be suspicious of the clowns you can recruit, the guys claim they want in."

Sharpetti wiped his mouth and frowned. "Alright, I can see I drove from Manhattan to waste my time," he said. "Fair enough."

"Sorry to put you out, but I would've told you the same thing over the phone."

Sharpetti nodded a few times. "These fuckin' feds," he said. "They went after the corrupt cocksuckers they work for in government, or those scumbags on Wall Street, they went after them the same way they come after us, this country be a lot better off."

"Except they're the ones with the power," Eddie said. "They aren't about to go after themselves. It is what it is."

Sharpetti took a sip of water. "Maybe," he said. He wiped his mouth with a napkin. "I'll tell you this much, I had seven hundred billion to lend out, I wouldn't have let the jerkoffs borrowing it set the terms. This jerk-off president we have. Got nothing to do with his being half a shine either. Motherfuckers on Wall Street, the shit they got away with, and the feds go after us for whacking each other?"

"You guys stay in the spotlight with violence," Eddie said. "People like the drama. They like seeing headlines, pictures of holes in the ground with a bunch of bodies from ten, twenty years ago. They see that stuff, they ignore the bankers."

Sharpetti wasn't hearing him. He said, "Fuckin' guys ran those banks like a casino, lost their stake and then they got rewarded for it. Seven hundred billion. The moron gave it away like fuckin' Santa Claus."

Eddie winked at Sharpetti. "And nobody on Wall Street went to jail," he said.

Sharpetti's face tensed. He dropped his napkin on his plate and stared at Eddie.

"It's the truth," Eddie said.

Sharpetti frowned again. He stood up and pointed at the table. "You mind picking up the tab on this?" he said. "I already wasted enough time here I could've been earning."

"No problem," Eddie said. He went to stand up and extend a hand but Sharpetti had already turned his back and was on his way out.

☐ ☐ ☐

An hour later Eddie was reading a book in a coffee shop near where he lived. He'd stopped there to pick up a slice of cake for his wife and saw he was still early. He was going to read one more chapter and head home when his cell phone rang.

Eddie saw it was Diane and answered, "Hey."

"How'd it go?" she asked.

"It's over. No problem."

"He wasn't angry?"

"Not at all. The kid wasn't looking to waste time or stroke me. He's no dope. He saw me for what I'd be, another headache he doesn't need."

"Why didn't you call?"

"You said you were busy until nine. Why I picked tonight to meet with him."

"Where are you?"

"Coffee shop on Main Street," Eddie said. "I was reading. Been here half an hour. It's a good thing I took that book with me."

"The one I bought you?"

"*The Guards*, yeah. I'm enjoying it. A private investigator hates his mother, loves his father. The author, this Ken Bruen guy, looks like he can put on a few pounds." Eddie could hear her chewing. "What are you eating?"

"Licorice."

"Then you won't want the slice of cake I was gonna pick up."

"I keep hearing noises."

"Probably you're chewing."

"No, really."

"I could skip the cake and come straight home."

"There it goes again."

"There goes what?"

"Like glass breaking. Probably the chimes next door. But it sounds like glass breaking."

"I'll skip the cake, be home in five—"

"The raspberry chocolate?" Diane said.

"It's what you like, no?"

"Get the cake. I'll have it in the morning."

"Anything else?"

"I'm wearing blue."

Eddie had named her lingerie by color. Blue was his favorite.

"I'll get the cake in the morning," he said. "I'm on my way."

□ □ □

Roger Daltry kept his left hand on Joseph Kincaid's shoulder to maintain his balance while quietly climbing the carpeted stairway. He held a Glock 9mm in his right hand. The two men had broken into the house a few minutes earlier. It was just past one in the morning.

Daltry wore a full-face ski mask to conceal his identity. He froze at the top of the stairway when he heard footsteps coming from one of the second-floor bedrooms. When he heard a doorknob turn, he extended his arm with the gun pointed down the hall.

The door didn't open. After a few seconds the footsteps headed away from the door. Daltry stepped onto the second-floor landing and quickly crossed the hall. He pressed his back against the wall and listened again. A night-light in the hallway straight ahead cast a silhouette much bigger than his smallish frame.

Joseph Kincaid, the Native American ex-convict Daltry had brought along to help, moved up onto the landing when Daltry signaled to him with his free hand. Both men heard the footsteps again, then the doorknob turning. Daltry held the Glock up and stepped toward the door.

□ □ □

It was to be a surprise for Eddie; the night he learned he would be a father again.

She had been eager to tell him since she first found out earlier in the day. It had been even harder keeping it from her parents and friends.

Earlier she'd picked up a bottle of champagne for Eddie and a bottle of apple cider for herself. She'd also bought two Waterford flutes so they would have something to remember this night forever. If all went as planned, Eddie would be happy to hear the news and they could make love.

He'd been against having another kid while his son from a previous marriage was young, but now that his son was abroad in graduate school, Eddie was more open to being a father again.

She was sure she heard another noise outside the bedroom after she rotated the champagne bottle in the bucket of ice. She crossed the bedroom to the door to listen, then remembered her cell phone was still on and stepped back to the night table to grab it. When she returned to the door this time, she was positive she'd heard something. She opened the door slowly and was startled to see a man in a ski mask holding a gun.

☐ ☐ ☐

"Wash was right," Roger Daltry said. He was looking at the woman on the bed, half naked in her tiny blue panties. "Except you too skinny."

"Please don't hurt me," the woman pleaded.

Daltry glanced at his partner. "Careful with that," he said.

Kincaid was drinking champagne from the bottle he'd just uncorked. The bubbling wine ran down his face onto his jacket.

Daltry held out his free hand. "Give some here," he said.

Kincaid handed him the bottle.

"What you think?" Daltry asked the woman before taking a sip. "We party until the man of the house gets home or what?"

Kincaid stood six foot six, weighed two hundred pounds and had spent twelve of his thirty-seven years incarcerated in correctional facilities in North Dakota and Canada. His face was scarred from self-inflicted burns and cuts. He smiled at Daltry's suggestion as he stared at the woman.

"Please," the woman begged. She pointed across the room at a pocketbook on her desk. "I have money in my purse. Take it."

"I come here for more than money," Daltry said as he made his way around the bed.

The woman cowered as he approached her. He grabbed her by an arm and spun her sideways on the bed. She tried to cross her legs but he was already there grabbing at her crotch. He tore her panties off.

Kincaid was opening his pants. Daltry saw him and held up a hand. "Get in line," he said. "Somebody got to stand guard."

The woman made a move to get off the bed and Daltry kicked her in the stomach. She gasped from the loss of air, then curled into a fetal position. Daltry poured champagne on her.

☐ ☐ ☐

Eddie Senta was nervous when he saw the car with New Jersey plates parked in the driveway. He looked through the driver's side window and saw a road atlas on the console, Port Washington circled.

When he saw the broken shards of glass in the side door, he removed his shoes and quietly stepped inside the house. He grabbed a baseball bat from the broom closet. Footsteps sounded in the master bedroom directly above him, followed by a loud slap.

Eddie ran for the stairs.

□  □  □

Daltry didn't want to hit the bitch so hard. Hell, he had wanted her awake while he raped her. Then she'd slapped him and he lost control. He'd used a sweeping backhand punch from left to right with the gun still in his grasp. The butt of the Glock slammed against her head just above her left temple and her head rose a few inches off the bed. She blinked wildly before her head dropped back down and she was unconscious.

Then the bedroom door flung open and a stocky man wielding a baseball bat was attacking Kincaid. By the time Daltry could react, it was too late. The bat caught Kincaid on the left side of his head. One of the Indian's eyes popped out of its socket.

Daltry shot the stocky man in the chest and got out of there.

## Chapter 3
## Mohall/Bismarck, North Dakota

Michelle Schmidt stood back from the small mirror in the trailer bathroom and examined her look. She turned her head to one side and reapplied the red gloss lipstick she had picked up at a Walmart on her way out of Minot earlier in the afternoon. A thick woman with full breasts and big brown eyes, she'd recently lost five pounds in anticipation of her Internet arranged date. When she was satisfied with the lip gloss, she adjusted the straps of her blue lace teddy and pulled down on the lingerie to expose more cleavage.

She had arrived at the trailer outside of Mohall a few hours early to prepare for the weekend tryst with Private Lester Gooden. After ten years of a marriage that had turned dull and a dozen unfulfilling extramarital affairs, Michelle had bought a computer. First she'd discovered the chat rooms that led to cybersex. When she was bored typing the sexual encounters she craved, Michelle moved on to meeting with men who'd emailed her pictures. To satisfy her attraction to black men, Michelle started flirting with a private stationed at the Minot Air Force base.

She had found private Gooden's emails both clever and charming and had decided to skip the prerequisite safety-first public lunch or dinner date. After speaking on the telephone a few times, they had planned the weekend-long tryst. She was excited as she slipped her feet into the black pumps she had grabbed from her bedroom closet back in Minot. She felt herself sweating and adjusted the thermostat to lower the heat inside the trailer. Outside it was ten degrees.

Michelle was playing a Lady Gaga CD and didn't hear the car when it pulled up outside the trailer. She gasped when she heard the knock on the door, took one last look in the small bathroom mirror, brushed her hair quickly and smoothed her teddy. She opened the trailer door and was confused when she saw a tall black man wearing a face mask that covered his left eye and extended down across his cheek.

Private Lester Gooden hadn't mentioned anything about a bad eye or a mask. Michelle cocked her head to one side and started to ask who he was when she was shot in the stomach. She folded at the waist from the impact of the bullet. She felt blood trickling out of her mouth as she slumped to the floor.

Then the man with the face mask was standing over her.

"Sorry," he said, just before he fired two more rounds and killed her.

□  □  □

Washington Stewart had left his ride where he'd planned to in Lansford on the way up to Mohall. He left the stolen car he'd used to drive from
Lansford to Mohall in the post office parking lot, walked three blocks on
Laurel Street and found the Dodge Ram exactly where he'd left it. He spent
the next few hours driving south to Bismarck to meet Roger Daltry at the
airport there. He watched from outside the baggage claim area until he
spotted the short man wearing a LeBron James, Miami Heat basketball jersey.

Ten minutes later they were on their way to the parking lot. "I hope you
smart enough to fly out of LaGuardia like you supposed to," Stewart said
to Daltry.

Daltry pulled at his jersey material. "Where I got this," he said. "Our
boy's jersey everywhere, man. They had a few Knicks on a couple hangars,
Stoudemire and Carmelo, but then half a wall of LeBron. That boy still be
killing, even after he fucked Cleveland over."

"You right about that. Prob'ly hundred niggers a day flying out New
York wearing LeBron."

The cold air was a shock when they stepped outside. The temperature
had dropped to two degrees. Their breath condensed upon contact with
the frigid air.

Stewart spoke over his right shoulder at Daltry. "We had some shit up
here you gonna need to handle."

Daltry was carrying a small gym bag that slapped against his right
thigh when they had to pass between parked cars. "What's that?"

Stewart unlocked the doors to his Dodge Ram and climbed inside the
cab. Daltry climbed into the passenger seat and set his gym bag on the
front floorboard.

"What happened?" Daltry asked.

Stewart started the engine, then turned the heat up. "You first," he said.

"Kincaid," Daltry said. "The Indian freaked."

Stewart waited for more. Daltry couldn't look him in the eye.

"That it? He freaked?"

"He too involved with the woman," Daltry said. "Saw her snatch and
went crazy. Had pussy on his mind the whole damn trip. Couldn't pay
attention."

"He couldn't or you couldn't?"

"That bitch too skinny for me, man. That was Kincaid."

"You're talking about Eddie Senta's wife, her snatch? The Indian saw it
how?"

"Tore off her robe," Daltry lied. "She wearing a bra and panties when she opened the door. He tore those off, too."

"He rape her?"

"Tried to," Daltry said. "Then she got loose and started to take off. I had to stop her. Kincaid wasn't watching the door."

"The man, Eddie Senta, he snuck up on you, that what you're saying? You had a gun, that big fuckin' Indian, but the man snuck up on you?"

"Your boy wasn't home when we got there," said Daltry, nervous now. He fumbled a pack of cigarettes onto the console. Stewart caught them and pulled one from the pack.

"Thanks," Daltry said. "Senta wasn't home we first got there. I went in with the Indian and we went upstairs, grabbed the woman. She all done up, too. Had a robe and some fancy panties and shit. Bottle of champagne in a bucket like she about to party. The Indian couldn't control himself."

"Cochise couldn't control himself, okay. What about you?"

"The man six-six, Wash. The Indian, I'm talkin' about. Had a fuckin' hunting knife like Daniel Boone. I let him have the bitch."

Stewart squinted at Daltry. "You could've knocked on the door, shot the woman, waited for the man, shot him and been on your way. You could've done that."

"We got in easy so we just went with it," Daltry said. "We didn't know he wasn't there. We went up the stairs quiet. She never knew it. She opened the bedroom door and there we were. She half naked in that robe, the way it was open. Kincaid went off, man. The Indian freaked."

"You keep sayin' that, 'he freaked,' but I still don't know what the fuck happened, do I?"

Daltry began to sweat. He removed his wool hat.

Stewart's eyes narrowed.

Daltry felt the stare and looked up. "What I just said, that's what happened."

"You shoot Eddie Senta?"

"Yeah, man," Daltry said, sensing some relief. "That was me. I shot him two times. Three maybe."

"Maybe?"

"It was crazy, Wash. I think so, yeah. Three times."

"He dead?"

"He should be. First one caught him in the chest. Took two more shots after that, he on the floor already."

"And?"

Daltry shook his head. "I don't know, man. I shot him, I know that."

"You shoot with a blindfold on?"

"Hey, it was scary, Wash. Kincaid on the floor, his eyeball out the sock-

et, blood all over the place. I shot the man and got out of there. I knew
there was no helping the Indian."

"He gonna die?"

"Probably."

"But you don't know."

"Wash, it was scary, man. Very scary."

"I don't suppose you shot the woman either?"

"She already unconscious. From Kincaid. Might be dead, too, all I know.
He hit her hard, knocked her out."

"I thought it was you stopped her?" Stewart said. "You confused or is it
me?"

"What? Oh, no, it was me stopped her, when she took off, but Kincaid
the one hit her. I think with that big ass knife he carrying, the back end.
The handle, I guess."

Stewart listed off his fingers. "She might be dead, the Indian might be
dead and Eddie Senta might be dead. Or they all alive. That what you're
telling me?"

Daltry started to shrug, saw the exposed half of Stewart's face start to
tense, and shook his head instead.

"It got out of hand, man."

"I have a mind take you out to Montana, the Rocky Mountains there,
and leave your dumb ass for grizzly bait," Stewart said. He let himself think
a moment, then added, "Meantime there's something happened back in
Minot while you playin' with yourself in New York."

Daltry was anxious to shift the conversation. "What happened there?"

"Some college kid overdosed."

Daltry tried for drama. "Uh-oh."

"You goddamned right, uh-oh," Stewart said. "And one of your flyboy
friends is selling in town. Nigger named Tyrone?"

"That's the guy I told you about from 'Lantic City," Daltry said. "He
servicing Minuteman IIIs. Came in from London six weeks ago. He about
to transfer over to Security Forces."

"That what they calling you now, Security Forces?"

"Used to be Military Police. Then we Air Police and now Security
Police. We have to know that shit, what we used to be called."

"You close with him, this Tyrone?"

"I know him. We met in Sioux Falls a few times before he come up to
Minot."

"He another fuckup?"

"He alright."

"You know that or you just blowing me off?"

"He okay."

Stewart could see Daltry was sweating. He turned down the heat. "You know the boy, forget him for the return trip you making in a few days."

"I'm going back to New York?"

Stewart stared at Daltry a moment, then said, "Unless you can kill Eddie Senta from here."

## Chapter 4
## Minot, North Dakota

Detective Dale Hehn had started digging the foxhole an hour before dawn. When he was finished chopping up the frozen ground, he dropped an old comforter on the dirt inside the hole for cushion and crawled inside. Hehn was part Norwegian, part German and half Sioux. He appeared somewhat younger than his forty-two years. At six feet and two hundred pounds, most of it muscle, Dale had to squeeze into a fetal position inside the foxhole. He covered himself with a blind he had built at the police station garage—a plywood board with brush stapled to one side. His face was covered with camouflage paint.

When he was settled inside the hole, he turned on his recording equipment and tested the radio connection between himself and the two undercover officers waiting in unmarked cars at either end of the parking lot. The wind added static to the connection.

"You guys hear me?" he said into the radio.

"Check," one officer responded.

"...a check," the other replied.

Dale's foxhole was settled along the grounds bordering the university football stadium parking lot. He had witnessed what he believed were two drug deals in the same location over the past few nights. A marine with special operations during the first Gulf War, he'd worked in Force Recon, as a scout/sniper and with reconnaissance battalions. Nineteen years later he was a fifteen-year detective with the Minot Police Department.

Now he looked through his night-vision binoculars and spotted a car approaching. A few minutes later a second car followed the first. Dale waited patiently in the cold foxhole, his eyes focused on the two cars as they pulled up alongside each other. He could see the silhouettes of the drivers through the windshields. It was a few minutes before both cars parked ten feet from the foxhole.

"Suspects have parked," Dale whispered into the recorder. "I'm not sure the recorder will pick them up with the wind up here, but they're close enough."

He heard the car doors open and the two men were soon audible to him. He pushed a recorder microphone out of the foxhole so it lay under covering brush.

One of the men outside the hole said, "It's too cold up here. We should meet down there next time, inside the student union building. I had a malted before I left work. Now I have a stomachache and the chills."

"You bring the money?" the other man asked.

"Two hundred, right?"

"Unless you want more."

"That's all I have, two hundred. Unless you can wait."

"Let's do this and get out of here."

The two men made the exchange and Dale spoke into the radio. "Bingo," he said.

Sirens sounded at each end of the parking lot as flashing lights illuminated the black sky. One of the men ran down a stairway that led to the football stadium at the bottom of the small hill. The other man froze.

Dale crawled out of the hole and shined the flashlight on his face. "Boo!" he yelled.

The man gasped, then stumbled backwards until he fell. He grabbed at the back of his pants and yelled, "Oh, God! Oh, no!"

□ □ □

"That kid really crap his pants?" Sergeant Don Ekroth asked.

Dale had just returned to the police station. He stepped out of his camouflage suit and feigned holding his nose. "Stunk up Freehan's cruiser no end," he said. "Go take a whiff for yourself."

"Oh, geez," Ekroth said. "The poor SOB."

"And all I did was say 'boo.'"

Ekroth chuckled. A bald man a few pounds overweight, he was a twenty-five year veteran of the Minot Police Department. He had thick eyebrows, wore metal framed glasses and usually chewed on a plastic coffee stirrer.

"Nothing to do with that heroin, though, I suppose," he said.

"No," Dale said. "It was cocaine this time. Cut stuff mostly. The seller we've busted before. Some dopey kid from Stanley. First time it was pot. The buyer was a surprise."

"The kid who couldn't hold it?"

"He was second team All-American last year in baseball. He's only a sophomore."

"From here?"

"Missoula."

"Montana? What the heck he come here for?"

"Married with children," Dale said as he folded the camouflage suit. "Wife's from Minot."

"That'll do it," Ekroth said.

"I already pressed them both about the Barron kid, but they didn't have a clue, either one. The kid from Stanley nearly shit himself too when I mentioned heroin."

"What about the baseball player?"

Dale shook his head. "He didn't live in the jock dorm," he said. "He didn't know who Nathan Barron was until he heard his name on the news."

"Speaking of which, the mother is coming in tomorrow morning," Ekroth said. "From Detroit."

"That has to be a nightmare," Dale said. "Poor woman."

"There's a contingent meeting her at the airport. People from the college, I guess."

"I hate this part of it."

"It's a shame alright," Ekroth said. "Kid goes off to college and dies, the mother gets to pick him up in a box. Damn shame."

Dale pointed to a clock high on the wall. "You staying through?" he said.

"Through and through," Ekroth said. "I'm home for a nap around noon but I'm back before five. You picking up that flyboy today or tomorrow?"

Dale took a deep breath. "Today is tomorrow," he said. "I think."

"I know what you mean."

"I'm not sure, tell you the truth," Dale said. He looked through the notebook on his desk. "Airman Tyrone Williams has been hanging around the truck stops on Fifty-two. He'll be carrying some heroin. A small amount, from what I was told to expect, but enough to book him? We shall see."

"Small fish catch big fish," Ekroth said.

Dale was pulling on his dungarees. "Let's hope so. Anyway, I'm not sure which day he'll be there. I've got someone at the diner to give me a call when he shows his face."

"That what the television shows call a CI?"

Dale smiled. "Something like that," he said. "It would be nice to find something out before this poor woman comes up tomorrow."

Ekroth sipped his coffee. "You get enough to bust them, these kids tonight?"

"Just enough," Dale said. "I almost wish I didn't. Especially the kid shit his pants. You'd think that would do it, eh? End his life of crime."

Ekroth winked and said, "It sure would end mine."

□ □ □

Dale went home to shower and catch a nap. When he was holding his wife in bed, he couldn't stop thinking about the woman who would come to claim her son's body the next day.

He had been around death before. He had smelled it firsthand and sometimes caused it, but the death he had experienced in war was expected and impersonal. For the woman from Detroit it couldn't be more personal.

*Mrs. Barron, I'm sorry to inform you that your son, Nathan, died last night....* Losing a son while he was away at college wasn't supposed to happen. Dale could feel his muscles tense as he pressed against his wife's back. He held Emily close. He kissed the back of her neck until she stirred, then leaned his head on his arm and watched her until she felt him watching and opened her eyes.

"You okay?" she asked.

"I'm fine," he said.

"You sure?"

"Not really," he said.

She reached back to touch him.

Dale said, "What time is your class today?"

"Eleven."

"Wake me before you leave."

She turned enough to kiss his forehead. "How about a little earlier?"

"I wish I had the energy. I'm exhausted."

"You're working a lot lately."

"I know. I'm sorry."

"We need to make some time."

"I will."

"I have a break at one. The departmental meeting is two thirty. I can meet you back here."

"I'll try."

Emily kissed his chin this time.

Dale closed his eyes. "I love you," he said.

"I love you, too," she said. She watched his eyes close and kept watching until she knew he was sleeping.

## Chapter 5
## New Hyde Park/Ossining/Queens, New York

Alex Pavlik glanced at his watch and saw visiting hours had begun. He headed through the lobby of Long Island Jewish Hospital where he'd been summoned by the wife of the man he had once believed was responsible for a Manhattan triple homicide. Two days earlier, he had been in the same neighborhood just six blocks from the house where Eddie Senta lived.

Pavlik wasn't sure what Senta's wife might want from him now, except she and her husband had been assaulted in their home again. From what he had learned from his former partner earlier in the morning, one of the perpetrators was a former convict from North Dakota. Eddie Senta had put the convict in a coma with a baseball bat.

Pavlik doubted there was much he could do for Diane Senta, but had agreed to meet with her from curiosity. Port Washington wasn't the kind of town that featured violent break-ins.

He stood at the foot of her hospital bed and did his best not to cringe. Her face was covered with ugly bruises. A gauze bandage was wrapped around half her head. Her lips were swollen, a hue of purple. "I'm very sorry," he said.

She struggled to maintain her composure. She swallowed hard a few times before she could speak. "I want that bastard to pay for this," she finally said. "I know it was him."

Pavlik knew who she meant. "James Singleton," he said.

"Yes," Diane said. She spoke slowly but with clarity. "I knew it was him the moment I saw those two animals."

"It could've been a break-in. You can't rule that out."

"It was him. I know it was James Singleton did this."

"The one in a coma," Pavlik said, "he's an Indian, Native American. He's from North Dakota. Detective Greene filled me in. Do you remember Detective Greene?"

Diane nodded. "Will he live?"

"The doctors don't think so. If he does, he'll be a vegetable."

"Good," she said. She reached for the cup of water. Pavlik handed it to her. She sipped slowly. "What about the other one?"

"He got away. But the police have good leads. They found the car he used in an airport lot. Stolen. He wasn't very careful. Left maps with your town circled in pen in the car. He'll turn up sooner or later."

"I don't trust the police," Diane said.

"They have more resources than I could ever have."

"I don't trust them. Or the FBI."

"I don't trust the FBI either."

"I'll pay whatever you want," she said. "All expenses. Anything. I want that son of a bitch to pay for what he did to us."

"I can't kill him, ma'am," Pavlik said. "As much as I'd like to, as much as he deserves it. I can't do much more than help build a case against him. If I can find him. If the police let me help. If the FBI doesn't stop me from looking. If it was him."

"It was him," she said. She sipped at the water again.

"The Indian was in the North Dakota penal system last year. He could've moved anywhere since then. The car the police found had New Jersey license plates."

Diane touched her stomach through the blankets. "I'm pregnant," she said.

Pavlik cringed.

"Eddie doesn't know. I was going to tell him last night. I bought champagne to celebrate. Those two animals drank the champagne. One of them poured it all over me while he was trying to rape me."

"Is the baby okay? Do they know?"

She started to sob. "They can't tell yet. He kicked me in the stomach. The one with the gun. In my stomach."

"I'm very sorry."

"Will you take the job?"

"I don't see how I can," he said. "If it was James Singleton behind this and he's still in the witness protection program, he's got a new name by now. It could become more frustrating than it's worth, trying to find him."

"What if he's not in the program?"

"I doubt he'd survive long on the outside. It wouldn't be long before he went back inside. I can check on that easy enough, but if he's in the program, his name won't come up."

Diane swallowed hard again. "Who else can I turn to?" she said. "You know the police won't do anything. The FBI was protecting the bastard."

"I don't know that I can get past them, the FBI."

"Please," she pleaded. "Or he gets away with it again."

Pavlik took a deep breath.

"I'll beg if you want."

"Ma'am...."

"Will you take the job?"

"I won't steal from you," Pavlik said.

He was looking at the bruises on her face while trying to imagine what kind of an animal would kick a pregnant woman in the stomach.

"You're our only chance to find this bastard," she said.

"If it becomes a waste of my time and your money, for whatever reason, I'll stop whatever I'm doing."

There were tears in her eyes now. "Thank you," she whispered.

"It might not have been him," Pavlik said.

"We both know it was."

"It could've been."

"If that man in the coma is from North Dakota, you know where to look."

"It's where he served time. He could've come from anywhere."

"You know what to do."

She was right. He did know what to do.

□ □ □

He asked a former friend on the force for information on the man James Singleton had testified against to earn his free pass for a life of crime and learned about Jamal Watkins, a mid-level dealer sentenced to serve fifteen years and currently doing his time in Ossining, New York.

When Pavlik sat across from the heavyset black man with broad shoulders and gold front teeth, he noticed how Watkins took his time before picking up the receiver on his side of the Plexiglas.

"Who you?" the convict asked.

"I'm a guy looking for Jimmy Singleton," Pavlik said. "I understand you knew him."

"You goddamn right I knew him, the rat, bitch-ass, motherfucka."

"Do you know where he is now?"

"I did he be dead."

"Do you know where he might be?"

"Who the fuck you to ask?"

"I used to be the law."

Watkins jerked a fist up and down. "I used to be a free man."

"I'd think you want somebody to find him."

"Only if they gonna kill him."

"Somebody has to find him first."

"It won't be me, I'm in here."

"Can you point somewhere? There anybody he dealt with he didn't snitch on?"

"You asking me, it means the law shut you out. How'm I supposed to know where the motherfucker is, I'm in here the last ten years?"

"I figured it was a waste of time, but I thought I'd give it a try."

"Yeah, well, you a stupid motherfucker."

"Except you're the one going back to your cage."

"Fuck you," Watkins said.

"Have a nice day," Pavlik said.

□ □ □

"Diane Senta is asking for a miracle I can't give her," he later told his girlfriend.

Pavlik had made the drive back to Brooklyn through the rush hour traffic. He was cranky from the delay but glad to be home. Aelish was cutting carrots. She had prepared another meal of the codfish she'd caught a few weeks earlier. Pavlik was tired of seeing it, much less smelling or eating it.

"Can you talk to Eddie Senta?" Aelish asked with a slight brogue.

"He's lucky to be alive. Still critical and might not make it."

"Then you'll be giving her hope."

"Like some charlatan selling an elixir."

"No, you lummox, like a former gold shield detective knows how to catch the bad guys."

"It's not my job anymore."

"Except you need something to do and this might be it."

Pavlik pointed to the fish laid out in a Pyrex dish. "Are you baking it or what this time, the cod?"

"Yes, with a topping. Seasoned bread crumbs."

"You sure you wanna get crazy like that, seasoned bread crumbs?"

Aelish stopped cutting the carrots. "You can order something, you don't want what I cook. And it's for your health, so you lose some weight. You've put on another ten pounds since Thanksgiving already."

Pavlik rubbed the small pouch that had formed above his waist. He looked down at the knuckles on his right hand and noticed one was swollen. He didn't remember banging it. He had boxed as an amateur and had five professional bouts before he joined the police force in his midtwenties. Most of the knuckles on both hands had been broken at one time or another. His nose had been broken seven times.

"I can take the weight off when I get back to the gym."

Aelish resumed her work with the carrots. She spoke as she cut. "Which you've been talking about for months now, but you don't go near the place."

"I'm not in the mood."

"And so I watch your diet for you."

"By cooking food I won't eat."

"You don't eat, you lose weight."

"Fine," he said, tired of fighting over the fish again. "I'm still left with a job I'm not sure I can do. The guy I'm supposed to look for, if it was him sent the other two, is protected. I probably won't find him. Maybe I shouldn't."

"Listen to you, Alex on his soapbox again. It's boring, yeah? You've been complaining about handling insurance claims since you retired from the force. Now you've got a chance to go find a genuine bad guy, get off your lard and do it."

"I'm just saying. Sometimes I wonder if this is the way it's supposed to be. The government protecting these pieces of shit and letting them do whatever they want. Sometimes I wonder if that's how it all balances out in the end. The world gets to deal with X amount of dirt bags to balance out the good people."

"You're daft, you know that?"

Pavlik went silent.

Aelish stopped cutting the carrots again. "What is it?"

"I didn't like him," he said, "Eddie Senta. Ten years ago I didn't believe him. I'm still not sure I believe he was all that innocent."

"That's when you were a cop. You didn't believe anybody."

"The guy was around it, the shit that happened to him. He was mobbed up. He wasn't so innocent."

"He saved his wife and kid," Aelish said. "From what you told me, he ran into a room and missed getting killed by inches to save his family. And he did save them. And then he went away for saving them."

"He went away for weapon possession."

"Oh, Jesus, Mary, and Joseph, you're just being obstinate now."

"It's what happened," he said.

Aelish waited for more.

Pavlik pointed to the computer on a desk across the living room. "I spent two hours trying to figure a way of checking with the bureau of federal prisons without tipping off the FBI, but I can't. I can't even think about asking anyone federal or they'll know someone is looking. They think that, they'll move the guy all over again. He can be anywhere, Aelish. Anywhere."

"You check Attica while you were at it?"

Attica penitentiary was a sore spot for Alex that he hadn't exorcised yet. It was where a serial killer of young boys Pavlik had arrested was being housed for the rest of his natural life.

"Yeah, I did, you wanna know," he said. "I did check Attica."

They had gone to therapy twice already to try and get him beyond what had happened back then. Pavlik continued to have nightmares about what he'd witnessed in the basement where he found Timothy Waller.

"And?" she asked.

Pavlik rubbed his face with both hands.

"Well?" Aelish asked again, doing exactly what she had been told by her boyfriend's last psychiatrist.

"Look, if Singleton is still in the program, he's using another name," Pavlik said. "And that makes perfect sense, so I'm wasting my time. If he's not in the program, he's a genius sending someone from North Dakota. How the hell can anyone be sure for less than twenty grand in investigative fees."

"Well, it's not like you wouldn't get paid," Aelish said. "If it costs, so be it. It's work."

"Except it be stealing," Pavlik said. "I'm not gonna find this guy. Nobody is. He's protected, for Christ's sake."

"If not you, then who?"

"How? What do I do?"

"You're the cop."

"Former cop."

"You'll figure something out."

"You're sure, huh?"

"Positive."

"And why's that?"

"Because you're one of the good ones, love, and you just can't let the bastard bad guys get away."

□ □ □

Pavlik spent the night tracking down three cops with federal connections and came up empty each time. Nine years after 9-11, the gap in communications between local and federal law enforcement agencies regarding anything but terrorism had widened severely.

Afraid he might alert the FBI into relocating Singleton again, Pavlik tried to follow up on the single lead he had from the second attempted murder of Eddie Senta. He used Google to research American Indian lawyers and was surprised when he couldn't find any. Instead, he saw what he'd always thought of as American Indians described as Native Americans.

"Shit," he said. "I guess that's right."

A few dozen searches later, he found an attorney through a Native American Programs site. He was in the middle of leaving a voice mail when someone picked up.

"Hello?" a male voice said.

"Is this Thomas Odakota?" Pavlik said.

"Speaking."

"My name is Alex Pavlik and I'm calling about a man I'm hoping you know something about. He was involved in an attempted murder during a home invasion on Long Island."

"Joseph Kincaid," Odakota said.

"The police contacted you?"

"No, I heard from a friend with the bureau of prisons here."

"Which prison?"

"I'm sorry, is there something I can help you with?"

"That depends," Pavlik said. "I hope so. I'm not looking for anything on Kincaid except for who he might've been working for and I'm pretty sure I know who that is."

"I'm sorry?"

"It's going to sound crazy, but it's a guy under federal witness protection I'm looking for. I think Kincaid might've been working for him, except I can't go near the FBI for help or they'll stop me cold and move the guy I'm looking for."

Odakota chuckled. "The federal government is giving you a hard time? Yes, we've heard that happens."

Pavlik wasn't sure what Odakota meant. "Well, not yet," he said, "but they will if they know I'm looking for the guy behind what happened on Long Island. I'm pretty sure Kincaid was working for him and if Kincaid was in North Dakota recently, and the suspended driver's license found on him suggests he might've been, then maybe the guy I'm looking for is there, too. In any case, North Dakota'd be the kind of place they'd relocate him."

"Joe Kincaid has been in North Dakota most of his adult life, too much of it in state prisons, if that helps, but I'd have no way of knowing who he might've been hanging around. I never met the man personally, but I can tell you without having to do much research that he's a direct product of historical racism. That's not an excuse for his behavior, mind you."

Pavlik rolled his eyes on his end of the line. "Is there any way to know how recently Kincaid has been in state?"

"I'm sure there is, but you do realize he could've gone to New York from anywhere."

"Would you meet with me if I flew out there? I can pay a research fee."

"Or make a donation."

"Huh? Oh, sure, I could do that."

"I'll be here through the end of the month, but then I have a conference to attend in Yankton, South Dakota for a few days."

"I'll be there tomorrow if I can book a flight."

Pavlik felt better after hanging up. Then he called Dexter Greene and asked for copies of any files he could get on James Singleton.

When he was finished with his phone calls, Pavlik took two of Aelish's Valium to sleep through the rest of the night. Sometimes a drug-induced sleep kept the nightmares at bay.

## Chapter 6
## Minot, North Dakota

At 6:15 in the evening the temperature outside was fifteen degrees below zero. With the winds gusting to forty miles per hour, the wind chill brought Minot's temperature down to fifty degrees below.

Sergeant Ekroth removed the plastic stirrer from his mouth to sip coffee from a cup that read *Magic City Police* as Dale finished the last of the paperwork on a truck-stop heroin bust.

With both of the other sergeants out sick, Ekroth was putting in long hours covering their shifts. He glanced at the arrest paperwork for Tyrone Williams and asked, "You think he can tell us anything?"

Dale was stretching his arms as he yawned. "He had to buy it from someone," he said. "And he doesn't appear to be a user himself."

"He say anything?"

"Soon as I cuffed him, he went mute. He's been schooled, Airman Williams."

Ekroth pointed to an envelope in Dale's mailbox. "That's from the coroner," he said. "The Barron kid from the college. He wasn't a user either. At least not habitual. The ME wants another opinion. The examiner from Fargo."

"He wasn't a user, except he's dead," Dale said.

Ekroth nodded. "You hear what happened up to Mohall?"

"Some woman, right?"

"Found in a trailer there. Shot in the stomach and a few times in the head. I have a friend up there, Jim Salinger, said she'd rented the place a week or so ago and was dressed for action."

"It's good to have friends," Dale said.

"Speaking of which, did your criminal informant give you this Williams character or was it good old shoe leather?"

Dale was up out of his chair. "It was Miss North Dakota and you know it. She tipped me off to the guy and a few people he was dealing to at the hotel. Most of those are into meth, but I grabbed one, some kid busses tables, and he gave up the good airman in exchange for his own ass. He said, 'the guy with the cornrows has the heroin.'"

"Nothing like the loyalty in crime," Ekroth said before he teased Dale. "Miss North Dakota, was it? You're a sly one, aren't you? Emily know about her?"

"What's to know?" Dale replied. "I stop by from time to time, see how she's doing, she tips me off to a few of the bad guys cross her path at the Lawrence Welk."

"But Emily doesn't know about it, does she?" asked Ekroth, a big smile across his face.

Dale pointed a finger at Ekroth. "Your mind spends too much time in the gutter."

"And I'm grateful for that much," Ekroth said.

A young officer stopped at the desk. He handed Ekroth a business card. "He wants his lawyer," the officer said.

"He'll have to wait until morning."

The patrolman pointed to the card. "He gave me that and said to call him now."

Ekroth read the business card, then glanced at Dale. "Becker," he said.

"Like I said, Airman Williams has been well schooled," Dale said.

Ekroth leaned back in his chair and yawned long and loud. When he was finished, he said, "Looks like your first real lead on that college thing."

□ □ □

The lounge at the Lawrence Welk Hotel was shaped in a horseshoe with two rows of tables surrounding a small dance floor. A small bandstand was set off to the right of the room. The bar faced the opened end of the horseshoe and featured, in neon lighting across the top, *"Drinks served by Miss North Dakota."*

"This an official visit?" Marsha Nordstrom said. An old girlfriend of Dale's, she was the former Miss North Dakota.

Dale had taken a seat at her end of the bar. He popped a few peanuts into his mouth. "Only if you'll serve me coffee," he said.

"I'm off in half an hour. I'll buy you a cup if you're still thirsty."

Dale tapped the face of his wristwatch. "That'll push me into official overtime," he said. "I need to be home at a reasonable hour tonight."

"Anniversary?" she asked.

Dale shook his head.

They had dated a few years before Dale was sent to Iraq. He had been promoted to Special Ops the month Marsha Nordstrom won the state beauty pageant. He had sent her a wire congratulating her. One year later she moved to Minneapolis to pursue a modeling career.

After both her marriage and modeling career failed, she moved to California and a series of dead-end jobs. When she became pregnant at thirty-six and the father of her child wouldn't help raise or support his kid, Marsha returned to Minot to raise her daughter as a single parent. She'd landed the job at the Lawrence Welk Hotel when the new manager of the bar realized her having been a former Miss North Dakota would be a draw. Marsha was one year younger than Dale. At forty-one, she was still an attractive woman. She had short blonde hair she wore in curls. Her eyes were sky blue, her skin pale. Her long legs and bright smile still turned heads.

Dale had a difficult time understanding why Marsha hadn't remarried or why she was serving drinks for a living. He remembered her as being one of the smarter girls he'd known. Although he was in love with his wife, he often found himself flirting with Marsha. Seeing her behind the bar was always bittersweet. Like any man, he was still attracted to her. Unlike most men, he felt sorry for her.

"You ever see that lawyer, Henry Becker, here with that little guy you fed me?" he asked. "I arrested him this afternoon, by the way."

Marsha put a hand to her chin. "I know who you mean, the lawyer, right? No, I don't think I've seen him here. I've seen his name in the papers. His picture, too."

"He's the best criminal lawyer in the state."

"He taking that case? The guy selling the heroin?"

Dale nodded. "Yes, ma'am."

"Don't call me ma'am," Marsha said. "It's too close to mom and I hear that all day."

"How is your Lilly?"

"Growing too fast and not fast enough," Marsha said. "She's a load. School, dance, gymnastics, and now hockey. Since when do little girls play hockey, Dale? I must've missed this someplace."

"It's not for beauty pageant winners," he said.

"My curse," Marsha said, "that stupid beauty pageant."

Dale grabbed another handful of nuts. "Anything else shaking down here?"

"Just that one-eyed guy I told you about," Marsha said. "The black guy with the eye patch, face mask–type thing."

Dale glanced behind him. "He here now?"

"No, not for a few days," Marsha said, before she opened a bottle of Olympia beer and set it on a coaster mid bar. "He was here a few times last week meeting different people," she said when she returned. "The guy I tipped you to was with him and another black guy I think is from the base. And the big guy I've seen around from time to time. He's white, the big one. Mean-looking, too."

"I never got the chance to follow up on that," Dale said. "This kid at the college has kind of taken all my time."

"That was such a tragedy," Marsha said. "I heard the mother is upstairs."

"I'm going to have to meet her sooner or later."

"I don't envy you."

"It sucks sometimes, this job. This is one of those times, having to talk to a woman just lost her kid."

Marsha poured a Budweiser on tap and handed it to an older man slurring his words. "That's it for tonight," she told him. "Last call."

"Thank you," the man said, then spilled some of the beer on his shirt.

Marsha turned to Dale and rolled her eyes. "You think your job sucks?"

"I'll try and look into that guy," Dale said. "Eye patch, right?"

Marsha wrinkled her nose. "And a sunken face, kind of," she said. She touched her own cheek. "You know, like some of his cheek is missing."

Dale nodded. "I thank you, ma'-lady."

Marsha pointed at him. "You were starting to say it again, weren't you?"

□ □ □

Emily cut the last of the carrots and added them to the pot roast she was cooking. She was a tall, slim woman with long blonde hair, blue eyes, and thin lips. She had turned forty-five years old the day before. She held up the gold bracelet her husband had given her as a present when he walked into the kitchen.

"I love this," she said.

"It cost enough," Dale said. "Least that's what the perp who was trying to sell it said."

Emily tossed a piece of carrot at him. He caught it in his right hand and popped it into his mouth.

They had been married two years and had met the night Emily was brutally mugged more than five years ago. Dale was one of the responding officers at the time.

"And how is Miss North Dakota this evening?" Emily asked. She knew Dale had once dated the former beauty pageant winner. At times his fishing for information where Marsha Nordstrom worked was an issue for her.

"Aging fast," Dale said. "She's starting to show those things around the eyes? What do you call them?"

"Crow's-feet," Emily said. "But you have to get awful close to notice those. Especially in that bar light, it's so dark."

"She gives me a hug whenever she sees me," Dale said, laying it on. "The poor woman can't help herself."

Emily closed her eyes as if in thought. "Hmm, I can't remember the last time we hugged," she said.

She finished cutting the carrots, washed her hands, then poured herself a glass of white wine. Dale opened his arms for her, but Emily ignored him.

"Did you hear about that woman in Mohall?" she asked. "It was all over the news tonight."

"Ekroth told me about it. He has a friend up there said they found her dressed up looking her best and it wasn't for her husband."

"Oh, Jesus," Emily said. "I hope that doesn't mean they won't take it serious."

"Of course they'll take it serious. It isn't about what she was doing behind her husband's back."

"Think he did it?"

"He supposedly wasn't in town."

"Supposedly."

Dale smiled. "You want a job down the station I can probably pull some strings."

"We might have some more time together that way," she said. "Anything new on Nathan Barron? The school is still in shock."

Dale stepped into the bathroom. He replied with the door left ajar. "Nothing," he said. "His mother is at the Lawrence Welk. I'll have to see her before she leaves. The ME at Trinity wants a second opinion so it might take another day or two. And I have a few kids I still need to talk with from the college."

Emily sat at the table and sipped her wine. When Dale was back in the room, she frowned at him.

"Sorry," he said. He stepped back inside the bathroom, flushed the toilet, then turned off the light.

Dale poured himself a glass of skim milk.

"I'm sorry about not being around," he said.

"Fair enough," Emily said. She raised her glass of white wine. They touched glasses.

"To pot roast," Dale said.

"To Miss North Dakota's aging," Emily said.

Dale drank half his glass of milk.

"A girl in my class mentioned that Nathan Barron was seeing an older woman," Emily said.

"Who's the girl in your class?"

"Nancy Wilkins."

"The guy on the car commercial? That Wilkins? His kid?"

"I guess so. She drives a brand new Camaro."

"Did she know Barron?"

"I don't know. She was talking with someone in the hall. I didn't see who. I just overheard her conversation. I heard his name mentioned and I listened in too late, I guess."

"I'll keep it in mind," Dale said. "If I don't hear about it myself. I'm waiting to interview one of Barron's former roommates. He's out of town right now. Jimmy Udahl. You know him?"

"Oh, Jimmy the hunk," Emily said. "He's such a cute boy. He hugs me every time he sees me. But he's aging fast. He's got those things in the corner of his eyes? What are they called again?"

## Chapter 7
## Williston/Lake Sakakawea, North Dakota

Washington Stewart squinted through his one eye as he sipped hot coffee from a thermos cup. It was 6:30. The sun was just rising across Lake Sakakawea. Stewart checked his watch and turned to see how his people were doing on the count.

"I mention half this haul is headed to Sin City?" a bald man sitting across the table said. "Like the man runs things down there doesn't have enough money already."

Stewart ignored the conversation.

"All that construction still going on in Vegas," the bald man continued. "You'd never know the economy is in the shitter."

Stewart looked out the clubhouse window across the golf course. "That's a beautiful view," he said, finally acknowledging the bald man. "It's hard to figure how a place like this didn't make it, but I know another one right near here didn't when it first opened. The Links at Red Mike. I know they were looking for investors there for a while."

Stewart told the bald man a lie about how he was considering buying shares in the golf course with some of the money he'd make from their deal that morning.

"But no more than twenty percent," he said. "A friend of mine told me never take more than twenty percent of a partnership unless you can afford the fifty-one percent gives you control. The problem here, I was told, was the traffic. Rich Canadians come down to play, but not enough of them. Farmers in state here haven't taken to it yet. Or they scared off when Tiger used to win. Before he got caught with all that white pussy, I mean. You see what I'm saying? They didn't want to play a game made popular by some brother back then."

The bald man stretched his skinny arms up and out as he yawned. "I could see how that'd be a problem," he said through the end of his yawn. "I'll sink mine in blue chips over time. I already got some real estate down south along the river, but they quit adding casinos. Your guy needs to step to and get people back to work already. Enough with the vacations on Martha's Vineyard and all the White House parties. Enough with the speeches. Two years in and no change anybody can believe in yet. He needs to yes we can it already or step aside and let someone knows what to do take over."

"Cut the brother some slack," Stewart said. "Good old boys aren't used to it yet, black man in the White House. Even some in his own party sabotaging the man. Plus he still catching flack for Bush. Ain't his fault the way things are."

"Well, I'll stick with the blue chips in the meantime, until he figures it out, what he's doing besides having parties with all those Motown groups from the friggin' sixties, they can barely walk, never mind sing."

Stewart rolled his good eye.

"In the meantime," the bald man said, "I found me a few guys from Vegas, investment bankers, know their shit. I'm sure they'll have some investment ideas, you're interested."

Stewart said, "There's nothing like clean money."

"Besides," the bald man said. "You sure they'd even let you in on a place like this? Being a minority and all, I mean. They don't much care for Indians up here, that goes without saying, but I'm not too sure they'd be thrilled sharing ownership of some private club with an African American. No offense intended, but you should check that out before you make an offer, get turned down, get yourself upset for something you could've avoided."

Stewart smirked. "African American, huh?" he said before lighting a cigarette. Ofay motherfucker, he was thinking.

The bald man yawned into a fist. "That's the problem with today, you ask me. All the political correctness. Be a lot less tension between people, they dropped the bullshit and called a spade a spade."

"Kind of what the Tea Party doing, right? Calling Obama a spade."

"Hey, you can't blame them for wanting their country back."

Stewart leaned forward, both elbows on the table. "You talking about Native Americans or the white man want they country back?" he said, laying on the street lingo this time. "Tea baggers get that confused all the time, about whose country this is. Native Americans, the ones you still calling Indians like John fucking Wayne, they the ones fucked over from the get go."

"Shit," the bald man said. "I didn't take you for a radical. Injuns seem to be doing okay to me. Free land, casinos, all the wampum they want, the way I hear it. Don't even pay taxes, some of them."

Stewart shook his head.

"What?" the bald man said.

"No, offense, but you one ignorant motherfucker," Stewart said. "Wampum. That like watermelon?"

The bald man looked confused. "Hey, all I'm saying is the Tea Party wants to return to what the founding fathers originally set up. That's all. Got nothing to do with the Indians."

Stewart was shaking his head again. He said, "Got nothing to do—the white man took it from Native Americans in the first place, you dumbass. They want it back now? From who? They the ones made the mess it is now. Never bothered paying the bill either. Native dude I listened to on some reservation here said the federal government never honored a single goddamn treaty since day one. Not a single one. If they wanted land, they pushed natives out the way. Natives put up a fight, government went genocide on them and gave out blankets with small pox. Killed off most the natives without blinking an eye, then pushed them onto reservations, fed them booze and whatnot to keep them in a stupor, same way drugs were let loose in the ghettos, and what land the government didn't build on wasn't theirs in the first place they stripped the natural resources from. Now they got natives bottled up and shit, they find themselves in trouble, natives get the same treatment niggers do. Government throws their asses into jail and for longer stretches than the average white boy. Or the ones can't handle it, they off themselves. Suicide rate just like the prison population. Same as for blacks in most states, way higher for natives than whites. Take our country back my ass. That Tea Party crowd got some American history to research before they spout that shit. Shame is, nobody calls them on it. All those cable news programs, all the so-called liberals out there on the networks, not a one has the balls to tell it like it is."

The bald man put both hands up. "Hey, sorry I brought it up, the Tea Party."

"You didn't," Stewart said. "You were taking shots at Obama. I brought them up, the Tea Party."

"Then I'm sorry for Obama. That help?"

Stewart shrugged. "It just a little hard to take these tea bagging, peckerwood motherfuckers with their take our country back signs serious is all."

The bald man forced a smile. "Tea baggers," he said. "Good one. What's a peckerwood?"

Stewart winked at the ofay. He was about to explain it to him when someone behind them yelled, "The count is good."

"Product's good," a man testing the heroin said. "Product's very good."

Stewart and the bald man shook hands across the table. Stewart gestured toward the door and the bald man directed his people to leave first. The small group of men gathered the bags containing the dope and left. The bald man was the last to exit the building.

Stewart waited until the cars had left the parking lot before he loaded the small duffel bag full of cash into his Dodge Ram. He had two airmen stationed at the Minot Air Force base working this morning. Roger Daltry and Tyrone Williams, both originally from inner cities, were twenty-five and twenty three-years old, respectively. Both young men had spent the morning counting more cash than they would ever see again in their lives.

Williams was tall and lanky. His hair was braided front to back in corn-rows. He had taken a bus from Minot the night before and spent the night at an Econo Lodge in Williston. Stewart offered him a lift back to Minot.

"I thought you at Sakakawea," Williams said.

Only a few people were supposed to know where Stewart was living. He squinted through his one eye again. "You learned that, huh? Somebody told you?"

"Roger," Williams said. "Why, it a secret?"

Williams was from Atlantic City. The Air Force had become his salvation from the streets. Selling drugs had become his salvation from the Air Force. The day before he had been arrested for possessing heroin with intent to sell. His lawyer, someone Stewart kept on retainer, had managed to knock the charge down to misdemeanor possession.

"I live on a boat there," Stewart said.

Williams's voice went up a full octave. "A boat? In this weather? You must be crazy."

"It's up on blocks until spring," Stewart said. "I got an RV parked at the marina, too, for bathing and what not, but I prefer the boat. I'm going up to Minot anyway. You want the lift or not?"

"Sure," Williams said. "Beats the bus, man."

□ □ □

Stewart stopped at the marina at Lake Sakakawea where he dropped off the duffel bag full of cash with a federal agent waiting inside the boat for him. When he returned to his Dodge Ram, Tyrone Williams was surprised Stewart had left the bag behind.

"I hope you got reinforcements somewhere on that boat," he said. "I don't believe I ever saw that much money in my life."

Stewart said, "That a legitimate question or you feeling me out?"

"Say what?"

"Maybe I'm stupid enough to tell you something you have no business knowing, you drop a dime, some ignorant brothers up the base try and make a score, get themselves killed instead."

Williams said, "What the fuck you talking about?"

An uncomfortable moment passed.

Stewart slowly smiled. Williams relaxed again. He said, "I thought you weirdin' out on me, man. After this morning, what went down on that golf course? Shit. Cops roll into the middle of that this morning and I'm away for life. Why I got out of Minot soon as I was released last night. Cops busted me on some bullshit possession. Somebody at the diner on Fifty-two gave me up. I owe that table-clearing motherfucker."

"Who handled it?"

"Becker. Backed those cops right down."

"Where'd you get Becker from?"

"Dude named Ahearn."

Stewart frowned.

Williams said, "Hey, you okay? I hope you don't think I'm playing you, man."

"I's just fuckin' with you," Stewart said.

"I hope we cool. I can use another payday like today. I can always use that."

Half an hour later Stewart shot Williams three times in the back of the head, then retrieved the two thousand dollars he had paid the airman. He stuffed the body inside a drainpipe one hundred yards off the highway, where they had stopped on the pretext of hiding some cash.

"Money to hide in the event something goes sour," Stewart had told Williams. "This way, I know where to go I ever need it in a hurry. It won't be much. Enough to get me across the country, I need to make a move. You can't keep it all in one place anyway. They find it, the cops, they'll keep it. Just remember, though, now you know where this is too. Just you and me, in case it goes missing someday."

Williams had been smiling as they walked through the small patch of trees off the highway. "You don't got to worry about me, brother," he said. "I can see you got things figured out. I like that. I can learn from you."

Stewart had handed Williams a spade to dig a hole for the paper bag he was carrying. "Just go down a foot or so," he said. "I need this in an emergency, I don't want to fuck with whatever ice forms in the turned up dirt."

"Right," Williams said. Then he'd gone down on his knees and speared the edge of the spade into the earth. Then Stewart shot Williams three times in the back of the head.

Now Stewart was on his way back to his boat at the marina at Lake Sakakawea, where he would await word on the results of the sting he had initiated at the golf club.

There were a few potential problems to handle before Stewart could escape the federal witness protection program forever. Tyrone Williams had been one. Another was about to take place on a highway somewhere in South Dakota.

## Part II

## Chapter 8
## Queens, New York/Minot Air Force Base/Mohall, North Dakota

Pavlik hated flying. Besides the cramped space for his long legs, there had been a particularly unpleasant father-son experience when he was eight years old. It was the year before his parents divorced. The Pavlik family had planned a summer vacation in Miami, Florida. Young Alex was excited to be the first kid in his family to fly. Because his mother suffered sunstroke their first day on the beach, his father took him to the Miami aquarium the next afternoon.

They watched sharks feed in a canal with clear railings on both sides. It was a popular attraction at the aquarium. Pavlik's father hoisted Alex onto his shoulders to see over the crowds blocking the railing. When his father stepped closer to the railing, Alex grew nervous. The panic Alex felt had paralyzed him; he thought his father was trying to drop him into the canal.

When he couldn't be coaxed down, Alex had to be removed from his father's shoulders by a stranger. It was the first of several panic attacks Alex suffered as a child from the rejection he felt from his father.

Flying revived the memory of his strained relationship. Father and son would learn how to deal with each other later in life, but their early relationship left an emotional scar Pavlik could never ignore.

He tried his best to suppress his darker childhood memories on his way to the airport. He looked to his girlfriend and thought of something that made perfect sense.

"You could come along," he said. "See the frontier, what used to be the frontier."

Aelish was driving. Her attention was focused on the parkway traffic. "Queens is frontier enough for me," she said. "Besides, this is work you're doing. You don't need me hanging around."

They were getting off the Grand Central Parkway, heading into LaGuardia airport. Pavlik watched a Delta MD-80 as it climbed in the sky after takeoff.

"I just hope this guy Odakota will talk to me," he said. "Or I'll be flying halfway across the country for nothing."

"Once you show him those pictures of Eddie and Diane Senta, it won't be easy for him not to help."

"At least I'm not chasing people faking insurance claims."

Aelish turned onto the ramp for departing flights. "Real police work is in your blood."

"Yeah, well, I'm not giving Diane Senta a stroke job, I'll tell you that much," Pavlik said. "This turns out as pointless as I suspect, I'm outa there, North Dakota."

"Just don't get yourself into trouble," Aelish told him. "Dexter won't be around to help you out."

"I'm not bumping heads with any locals out there. I'm gonna talk to this Odakota and if he turns out to be the wrong type, he feels he has to notify the FBI, I'm done. The feds will put the lock on it anyway, he talks to them. I'll deal with somebody with the police up there as a last resort, but I'd rather not. One guy looking to kiss federal ass and that's the end of finding James Singleton."

Aelish followed the signs for Delta Airlines. "You know how to maneuver," she said. "So quit your whining."

"What's that supposed to mean, I know how to maneuver?"

"Just what I said. You know your way around. You'll do what you have to. You'll get it done."

"If there's anything to get done."

She pulled over to the curb to let him out. "Give us a kiss," she said.

Pavlik leaned across the console to kiss her. He said, "I don't maneuver, Aelish."

"Excuse me?"

"I don't maneuver."

"The hell are you talking about, man?"

Pavlik felt himself blush. "Because the way you said it, I mean. Maneuvering."

"You mean cheating?" she said.

"I thought that's what you meant."

"Oh, Jesus, you're daft." She pointed to the terminal. "Go, before you puke on yourself."

Pavlik slid out of the car, then pointed a finger at her before closing the door. "I don't maneuver," he said.

"Have a good flight," she said.

"I'll call you once I'm settled. Every night I'm there."

She motioned at him to shut the door. He did so and then swore he heard her laughing as she pulled away.

□ □ □

Colonel Robert Schmidt spent two hours discussing his dead wife with two Mohall city policemen. Although one officer seemed especially suspicious, Schmidt could tell the police were frustrated by the lack of evidence surrounding his wife's murder.

When he was finished with the police, Schmidt drove to the Minot Air Force Base to log a few hours of flight time. In a few days he would use an Air Force helicopter to begin his escape from the country.

When he arrived at the airfield he asked the airman handling vouchers if he was interested in taking a ride. The airman politely refused the offer.

Schmidt pointed at the Sikorsky Pave Hawk helicopter. "Is it fueled?" he asked.

"Yes, sir."

"Sure you don't want a ride?"

"Positive, sir."

"You can impress your girlfriend, airman," Schmidt said. "Unless you're married. Are you married, son?"

"Ah, no, sir."

"Smart man. Stay single."

"Yes, sir."

"I could hover over your girl's place while you call her on the phone, she can come out and wave hello."

"My girlfriend lives in Nebraska, sir. Thank you anyway."

"Okay, then," said Schmidt, giving the airman a pat on the shoulder. "Don't say I never asked."

The airman stood back as Schmidt walked across the short tarmac to the helicopter stations. Next the airman noted the time and recorded it in his log. He stepped outside the glass partition and leaned into the wind as the chopper blades started to rotate. The airman stood shivering in the cold a full five minutes before the helicopter finally lifted and turned west.

□ □ □

Twenty minutes later Schmidt swung the Pave Hawk chopper down low across a tiny trailer camp just outside of Mohall. The sun was blinding until he repositioned the chopper. He searched for his wife's car and spotted it alongside the last trailer in a row of three just off the main road. The police had not removed it yet.

Schmidt pictured his wife being killed inside the trailer and smiled from the images in his head. The Mohall police had tried to be delicate after they first informed him of her murder. It was a conversation he now found amusing.

"Sir, your wife seemed to be waiting for someone," the police officer had told him.

"What do you mean, waiting for someone?" Schmidt had asked.

"We think she might've been waiting for someone she knew."

"I don't understand."

"An affair, sir. Someone she might've been seeing behind your back."

It was then Schmidt had turned and used an accusatory tone. "Excuse me? What are you telling me, officer?"

One of the Mohall policemen had smirked at Schmidt's performance.

"Is there a problem?" the colonel had asked the doubting cop.

"We figure it isn't the first time," the officer had said.

"And?"

"You make many trips away from home?"

His arrogance had unnerved Schmidt. It was difficult not to show it.

"What's your point?" he'd asked.

"Your surprise, quite frankly," the officer had said. "I don't understand how she could be having affairs behind your back is all. Usually a man knows when something like that is going on?"

"Really?" Schmidt said. "You've taken polls on the subject?"

He knew it was a mistake to engage the cop, but he'd lost his temper and couldn't control himself. What bothered him more than the officer's arrogance was the way he had tried to stare Schmidt down afterward.

When he first saw Michelle's body at the morgue, it wasn't difficult to feel disgust for the way she had prepared herself for her date. Schmidt thought it repulsive. Who did she think she was kidding? She was way too chunky for lingerie. He hoped she felt foolish the few moments before she died.

Now he swung the chopper back south. He had purposely avoided flying north the last time he used the helicopter because the flight path was recorded in a log. He had flown west, south, and east while logging his time. The next time he wouldn't have to log his flight hours for the Pave Hawk; he wouldn't be bringing it back. The plan was to fly south and leave it somewhere close to the state border where a prearranged car would be waiting.

He wondered what the weather would be like in Mexico as he flew over the snow-covered ground. He spotted a pack of deer below and wondered how many of them would survive the frigid winter.

Then the deer were gone and Schmidt wondered about Mexico again. It would be a nice change to walk around in a T-shirt and shorts.

## Chapter 9
## Minot, North Dakota

When he was ten years old, Dale watched his father get beaten by three men. It was the end of a holiday weekend. His parents had gone to a party at a bar in the next town. A group of rednecks were there and had started to pick on Dale's Norwegian father for marrying a Sioux woman.

Dale's parents left after the fight was broken up, but a few of the troublemakers had followed the couple home to Cando, where they attacked John Hehn in his front yard. Dale had woken up from the noise and witnessed the beating through his bedroom window.

When Dale ran out of the house to help his father, his mother dragged him back inside. He screamed at the men to stop while his mother phoned the police. The beating went on for several minutes before they grew tired of stomping John Hehn.

When it was finally over, Dale's father showered and let his wife tend to his injuries. He had been badly beaten. His face was bruised and swollen. Three fingers on his right hand had been broken. He spent the rest of the night sitting in silence in his chair in the living room.

Dale had crawled onto his father's lap and fallen asleep there. His father didn't move the entire time. It would be the night by which Dale forever defined their relationship.

The next morning, after his father woke him from a sound sleep, Dale knew that he would spend his adult life protecting people. It was why he had joined the army as soon as he graduated from Jamestown College. It was why he had joined the Minot Police Department once his mother had passed in 1995.

Now he was viewing the OD awaiting shipment back to Detroit. A once attractive, nineteen-year-old, white male had died from an overdose of heroin. The chief medical examiner from out of town had concurred with the local examiner. Both believed the fresh needle marks were probably the first two times Nathan Barron had ever mainlined a drug.

"You want a closer look?" Dr. Thomas Olsen asked Dale. The two men were standing in the morgue doorway while two orderlies bagged the Barron body.

"No, thanks," Dale said.

"This was a real shame," Olsen said. "The kid wasn't a user. We found traces in his nose but not enough to suggest it was habitual."

"Wrong kid playing the wrong game?"

"Kieffer up at the university said he was a hell of a tennis player."

"I heard he was a good student."

"The writing thing, that's right," Olsen said. "He won some award for that at the college."

Dale rubbed the knuckles on his right hand; an arthritic barometer for frigid weather he'd become used to.

"You see the mother yet?" Olsen asked. "The poor woman was beside herself when she got here, and then we had to ask her to let us hold the body another few days. I wanted ME Nance out to Fargo to take a look. He wasn't in town until yesterday. He made the trip up last night. Like I said, he confirmed what I found. I wanted to be sure. The mother was so out of it she didn't get upset. I heard the college put her up at the hotel."

"The least they could do," Dale said. "I'm hoping to have something for her before she leaves, although right now I don't have anything. I'm not looking forward to it, I can tell you that."

Both men stepped aside as the orderlies wheeled the bagged body of Nathan Barron on a gurney out of the morgue.

"There a chance this kid was forced into shooting the dope?" Dale asked.

"No signs of a struggle. Nance didn't find any either. No bruises anywhere on the body. No scratches around the two needle marks."

"Both fresh?"

"Both. He probably shot up again too soon after the first time."

Dale watched the orderlies turn the corner further down the hallway.

"Is there something I should know about?" Olsen asked.

Dale was lost in thought. The question caught him off guard. "Huh?" he said.

"Is there anything else I need to know?"

Dale shook his head. He was thinking maybe there wasn't a struggle and that Nathan Barron might've had unsolicited help shooting a second time.

"Dale?" Olsen said.

"Sorry," Dale said. "No."

□ □ □

He had been waiting to meet with a former roommate of Nathan Barron's, Jimmy Udahl. The junior from Towner, North Dakota had gone to Florida to visit with his girlfriend attending school there and was scheduled to be back in Minot sometime this morning.

A wrestler, Udahl roomed at the athletic dormitory. Just before noon Dale caught up with him outside Pioneer Hall. He invited Dale into his room, then excused himself as he changed clothes during the interview.

"How was Florida?" Dale asked.

"A lot warmer than here," Udahl said. "My girlfriend goes to Miami. It's another world compared to here."

"I hear you," Dale said. "You roomed with Nathan last year, correct?"

"Our freshman year," Udahl said as he pulled his sweatpants off. "I lived off campus last year. It was too expensive so I came back to the dorms this year. Nathan and I roomed together our freshman year."

Dale took notes. "How was it living with him? What was he like?"

Udahl was stepping into a pair of faded dungarees. "Nate was a tough roommate," he said. "He was a nice guy and all, he wasn't obnoxious or anything, but he kept late hours. Writing and listening to music mostly. He did everything on a reverse schedule. I had problems with the hours."

"What about drugs?"

"I never seen him do any," Udahl said. He pulled a Mr. Taco shirt off a hanger. "He didn't take drugs in front of me, if he took them at all. I was pretty surprised when I heard he overdosed."

"And outside the room? Did you know him to use drugs with other friends?"

"We didn't hang together," Udahl said. "I'm from Towner here in state. I went home a lot on weekends. I invited him a few times, but he never came."

"You never knew him to get high? Not even a joint?"

"Not really, no. A few beers once or twice, but never any drugs."

Dale made another notation. "What about a girlfriend? Did Nathan have any girls he hung around with?"

"Not our freshman year," Udahl said. He was lacing his sneakers. "He had a girlfriend back home he wrote to, they talked on the phone once in a while. Nobody up here that I know of. Not back then. I heard he was seeing a waitress or somebody from downtown, but that wasn't mentioned until after what happened. I don't know it's true."

"You remember who told you about the waitress?"

"Somebody at our table in the union, the student union. It was at breakfast the day after he died. Somebody called her a skank, the waitress. I remember that."

Dale handed Udahl a Minot Police card with his office and cell number. "Okay," Dale said. "Thank you. But if you remember anything else, please give me a call at that number. You can leave a message on the voice mail if I don't pick up."

"Sure," Udahl said.

"Thanks," Dale said.

□ □ □

In one of the dead student's notebooks Dale found home and cell telephone numbers scribbled below a heart surrounding "Kathy and Nate." The handwriting was different from that of the history notes in the book. Dale had figured it was the woman's, Kathy's. Kathy Ljunndgren lived in Minot. His first two attempts to question her had been thwarted on consecutive days by the doctors at the treatment center where she was recovering from a heroin overdose. At work they had told him she was out sick with the flu.

When he finally caught up with her, it was at the small diner on South Main Street where she worked as a part-time waitress. Kathy was twenty-eight years old, divorced, and the mother of two girls, ages six and three. She was tall and slim with short brown hair. When she was healthy, she worked at the coffee house while her mother watched her girls.

Dale waited until her break to interview Kathy. Then they stepped out and sat in Ljunndgren's car in the parking lot behind the coffee house.

"I only knew Nathan for six months or so," Kathy said.

"And?"

"Look, I can't afford to lose this job, officer."

"Detective," Dale said.

"Whatever. I really can't afford to lose my job. Please don't tell my bosses."

"I won't tell them anything, but I can't guarantee they won't learn about it through an investigation. It depends on how much you tell me and how much of it is true. Do we understand each other?"

Ljunndgren huffed.

"Kathy?"

"What is it you want to know?"

"Tell me about your relationship with Nathan Barron and about the drugs he overdosed on."

"I met him at a flyboy party," Ljunndgren said. "He was there with a friend of his from the college. I was there alone. I knew the flyboy."

"And his name?"

"Jesus Christ," Ljunndgren said.

Dale said, "His name, Kathy."

"Ahearn," Ljunndgren said, stomping her right foot. "John Ahearn, okay? He's not from here. Wisconsin, I think. He's here through the Air Force. He used to be in the Air Force. He's not anymore."

"You know him well?"

"I know him, that's all. I know who he is."

"How old is he?"

"Forty-something," she said, then added, "and he's married."

Dale was pretty sure he knew the answer to his next question, but he asked it anyway.

"Were you and Mr. Ahearn involved?"

This time she rolled her eyes. "Jesus Christ."

"If you don't tell me, I'll find out from somebody else, if not Mr. Ahearn himself. You might as well tell the truth."

"Yes," Ljunndgren said. "Yes, we were involved. But he's married."

"Do you know his wife?"

"Shit."

"Kathy?"

"Yes, damn it."

"Is Mr. Ahearn a drug user?"

"Oh, fuck."

"That a yes?"

"Yes, yeah."

"Heroin?"

"Fuck."

"Kathy?"

"I don't know about heroin. I seen him use other drugs, not heroin."

"Is he the one Nathan got the heroin from?"

"I don't know."

"Kathy?"

She was squirming. "I don't know," she said. "I don't. He did some with me, but I don't know who gave Nate the stuff that he overdosed on. I don't think it was John Ahearn. We saw he was sick and called the ambulance."

"How often did you two use?"

"Nate wasn't a user."

"How long?"

"He just did it that one time. He snorted a few times before that."

"When did he start injecting?"

"I swear to God, I don't know if he did it before that night," Ljunndgren said. "I don't think so." She was pleading now. "You have to believe me," she said. "I only snorted with Nate. He never mainlined in front of me. I just started mainlining a few weeks ago myself."

"And then you were sick. Doctors already told us."

"The next day, once I found out about Nate."

"Was it the stuff you used or something you did on purpose?"

"I wasn't looking to kill myself. They asked me that a thousand times already. I screwed up is all."

"Where'd you get the stuff, Kathy?"

"I didn't get it from anybody. I didn't buy it. Someone gave it to me and I don't remember who."

Dale knew the interview was over. Kathy Ljunndgren couldn't help but lie. She still had too much to hide and there were people she was protecting. He handed her his card.

"I'll be in touch," he told her. "So don't think I'm going away."

□ □ □

It was the thing he'd been dreading since learning about the Barron kid; having to meet the mother of the child that had died. He'd always dreaded notifying loved ones of a sudden death in their family. Although Mrs. Barron was already aware of her son's passing, Dale had no way to try to make sense of it for her. A kid had gone off to college and died. What could he say?

He found Jennifer Barron at her room in the Lawrence Welk Hotel. She had been napping when he knocked on her door. He could see her eyes were still swollen from crying when she answered his knock. She told Dale it was the first sleep she'd had since she'd arrived.

"I'm sorry to have to bother you, Mrs. Barron," Dale said.

"Jennifer, please," she said. She invited him to sit.

"Thank you, ma'am," he said.

She sat on the edge of the queen-sized bed. She was an attractive middle-aged woman with long dark hair. She wore the emotional stress and pain of losing a child. "I'm a wreck," she said. She glanced at herself in the mirror across from the bed. "Sorry."

"I've been talking with some of the kids at the college who knew Nathan," Dale proceeded. "I learned a few things I'd like to share with you."

Mrs. Barron nodded.

"He was involved with a woman from town," Dale said. "Did you know about that?"

She shook her head. "He had a girlfriend back home but they broke off during the summer. He didn't mention that he was seeing anybody from here."

"She was a few years older than Nate," Dale said.

Mrs. Barron sat up straight. "Who was she?"

"A single mother. She was also a drug user," Dale said. "We don't think Nate was a user, not habitual by any means, but...."

"This woman and Nate... the drugs?"

"Yes, ma'am," Dale said. "I think so."

Mrs. Barron rubbed her forehead. "I promised myself I wouldn't be one of those parents who sat in judgment about the people my kids became involved with. I have a daughter back home who just dropped out of her senior year in high school because she's in love with a truck driver seven years older than she is. I know it's wrong and I screamed when I first heard about it, but Gwen is stubborn and getting angry only makes it worse. But Nate was so much more mature."

She stopped to cry.

"Are you okay, ma'am?" Dale asked. He handed her the box of tissues on the table.

"Did she get him started on heroin?" she asked. "This woman he was sleeping with. Did she start him?"

"I'm not sure," Dale said. "She claims that Nate was against doing the heroin with a needle. He hadn't done it before. The pathologist confirmed that. This woman claims she snorted with Nathan."

"Please don't tell me she's pregnant," Mrs. Barron said. "Please don't tell me that. Not on top of this."

It was something Dale hadn't even thought to ask Kathy Ljunndgren. "Not that I know of, ma'am."

Mrs. Barron took a long slow breath.

"I'm going to do my best to find out what happened," Dale said. "I promise you that."

Mrs. Barron forced a weak smile. "I don't know if I care," she said. "Nathan's gone. He's not coming back."

"We want to know if someone else is responsible," Dale said.

"Does it make a difference?"

Dale reached out and took her hands. "I can't begin to understand your pain, ma'am," he said. "And I'm very sorry for your loss. We all are."

Mrs. Barron used a tissue as she sniffled. "Do you have children, Detective?" she asked.

"No ma'am, I don't."

She was choking on her emotions.

Dale said, "Ma'am?"

"I think I need to be alone," she said.

"Yes, ma'am," he said. "Of course."

## Chapter 10
## Minneapolis/St. Paul, Minnesota; Lake Sakakawea, North Dakota

Pavlik had taken two more of Aelish's Valium before the flight. The sedative worked until he woke up from a baby crying a few rows behind his. Pavlik looked out the window at the endless fields of white and wondered what the hell people did for entertainment surrounded by all that snow.

As the jet made its final descent into the Minneapolis-St. Paul Airport, he spotted what appeared to be a farmhouse and barn, then strained to see movement around the buildings and was surprised when he spotted cows. He smiled at the sight and couldn't wait to tell Aelish about it.

Twenty minutes later he was enjoying a Bloody Mary at one of the airport bars. He was mesmerized by the number of people with blond hair. He had heard about the Norwegian and Swedish influence in the region, but seeing it firsthand was something else.

He finished his drink, paid his bar bill and headed to the gate for his flight to Grand Forks. He stopped when he saw a long line of angry passengers waiting at the check-in desk. Then he learned his flight had been delayed.

He had forty minutes before another flight would take him to Sioux Falls, South Dakota. Another flight would take him to Grand Forks and then Bismarck, North Dakota. He had reserved a room in Bismarck close to the state penitentiary where he planned on meeting the lawyer he'd made contact with over the phone. Pavlik was hoping he might gather information about the Native American without resorting to prison protocol. If the lawyer couldn't help, he'd have to pursue Joseph Kincaid's recent past some other way. He didn't have a clue how.

Still, Aelish had been right, Pavlik was grateful for the opportunity to chase bad guys again.

□ □ □

Special Agent in Charge Eugene Morris checked his watch while he waited for Washington Stewart's undivided attention. Stewart was sitting in his recliner inside the dry-docked sailboat. He took a drag from his cigarette and tried puffing out smoke rings.

"I'm tempted to give you a gold star," Morris said. "This thing went off without a hitch."

Morris was a stocky black man with a thick neck and broad shoulders.

He had just turned fifty-five. His short hair was showing gray along his temples.

"We got the two fronting the Vegas money," Morris added. "A pair of yuppies so scared of what they stepped into, they were taking notes on what they could do to stay out of the joint."

Stewart smirked. "You got yourself a new pair of snitches is what you telling me," he said. "Some white boys connected to the real money."

"Indeed they were," Morris said. "You got coffee?"

Stewart pointed toward the galley. "Help yourself. But if you gotta use the bathroom, it better be number one, because the pipes froze on number two."

"You using the RV?"

"When I gotta shower or shit, I do."

Morris poured himself a cup, added two spoonfuls of sugar, and sipped a few times before continuing his conversation.

"They're investment bankers from the coast," Morris said. "They were working for somebody in Vegas. They couldn't shit their bricks fast or hard enough. One of them was literally shaking. Had a full-blown panic attack. They want to deal."

"What's it mean to me?"

"Nothing yet."

"Then why mention it?"

"They both have a hell of a lot to lose."

"They white they do."

"White investment bankers," Morris said. "Appears they were brokering for Vegas hard guys."

"Investment bankers use other people's money. There was a movie about it with that short actor-dude with the Italian name. What was it again?"

Morris didn't bite.

"Anyway," Stewart said, "that bald motherfucker back at the golf course did all the talking said he's got money in blue chips, then mentioned casinos down south. That true? Your boys gonna make a deal with him too, a racist like that?"

Morris sipped his coffee. "What do you care, Jimmy? You looking to make investments?"

"The name's Washington," Stewart said.

"Okay, Washington, let's forget the Missouri racist and let me ask you how come your count was light?"

"Expenses. My crew had to do the counting while I played the Great Black Drug Lord of the North. They doubled as security, too. Had to pay them something."

"Expenses my, ass. Those two punks couldn't cost you any more than a grand apiece."

"They could sell crack on a corner and make a grand in six hours."

"On a corner in Philly maybe. Or Atlantic City, where that one punk is from, Tyrone Williams is it? Maybe there he could earn some scratch selling H, but not out here, my friend. Not in North Dakota."

"You'd be surprised the traffic interested in that kind of trade," Stewart said. "Even out here. You watchin' too much television you think it's just meth these crackers are into."

"Yeah, well, just in case you forgot the last time I mentioned it, your boys don't do you any good getting busted up here. We already know they're both hustling on and off the base, Jimmy. The locals bust them, they name you, it's not some place you want to go. Not again, you don't."

"Washington," Stewart said. "The name is Washington."

"Right," Morris said. "In the meantime I have to head down to Bismarck."

Stewart pointed to the small bag of cash. "Feel free to take something for yourself," he said. "Seeing you're out here with nothing to do anyway. Take some and go to the reservation. Play some blackjack. Get yourself a squaw. They pretty good. Look more Latino than Indian. Can pass for Puerto Rican, you squint hard enough."

Morris set the cup of coffee on a table alongside the recliner. He turned on a light next to the computer. The screen saver showed Teddy Roosevelt charging up San Juan Hill. Morris clicked the mouse and Teddy Roosevelt disappeared. A program page with photos appeared in its place.

Morris said, "What's Adult Intimate Companions?"

"You asking, you already know," Stewart said.

"Why don't you tell me?"

Stewart struggled to get out of the recliner. He moved to the folding chair in front of the computer and clicked on one of the small pictures listed top to bottom.

"It's a personal ad service," he said. "How you find snatch over the Internet. How snatch finds you."

Morris squinted at the picture Stewart had clicked on. It was a skinny woman with short blonde hair. Her neck and shoulders were covered with tattoos. He waved it off and stepped away.

"The women on those things, the ones put the ads in, they really out there like that?" he asked.

Stewart measured Morris before he spoke again. He enjoyed using street talk on the man. It kept the agent off balance.

"Some of them," Stewart said. "The ones up in age. The pigs. The desperate ones. The young ones are usually escorts. Probably the services they work for pay for the ads. Or they business women. Professionals."

"And you get women with those ads?" Morris said, still unsure whether or not Stewart was talking shit.

"My lady does," Stewart said. "They a lot of white girls want the dark meat. Sometimes they go both ways. My woman seems to find them easy enough. She find one for you, you interested. Give you something to do to keep warm up here."

"I'm not that desperate I need you to find me a girlfriend."

"Who said anything about a girlfriend," Stewart said. "We got one now, not far from here, living with two white guys can't do anything for her. She a white girl, too. You can spend some time with her, maybe teach her a thing or two."

Morris ignored the commentary.

Stewart said, "She from the South. You can get some payback for all that slavery, having one of they women. Probably what Obama's daddy did before he split. Got him some revenge."

"Obama's father was from Kenya, moron."

"Where they took us from in the first place. Good for him. Too bad he didn't see his boy grow up white enough to become President."

"Except he married a black girl and has two black kids."

"He lucky they didn't come out white is all. He still half ofay, no matter you work for him or not, Tom."

Morris glared at Stewart then. "Call me Tom again and see if I don't knock your teeth down your throat. How's that?"

Stewart smiled. "It's good to see a black man defending a brother," he said, then made a fist and raised it over his head. "Power to the people, bro. I gots to wonder, though, you get upset when Michael Jackson died. He a brother, too."

Morris flipped Stewart the bird, then looked back down at the picture of the woman on the computer. He said, "Still got it for blondes, I see."

"Slim blondes," Stewart said. "Like my sweetheart."

Morris made a face. "That woman is a skank."

"Is that nice?"

"She's ugly and flat as a board."

Stewart lit a cigarette. "Beauty in the eye of the beholder, my brother."

"You're half fucking blind, maybe that explains it."

Stewart thought about shooting the agent right there and then. He took a moment to calm himself, then forced a smile. "She keeps me informed," he said. "Updates the computer lists for me. Lets me know if there's any new tail in the area. She likes the group thing, too. Likes to invite another woman to join us from time to time."

Morris held up a hand. "I don't have the stomach for that image."

"Like I said, beauty in the eye—"

"I'm leaving," Morris said. "You going to Minot?"

"Tomorrow. Too tired now. Gonna watch Kobe and the Lakers, have a steak, drink some brews and go back to sleep."

Morris was at the small ladder that led to the deck. He stopped, turned to Stewart and said, "You need to reign in Daltry and Williams. We can't have that kind of exposure now. The kid from the college in Minot OD'd from heroin and that had to come from your friends, either Daltry or Williams."

"Tyrone Roger's friend," Stewart said. "I don't know the kid, and besides, the college kid could've got it somewhere else. You need to get out more often. The Air Force base isn't the only source for drugs in this state. Go north to Canada, it isn't that far. Or Minneapolis-St. Paul. I suppose they get it from my guys, too? Or the Indians. They all clean, too, right?"

"I'm just saying," Morris said, not so sure of himself then. "We don't need the extra attention. We're operating up here pretty much without interference. We don't need the locals educating themselves from Daltry or Williams' extracurricular activities."

"Daltry drives a Volkswagen Rabbit," Stewart said. "Used to drive it. The transmission went and he can't even afford to have it fixed. Was driving it around without heat the last month or so. In this weather? Shit. Boy don't have a dime to his name, poor Roger."

"The man is a punk drug dealer," Morris said. He took a step back toward the cabin ladder. "Not too different from yourself, come to think of it. Except he has both his eyes."

Keep it up, Tom, Stewart was thinking. He forced himself to clap. "You should do stand-up," he said. "You a funny motherfucker, you make the effort."

"Your skank off the horse?"

"Four months now," Stewart said. "Lynette off the junk and much more aggressive in the sack. Likes to tussle with the snake."

"Because nothing should go wrong," Morris said. "This really is your last chance, Jimmy."

"The name is Washington," Stewart said.

"You letting her stay with you?"

"No."

"Maybe keep an eye on her? That investigation up at the college is still fresh. You don't need her getting picked up for using."

"She with Roger tonight," Stewart said. "Daltry. They both fine."

"I'd feel better knowing you were in more control of your crowd," Morris said.

"I'm more focused when I'm alone. I can't relax I know somebody else is on the boat while I'm trying to sleep. It's a personal preference I developed from the joint. I don't like people in my shit, they don't have to be."

"And what happens when she goes off and gets herself a fix and comes back flying? Or she gets herself arrested with a bag of heroin? You got a game plan for that?"

Stewart popped a peanut into his mouth. "Lynette knows better than to fuck with me. Besides, I told you she clean. I'm like her father figure. She don't like to disappoint daddy."

Morris raised his eyebrows. "That's a scary thought, you a father."

Stewart winked at Morris.

Morris said, "By the way, Michael Jackson was a pedophile piece of shit should've died in the joint choking on some skinhead's cock."

Stewart said, "But the boy could represent. Could dance like a motherfucka."

## Chapter 11
## Bismarck, North Dakota

"How was the flight?" Tom Odakota, Esquire, asked Alex Pavlik.

He'd met Pavlik outside the North Dakota State Penitentiary on Railroad Avenue and drove him to his office across the Missouri river in Mandan. Odakota's private office was in the rear of a railroad storefront on East Main Street. A small room with little space between the attorney's desk and the two folding chairs facing it. Pavlik shifted sideways on his chair to stretch his legs. Odakota, a much smaller man, smiled from across his desk.

"The flight was torture," Pavlik said. "There was a detour to Sioux City, where I was squeezed inside a tiny prop thing. Not easy to adjust at my height. Pure torture."

"You're too tall for air travel," Odakota said.

"I'm thinking of driving back."

"Can't say I'd blame you. How can I help you?"

"Call me Alex, please," Pavlik said. "A number of ways, I think." He opened a folder from his briefcase and pulled three pictures. He shuffled Joseph Kincaid's picture to the top and handed them to Odakota.

"You know he was in Bismarck," Pavlik said.

"Twice I know of," Odakota said. "He was also incarcerated up in Canada once."

"Violent crimes?"

"Almost always for guys like Kincaid," Odakota said. "Usually from getting drunk but nothing as serious as what you mentioned, trying to kill someone. Prosecutors have a way of turning a bar fight into assassination attempts."

"Not this time," Pavlik said. "Look at the pictures."

Odakota did so. "You mentioned there was a third party on the phone," he said. "Maybe it was him who did the violence."

"Maybe, but either way, I'm pretty sure they were sent to New York to kill my client's husband," Pavlik said. "They banged her around pretty good. Tried to rape her, too. The husband walked in on it and was shot. He's the one they were after."

"And Kincaid?" Odakota said. "He still in a coma?"

"The doctors aren't sure he'll make it."

Odakota waited for more.

"Like I told you over the phone, the guy I'm looking for is a killer under federal witness protection," Pavlik said. "His name was James Singleton. If it is him, I'm sure they've changed his name. It could be Frederick Douglass by now. He's black, about forty-three years old, six two, two hundred pounds. That was his weight a couple years ago. But there is a distinguishing physical trait that I don't think plastic surgery could've changed much."

Odakota nodded.

"His right eye was shot out," Pavlik said. He pointed to one of the pictures on the desk. "That guy did it, the one Singleton is after. He shot out an eye. I'm sure Singleton's had it touched up. In fact, if he's still working for the government, I know it's been touched up, compliments of Uncle Sam, but I doubt they could do much about his eye and the damage the bullet did surrounding his eye."

"He may not be in North Dakota," Odakota said. "The guy you're looking for. Natives here are no different than anybody else in state. Unless they have ties, they tend to roam. White kids graduate college and tend to take off. Same with us. Unless the kids have a job to go to, it's reservation to reservation, state to state. Up in Canada, too sometimes. So, even if you're right about this, it could've started from anywhere."

"He can be in Rio, I know," Pavlik said. "But the attempt made on the other guy, the one shot him and his wife, that was very specific. And Kincaid was involved. The other thing, he had scars all over him, Kincaid. They appeared to be self-inflicted scars."

Odakota nodded. "It's a rite-of-passage phenomenon. Sometimes it's decorative and sometimes it's just dumb shit like bragging-rights tattoos. They used to do it inside the prisons mostly. Then it spread out to the reservations. I guess when they get themselves good and drunk. There are all kinds of theories on what it's about, but I tend to think it's just another form of a pissing match. My scars are bigger than yours, like that."

Pavlik nodded.

"Look, I doubt the FBI will provide me with the kind of information you're searching for," Odakota added. "Native Americans aren't top priority to the government unless they're looking to take something else from us."

"Which is why I asked you to meet me instead of going the formal request route," Pavlik said. "The feds won't help my client or her husband. The feds are the reason this happened in the first place. You can blame their bullshit witness protection program."

"I blame the federal government for a lot more than that," Odakota asked. "What can I do for you?"

"Good old grunt work, which I'd be more than willing to help with, provided the access." He presented Odakota with another folder. "Look this over before you make a decision. I was one of the homicide detectives assigned to the original case when the guy there, the one they're trying to kill, was a suspect. Singleton murdered three people in Manhattan before Eddie Senta stopped him from murdering his wife and kid. There are copies of the police scene report, the case report, and whatever else you might need. Like you said, contacting the FBI would just alert them. I'm not so sure they don't already know about this. The local police on Long Island were also familiar with the case I was assigned two years ago. They were there when Singleton was shot."

Odakota took a deep breath. "I can make calls," he said. "See what I can dig up for you, but I'm not sure it'll help. Guys like Joe Kincaid either alienate or scare the people they come into contact with. You might do better with local police, but then you'd be jumping town to town and there are a lot of them."

"Any Indian—sorry, Native Americans on the police forces up here?"

Odakota smiled. "A few," he said. "Very few, but there are some sympathetic to our cause."

"This the cause I'd be making a donation to?"

"It's called the Republic of Lakotah," Odakota said. "Look it up on the Internet."

"And how much am I donating?"

"Whatever you feel. We're a peaceful organization, Alex, but we're also serious. We know the fight for independence won't come easy or be cheap. We also know until more people are informed about our situation, there won't be much sympathy for our cause."

"Independence?"

"You'd best look it up before you decide on a donation."

"Can I at least leave you something for now?"

"I'd rather you looked up our organization and made your decision then."

□ □ □

He had dinner in the hotel restaurant. Between bites of liver he checked the local papers for crimes that might suggest James Singleton was in the area. He saw where a Native American bar featured karaoke between nine and closing and wondered if he might stop by and ask some questions there.

So far he'd had one hit in one try, a very good start. Odakota had known of Joseph Kincaid and had an even bigger beef with the federal government than Pavlik. Hopefully, tomorrow morning the attorney might know something more and maybe steer Pavlik in the direction of a one-eyed black man with at least two identities.

A heavyset older man with an eye patch entered the restaurant with a much younger woman. Pavlik wondered whether James Singleton was using a glass eye in place of the one Eddie Senta had shot out, or if he was also wearing an eye patch of some kind.

He watched the couple across the lounge. They looked like a grandfather and granddaughter or maybe a father and his daughter, or a prostitute and her john. Being suspicious was an old police habit he hadn't broken yet.

The waitress, a middle-aged woman with a big chest and thick legs, brought him a fresh cup of coffee and asked if he'd like to order something else. Pavlik asked for a slice of hot apple pie.

She gave him a wink. "New York?" she asked.

Pavlik was caught off guard. "Ah, yeah, yes, I am. That obvious, huh?"

"I was there once. Long time ago. It was so busy, all the people and traffic. Exciting, though. Very exciting."

Pavlik nodded politely.

"Shame what happened to them towers," she added.

Pavlik nodded again. He knew a dozen of the cops who had died when the buildings collapsed.

"Closest we had to something that bad here was a few years back," she said. "Some train run off the tracks outside Minot spilled some kind of chemicals. Ammonia or something. Killed one poor guy."

"Scary stuff, chemical spills," Pavlik said for politeness sake. He wished she would get his pie and leave him alone.

"You staying here? Upstairs?"

He nodded.

"Staying the night or longer?"

"Just tonight."

"Where to?"

"Minot, as a matter of fact."

"Oh, where the train wreck was. It's clean now. Nothing to worry about."

Pavlik half smiled.

"I'll go get your pie," she finally said, adding a wink for emphasis. "Ice cream with that?"

"Ah, no, thanks," he said.

She winked at him again. It made him uncomfortable. He wished he were back home.

## Chapter 12
## Minot, North Dakota

"Your girlfriend can use a makeover," Colonel Robert Schmidt told Washington Stewart.

They were at Schmidt's medical office on North Hill in Minot. Stewart's girlfriend, Lynette Nichols, was busy working on a crossword puzzle in the empty reception area. Roger Daltry, sitting alongside her, was playing with a portable video game. The office was closed for business. Schmidt could see the scarred woman from where they stood inside an examination room.

"I prefer her that way," Stewart told his partner.

"Not that it's any of my business," Schmidt added.

"You right, it's not, but there is something I need to know."

Schmidt nodded.

"Your wife's computer?"

"At the bottom of Devil's Lake."

"Good."

"One of the cops is still suspicious, but they could verify my whereabouts at the time of her murder. Now they have to live with their suspicions."

Stewart said, "I saw it on the news how the husband was out of town."

"She died like the slut she was," Schmidt added. "A woman fooling around on the Internet wound up in over her head. One of those Internet predators caught up with her."

"They'll eventually find her computer accounts," Stewart said.

"They already did. She had her own credit cards. I told the police. Where she kept her computer, possibly a laptop to keep it from me, I don't know where that is. I do, but I won't tell them to look in Devil's Lake. They already confirmed she was a slut. She was living a clandestine life, how was I supposed to know anything? I'm having the body shipped to her family. I'm still too distraught from what she must've been involved in to handle a funeral."

Stewart nodded again. "Good," he said. "We only need another few days."

"I'm on schedule," Schmidt said.

Stewart was there to pick up his half of the Afghani heroin shipment Schmidt had confiscated by accident months ago. Stewart thought it had landed at the Air Force base recently. "I believe you have something of mine," Stewart said.

Schmidt leaned against a file cabinet. "I was wondering about something," he said. "Regarding what you intend to do with your half of the product."

"Except that isn't your business," Stewart said.

"Maybe it should be."

"You have to be more specific. I'm a simple man."

Schmidt said, "You had mentioned potential buyers for your half. I'm wondering could I piggyback some of my half onto it? For the sake of facilitating a cleaner transition out of the country. Cash will be much easier to negotiate with than product once we're gone. If your buyers are interested, of course."

It was something Stewart had already considered, dealing the heroin all at once. Until he realized Schmidt could fly them out of the country safely, he had thought that he would have to kill the doctor to get it done.

Now the man was making it easier for him by finally showing he was nervous about something.

"Buyers are always interested in a bigger score," Stewart said. "Except then I'm the one taking all the risks."

"You're talking about a broker's fee."

"About fifteen percent."

"Ten."

"Twelve."

"Deal."

They shook on it.

Stewart said, "Where's the product?"

"Yours is in the trunk of my car in the garage," Schmidt said. "Mine will come after your negotiations are completed."

Stewart nodded. "Fair enough," he said. He started to leave when he remembered something. He pulled a small cassette tape from his pocket and tossed it to Schmidt.

The doctor was all smiles. "Michelle?" he asked.

"And Lester," Stewart said. "Their last conversation before she was killed."

□ □ □

If not for her scars, Lynette Nichols would have been an attractive woman. She had a slim body with good muscle tone, straight blonde hair and blue eyes. Most of her scars were from the time she spent living with Native American ex-convicts. Lynette had willingly adapted to the peculiar masochistic rituals of self-mutilation.

She had come to North Dakota from Oklahoma eight years ago. She had met Stewart at the state fair in Minot a year ago when a group of drunks were teasing her about her facial scars. Stewart had chased the drunks with a broken beer bottle. He took Lynette home that night and the two became intimate.

The burn marks up and down her legs were random. The scars on her stomach were symmetrical but ugly. Given the brutal North Dakota weather her stomach and leg scars were mostly hidden with clothes, but it was hard to look at her face without seeing the scars. She had told Stewart they were from cigarettes. He wasn't so sure they weren't from heated metal.

"So, the doctor wants to play too now?" she asked him.

They were in the Dodge heading south to Lake Sakakawea. Five kilos of pure Afghani heroin were riding in a container under a galley floorboard. Stewart had already dropped Daltry off back in Minot.

"The doctor wants to keep his hands clean," Stewart said. "But, yeah, he wants in. Wants the cash."

"Is that okay?"

"It's fine."

"What if they don't have enough money?"

"They'll have it."

"What if they don't?"

Stewart turned to her. "I said they'll have it."

Lynette apologized. Stewart turned the radio on. They drove a few miles listening to an oldies station before he turned the radio off again.

"You need to stop worrying," he told her.

"You're getting ready to leave," she said. "I can feel it."

"Except I'm taking you with me," Stewart said. "I told you that."

"I can't stay here without you," she said. "I'll kill myself."

Stewart reached across the console and put a hand on her arm.

"Everything will be okay," he told her.

Lynette forced a crooked smile. She saw herself in the rearview mirror and noticed her eyes were tearing. She wiped them before Stewart noticed it too.

□ □ □

First there was a voice message from the Mohall cop that had irritated Schmidt. It had come shortly before he closed the office. The woman who served as a receptionist had heard the message and would no doubt discuss it with her husband and friends when she got home.

Schmidt replayed it again now.

*Doctor, this is Jim Salinger up in Mohall. I was going over a few things and wondered if you could give me a call back in regards to what I had mentioned the other day. It seems your wife was involved in several affairs and I'm still having trouble understanding how you didn't know. Anyway, if you get a chance, please give me a call. On my cell is fine. Thanks.*

Then the cop from Mohall had set a speed trap for him. Schmidt was on his way home when he saw the flashing lights in his rearview mirror.

When he saw it was Salinger standing alongside his car, Schmidt thought it was about the phone call he hadn't bothered to return. Then the cop asked him for his license and registration without so much as saying hello.

"My license and registration?" the colonel had asked. "What the hell for?"

"You were speeding, sir," Salinger said.

"Speeding? Are you kidding me?"

"License and registration, please."

Schmidt realized the cop was trying to get under his skin again. He was determined not to let it happen this time. He handed over the paperwork and sat in silence until Salinger wrote the ticket.

Schmidt didn't bother to check for the amount because he had no intention of paying it. Instead, he set it on the console and waited for Salinger to repeat what he had asked on the voice mail.

Salinger seemed to be playing the same waiting game and said nothing.

"Can I go?" Schmidt asked.

"Did you have regular sex with her?" Salinger said.

"Yes," Schmidt lied.

"Regular a lot or once in a while?"

"Once a week. Sometimes it was two weeks. You know how marriages can get stale that way."

"And you still couldn't figure it out, that she was sleeping around?"

Schmidt didn't respond.

Salinger said, "She ever get infected or anything like that?"

"May I go now?" asked Schmidt without answering the last question.

"Sure," Salinger said. "But try and think if maybe you did suspect something and just didn't realize it. Sometimes that happens. It might help us in our investigation if we could find a time line that places a certain individual in it."

Schmidt knew the cop was bullshitting now. He nodded for the sake of going along with the routine.

"Okay, then," Salinger said. "Give us a call if you remember anything."

Schmidt cursed under his breath as he headed for home. Salinger thought he was being cute setting him up like that. First the bullshit phone call to unnerve him and then the speeding ticket. It was harassment, pure and simple, except Schmidt didn't have time to waste with a lawyer to back the cop off.

His wife had thought she could outmaneuver him and look how things had turned out for her, Schmidt was thinking.

Maybe the cop needed to learn a lesson as well.

## Chapter 13
## Minot/Velva, North Dakota

Emily Hehn's interest in petroglyphs first developed when she was thirteen years old. It was the first time she and her father had vacationed together in Glacier National Park. While there they visited a paleontology dig and Emily became fascinated with rock paintings.

The following summer her father brought Emily to a Native American reservation and she became enthralled with cave paintings depicted in a Native American art book. She went on to study petroglyphs at New Mexico State College and eventually became a humanities professor specializing in the same field.

As she prepared for an evening lecture, Emily highlighted the relevant points she would make, then read them aloud to herself in her office.

"Most of the petroglyphs were created between 1300 and 1650 AD," she said. "Some petroglyphs could be as much as two or three thousand years old. Other petroglyphs are historic, dating from the Spanish colonial period."

Emily circled "origins" on her outline and drew an arrow to the word "reasons."

She smiled as she remembered the first time Dale had showed interest in her field of specialty. It was shortly after they started dating. She had just taken the humanities position in Minot and had been so excited by his enthusiasm she talked for forty minutes before she recognized the stupefied look on his face.

She wrote "KEEP IT SHORT" on the top and in the middle of her lecture notes, then she underlined the words three times.

□ □ □

Dale had made it in time for the last few minutes of his wife's lecture. Sergeant Ekroth had come along for the ride. The two lawmen stood out in the back of the room full of students.

When it was over, Ekroth shifted the plastic coffee stirrer to one side of his mouth with his tongue and said, "You have a clue what she was talking about?"

"Something to do with cave paintings," Dale said. "That stuff on the walls. I once called it caveman graffiti, but I learned not to crack those jokes in front of Em again."

Emily made her way down the aisle to meet them.

Ekroth removed the coffee stirrer from his mouth. "It was great, Em," he said. "Really."

Emily rolled her eyes. "The last thing I said or the next to last?"

"Both," Ekroth said.

"I'm sorry, honey," Dale said.

"It's okay," Emily said. "I don't expect miracles. I'm glad you bothered to come at all."

"Don and I have got to head out to Velva. I shouldn't be home too late."

"It's okay," Emily said. "I'm going for drinks with some of the faculty before I head home."

Dale turned to Ekroth. "Drinks? Uh-oh."

"This coming from a man who drinks milk with his dinner," Emily told Ekroth.

"We had him figured for a bit of a wuss down at the station," Ekroth said.

Emily kissed Dale on the mouth, then pinched his ass. Dale jumped from the surprise.

Ten minutes later he and Ekroth were on their way to the small town of Velva. John Ahearn had moved there after leaving the Air Force seven years earlier. He had been arrested several times for driving under the influence and for a few assaults. Ekroth was familiar with Ahearn from an incident at the Minot Police Station a few years earlier.

"You're thinking Ahearn had something to do with the Barron kid?" he asked Dale.

"I'm thinking he knows something about what happened," Dale said. "His name came up and I ran it before I talked to you. He seems to gravitate toward trouble."

"He's a character alright. Nearly took Peterson's weapon at the station house the last time he was brought in. I had to whack him pretty hard to drop him."

"Six three, two twenty," Dale said, "according to his sheet. A guy that size hopped up on booze or drugs can be more than a handful."

Velva was twenty-three miles from Minot. It took Dale twenty minutes to get there. He turned off Highway 52 and crossed the railroad tracks into the small town.

"Let's just hope he's got heat," Ekroth said. "Unless we do the interview in here."

Dale read the temperature gauge on the dashboard. "Thirteen below," he said. "You think we'll ever get a break from this weather?"

"Around about April," Ekroth said.

They found the address on Fourth Street Northwest. Dale knocked on the door several times before John Ahearn finally answered.

"Yeah, what is it?" the big man said when he opened the door.

Dale introduced himself and Ekroth. Ahearn wasn't impressed. Dale asked if they could ask a few questions. Ahearn braced both his thick forearms against either side of the door frame.

"Ask away," he said in a gruff voice.

Dale rubbed his hands together. "Could we maybe come inside?"

"Not without a warrant," Ahearn said.

"Right," Dale said. "Well, do you know a college kid named Nathan Barron?"

"No."

"You don't?"

"No."

"Maybe you know him by another name? Nate, maybe?"

"No."

Ahearn was staring at Dale now.

"Do you know a Kathy Ljunndgren?" Dale asked.

"Yeah," Ahearn said.

"And?"

"I know her. So what?"

Dale looked to Ekroth.

Ekroth removed the coffee stirrer from his mouth. "Bring him in," he said.

"For what?" Ahearn said with attitude.

"Being uncooperative," Ekroth said.

"You have to subpoena me for that," Ahearn said.

"Technically," Dale said.

"What do you mean, technically? That's the law. I know my rights."

Dale looked to Ekroth again.

"Maybe we should get a warrant while we're at it," Ekroth said.

"Warrant for what?" Ahearn asked. "For knowing Kathy?"

"I was thinking we just grab him by the ears and drag him out to the car," Dale said.

"I'd like to see you try," Ahearn said.

Now Dale was fully engaged in his own stare-down with the big man. Ekroth put a hand on Dale's right shoulder. "Let's go," he said. "We'll come back with the warrant and a subpoena. He just gave us enough for that."

Ahearn turned to Ekroth and said, "And I remember you. You're the one hit me in the back of the head with that nightstick. Big tough guy with six of your best friends there."

"Actually it was the back of my weapon I struck you with," Ekroth said. "You're right, though, I had six of my best friends with me."

"Yeah and you almost scared me," Ahearn said.

"We'll be back," Dale said.

Ahearn feigned shaking his hands from fear.

□ □ □

Dale had infiltrated the small town of Safw6near the Iraq-Kuwaiti border a few days before the ground invasion. He was living in a hole he had dug and covered with rubble from a collapsed building. He had provisions to last a week. He was there performing reconnaissance for the invasion. The Iraqi Republican Guard had leveled and occupied the town a few days earlier. Republican Guard soldiers had raped many of the women and executed most of the men. Children had been herded into trucks and taken away. The night before the invasion two Republican Guard soldiers had found a young girl hiding in a nearby building. They took her to an area where air mattresses had been thrown down side by side. They began to beat the young girl until Dale could no longer watch. He used a sound suppressor and shot both men in the back from fifty yards. The girl was in shock and didn't move for hours.

Dale never reported what had occurred. The next day, when the ground invasion began, he buried the two Iraqi soldiers he'd killed. He never knew what had happened to the young girl.

"You okay?" Ekroth asked as they drove back to Minot.

"Huh?" Dale said. "Oh, yeah, sure. I'm just daydreaming."

"About what? You looked troubled."

"How does a guy like that make it through life?" asked Dale, switching his thoughts back to John Ahearn.

"Ahearn's a survivor," Ekroth said. "Air Force pension probably keeps him under a roof. He was injured on the base and wound up with permanent disability, believe it or not."

Dale made a face of disbelief. "You have to be kidding me," he said. "Disabled? That guy?"

"Ahearn probably plays every angle he can," Ekroth said. "He even tried to sue us, the department, once. Had a lawyer look into it."

"And?"

"Wasn't Becker, the lawyer," Ekroth said. "Some young kid fresh out of law school, I suppose. Advised our friend that while he might have a case, his client could also spend a year or so in jail. I guess the trade-off wasn't worth the risk."

"Unbelievable."

"Sure is, but I don't think Ahearn will get through the rest of his life without spending some of it in jail. He's a bad customer and not very smart."

"Sometimes I think life never catches up to people like that."

"Don't think so much," Ekroth said. "Although you can probably count on Ahearn having something to do with the drugs that killed that college kid."

Dale said, "That woman I told you about, the one down at the coffee shop, she was his girlfriend for a while. That might jar him."

"Ahearn didn't seem too impressed," Ekroth said. "He's probably got her scared out of her bra already. I wouldn't count on any fear of his wife either. Ahearn isn't the type to worry about his wife or any other woman catching him fooling around."

Dale let out a breath of frustration. "I guess you're right," he said.

"You let him get to you," Ekroth said.

"Yeah, I did."

"You need to be more subtle. Like I was with that remark about hitting him with the gun. Play along and drop one on him. He's easy enough. Hell, the man's a psycho. His only advantage is playing the tough angle and getting you to take a swing at him first."

Dale bit his upper lip.

"So, you do the next best thing to nailing him," Ekroth continued.

"Which is?" Dale asked.

"Bother the people around him," Ekroth said. "He's not a bright guy. You can aggravate him from a bunch of different angles."

Dale smiled.

"What?" Ekroth said.

"You're not as dumb as you look."

"It don't take a genius to spot a goat in a flock of sheep."

"Say what?"

Ekroth removed the coffee stirrer from his mouth. "If I was so smart, I wouldn't be a policeman this long," he said. "I'd have gone in with my brother-in-law and sold cars down to Bismarck."

Dale furrowed his eyebrows. "Selling cars? That's not you, my friend."

"That feller makes six figures a year, has a big house down there and his summer joint in Montana is bigger than my house here in Minot. Goes there twice a year to hunt and fish. Has at least three cars in his driveway at all times and a full lot of them to pick from he grows tired of the colors. Thirty years down the road, what do I have besides a mortgage?"

"Peace of mind?"

Ekroth bit down on the coffee stirrer. "Hemorrhoids," he said.

## Chapter 14
## Bismarck/Lake Sakakawea, North Dakota

Pavlik drank from a can of Olympia beer while he watched a local sporting show on ice fishing. He had been skipping through channels when an aerial view of shacks and tents scattered across a frozen lake stopped him. Now he was fascinated.

He listened intently and learned how crappies were a favorite catch for those into night fishing and how walleyes often looked for prey immediately after the sun set.

He was amazed to learn there was an entire ice fishing industry that included customized ice shelters similar to mobile homes.

He turned up the volume during a commercial for ice fishing equipment.

*We pride ourselves on building you the best shack you will ever buy for your investment. Have all the comforts of home while you relax and wait for that catch of a lifetime. As most fishermen know, the more comfortable you can make yourself, the more enjoyable the experience will be! Our shacks and toy haulers have all the latest advancements in the RV industry. Make your first purchase of a Lodge a lifetime investment. We also offer a full one year end-to-end warranty on every trailer.*

*You want something different? We specialize in customizing your shack or toy hauler to fit all your needs! If you want it we will build it for you!*

Pavlik tried to imagine himself with Aelish living on the ice when she called his cell phone.

"Hey," he answered, "I was just thinking about you."

"I would hope so," Aelish said.

"I'm watching a local show about ice fishing. They have these made-to-order shacks you can have built. Pretty cheap, too."

"And you were thinking about me?"

"Just, you know, picturing us living in one."

"On the ice."

"Well, fishing on it. It's a big deal out here."

"Alex, you don't have the slightest clue how to fish."

"Says you."

"Says me. You get green talking about it."

"Because we live near the ocean. This here is lake country. No rogue waves to worry about."

"Rogue waves. Listen to you."

"I'm just saying. This kind of fishing doesn't require you use a boat. They have shacks and tents and stuff. You just pull up a chair, pop a beer and drop the line in a hole in the ice."

"In temperature cold enough to freeze a lake."

"Yeah, but you're all warm inside. It's not like you're out on the high seas. No need for sea legs."

"Sounds pretty boring, Alex."

"It's a big business out here."

"I was calling to say goodnight, love."

"Don't you want to hear about my day?"

"In the morning."

"Oh, okay."

"I'll wake you before I leave for work."

Pavlik was watching a heavy man unhook a long fish he'd just pulled from the ice hole. "Wow," he said.

"Wow? You're preoccupied."

"Huh?"

Aelish kissed him through the phone. "Night, love," she said.

"Oh, right. Love you, too," Pavlik said.

He set the cell phone down and turned up the volume on the television one more time as the heavy guy showed how to fillet a walleye.

□ □ □

They stopped at the RV at the marina to use the bathrooms and shower. When they were back on the boat and the cabin was warm again, Lynette gave Stewart a blow job before he took a nap. When he woke up, he sat in front of the television and watched a Lakers game.

At the half he was feeling tired again. He needed coffee and called to Lynette to make a pot. She didn't answer.

Stewart went to her room and saw she was wearing headphones while she worked on her computer. A stick of her favorite candy, Twizzlers, hung from her mouth as she worked the mouse with her right hand. She leaned in close to the screen to read and didn't notice him.

Although he was originally attracted to her hair color, Stewart also felt an affinity with Lynette because of her scars. There was something beyond the physical attributes of their wounds he could relate to. She was a loner; so was he. She was a drug addict; he had been one himself. Until she met him, Lynette seemed to have nothing to live for; he had learned to live for revenge.

Now he turned the volume off on the CD player. Lynette tugged on her headphones before turning to Stewart. "Oh, I didn't see you," she said.

He had become protective of her. Sometimes he would let her spend the night with him. Sometimes, when he traveled without letting the federal agents know where he was going, he would take her with him.

He stared at the long burn scar that ran from the base of Lynette's nose around her mouth and down her chin to the base of her neck.

"You always got that shit kicking music on," he told her, "of course you didn't see me. You can't hear me. I been calling you for ten minutes."

Lynette frowned. "Sorry."

It was a pathetic sight when she frowned. It made him feel shitty for hassling her. "I'd like some coffee," he said, "it's not too much trouble."

"Sure."

"I'm lucky the heaters are working tonight. It's cold enough out there they don't."

"You can always stay in the RV."

"I can set myself on fire, too. I don't like the RV. I like it here." He motioned at the computer screen. "What you got there?"

"Our girl in Montana."

"Okay," said Stewart, smiling now. Lynette turned the screen so he could see it. "Let's see what she has to say."

Lynette read the email from BLNDMONTANAHOT14U. "'I'm still waiting for that picture, lover,'" she read. "'In the meantime, instead of Internet sex, how about phone sex? If I like your voice, maybe I can ignore what you look like.' Then she gives a number."

"Let me have it," Stewart said. He wrote the number on a piece of newspaper as she repeated it.

"Should I respond?" Lynette said. "I have to leave soon. Selma asked me to spend the night. The other two aren't supposed to be there."

Selma was a junkie Lynette had brought over for an occasional threesome. Stewart had thought it was good Lynette had another woman living at the place she shared with two other junkies, a pair of cowboy rednecks he had threatened with a gun more than once.

"No," Stewart said. "I'll call." He motioned toward the galley. "How 'bout that coffee before you go?"

Lynette grabbed another Twizzler from the bag when she stood up from the desk. She took a bite as she sidestepped Stewart on her way to the galley. Stewart sat at the terminal and used the mouse to scroll down a list of pictures alongside personal ads. He stopped when he spotted a blonde posing in a white bikini.

He read aloud from the profile caption. *"Former cheerleader, single mom, seeking self-sufficient generous man. Must be single, polite, and must like children. Send pic or don't expect a reply. No pics to trade, so please don't ask."*

"But are you really blonde, honey?" Stewart asked the screen. "And how'm I supposed to know, I don't see for myself?"

□ □ □

He closed the bedroom door before he spoke into his cell phone. "You still with that Montana girl?" Stewart asked. "The one with the perky ass?"

"For at least another week or so," Joe Mayo said.

"She still on the Internet?"

"'Blonde Montana hot one for you.' Take a look, that's her picture."

"Just checking. I already did. She lovely alright."

"We still on?" Mayo asked.

"Why wouldn't we be?"

"I show mine, you show yours?"

"Fair enough," Stewart said. "We both rats, it wouldn't be a surprise one of us stiffs the other, the stiffed party drops a dime."

"Let's not get confused here," Joe Mayo said. "It's my father in the program, not me. This is his game."

"And I'm a firm believer in apples not falling far from they trees," Stewart said. "Or I wouldn't agree to the terms."

"I'll see you soon."

"Sooner the better. And I may have a present for you and your dad."

"I'm not into surprises," Joe Mayo said. "Neither is the old man."

"Trust me," Stewart said, "he'll like this one."

□ □ □

When Stewart awoke, it was from the telephone ringing. He glanced at the digital alarm radio. It read two o'clock. He yawned as he answered the phone.

It was Lynette. The woman she was supposed to babysit had wandered off somewhere. Stewart rubbed his good eye. "What you mean, she's gone? How the hell that happen?"

"Tommy and Olafsen weren't supposed to be there but they were," Lynette told him. "They cranked up before I got home." Her voice was nervous. She said, "They were skying when I walked in. Selma was gone. She had a jacket, but not her heavy one. I took a quick drive around the streets here. I didn't see her."

"Fuck," Stewart said.

"What do we do?"

"I'll be right there."

"You're coming over?"

"What I just say?"

□ □ □

It was a few minutes before dawn when Stewart found the woman they had been searching for. She had passed out on a dirt road near Lake Sakakawea about two miles from the town of Pick City, where Lynette lived with the rednecks and her friend Selma. The woman was close to freezing to death from exposure when Stewart put his flashlight on her. He had brought his Glock but thought better of shooting her. Selma had been a good friend to Lynette and didn't deserve a violent death.

He pinched her nose with two fingers and then covered her mouth with his free hand until he was sure she was gone. When he caught up with Lynette again, he told her there was no point in looking anymore; either her friend had hitched a ride somewhere or she was lost and would probably freeze to death. Lynette accepted the news without comment. She let Stewart take her hand and guide her back to the Dodge. They shared a joint in the cab before he drove back to the boat. Half an hour later, she cuddled against Stewart in his bed. Outside the wind chill was twenty-five degrees below zero.

"I'm real sorry about Selma," Lynette said.

"The girl was junkified," Stewart said. He was facing away from her. He spoke with his eye closed. "Nothing you can do for somebody like that, they don't want to help themselves."

Lynette had been stroking his ass with her fingertips. He reached behind to slap at her hand.

"Not now," he said. "I need my sleep."

"Sorry," she said.

Sometimes he put it on for her, the street talk he often used to throw people off. Sometimes, like now, when he was tired, Stewart forgot which talk to use.

"That's twice you sorry," he told her.

"Sorry," she said again.

He turned to face her. He was angry, but the hurt look in her eyes kept him from saying anything cruel. He kissed her forehead instead. She smiled. It was a grotesque smile that always touched him. He kissed her again before he turned back around.

"We got business to take care of," he said.

"In Minot?"

"Yeah. So you stay clean, you hear?"

"I am. I didn't do anything. I've been clean. You know that."

"Good."

"I didn't even drink."

"Good."

"I stopped for something to eat after I left and then I went straight home. I probably shouldn't have. I probably would've run into Selma if I didn't stop. I could've kept those two assholes from getting her high."

"Forget Selma."

"I still should've went home first," Lynette said.

Stewart turned his head to speak over his shoulder. "Well, you never went home, anybody asks."

"Huh?"

"You never went home."

"Okay."

"You went and got something to eat and then came back here."

Lynette nodded. "Sure, hon."

Stewart turned back around and pulled the covers tight over himself.

"I sure hope Selma hitched somewhere," Lynette said. "The way she was dressed. Her heavy coat was in her room when I got there."

Stewart had started to snore lightly. Lynette listened to him a moment before curling up alongside his back.

"I love you," she whispered.

Stewart snored.

## Chapter 15
## Minot, North Dakota

When he woke up, Dale saw his wife was wearing white lace garters with a matching bra.

"I died and went to heaven," he said.

"Good response," Emily said.

She had been brushing her hair in front of the mirror. She picked up the cup of coffee she had poured earlier and brought it to him.

Dale looked into the cup, saw it was half filled, and said, "What happened to the rest?"

"We don't have time for the rest," she said. "Drink up."

He followed her instructions, then set the cup on the night table.

"Use the bathroom now if you have to," she said. "I have a nine o'clock meeting at the office."

Dale jumped out of bed and headed for the bathroom. He wondered what was going on until he remembered the stunt Emily had pulled during the summer when she had shown up at his job naked underneath a raincoat. It was something he never could have expected back then. Just the thought of it now excited him.

That day she had made love to him in one of the janitor closets in the basement. Now at least he wouldn't have to worry about someone walking in on them.

He was still hard when he came out of the bathroom. Emily gave him an approving wink.

"Very good," she said. "Now, we have exactly twenty-five minutes before I have to leave."

Dale looked at the clock and saw it was ten to eight. "You'll never make the meeting on time."

"Not if you're gonna talk I won't."

He went to her and they began kissing. Dale stole looks at his wife's body in the mirror as he groped her. She pulled him to the bed and Dale tried to go down on her. Emily stopped him. She motioned for him to lie on his back and then mounted him. She removed her bra and leaned forward enough to tease his lips with her nipples. Then she reached back and fondled him with her right hand and guided him inside her.

Emily closed her eyes as she rocked back and forth. Dale grew conscious of the time and started to buck underneath her. She met his thrusts and soon had his shoulders pinned with both her hands. She leaned into him until she felt the first rushes of orgasm. She was loud when she came. Dale was caught up in the moment. He tried to keep her on top, but she rolled off and lay on her back.

When he tried to climb on top, Emily turned away.

"Later," she said. "I'm too tingly now."

"Later?"

"Tonight."

"Tonight?"

"After dinner, I promise."

"Jesus, Em, this isn't right."

"It was great, honey. Thank you."

"But I thought it was for me."

"It was for both of us."

"But I didn't come."

"Not this time. Tonight you will."

Dale sighed.

"Don't be a baby," she said. "You made your wife very happy this morning."

"I have a feeling it wasn't me."

"It was, trust me. It's nice to know I can still excite you."

"In that outfit, Jesus Christ'd get excited. I can't believe I have to think about it all day."

She rolled onto her side to face him. "That's the point, detective. You'll think about it and then it'll be that much better."

"Yeah, great, thanks," Dale said. He saw the time on the radio clock. "Aren't you gonna be late?"

Emily saw the time and waved it off. "I have a few minutes."

"Don't you have to shower, get dressed?"

"Nope."

"Nope, you don't have to shower, or nope, you don't have to get dressed? You're not going to work like that, I hope?"

"Yep, it'll be under my dress."

"What?"

"It'll be under my dress."

"Something else for me to think about?"

Emily leaned over to peck him on the lips. "Who ever said cops were stupid?"

Dale watched his wife roll off the bed, grab a dress from the closet, and head into the bathroom. Then he looked down, saw he was still hard and cursed under his breath.

□ □ □

He was cranky the rest of the morning. His mood didn't improve when he was called to the scene of an apparent train accident victim under the Broadway overpass. A hobo had probably frozen to death too close to the tracks and was hit by a train. His body had been severed in half.

"How the hell do you get hit by a train?" Dale asked no one in particular.

"You get drunk and then freeze to death," Ekroth answered. "Or maybe you fall asleep before you freeze to death."

Dale hadn't seen the sergeant drive up. He shook Ekroth's hand. "I thought you were in later today?"

"I was supposed to be," Ekroth said. "Couldn't sleep once the sun came up."

"You should try using shades."

Ekroth nudged Dale with an elbow. "Come on, let's grab some coffee. They'll be scraping that poor bastard off the tracks the rest of the morning."

Dale followed Ekroth to a Mr. Donut near the university campus. They sat at a table and ate a donut breakfast.

"Some kids found another body late last night," Ekroth said before taking a bite from a donut. "It's up at the morgue now. Couple, three shots in the back of the head."

Dale was listening. "And?"

"Black feller with cornrows."

"Williams? The flyboy?"

"Looks like it."

Dale looked ready to jump. "Shouldn't we get over there, the morgue?"

Ekroth waved it off. "Body isn't going anywhere and the ME said it'll take a while for it to thaw. Some kids found him near a drainpipe half a mile from Fifty-two. Frozen solid. We're trying to keep a lid on it, but the kids that found him will probably blab it anyway."

"Executed, huh?"

Ekroth nodded. "Got me to thinking," he said. "That thing up in Mohall, that doctor's wife they found murdered up there."

"Not for us to think about," Dale said. "Not our jurisdiction."

"Yeah, but the woman and her husband lived here in Minot."

"Wasn't she caught in a kind of compromising situation? I mean, the doctor didn't seem to know where his wife was. Didn't he put out a missing person report or something?"

"He was visiting her hometown in Montana. Even bought her some presents from her old high school. A hat or something. Pretty convenient, you ask me."

"Could be. So?"

Ekroth dunked the last of a donut in his coffee. "This is still North Dakota," he said. "That woman one day, the Barron kid, then this feller they found at the drainpipe, whether it's Williams or not."

"Except Barron is an overdose."

"Probably."

"I'm back to so," Dale said. "What?"

"And this mess this morning," Ekroth said.

"The poor slob probably froze to death before the train got him."

"Probably froze to death first. Maybe so."

Dale rubbed his face. "I've already had a rough morning," he said. "You'll have to be more specific about whatever is bugging you."

Ekroth shook his head. "I don't know," he said. "It's just a lot of death, I guess. These aren't the usual highway accident fatalities. There's been a lot of curious death for here. Makes a man wonder."

"That it?" Dale asked. "That's what you were thinking about?"

"That's it."

Dale shook his head.

"I didn't say it was anything profound," Ekroth said.

## Chapter 16
## Bismarck, North Dakota

In the morning it was bitter cold outside. Pavlik draped himself in a blanket and wore it to and from the bathroom. He used the portable coffeemaker to brew a quick pot, then stood at the window and looked out at the barren land that was once the American frontier. He shook his head at the vastness of it.

When the coffee was ready, he sipped from the cup several times before he picked up the telephone to call home.

"Hey," he said when Aelish answered.

"Good morning," she said with energy in her brogue. "You're up early. I wasn't going to call for another half hour. You going ice fishing?"

"Very funny."

"You might as well while you're out there. Get it out of your system."

"I wouldn't mind trying it, smartass. In the meantime, you know where I am?"

"North Dakota."

"Bismarck, North Dakota. It's where the Raccoon National Cemetery is. Where Ralph and Alice could've been buried if he won Raccoon of the Year?"

"What the hell are you talking about?"

"*The Honeymooners.*"

"The what?"

"Never mind," Pavlik said. "The television here says it's five degrees outside."

"The television here says it isn't going much higher where you are. I've had the weather channel on since last night."

"It really is cold. You're lucky you're home."

"How's it going?"

"The attorney here is going to help, but I'm in for a lecture."

"About what?"

"Historical racism. The attorney is part of some movement looking to break away from the United States to form their own country."

"And what's wrong with that?"

"Nothing, except I don't have time for it now. If Singleton is out there, I can't waste time relearning American history and this guy sounded like he couldn't wait to tell me about it."

"You ask me, it's a damn shame you don't already know your own history. It's an arrogance about too many Americans, how they like to bathe themselves in patriotism based on fairytales. My Da used to say it takes a particular blindness to be so self righteous."

"Not you, too."

"Don't be cute, love. My Da spent five years in a British jail for Irish independence, which he never lived to see and we still don't have."

"And you support what they did, the IRA? Not the cause, what they did."

"When it wasn't indiscriminate violence I did. But what did peaceful negotiations ever get them except token gestures of half-assed freedom? You should listen to what this attorney has to say. Learn a little something more about your founding fathers than what you've been brainwashed to believe. A bunch of rich white men formed a government to protect what they had. They didn't seem to mind the slavery issue, not enough so they didn't let it continue. Then again, some of them were slave owners themselves."

"And here I would've thought you would've admired their fight for independence, especially from England."

"The revolution was one thing, but then once they had their independence what did they do with it? Ask the slaves how they felt about your independence."

"Uh-oh."

"Never mind," Aelish said. "And those poor bastards out there, American Indians, what's happened to them ever since?"

"That wasn't fair, I'll give you that."

"You'll give me? How about the small pox?"

"Excuse me?"

"Christ, you really are daft."

"What about small pox?"

"America didn't need discovering, Alex. It was already populated. Long before Europeans stumbled onto its shores. Part of the move west included trying to kill off the native population with small pox. The fact you don't know that is shameful."

"I guess I skipped that part of the movie when I went to get popcorn."

"Don't be a smartass. You make jokes about it, but it's close to my heart what those people go through. You tell me the difference between what Israel does to Palestinians, the Brits do to the Irish and Scotts and how native Americans are treated."

"Hey, lighten up, it isn't my fault."

"If you support this government it is."

"Oh, Jesus."

"Oh, Jesus yourself."

Pavlik gave it a moment. "You're angry now?"

"Maybe we should talk tomorrow."

"Aelish, I don't want to fight."

"It's too late for that now, isn't it?"

"Oh, come on."

"Have a good day, Alex."

"Aelish, don't—" but she had already hung up

◻ ◻ ◻

He met Thomas Odakota in the coffee shop downstairs an hour later. When the attorney handed back the folder, Pavlik frowned as Odakota pointed to it.

He said, "There's an extra sheet of paper in there. Kincaid got himself in trouble a few times. He's off the Turtle Mountain Reservation. It can be a nasty place. When they come out of there, Turtle Mountain, they can be violent hard-liners."

"When did he leave Turtle Mountain?" Pavlik asked.

"He was nineteen, the first time. He did a stretch at the state penitentiary here in Bismarck, was out at twenty-two, and was back again for manslaughter by twenty-five. He killed a Native American inside the prison, but he got away with that one. The guy he killed inside was from the reservation at Standing Rock, another resort for some violent offenders. It's a reservation like the one at Turtle Mountain. It's another prison if you're on the lower end of the income scale."

"How might Kincaid associate with blacks?" Pavlik asked. "I read somewhere they didn't get along, Native Americans and blacks."

"Some don't," Odakota said. "We're no different than any other group, except we were shit on a lot more than the rest. Some don't get along with others. I don't know how Kincaid wound up working with blacks, unless it had something to do with drugs."

"That would fit the guy I'm looking for, the drug angle," Pavlik said.

Odakota pointed to the envelope. "There was an instance where Kincaid had some trouble with the police in Minot," he said. "That's straight north of here. Somebody bailed him out. Could've been a black guy, but it doesn't say there. Just the name. John Ahearn."

"Did he have an eye patch or something like that, this Ahearn guy bailed out Kincaid?"

"I have no idea."

"There's an Air Force base up there, right, in Minot?"

"There's another in Grand Forks, but, yes, there's one in Minot, too."

"Did the guy who bailed Kincaid come from the base?"

"No. If he's moved there, you'd better forget about snooping around. The Air Force isn't receptive to outsiders walking their grounds."

Pavlik touched the envelope. "Anything else?"

"No," Odakota said, "except I have friends in Minot should you need any help once you're there. Give me a call if you do and I'll see if one or two are available. Better yet, I'll give you a call. Where are you staying?"

"The Lawrence Welk."

Odakota smiled as he shook his head. "The band leader," he said. "That makes me chuckle every time."

Pavlik said, "About a donation. Can you give me a hint here. I wrote a check here for two hundred. That okay?"

Odakota shrugged. "Just remember to look us up on the Internet," he said. "For your own edification."

"Oh, believe me, I will," Pavlik said. He went to hand the check to Odakota, but the attorney waved it off.

"After you look us up," he said.

## Chapter 17
### Lake Sakakawea/Minot, North Dakota

Special Agent in Charge Eugene Morris was anxious to confront his key player in the North Dakota drug operation. After learning about the attempt on Eddie Senta's life back in New York, Morris had requested a security check on the Senta couple. When he learned Senta's wife had retained a retired New York police detective, Morris extended the security check and was informed that the retired cop was Alex Pavlik, one of the two NYPD homicide detectives on the scene the day Eddie Senta shot James Singelton/Washington Stewart's eye out.

This morning he had learned that Pavlik was already in North Dakota asking questions and that he'd booked a room at the Lawrence Welk Hotel in Minot, the same place Morris had pre-booked a room for Washington Stewart.

The special agent in charge found Stewart urinating at the edge of Lake Sakakawea. Standing with his arms folded, Morris waited for Stewart to zipper up before starting in on him.

"You couldn't let it go, could you?" he finally said.

"Let what go?" Stewart said.

"Eddie Senta," Morris said. "You couldn't leave him alone."

"Afternoon to you, too," Stewart said.

Morris grabbed Stewart by the jacket collar. "I should run you into the river and toss you a rock," he said.

"Let go of me!" Stewart said.

"Let go of you?"

Morris punched Stewart hard on the exposed side of his face. Stewart went down. He rubbed his jaw a few times before getting up.

"You sent one of your boys off to New York with some Indian convict to kill Eddie Senta and his wife, and then they left a trail back here any moron could find."

"Man shot my eye out," Stewart said. He continued to rub his jaw.

"The man isn't my concern, fuckhead!" Morris yelled. "The man is a nobody. You put a federal investigation at risk because you're holding a vendetta for something you deserved. You deserved a lot worse, but Eddie Senta was a bad shot."

Stewart examined his hand for blood. There wasn't any.

"And there's something else," Morris said. "There's a man out here looking for you now. An ex-cop. An ex-cop Eddie Senta's wife hired to find you. He's already on your trail, thanks to the Indian."

"Yeah, where'd you hear that, there's somebody on my trail?"

"Like it makes a difference. The Indian was carrying his wallet when Eddie Senta knocked one of his eyes out with a baseball bat. The man knows you're here, in North Dakota."

"He know where?"

"Don't push me, asshole."

"I'm serious. The man know where in North Dakota? This a big fuckin' state. Huge fuckin' state."

"Except you're supposed to be under the radar. You were. Now you're not."

"So, you about to flip those investment bankers anyhow, the ones you nailed in that little sting I did for you the other day. Step your plans up, brother. Move them in and me out."

"Just like that, huh? We're here to service you."

Stewart said, "Look, I took a shot and missed. If it'll help, I promise not to do it again." He held up two fingers. "Scouts honor."

Morris floored Stewart again. This time he drew blood.

"I have your attention now?"

"Don't hit me again," Stewart said. He wiped blood from the corner of his mouth.

Morris said, "He was one of the cops in the house the day Eddie Senta shot you. We had a beef that day, me and him. He didn't like that we were protecting you and I didn't like that he was in the middle of my investigation, although that was only because you thought you were so smart you were gonna rob some gold and get out of the country."

Morris gave Stewart a moment to think about it, then added, "Eddie Senta's wife contacted him."

Stewart wiped at his mouth with the back of his sweatshirt sleeve.

"The guy knows he can't do anything to you while we're protecting you," Morris said. "He's looking for a way around it."

Stewart remained silent.

"You'd better think about it before you shrug it off," Morris said. "There are people in New York want you killed. That make you nervous? It would me."

Stewart said, "You gonna tell me the man's name? The one here looking to have me killed."

"No," Morris said. "It'll keep your half blind, ignorant, black ass a little more honest if you're worried about dying."

"And if he manages to kill me before I do finish my gig for Uncle Sam? Where's that leave you?"

"Now that shouldn't concern you, dumbass, what happens to me after you're dead."

☐  ☐  ☐

"You're making kumla?" Marsha Nordstrom asked Dale.

She had followed him inside the kitchen at the Lawrence Welk Hotel. He set two bags of groceries and some precooked food he had brought from his house on a chair. He pulled a bag of potatoes from one bag and set it on a stainless steel counter.

"Yes, ma'am," he said. "Got the chef's permission to borrow your kitchen here at the hotel in exchange for the use of my new shotgun so he can shoot some wild turkeys over in Minnesota."

"Excuse me?" Marsha said. "Ma'am?"

"Miss," Dale said. "Yes, miss."

"Smart, good-looking, and you cook," Marsha said. "I really did blow it."

"Except I have to make two batches," Dale said. "Em likes her kumla spicy. I can't handle the spice."

"You never cease to amaze me, sir."

He emptied the ham broth into a pot and set a low flame. "You on break?" he asked.

Marsha nodded. "Half an hour."

Dale held up the plastic bag filled with ham steak slices. "Feel like cutting this up?"

"Sure," Marsha said. She tied an apron around her waist and grabbed the plastic bag filled with ham.

"That guy you fed me turned up dead," Dale said. "The one with the cornrows."

"Oh, my God," Marsha said. "How?"

"Shot in the back of the head, his body is still thawing out."

"What's going on in this place, Dale? What's Minot turning into?"

"Don Ekroth and I drove out to Velva to talk with that mean guy you mentioned," Dale said. He ran a potato through a cheese grater. "His name is Ahearn. John Ahearn."

"The name isn't familiar, but I sure can picture him," Marsha said. "Curly blond hair, thick beard. Big hands. I remember his hands because he palmed one of those bar mugs the hotel was using for Octoberfest last year. Most people needed two hands to hold it. He have something to do with the one who was killed?"

"We don't know yet, but I'm thinking he might."

"How big should I cut the ham slices?"

Dale turned to look at the meat. He closed one eye as he tried to visualize a ball of potato and cheese with a piece of ham in the middle.

He held two fingers an inch apart. "Like that," he said.

Marsha smiled at him.

"What?" he asked.

"You're too cute."

Dale blushed.

"What about that other guy?" Marsha asked. She started to cut the chunks of ham steak. "The one with the mask. The mean guy know him?"

Dale was feeding another potato through the grater. "Ahearn wasn't very cooperative," he said. "Don Ekroth put a call to the base, but we're not expecting much help from them. Ahearn was with the Air Force at one time. We know the dead guy was. Tyrone Williams was his name."

"I still can't believe this is happening here."

Dale said, "It amazes me how cryptic that place can sometimes be, the base. You call up and tell them you arrested one of their people for possession of heroin and it's as if the guy was holding national secrets."

"You'd think there would be charges," Marsha said.

"Civil rights," Dale said. "There probably are but nothing can happen until he's proven guilty of something in a criminal court. Enter Mr. Henry Becker. Exit criminal case. Most of them anyway."

Marsha was finished with the first ham steak. "Did you meet with that kid's mother? The one that died?"

"Yeah," Dale said. He turned to her. "And I made a promise that I don't have a chance in hell of keeping. Not yet."

"That's because you're a good guy," Marsha said. "You wanted to make her feel better."

Dale finished with the first few potatoes and transferred them into a mixing bowl. "I don't kid myself about that," he said. "There's no making that woman feel better. I realized that after I told her that I would find out if there was anyone else responsible for her son's death. She told me it didn't matter. She said her son was gone. He isn't coming back."

It was an uncomfortable moment. Marsha pointed to the mixing bowl. "You need to add the flour," she said.

"Right," Dale said. He grabbed the bag of flour from the grocery bag and opened one end.

"Well, I'll keep my eyes open. If that guy or anyone else shows up at the lounge again."

"They green or blue, your eyes?" Dale asked. "I forget."

Marsha tossed a piece of the ham at him.

"Oh, right. I remember now. Green, right?"

"And Em?" Marsha asked. "What color are your wife's eyes?"

Dale turned to point a finger at her. He said, "Oh, no, you don't."

They worked fast the next several minutes. When he was finished mixing the flour and potatoes, he added the oatmeal and mixed again. He formed potato-sized balls with the mix and poked a hole for the ham. He remolded the mix around the ham and set each ball into the ham broth.

"I'm impressed," Marsha said.

"You need to get out more."

"Tell me about it."

"What is going on with that, your love life?"

"Nothing, to be honest. That guy I was dating in the summer wanted to move in. I wasn't that interested."

"Where is he now?"

"South Dakota. Still looking for a wife, I suppose. He wasn't so interested in me as he was in being married."

Dale said, "Well, you're still the best catch in Minot, you ask me."

Marsha said, "So are you, Dale. Emily is a lucky woman."

They smiled at one another until they were both uncomfortable again. Marsha removed her apron and Dale started on the second batch of kumla. Then he remembered his wife's lecture at the library. He glanced at his watch and frowned when he saw he was already late.

☐ ☐ ☐

Stewart found Henry Becker, Esquire, at his Minot law office in a building on South Main Street. The old Montgomery-Ward Department store had been renovated to accommodate both commercial and residential space. Becker was one of the most successful criminal defense attorneys in the state. His law offices were on the main floor. He also rented a one-bedroom apartment upstairs.

Becker spotted Stewart in the lobby and immediately rushed out of his office.

"You know who I am?" Stewart asked once they were in the elevator.

"I have an idea," Becker said.

They remained quiet until they were inside Becker's apartment. They sat across from one another in the modernly furnished living room. A glass cocktail table with fresh white orchids in a vase was centered on the table.

"This isn't bad, your little getaway," Stewart said.

"It works," Becker said. He pointed to a rolling bar in one corner. "Drinks?"

"No, thank you," Stewart said. "You know, I spotted two good ones down there before you rushed me into the elevator. The two brunettes working your reception. One has short hair, the other long."

"They're lovely girls," Becker said. "The one with the curls works reception. The other is my secretary."

"Whatever," Stewart said. "They both have some fine butts. These white girls up here, some of them got robust butts like the sisters back East. Big puffy butts. They can get out of control sometimes, don't get me wrong. Start to spread all over the place once the kids come, but you can't beat the feel of one when they still young."

Becker patiently waited for Stewart to finish. "You through?" he said.

Stewart said, "Floor's yours, counselor."

"Thank you," Becker said. "Tyrone Williams was an easy one, but I don't know that you want to let them get any more practice at this. The police up here may seem naive, but they're not. They're not stupid either. Sooner or later they'll figure out who to look for and how to catch them, especially when people start turning up dead."

"At least Tyrone won't be a problem anymore," Stewart said before he lit a cigarette. "You don't mind I smoke?"

"No problem," Becker said. "There's an ongoing investigation into the kid from the college. That one you can't make go away. It's why the Tyrone Williams thing isn't smart. I understand Ahearn passed out my card to a few people. That wasn't smart either."

Stewart ignored the mention of John Ahearn. "Kid from Detroit, right?" he asked. "The one from the college? That one shouldn't have happened."

"It isn't good press for the campus," Becker said. "You'd be surprised how much clout they have in this city, the university."

"That was out of my control," Stewart said. He reached for a crystal ashtray on an end table.

"I'm mentioning it because people are alert to the problem. The meth problem is bad enough. Knowing there's heroin moving across state borders was overlooked until this kid turned up dead. Now there are headlines to contend with. Heroin won't be overlooked in Minot. It scares people. People here'll want something done about it."

"And well it should scare them," Stewart said. "It's a nasty drug, heroin is."

"I think you get my drift," Becker said. "Heroin-dealing won't be a long-term profitable business here. Nothing near worth the risk it'll involve."

Stewart removed an envelope from inside his coat. He set it on the cocktail table and pushed it across to Becker. "The balance for your trouble with Tyrone," he said. "And for whatever else might occur the next few weeks. I'll be going on a vacation after a week or so. I'm thinking Glacier Park or Yellowstone. I haven't decided yet."

"It's a little cold for those parts this time of year," Becker said.

"It's how I like it," Stewart said. "Besides, I'm used to the cold now."

Becker motioned at the envelope. "How much is in there?"

"Five thousand."

"Plus what's left of your original retainer makes it seven grand," Becker said. "I'll be sure to return whatever isn't billed."

"Or you can buy those girls with the robust butts those lacey thong underwears they have in the Victoria Secret catalogue," Stewart said. "Have them parade around here cleaning up the place. Certain angles, big butts like that, the thong gets lost in the crack."

Becker smirked as he reached for the envelope.

"It's a beautiful image," Stewart said. "Don't you think?"

## Chapter 18
## Minot, North Dakota

Pavlik checked in at a hotel close to the Minot airport. Lawrence Welk smiled at him from a big picture over the front desk in the lobby. Twenty minutes later, he settled into his room, turned on the news, and scanned the local newspaper for anything resembling a police blotter. He looked up from the paper at the television when he heard: *An Air Force soldier was found murdered outside of Velva early this morning. Tyrone Williams, a twenty-five-year-old airman from Atlantic City, New Jersey....*

Pavlik listened intently. When the story about the murdered airman finished, he turned the television off and searched the newspaper for anything else suggesting James Singleton was in Minot.

After going through the bulk of the paper, he found something about a college student who had recently died from a heroin overdose. The university was holding a candlelight celebration for the life of the nineteen-year-old Detroit native later in the evening. A Detective Dale Hehn was handling the investigation.

Pavlik circled the end of the article with a pen and underlined the name Dale Hehn. If all else failed, he'd have to give the detective a call.

□ □ □

They had sex while the surprise dinner Dale had cooked for her warmed. Dale tried his best to be slow and deliberate, but Emily had kept her garter outfit on. He was too excited. She did her best to control his pace, but it was over sooner than either had wanted it to end.

"I love that roast of yours," he said when she was up and headed to the bathroom. "Or is it your rump?" he asked when she returned wearing an open robe minus the garters.

They kissed again when he was out of bed. He groped her through the robe and let go when the telephone rang. Dale stopped before he picked up.

"You expecting anybody?" he asked.

Emily shook her head. Dale answered the phone.

"Hello?"

It was Don Ekroth. "I hope you ate dinner already," he said.

"Just about to."

"Then you might want to finish before you come see this."

"What is it?"

"Yet another body."

"You serious?"

"Some woman. Young woman. She was dressed for a spring afternoon in the middle of winter. She's an icicle now."

"Can it wait?"

"Until spring before she thaws."

"I'll see you after I eat then," Dale said.

"Enjoy your supper," Ekroth said.

□ □ □

Pavlik went down to the bar to fish for information there. A sign in the lobby advertised a former Miss North Dakota as one of the bartenders. It read: *"Have a drink with Marsha Nordstrom, our own former Miss North Dakota."*

Pavlik wondered what year it was Marsha Nordstrom had won the state pageant as he sat at the bar. She looked to be no more than thirty-five or so.

"Miss North Dakota?" he asked.

"Marsha," the bartender said. "And, yes, I was Miss North Dakota. Back in the 1990s but that's as close to a date as you'll get. Obviously, it wasn't a life-changing event. So, please, don't tell me how cool it is."

"Can I have a beer?" Pavlik asked.

Marsha Nordstrom squinted at Pavlik. "Sure," she said. She laughed to herself as she poured him an Olympia.

"It is pretty cool, though," he said. "You're my first Miss anything."

She pointed at the beer and rapped the bar top with her knuckles. "That's with me," she said. "Just for getting me to smile. I can use it today."

"Cheers," Pavlik said as he toasted her.

"That an East Coast accent?"

"New York."

"What brings you to Minot?"

"Visit a friend."

She examined him a moment. "What's his name?"

"Kincaid," Pavlik said. He picked up a menu and glanced through it. "What's good?" he asked.

"Nachos," she said. "Or the bacon burger, if you like bacon. The pizza isn't too good. I'd avoid that."

"Let me ask you something about the pizza here," Pavlik said. "I saw some pictures of it in the newspaper and on some posters at the airport in Bismarck. What's with cutting it? Why would you use a knife and fork on pizza?"

"I heard they fold it back East," Marsha said. "I don't know, tell you the truth, but it's been like that since I can remember. I'd avoid it anyway, though, if you're hungry."

"I like bacon," Pavlik said.

"Bacon burger?"

"With well-done fries, please."

"Hey, I like them crispy, too, my fries." She put the order into the kitchen through an intercom before returning.

"It true some kid overdosed on heroin at the college?"

"You know about that?"

Pavlik pointed at a newspaper on the bar. "I read something in there, I think. Minot Daily News?"

"Weird, huh? I'm friends with the detective assigned to the case."

Pavlik sipped his beer again. Marsha glanced at his fingers. Pavlik checked his watch.

"I hope you don't mind my saying, but you look like police?" Marsha said.

Pavlik shook his head. "Insurance," he said.

Marsha tilted her head to one side. "Really?"

Pavlik shrugged apologetically. "Sorry."

"No, I'm sorry. Just let me know when I'm being too nosey."

"No problem. I get it at home, too."

Marsha was caught off guard. "Geez, I didn't see a ring. I was getting my hopes up."

Pavlik blushed bright red.

"I-uh, I'm, uh, not married," he managed to stutter.

"Neither am I," Marsha said.

"Huh?" Pavlik said. "She's my girlfriend," he was able to add.

"I see."

He was getting nervous. "And she's not that bad, really. I mean, about the questions. Just involved. That sounds better, right? She's involved."

Marsha nodded.

"She means well," Pavlik added.

An uncomfortable silence followed.

Pavlik said, "Let me know if I sound like a jerk."

Marsha said, "Not at all, but you sure do look like the law."

## Chapter 19

They ate at the dining room table. Dale was on his second serving of the kumla he had prepared as a surprise when Emily remarked on the latest death reported in the news.

"The woman Ekroth mentioned," he said. "They found her frozen near the lake. Ekroth said she was dressed for a spring day."

"From the college?"

"I don't think so, but he didn't say."

"Don't these people know what they're doing to themselves?"

"My guess, it's coming from the base. We already have two leads pointing there. God knows where they get it."

"Except there has to be a demand," Emily said. She picked at fresh steamed string beans. "It's certainly like that with meth around the Midwest now. They should treat it like the epidemic it's become."

"I can't argue with that."

"What time do you think you'll be finished tonight? I was hoping we'd have some more time together."

"You wearing the garters again?"

Emily sighed. "Dale?"

"You women. Honestly, I don't know how I handle it."

"Unless you're pre-booked with Miss North Dakota. Then I'll just go to sleep early."

"Don't do that," Dale said. He quickly downed half a glass of skim milk. "But feel free to surprise me with something else."

"Don't push your luck, husband." Emily pointed to the clock to the right of the dining room cabinet. "You have until ten thirty," she said. "Then I turn back into a professor with a long day ahead of her tomorrow."

"Another lecture?" Dale said, his eyes wide open.

"You did forget. But I forgive you."

"No, no, I didn't forget, really. Is there another one?"

"Yes, but don't sweat it. Come if you can. It's okay if you can't make it."

"Nothing special I know of."

"Well, if you've nothing better to do. It starts at three o'clock sharp. At the library."

He bit another piece of the broth-soaked bread. "This was great," he said. "Don't you think?"

Emily was pointing at the clock again.

"What?" he asked.

"You're running out of time," she said.

□  □  □

The big man slipped on ice and just missed taking Pavlik's nose off with a roundhouse right. They were in the parking lot behind the hotel. It was dark and cold and the big man was holding his right knee after hyperextending it trying to stop himself from falling. Holding onto his injured knee with both hands, he stood in an awkward position.

Pavlik had already measured him for a return punch, but stopped when he saw the man was in pain.

"Tear cartilage?" he asked.

"Fuck, I think so," the big man said.

"Why'd you take a swing at me?"

"Man paid me. Fifty dollars."

"What man?"

"Some nigger in a suit. I was supposed to wait for my brother and a friend but they're probably still at the bar. They never showed."

Pavlik quickly turned and surveyed the area.

"He's gone a few hours now," the big man said.

"He wearing an eye patch?"

"Huh?"

"An eye patch or a glass eye. Could he see out of both eyes?"

The big man twisted some more and finally hit the ground. "Fuck," he said. "I think I tore it bad."

Pavlik stood over him. "What the black guy look like? And don't tell me he was black."

"Stocky, thick neck, square head. Had a suit on. I don't know, maybe a football player when he was younger."

"How old was he?"

"Fifty? I don't know. He was no spring chicken, not that you can tell with them people."

"He look like a cop?"

"A what?"

"A cop."

The big man gave it a moment. "Yeah, I guess. If he wasn't from here. There aren't many niggers on the police department here."

"You use that word when he gave you the money?"

"What, 'nigger'? I look shy to you?"

"Not shy, stupid. Where'd he find you?"

"Bar downtown. Saintly Sinners."

"That your place, where you go?"

"Yeah."

"You ever see him before?"

"No."

"He say where he was going?"

The big man shook his head. "He was on his way out of town. Gave me the fifty and drove me up here to the hotel. Pointed you out from the lobby. You were at the bar."

"You see him leave?"

"I saw him drive away. I don't know where he went. You think you could call me an ambulance or something?"

Pavlik kneeled down to look the big man in the eyes. He said, "Not if you were on fire, asshole."

□ □ □

Pavlik checked the time and saw it was a little before nine o'clock. He knew his ex-partner back in New York would be home in a few minutes. While he waited, Pavlik looked out over the valley and the downtown section of Minot. The city lights spotted the darkness. He wondered if James Singleton was somewhere in that valley.

At 9:10, Pavlik called his ex-partner and didn't bother saying hello when Dexter Greene answered.

"What was the name of that moron with the FBI when we were on that Eddie Senta thing?" Pavlik asked. "You know the one, the black guy in the house arguing over jurisdiction on the stairway while Senta was in a gunfight in the bedroom."

Greene hesitated a moment. "Morris, I think, but I can find out for sure."

"No, that's it, Morris. Eugene Morris."

"Why, what's going on?"

"He just paid some local goon to take a swing at me."

"What?"

"The guy missed, slipped on ice or something and blew out his knee. He gave up Morris, though. He didn't hesitate."

"You're sure?"

"I'm positive. At first I thought it might be Singleton, but that didn't make sense. First of all, he would've shot me, not had some drunk take a swing. Second, he wouldn't know. Morris would. From what happened on Long Island. Morris would know that and he'd probably keep it from his star witness just to keep him out of trouble."

"How'd you find them so easy?"

"I didn't find them, but I sure know they're here now."

"Can you get help there?"

"I'm gonna try."

"Where?"

"There's a detective here working an overdose case I may reach out to."

"Don't step on any hick toes. They won't appreciate the city input."

"Thanks for reminding me."

"You're not in Brooklyn anymore."

## Chapter 20

A car accident fatality near the campus kept Dale busy through the evening. When he finally made it home it was after midnight. He had expected Emily to be angry at him for being late, but instead found her preparing one of his favorite meals for next night's dinner, the Scandinavian specialty dish called lutefisk. One of Emily's art students, Traci Muller, a sophomore from Minot, was at the house helping. The girl had been to a party earlier and was approached by someone offering heroin to sample.

"I called Ms. Hehn because I know you're a detective," Traci said. She was an athletic girl with brown hair and glasses. She wore a college sweatshirt and dungarees. "Ms. Hehn mentioned it to our class that you were handling the investigation of Nathan Barron's overdose," she added. "I'm sorry to bother you."

"Thank you for coming forward," Dale said. He had just poured himself a glass of milk. He sat at the kitchen table across from the girl. "Tell me what happened."

"She's a little concerned about this, Dale," Emily said. "About her name being circulated. She was at a party and called here around ten o'clock. She was afraid to go home."

Dale held up his right hand. "It'll stay right here. I promise. Unless you're talking to somebody else. Have you?"

Traci shook her head no. "Just my mother. And I had to stop because she was getting all weird on me."

"I understand," Dale said. "Tell me what happened."

The girl explained how she'd gone to a party for the basketball team and how there were several people from the Air Force base there.

"Friends of the players?" Dale asked.

"Mostly," Traci said. "The guy that approached me is a friend of Stephan Barker. I think they knew each other from back home."

"He's one of the stars on the team, right?"

"One of the captains, yes. But I know he isn't a druggie. He's, like, one of the nicest guys at the university. He doesn't do drugs at all."

Dale nodded. "How did his friend approach you?"

Traci blushed. Dale looked to Emily.

"It's alright," Emily said. "Dale won't pass judgment."

Dale was confused. "Traci?"

The girl spoke while she looked at the table. "We were making out," she said. "In one of the bathrooms."

"And?"

Traci looked up again. "His name is Chris," she said. "He's from New York. He's in the Air Force."

"And?"

"He showed me some of the heroin he had with him," Traci said, again without looking at Dale. "He asked me if I wanted to try some. He said we could snort it or use a syringe. He had a syringe with him. He had a few of them."

"And?"

"It scared me. I told him no. When he tried to kiss me again, I pushed him away. I was really scared. I wanted to leave."

"You're a smart girl," Dale said.

"I wouldn't have done anything more with him," she said. "Not tonight. Not after seeing the drugs and all."

"It's okay," Emily said. She put a hand on Traci's left shoulder. "You did nothing wrong."

"Did he sell any drugs while you were there?" Dale asked.

"No," Traci said. "Not that I know of."

"And he's from the base?"

"Yes, I think so. I'm pretty sure. Like I said, he's friends with some of the guys on the team. I think his last name is Ryan, but I'm not sure. I thought one of the other players called him Ryan. He introduced himself as Chris."

Dale wondered who else was at the party. He asked about the black man with the face mask, but Traci didn't recognize the description.

"What about a man named Ahearn?" he asked. He held one hand up high. "Big guy, about six two or so? Curly blond hair, thick beard, kind of mean-looking?"

Traci remembered him from the description of his hair and beard. "Yes!" she said, somewhat excited. "He was there. He showed up as we were leaving."

"As you and the guy with the heroin were leaving?"

Traci was confused a second, then shook her head. "Oh, no, not him," she said. "I meant my girlfriend, the one I went there with. The big guy said something to Sarah, my girlfriend, as we left."

"What did he say?" Dale asked.

"It was rude."

"It's okay."

"It was about her breasts."

Dale looked to Emily. "Only he didn't call them breasts, right?"

"No," Traci said, "he didn't."

□ □ □

Dale dropped Traci Muller off and headed back to the party where she'd been earlier on Tenth Avenue Northwest. He could see lights in the house from half a block away. It was a few minutes after one o'clock in the morning. The party appeared to be going strong.

He decided to wait a few minutes to see if John Ahearn was still inside. He parked at one end of the block and walked back and forth to keep warm. He was on his second trip when Dale saw Ahearn and a woman walking away from the front door. Ahearn was counting money. The woman was stumbling until Ahearn helped her.

Dale watched as the two got into a pickup parked in the curb a few doors from where the party was still going on. They sat there a while before the engine started. Dale noticed one of the rear taillights wasn't working. He returned to his car and called for patrol backup. He instructed a patrolman to stop the pickup once it turned onto Broadway. He would follow and block off any attempt Ahearn made to escape.

□ □ □

"Your wife is flying on heroin," Dale told John Ahearn half an hour later.

"Fuckin'-A right, she is," Ahearn replied. "No wonder they gave you a badge."

They were at the Minot police station. Mrs. Ahearn had been taken to the emergency room at Trinity Medical Center. John Ahearn sat across from Dale's desk and leaned both elbows on his knees.

"You were carrying more than seven hundred dollars in cash," Dale said. "In small bills."

"That's not against the law," Ahearn said.

"Where did your wife get the heroin, sir?"

"I have no idea."

"Did someone at the party sell it to her?"

"Fuck do I know? Ask her."

Dale shuffled papers on his desk. "Right now, your wife doesn't know what planet she's on."

"I guess you're out of luck then."

Both men stared at each other. A short man with a full head of gray hair was ushered into the room. Dale frowned at the sight of Henry Becker, Ahearn's attorney.

"John, shut up!" Becker yelled. He was pointing a finger at his client from across the room.

"Yes, sir," Ahearn said, all smiles then.

"Officer, this interrogation is over," Becker told Dale.

"Detective," Dale said.

Becker stood alongside his client. "Detective? Fine. Then you should know better. No more questions."

"We're still booking his wife when she gets out," Dale said.

"Not my concern," Becker said. "I understand you stopped Mr. Ahearn for some traffic violation. Is that correct?"

"Turning without a signal," Dale said. "I was behind him. I radioed the nearest patrol car."

Becker smirked. "That just happened to be in the exact same area at one o'clock in the morning? That's rich. And you were doing what there? In the same area, I mean."

"My job," Dale said.

**Part III**

**Chapter 21**
**Minot, North Dakota**

With wind gusts up to thirty miles per hour, it was twenty-seven degrees below zero one hour after the sun had come up. Dale and Don Ekroth were waiting for Kathy Ljunndgren. They sat in Ekroth's Blazer outside the coffee shop, both men sipping hot chocolate from Styrofoam containers. Kathy Ljunndgren was already ten minutes late for work.

"I appreciate this," Dale said.

"I have nothing scheduled for today," Ekroth said. "Sally's still down to Bismarck visiting her mother."

"How's she doing, Mrs. Norquist?"

"Not bad, considering. The old girl's had two strokes now. It's her movement that's restricted."

They watched a young nurse they both knew as she passed the Blazer and headed inside the coffee shop.

"That girl is beautiful in six layers of winter clothes," Ekroth said.

"Makes you appreciate spring," Dale said.

"Speaking of which, we going ice-fishing before the lake thaws?"

"Please, don't remind me. I've been itching to fish since Thanksgiving."

"Well, it's your call, detective. I banked some time. I can take a few days to a week."

"I know, I know. I have to wait until Em has something. Or she'll just get pissed off I'm not spending time with her."

"Speaking of marital bliss, they release Ahearn's wife yet?"

"No clue," Dale said. "The woman is a mess. Body bruises, needle tracks. Unbelievable. And a lawyer to protect her husband."

"That's two now," Ekroth said, "Tyrone Williams and John Ahearn that Becker's defending."

"You mean Ahearn's wife," Dale said.

"That's right," Ekroth said. "Ahearn wasn't charged with anything. He gets the blinker fixed and shows up to court, he beats the traffic ticket as well. Becker didn't do much for Tyrone Williams, though."

"Kathy Ljunndgren might help us," Dale said. "I shook her up the other day. She's the one was seeing the Barron kid from the college. She told me some half-truths. She left out a few of the details. I think she knows who gave the Barron kid the heroin that killed him. Except she's a user."

"I hope she's not flying this morning."

Dale saw Kathy Ljunndgren turn the corner. He pointed to her. "We can find out right now," he said as he opened the passenger door.

Ekroth had just started to sip his hot chocolate. Dale was out of the Blazer before the sergeant could stop him. "Or we could invite her inside," he said, "where it's warm."

□ □ □

Kathy Ljunndgren started cursing as soon as Dale was within earshot. "Jesus fucking Christ, mister, I have kids I have to feed. You're going to get me fired you keep coming around my job."

"And you're going to lose your kids if you don't start telling me the truth," Dale said. He had walked up to within a few inches of her. They stood face to face.

"I don't know anything!" she yelled.

Dale turned to Ekroth. "I told you," he said. "It's a waste of time with this one. Let's just book her and have social services put her kids with somebody safe."

"You can't do that!" Ljunndgren yelled. "You can't report me without a reason."

Ekroth played good cop and guided Dale away from Ljunndgren. "Let me try," he said. When Ekroth turned to her again, she was looking at her watch.

"I'm already late," she said, pointing to the coffee shop.

"Just give me a few minutes," Ekroth said. "Or would you rather we talk inside? We don't have to tell them what it's about."

"Oh, shit, what's the difference anymore," Ljunndgren said. She looked to Dale. "What do you want now?"

"Ahearn," Dale said. "Is he a drug dealer, yes or no?"

"Why don't you just shoot me here?"

"Ma'am?" Ekroth said.

"Did you ever get drugs from him?" Dale asked. "Heroin, specifically."

"Yes, but I didn't buy it from him," Ljunndgren said. "You already know that." She pointed at Dale. "I told you that. I never saw him sell anything."

"Who sells it to him?" Dale asked.

"How the hell would I know that?"

"Who gave Nathan Barron the heroin that killed him?"

"I already said. I don't know."

"Were you at the party last night? At the house on Eleventh Street Northwest?"

Ljunndgren was surprised at the question. She stuttered. "What? No.

Where?"

"Ma'am," Ekroth said again.

"I left early," Ljunndgren said, her voice somewhat subdued. "I was gone before John showed. I didn't see him."

"Were there drugs in that house?" Dale asked. "While you were still there."

"Some," she said, her voice almost a whisper now. "Not heroin. I didn't see any."

Dale frowned. "Kathy?"

"Some pot, maybe. Beer and pot, that's all I saw."

"Did you and Nathan Barron mainline together?" Dale asked.

"What?"

"Nathan Barron. Did you and he—"

"Just once!" Ljunndgren yelled. "I already told you. Just once."

"You told me you snorted, Kathy. Now, I know otherwise. I know he shot up twice."

"Who was it then?"

She looked away from both of them. "I don't know."

"Kathy?"

"I don't fucking know! What do you want from me? You want me to lie?"

Dale and Ekroth waited for more.

"Can I please get to work?" Ljunndgren asked. "I need this job."

Ekroth deferred to Dale.

"Go 'head," Dale said.

"Thank you," Ljunndgren said.

They watched her head inside the coffee shop.

Dale was frustrated. "Shit," he said.

"You need to go all the way with druggies," Ekroth said. "You can't bluff them."

"Except for her kids," Dale said.

"She lives with her mother, this one, right?"

"Yeah."

"Then the mother is probably bringing up the kids anyway."

"I guess."

"Then you can't bluff her."

□ □ □

Ekroth found two bags of heroin in Kathy Ljunndgren's purse when he searched her possessions at the coffee shop. Dale arrested Ljunndgren on a heroin possession charge and cuffed her hands behind her back.

Ljunndgren was cursing both men in a rage as they led her out to

Ekroth's Blazer. Dale whispered to Ekroth, "If Becker shows up to take her case, I'm shooting the son of a bitch."

"Don't be surprised," Ekroth said.

Ekroth dropped Dale and Ljunndgren off at the police station. Dale walked Ljunndgren inside and had her fingerprinted. He offered to release her with a desk ticket if she cooperated. She spit in his face.

## Chapter 22

Stewart met with two men in the parking lot of I-Keating Furniture World on South Broadway. The sun was bright, but the temperature remained a frigid twelve degrees below zero. John Ahearn tugged down on the baseball cap he was wearing over his curly blond hair. He smoothed his thick beard with a gloved hand and turned his back to the wind. Roger Daltry also turned his back to the wind. He was anxious to get out of the cold.

"I'm heading inside in two minutes to pick out a clock," Stewart said, "that I'm sending to you as a gift, John. They'll be a card on it. It'll read: To John, Love, Garth."

A gust of wind forced Stewart and Daltry to dig their hands deeper inside their jacket pockets.

Ahearn looked confused. "Garth?"

"It just a name," Stewart said. He noticed Ahearn's ears were red. He pointed at them. "You okay out here? Your ears look about to fall off."

Ahearn touched his right ear with his gloved hand. "Fuckin'-A," he said. "I'm fine. Who's Garth?"

Stewart winced. The big man was downright stupid. "Garth Brooks," he said, trying one more time. "Abraham Lincoln. Britney Spears. Lady fuckin' Gaga. You see what I'm saying? Garth is nobody. He can be anybody."

The big man nodded, but Stewart wasn't sure Ahearn was getting it.

"I'm sending you a clock big enough you can fill the thing with product," Stewart said. "You'll get that later tonight. They'll be an extra bag in there, too, a small bag. The one you get to keep. The small bag, John, but make sure it's the small one. That'll keep you flying a good month or so, you use it right and don't invite deadbeats over to party every night. I'll send you another small bag when the job is done, keep you flying through the spring."

Ahearn nodded.

"You load the clock and I'll get you an address where you'll bring it," Stewart continued. "You get stopped along the way for something dumb, speeding or something, you delivering a clock is all. That's worth another two grand you get it there without a problem. Half up front, half when the delivery is made and the product is still inside."

"No problem," Ahearn said.

"I hope not," Stewart said. "Or some vicious people will look to see your big farm ass is butchered."

Ahearn didn't blink.

"Now you can go," Stewart said. "Stop at the Walmart on the way out of town. Buy yourself some earmuffs or something. Your ears, man. Seriously."

Stewart and Daltry watched the big man lumber his way to his pickup at the end of the lot. The engine started without hesitation.

"You see his ears?" Stewart asked Daltry.

"Man's a Sasquatch," Daltry said.

Daltry and Stewart waited for Ahearn's pickup to turn south on Broadway before they jogged the few steps to the furniture store. They stood inside the doorway rubbing their hands while they talked.

"It's brutal out there," Daltry said.

"You get your man?" Stewart asked.

Daltry nodded. "Meeting me at King's," he said. "Another friend of Ahearn's. Sasquatch say the dude likes the burgers at King's up the hill."

A saleswoman in beige pants and a brown blouse approached them. At first she was startled at Stewart's face, but recovered professionally and asked if she could be of help. Stewart played it off and asked if he could see the grandfather and cuckoo clocks. The woman took him toward the rear of the store and up a short flight of stairs. Stewart checked out her ass as he followed.

"Thank you," he said. "I'm gonna pick one out myself and I'll come get you to write it up. That okay?"

"Sure," the saleswoman said. "I'll be right down the stairs. Would you like some coffee to help warm up? We also have tea or cocoa."

"That might be nice," Stewart said. "Some cocoa. But we'll help ourselves. Thanks."

"For sure," the saleswoman said.

"I can for sure take that booty for a ride," Daltry said when the woman was gone. "That why we come here, the salesgirls?"

They both watched the saleswoman walk out onto the floor directly below them.

"This place the best in the state for furniture," Stewart said. "That's word of mouth. Heard it from a dozen people at least since I'm up here."

"I know they out to the base a lot," Daltry said. "I see their trucks making deliveries."

Stewart moved away from the railing and whispered at Daltry. "You extend your pass?"

Daltry nodded. "Three days," he said.

"When you leaving?"

"Later today."

"And your man?"

"Ahearn says his boy will be there," Daltry said. "Needs the money."

"And you need to get it done this time," Stewart said. He glanced around them before handing Daltry an envelope. "You need to count it, go do it now. There's money enough for your new man plus expenses." Daltry stashed the envelope inside his pants. "You been good to me," he said. "I don't need to count it."

"Not good enough for you to get it right, though," Stewart said. They exchanged stares until Daltry looked away. Stewart looked at a few of the clocks lined against the wall.

"Why do you think those moons are on all the faces?" he asked, pointing at one of the clocks.

Daltry didn't understand the question. "What moons?"

"Never mind," said Stewart, moving on to another clock. "I shouldn't offer but the bonus still stands, payable upon completion. When Eddie Senta is dead, you get an extra grand."

"I appreciate it."

"You should," Stewart said. "But if anything goes wrong this time, you owe me. Work or money. Something. Fair is fair."

Daltry wiped sweat from his forehead. "Now it's too hot in here," he said.

"You got too many layers on. I can see that outside. You bundled way too much."

"I'm gonna meet the dude in a few," Daltry said. "Up at King's. I gotta walk there from here, I need the extra layers."

Stewart nodded. "You know this dude you're meeting?"

"No. Ahearn says he's a big farm boy from Canada someplace."

Stewart was looking at a cherrywood cuckoo clock hanging from a wall.

Daltry said, "Ahearn say the man can lift cars off the floor by their bumpers. I figure we get inside the hospital, the man breaks Eddie Senta's neck with his hands, and out we go."

"Just make sure you get it done this time," Stewart said. "Make sure the man is dead before you leave. You ditch the car you driving first chance you can, too. Find another one and drive back. Even you have to go AWOL a couple days. Then you coast on what you got, run out your time up here, and you come work for me full-time. What is it, another six months?"

"Five."

"Five months. You ride that out, get a clean bill of health from Uncle Sam, the GI benefits, all the rest, you come work for some real scratch."

"I could get used to that," Daltry said. "Specially those paydays just to count money. I can get used to that easy."

"You still thinking small," Stewart said. "But it's good you still humble. Help you appreciate the bigger scores when they come."

Stewart pulled the tag on the cherrywood clock. It read twenty-five hundred dollars. "I get this sucker for less than two thousand," he said. "Wave some cash in these farmers' faces, shit, they'll massage your balls while you sip their free coffee."

"I wouldn't mind that salesgirl massage mine," Daltry said.

"She still too scared of my face," Stewart said.

"You wave that cash, she might get used to it."

"True dat."

☐ ☐ ☐

Pavlik figured he had an ace in the hole with the paid for assault by a federal agent, at least so long as the local police were in the dark about the feds in town protecting James Singleton. Chances were Morris wouldn't inform the Minot PD about anything going on in their city. He also knew Morris would deny ever seeing the guy he'd hired to take a swing the night before, except it all the more suggested hiring a local yahoo in the first place was something personal Morris hadn't let go of.

Or why the hell would he do something so stupid?

Pavlik figured Morris had to know he wouldn't back down, which brought it back to being personal. Maybe Pavlik would teach the federal agent a thing or two about throwing a punch.

In the meantime, he decided to risk trying the local police. If it was one thing he knew for sure, it was that local police never liked learning the feds were in town.

He'd slept in late, but the first thing he did after a quick cup of coffee was try the Minot police department. He asked for Dale Hehn and was put on hold. When nobody picked up, he hung up, then called back. A surly voice explained that he'd patched the first call through but the detective said there was nobody on the line.

Pavlik asked the surly man if he might try the detective again. When he was on hold for another two minutes he gave up and drove to the police station instead.

It was a few minutes after ten o'clock when he asked for Detective Dale Hehn at the front desk. The officer sitting the desk asked Pavlik if he was the guy who'd hung up earlier.

"I was on hold forever," Pavlik said. "I figured the call didn't go through."

"It went through," the officer said, "both times. You were gone when I went to connect you."

"Sorry," Pavlik said.

The officer frowned.

"Is he around now?" Pavlik asked.

"No and I'm not sure if he's coming back."

"Can you call him?"

"What's it about?"

Pavlik didn't like the officer getting into his business. "It's personal," he said. "I need to talk to the detective."

"Give me a few minutes," the officer said. "Take a seat over there and I'll call you when I have him on the line."

Pavlik took a seat near a small trophy cabinet. He picked a local newspaper from a rack of magazines and went through it. He was glancing through the sports section a second time before he realized he'd been sitting there five minutes already. He stood up and saw the officer behind the desk was on the phone. The officer waved him off.

Pavlik glanced at his watch. He sat back down and read the editorials this time. After a few more minutes he went back to the desk.

"Any luck?" he asked.

"No, not yet. I left a message but he hasn't called."

"Can I have his number?"

"His personal number?"

Pavlik huffed. "His phone mail, anything."

The officer took his time staring down Pavlik.

"Hello?" said Pavlik, pissed off now.

The officer looked up past Pavlik, saw Sergeant Donald Ekroth and waved him over.

□ □ □

Roger Daltry did a double take when he saw the man he would be traveling to New York with to kill Eddie Senta. After watching him eat three double King burgers and two milk shakes for breakfast, Daltry was afraid of leaving the place before the big man used the bathroom.

They had taken US 52 out of Minot to Jamestown, where Daltry picked up 281 south. They were heading to Aberdeen, South Dakota, where they would take a morning flight to Chicago and then a late afternoon flight into Newark, New Jersey. Stewart had made it clear that Eddie Senta had to die this time. Daltry was to go to the hospital where the man was recovering and finish the job he had botched nearly a week ago.

The problem was controlling somebody as big and dumb as the monster John Ahearn had hooked him up with. Daltry hadn't been told how mentally slow the ex-con was. Daltry thought the man might be retarded.

When he first asked the monster's name, "Ox" was the response he was given.

"Ox?"

"Ox," the beast had said. "What everybody calls me."

"What's your last name?"

"Oxton, where the nickname comes from."

"Then you must have a first name, right?"

"I don't like it."

"What is it?"

"Just call me Ox."

"Ox. I call you Ox?"

"What everybody calls me."

Daltry thought about dropping the guy off along the road and doing the job himself this time, but then thought better of it. He could use the guy to kill Eddie Senta and then lose him.

Or he could kill Ox immediately after Ox killed Senta. Getting rid of loose strings, it was called in some of the movies he'd seen.

The thing he wouldn't do was get on a plane with the man. He decided to drive instead. He wasn't supposed to kill Eddie Senta for another two days according to Stewart's instructions, so what was the point of drawing all that attention by flying alongside a monster. There was no way they wouldn't go noticed in an airport, much less on a crowded flight from Chicago to New York. The last time, flying with the big Indian, Daltry had been uncomfortable wearing a blond wig, the matching mustache and the Miami Dolphins football cap.

When he told Ox the new plan, that they were going to drive to New York instead of fly, the beast seemed relieved.

"Good," he said.

"You like that, huh?" Daltry said.

"I don't like the shitters in planes," Ox said.

"I can see why."

"I don't like the little meals either."

"Two for two," Daltry said.

"And the waitresses always make me horny," Ox added.

"Huh?" Daltry said. "You mean stewardesses."

"The women, yeah. They make me horny."

The big man licked his lips. Daltry did a double take at the monster and swore to himself he wouldn't say another word the entire drive.

◻ ◻ ◻

Pavlik explained what he was doing in Minot to Sergeant Donald Ekroth over coffee and sweet rolls. The sergeant seemed to listen attentively as Pavlik stressed the importance of the situation, especially because of what had happened the night before, but the sergeant was suspicious about the attack in the hotel parking lot.

"Why didn't you call it in?" Ekroth asked.

"To keep it from Morris," he said.

"He's the fed you mentioned."

"Yes, and he obviously already knows I'm here. But unless he has a reason to stay, something he needs the guy I'm looking for to stay, Morris can pull stakes and be gone in an hour. That happens, the guy I'm looking for walks away again. You don't understand how the feds operate. It's all about them, nothing to do with anybody else, least of all the victims."

"Actually, we have worked with the FBI before," Ekroth said. "Several times, in fact. We only look dumb."

"I don't mean to offend," Pavlik said, "and I know it sounds crazy, but it's what they do with cases like this. They have somebody they're protecting and they let the piece of shit do pretty much anything he wants. It's all about making their case. They don't care who gets screwed in the process."

"And we can't go to them and ask because they'll cover it up anyway," Ekroth said. "That what you're trying to say here?"

"They'll tell you to back the fuck off first," Pavlik said. "Then they'll leave town, yeah. And the guy who sent two people to kill my client and her husband will walk away one more time. He's already killed at least three people we know of."

"We?"

"NYPD for one. The Port Washington Police Department also. They're on Long Island. Call them if you don't believe me. I gave you the file. Make a copy and follow up on it. But they're probably anxious for a lead on what happened in their town a second time. They might go straight to the feds to find out if they haven't already."

Ekroth nodded.

Pavlik said, "Look, I'm not looking to push any buttons here. I'm here looking for this guy because of what he did to my client. I don't like it that the feds protect scumbags like this, but I know I can't do much about it, except maybe point him out to you guys and hope to hell you don't let the feds make assholes of you, too."

"That's about three different times you've insulted us now," Ekroth said.

"I'm sorry," Pavlik said. "I don't mean to. It's just that now Morris knows I'm here time's an issue. If you guys don't move fast, he'll up and leave and that'll be the last chance I have to catch this piece of shit."

"Which you already said you really can't do, not legally," Ekroth said.

Pavlik closed his eyes in frustration. When he opened them again, Ekroth was handing off the file to another officer.

"Make copies of everything in the file and bring it back here," he said.

"Thank you," Pavlik said.

"I can't promise you anything," Ekroth said.

"I understand that, I do."

"You're staying at the Welk?"

"Room three-sixteen."

"I'll do what I can," Ekroth said.

"Thank you. And I'm sorry if it sounded like I was insulting before. I didn't mean to."

The two men shook hands and Pavlik left the station without acknowledging the desk officer. He got in his car and drove back to the hotel where he had a quick breakfast in the restaurant before heading up to his room to call Aelish.

He opened the door and was surprised by the two men waiting for him.

"Feds?" he asked.

Both men produced their identification. The taller of the two said, "FBI."

Pavlik stepped inside the room. "Where's Morris?" he said.

"I'm special agent Mears," the tall agent said.

"Special agent Feller," the short one said.

"You got first names?"

"Michael," the tall one said.

"Greg," the short one said.

Agent Mears shut the door and blocked it. It was then Pavlik noticed the drapes had been drawn.

"I gotta tell you, there are people back East know I'm here," he said. "Some police friends included."

Mears pointed to the chairs. "Why don't you take a seat?"

Pavlik said, "Why don't you go fuck yourself?"

Mears continued pointing to the chairs. Feller leaned against the window frame across the room. Pavlik stood with his arms folded across his chest.

"What's it about?" he asked.

"A federal operation involving different branches of law enforcement," Mears said. "We're here to make sure you don't interfere."

"You're protecting a murderer," Pavlik said. "Just so you know."

"We have our orders, sir," Feller said.

"Which of you is the senior agent?" Pavlik asked.

Both agents ignored the question.

"I'm Alex Pavlik, but you already know that."

"We're not looking for trouble, sir," Mears said.

Pavlik shrugged. "Am I under arrest?"

"No, sir," both agents said.

"But you're gonna hold me here anyway."

"Yes, sir," they said.

## Chapter 23
## Velva/Minot, North Dakota

John Ahearn leaned his big body on one arm of the couch and pointed a finger in Kathy Ljunndgren's face.

"What the fuck did you tell them?" he said.

Ljunndgren flinched away from his finger. "Nothing," she said. "I spit in his face." Ahearn held the pose a few seconds longer. "I swear it," Ljunndgren said. "I spit right in his face. I didn't tell them anything."

Ahearn grabbed a can of Olympia beer from the top of the television and guzzled half of it. He set the can down and belched.

"I've had about enough of those cops fucking with me," he said.

"It's about Nate," Ljunndgren said. "They're investigating the overdose." Ahearn sat in the recliner to the left of the couch.

"That cop got me fired," Ljunndgren said. "And I needed that job. I haven't even been home since I got fired. I can't deal with my mother over this. She'll make me stay home now. She'll take the kids."

Ahearn wasn't paying attention. "What about those two coons, Roger and Tyrone? That cop mention either of them?"

"Just you."

"Fuck."

"He arrested me for possession. They took my last two hits from my purse."

"Huh?"

"He took my last two hits."

"And I suppose you want some more. That why you came?"

Ljunndgren shook her head. "I tried Roger but he wasn't home. I got some from a friend. I can use more, yeah, but I came here to tell you about the one cop, that detective."

"What do you know about him?"

"What do you mean?"

"The fuck I just say? You know where he lives, he's married or not? He got a girlfriend? Any kids?"

Ljunndgren shrugged. "I could find out."

"You followed out here?"

"I don't think so."

"You check?"

Ljunndgren fidgeted first, then shrugged again. Ahearn lit a Marlboro. "Fuckers stopped me the other night, too," he said. "After the party. Took my cash, but I got it all back."

"He mentioned the party," Ljunndgren said. "He asked me if I was there and if there were any drugs around. He asked about you specifically."

"Fuckin-A right he did," Ahearn said. He folded his arms across his chest. "They were waiting for me to leave. They arrested Kelly. Bullshit arrest. Just to make trouble. She's still at the hospital."

Ljunndgren scratched at the crook of her left arm inside the elbow. "I can use a hit, John," she said.

"For free, I suppose."

"I'm broke now that I don't have a job anymore. That same cop did that, cost me my job."

Ahearn wiped his mouth with the back of his hand.

"I really need the hit," Ljunndgren said. "For later, I mean."

Ahearn checked his watch, then started to unbuckle his pants. "Kelly won't be home until they clean her up," he said. "You can work it off."

Ljunndgren crouched down to help him with his pants. "Sure, John," she said.

"I'm gonna fuck with that cop," Ahearn said. "I'm not through with him."

"I'd like to help you there," Ljunndgren said.

"Find out he's married, got kids and whatnot."

Ljunndgren smiled cautiously as she pulled his thermal underwear down to his thighs.

Ahearn said, "Aren't you the happy hooker?"

Ljunndgren took him inside her mouth.

◻ ◻ ◻

Emily was checking the outline for her third lecture in six days. She was in her office in the humanities building when Dale stopped in with a bouquet of flowers.

"You're forgiven," she said.

Dale crossed himself after handing her the flowers. "And I swear on my favorite fishing pole that I'll never be late for another one, although yesterday it was for a good cause. Remember?"

Emily breathed in the scent of the flowers. "Didn't anyone ever tell you not to make promises you can't keep?"

"Yes. And I promised I'd never do it again."

They kissed as they embraced. Dale grabbed her ass. Emily slapped his hand away.

"You're not that forgiven," she said.

"Maybe we should head home for a quick lunch," he said.

"A quickie? How romantic."

"I know, but I'm waiting on another ME report back at the morgue. I have to head there later and then Don wants me to check in with some New York guy at the hotel. He thinks the guy might know something about what's going on around here lately."

"New York, huh?"

"A former cop from there. A detective, Don said."

"Okay, well, maybe we better grab lunch or something. I have to be at the library for three, or did you forget again?"

Dale noticed the outline on Emily's desk. "Actually, I'm not going to make it today," he said. "Sorry."

"I don't expect you to attend these things when you're working, but I really do wish you wouldn't say you will."

"Well, I am sorry," he said. He pointed to her outline. "Reliving the moment?"

"Actually, I've been invited to do it again. In Fargo, next month."

Dale took out his detective's notebook and pen. "When?"

"Please."

"I'm serious, Em. I'll do my best."

Emily rolled her eyes. "Next month, the fifteenth."

"I'll be there."

"Yeah, right," Emily said. "Let's go."

They went home and made love in the kitchen. They used the counters, the table, and eventually climaxed on a chair. They were both sweating when they were finished. Emily had just enough time for a quick shower. Dale didn't.

He headed back to the morgue for the ME report on Tyrone Williams. It was troubling Dale that the young airman had been found so close to the same town where John Ahearn lived.

Statistically, Williams was the third murder of the year in the county. Dale couldn't recall when there had been three murders within the first month of a new year in Ward County. 2010 had started ugly. He wondered if it could get any uglier.

□ □ □

Emily had less than forty-five minutes before her library lecture. She took a hot shower and was so relaxed she nearly forgot the time. She quickly applied skin cream to her neck, arms, and hands and then dressed while a fresh pot of decaffeinated coffee brewed in the kitchen.

The telephone rang at the exact moment she reached for the coffee. She spilled some onto the counter.

"Damn," she said, then crossed the room and answered the phone on the third ring.

"Hello?" she said, her voice somewhat frustrated.

"Emily Hehn?" a gruff voice asked.

"Speaking."

"You the teacher from the college?"

"Yes, who is this?"

"You have nice tits for a teacher."

Emily frowned at the comment and hung up. "Asshole," she said. She hit the callback function but the call had come from a blocked number. She set the receiver back in the cradle as it rang again. She let the answering machine pick up.

"I'm gonna fuck you, bitch," the same gruff voice said.

She picked up her cell phone and dialed Dale's cellular number.

□ □ □

Pavlik argued on and off with the two special agents until he was fed up and started for the door. Agent Feller pulled a pair of handcuffs.

"We'll use these if we have to," he said.

Pavlik said, "You spending the week here or just a couple days?"

Agent Mears glanced at his watch. "Just another few hours."

"He's here, isn't he?" Pavlik asked them. "That's what this is about? James Singleton is here, in Minot someplace, and you two are making sure I don't walk into him."

"We're just doing our jobs, sir," Feller said.

"Without any legal authority, I might add," Pavlik said. "And I have been pretty decent about it, haven't I? The bullshit stunt that asshole Morris pulled."

"No need to get excited, sir," Mears said.

Pavlik had had enough. "There isn't, huh?" He pointed at the two agents. "Okay, well, you guys let me know how they go, the next few hours. In the meantime, I'm going down for a beer."

Agent Mears reached inside his jacket. "Sir, please sit back down," he said.

"Fuck you," Pavlik said.

Feller took a defensive pose at the door. "Sir, I advise you to sit down."

Pavlik said, "And I'll ask you just once to get away from that door, kid. Then I'll move you out of the way."

Pavlik felt the jolt somewhere in his left rib cage and was on the floor before he knew what had happened. He felt his body spasm a while before he could hear again. When he looked up, both agents were kneeling alongside him and speaking in calm voices.

"Just breathe easy," Agent Mears said.

"Just relax, sir," Agent Feller said.

## Chapter 24

Dale took the call from Emily outside the morgue. He ducked into an empty hallway and asked his wife to repeat what the caller had said word for word.

"Are you alright?" he asked when she finished telling him.

"Yes. I'm fine."

"Do you want me to come home?"

"Eventually, yes," she joked.

"Em, please."

"It was just some asshole, I'm sure. I was frightened because I was alone. I'd just got out of the shower. I felt vulnerable. I'm fine now."

"I want you to call the station and ask someone to come by."

"No. I have to leave."

"Em."

"Dale, I'm okay. I thought you should know is why I called."

"I should know. I can be there in ten minutes."

"I'm already on my way. The library, remember?"

"Right, damn. I'll call it in anyway."

"Where are you now?"

"The morgue."

"Yuck," Emily said. "I have to go. I love you."

"I love you, too," Dale said.

He returned to the morgue as a body was brought in on a gurney. Dale squinted at the sight. Paperwork from the Air Force base had identified the body as that of Tyrone Williams, the man Dale had arrested earlier in the week, but except for the tattoos and braided hair, there was no way of knowing that from the body on the table. The exit wounds had obliterated the dead man's face.

"He took three shots in the back of the head," said Dr. Thomas Olsen, touching the back of Dale's head approximately where each bullet had entered Tyrone Williams's skull. "At least two exited through his face, what caused all the damage. I doubt he saw his killer."

"Or he wasn't looking at him," Dale said.

The doctor was confused a second. "Huh? Oh, yes, right. I guess."

"What caliber?"

"Looks like a nine millimeter."

"Can you tell how long he's dead?"

"I can approximate and say a few days."

"I arrested him for possession this week."

"Then he was killed shortly thereafter."

"Executed, looks like."

"Huh? Oh, yeah, I'd say. For sure."

□ □ □

"What time is it?" Pavlik asked.

"We'll be leaving soon," Special Agent Mears said.

Pavlik was resting in the bed. His hands were loosely cuffed. The agents were seated on either side of him. They were watching an HBO movie on the television.

"Aren't you worried the cuffs might leave marks?" Pavlik asked them.

Neither agent answered.

"You gonna leave money for sharing the room?" he asked next.

Again the agents remained silent.

"Did anyone call? Can you at least tell me that?"

"No one has called," Mears said.

"You sure? You check messages?"

"The telephone would show it."

Pavlik was grinding his teeth from frustration. He said, "If there's any way I can prove this, I will. I'll have both your asses six ways to Sunday. I'll sue the shit out of the Bureau."

The agents remained silent.

"We used to piss on you guys back in New York," Pavlik said. "NYPD had you all figured for college boy sissies liked to wear sunglasses and suits."

The two agents smirked at each other.

"One for me," Pavlik said.

"Check this out," Special Agent Feller said to Mears.

Pavlik looked up at the screen and watched as Morgan Freeman walked across water.

"Cool," Mears said.

Pavlik saw it was a Jim Carey movie and rolled his eyes. He said, "And you can tell Morris that I'll find him someday. I'll do whatever I have to do to find him, but I will find him. And then I'll kick his ass up and down whatever street we're on. That's a promise."

Special Agent Feller said, "If God is a black man, I'm glad he's Morgan Freeman."

□ □ □

Elvira Ljunndgren answered the door. A frail woman of sixty-five years, she was holding onto a cane that helped her walk. Her hair was thin and white. She wore brown glasses, a wool housedress, and thick-soled flat shoes. She squinted at Dale's badge from inside the house.

"I need to speak with your daughter, Mrs. Ljunndgren," Dale said.

"I knew it would come to this," the old woman said.

"Ma'am?"

"The police. It was only a matter of time. Next will come the department of family services. I'll call them myself, though, they aren't here in another day or two."

"I need to speak with Kathy, ma'am," Dale said. "Is she in?"

"Where else would she be? Upstairs, stoned high on whatever junk she put into her system this time. She lost her job again, so now she has the entire day to get high, when she bothers to come home."

Dale was waiting for the woman to step aside and let him in. "Ma'am?" he asked.

Elvira Ljunndgren waved him in, then turned to one side. "She's upstairs in her room with all that damn music blasting."

Dale found Kathy Ljunndgren's bedroom at the end of the hall opposite the stairs. A Black Sabbath song he was sure was at least forty plus years old played loud behind the door. He knocked a few times, but there was no response. Finally, after checking behind him for the mother, he turned the doorknob and entered the bedroom without permission.

Kathy Ljunndgren lay on her back, breasts exposed, wearing sunglasses and red panties. She waved a long feathered roach clip in time to the loud music. Dale tossed a robe he found hanging on a chair across her chest. He went to the receiver and turned down the volume. Kathy laughed.

"We need to talk," Dale said. He pulled the chair out from under a desk and straddled it.

It took Kathy two tries to sit up. The robe fell and her breasts were exposed again. Dale pointed to them. Kathy covered herself.

"I'm a little high," she said.

"You're stoned," Dale said.

"Yeah."

"Do you need the glasses?"

Kathy removed them. Her left eye was swollen and bruised.

"What happened?" Dale asked.

"Huh?"

He pointed to her eye.

Kathy seemed confused. "Oh," she finally said. "John got a little wild. He does that sometimes."

"Ahearn? You were with him today?"

Kathy cocked her eyebrows at Dale. "We had sex. I gave him head and then he fucked me."

"Lucky you."

"He prefers me to his wife."

"Why'd he hit you?"

She was looking at something across the room. Dale followed her gaze to a curtain.

"Kathy?"

"Huh? Oh, he gets overexcited sometimes. It's part of his routine, having sex with him. I do it for the dope when I have to. He didn't hurt me, though, if that's what you think."

"Because you couldn't feel it," Dale said. "You're stoned. I suspect you will later, though, feel it."

Kathy was gazing across the room again.

"Anyway, I have some pictures I need you to see," Dale said. "They're a bit gory. It's a dead man."

"Gimme," she said.

He pulled an envelope from inside his jacket and stood up. He walked the pictures to the bed and handed them over. She squinted at them a while before setting them down.

"Do you know that man?" Dale asked.

"It's Tyrone, I think," Kathy said. "Those are his tattoos."

"And? Can you tell me anything else about him?"

"He's from back East. Atlantic City, I think."

"And?"

"He deals horse. Him and Roger."

"Roger?"

"Roger Daltry. I had sex with him, too. John made us do it." She suddenly laughed hysterically. "He said I needed to do my part for the troops."

Dale waited for her to calm down.

"Kathy?" he said.

"Sometimes John just watches, when he's really high," she said. "Then he doesn't get so wild. He made his wife do it with Roger too once."

"Kathy, tell me more about Roger, please. Who is he?"

"John likes me better than his wife."

"Kathy, who's Roger? Roger who?"

"John's friend. Roger Daltry."

"Where does he live ?"

"Roger will be upset about Tyrone. They were buddies."

He tried again. "Where does Roger live?"

"He's the one who spiked Nathan first," she said. "Roger was."

"Nathan Barron?"

"Roger spiked him first, and then John did it the second time. Nate wasn't used to it, though. It was too much too soon."

"John Ahearn? Ahearn gave Nathan Barron the heroin?"

Her eyes were closed. "Roger did it first and then John. It really was an accident."

"Did Nathan Barron want to spike up?" Dale asked. "Was he forced?"

"John was pissed because his wife was flirting with Nate. John was jealous."

"Did John Ahearn force the needle into Nathan's arm?"

"Nathan was already high," she said. "He didn't know what was happening."

"Jesus Christ," Dale said. "Kathy, I need you to come down off the drugs. I need to check you back into Trinity."

"I just spiked up," she said.

"I know, but no more today, okay? I'm going to call an ambulance and they'll help you dry out."

"I lost my job because of you," she said through a giggle.

"Yes, I know. I'm sorry."

"It's okay. I didn't like working there anyway."

"Of course not," Dale said, then he dialed for an ambulance.

□ □ □

"You're both young, maybe you aren't aware of what the bureau did in Boston," Pavlik said.

He was on his back on the bed. His hands were still cuffed to the bed frame. The two agents were seated on chairs between the bed and the door. They were watching another movie.

"Two handlers there wound up getting arrested," Pavlik continued. "The guy they were watching, the one they cut the deal with, Whitey Bulger, they still haven't found him, your precious bureau."

"We're not handlers," Special Agent Mears said.

"Well, Morris is," Pavlik said. "And the guy he's protecting has killed before and he'll kill again. This is gonna blow up sooner or later. Whether it's the wife of the guy Singleton tried to kill back in New York or somebody else, it's gonna blow up. You guys find yourself in the middle of that, you'll wish you listened to me."

"We don't know what you're talking about, sir," Feller said.

Pavlik frowned when he saw both agents were staring at the television. "Technically, this is kidnapping," he said. "Whether you know why you're doing it or not, it's still kidnapping. Unless you intend to kill me, I'll make sure you're both brought up on charges. How hard you think it'll be for me to pick you up out of a bureau yearbook?"

"We're doing our jobs, sir," Feller said.

"And nobody is going to kill you, sir," Mears said.

"Yeah, and you were leaving in a few hours before," Pavlik said. "How long ago was that?"

"There was a change in plans," Mears said.

"I'll bet."

Pavlik closed his eyes and tried to think of a way to make enough noise to draw attention to the room. When he opened his eyes again, he saw Steven Segal on the television screen.

"Jesus Christ," he said.

"Sir?" Feller said.

"There's nothing else to watch?"

"This is almost over," Mears said.

"It's pretty good, too," Feller said.

"Kids," Pavlik said.

"Check this out," Feller said.

Pavlik watched Steven Segal use martial arts to toss a bad guy into a garbage can.

"Cool," Mears said.

"He runs like a girl," Pavlik said.

"Huh?" Feller said.

"Watch him," Pavlik said. "The guy runs like a girl."

Segal was chasing a man chasing a kid.

"Look, his arms flailing all over the place," Pavlik said. "Guy probably squats to pee."

The two agents smirked at each other.

"I'll bet you two run like that, too, huh?" Pavlik said.

"Yep, we do," Mears said. "How 'bout you?"

Pavlik waited for the agent to look at him. Then he winked and said, "Sonny, you untie me and lose the stun gun and any other toys you're carrying and I'll kick both your asses into next week."

"I'd almost like to take you up on that, sir," Feller said.

"Almost don't count, sonny. Just means you're full of shit."

Mears chuckled.

"And a pussy," Pavlik added.

## Chapter 25

When Special Agent Eugene Morris arrived at the Minot Ryan High School, he found Washington Stewart eating Spanish olives from a tall, thin jar as he slouched behind the wheel of the Dodge Ram. With the wind chill factor the temperature had dropped to forty-one degrees below zero. Morris got into the Dodge and rubbed his gloved hands together.

"Game start yet?" he asked.

"Half an hour ago," Stewart said. "I can't bring myself to watch these white boys play. Not this early. I wait till the finals. There's at least a couple good players come the finals."

Morris glanced around the parking lot. An open field lay beyond one end. The gray sky seemed to extend forever. Morris said, "It's a different world, North Dakota."

"Yes, it is," Stewart said. He speared an olive from the jar and offered it to Morris.

"No, thanks," Morris said. "Olives give me the shits."

"Lovely image," Stewart said.

"I'm back and forth to this place and Missouri and I still can't tell the difference. Just as cold there. Nobody lives there, either. Except St. Louis. The rest of the state is the same as here, flat and cold."

"I'm assuming you here for something other than geographical commentary," Stewart said before eating the olive.

Morris checked his watch. "Matter of fact, a few things. You kill Williams?"

"Excuse me?"

"Tyrone Williams. You kill him?"

"No."

"I'll make believe that's the truth for now," Morris said.

Stewart was picking another olive from the jar.

Morris said, "One of the guys we scooped up was a tester with a small bankroll of cash in his place back in Hawthorne where he lived. Hawthorne, California. It's a tough one to digest, the amount of cash this guy had. 'Specially since he taught chemistry at a junior college."

"This supposed to interest me?" Stewart asked.

"They were pitching for the hard guys, according to the investment bankers. Somebody in Vegas."

"Sin City," Stewart said. "I never been."

"You should go, you get the chance. Prostitution is legal in Nevada. You can have all the blondes you want."

"I have all the blondes I want here."

Morris was staring at Stewart, searching for something. When Stewart didn't flinch, Morris said, "We flew up the investment bankers."

"Like I didn't know this was coming."

"This sting is bearing fruit. We need you to bring it to fruition."

Stewart popped another olive into his mouth.

"You were right about the investment bankers," Morris added. "It wasn't their money."

"It never is. So? What, they went on the street for it?"

"Not exactly. We believe them when they tell us they were brokering for the mob in Vegas. They want to meet the man set them up."

Stewart jerked his head toward Morris. "The fuck you talking about? They want to meet the man set them up, for what, insurance?"

Morris chuckled. "Something like that. What the hell do you care, Jimmy? We'll give you a different colored face mask and another name."

"You fuckin' serious here, aren't you?"

"As a heart attack," Morris said. "The bankers want to meet you and we need them. They testify and you change identities all over again. You're gonna have to anyway, the man looking for you already checked into town. Here, right here in Minot."

Stewart turned on his seat.

"You're interested now, huh?" Morris said. He waited a beat and added, "Daddy already took care of it. These bankers are the important thing now. They become your neighbors, theoretically. They get new names, too, but you don't live anywhere near each other."

"Unless you fuck up," Stewart said. "The government, I mean. Unless you fuck up, somebody finds me, the man you claim is looking for me."

"And whose fault is that, there's a man looking for you?"

"Fuck you."

"Look, let's not jerk each other's chains, okay? I already took care of the guy looking for you. And you agreed to become a point man for us after that fiasco in New York, because the alternative sucked, life in the joint. You'd already be dead you didn't work for us."

"These bankers in Minot, too, now?" Stewart asked.

"Yes. And I want you to meet with them later."

"I need to get home."

"What, the skank throwing you a party?"

"Yeah. She taking me to the policemen's ball."

"I'll call you when they're ready," Morris said. "I booked you a room at the Lawrence Welk up the hill. Just make sure you're around. They're going back overnight."

"Want their investors back in Vegas to sweat, huh?"

"Sure, if it makes you feel better," Morris said. He had both his gloves off. He lit a cigarette, thought about opening the window to toss the match, but decided to drop it inside an empty coffee container.

"They dead anyway and you know it," Stewart said. "That amount of horse and the money involved. Hard guys already know they flipped. Probably made plans already. You kidding yourself. Or the bankers are kidding themselves. But I'm not kidding myself. I know exactly what's going on with this cluster fuck you in charge of."

"Oh, yeah? And what's that?"

"You maximizing the potential. You got one fell into your lap, some white boy investment bankers frontin' for the Vegas mob and now you can't wait to see where it goes. You all giddy and shit, like somebody thinks they did something big."

Morris shook his head. "You're almost amusing sometimes, you know that?"

"Yeah, I'm a motherfuckin' riot, I know. Maybe the Vegas guys whack the bankers, or myself, and then you get them, or whoever the fuck they send, on a murder rap. You flip whoever is willing to change names and another cycle of bullshit starts. You covering your bases is all. But you know what?"

Morris smirked. "Tell me, Jimmy, I'm dying to hear the rest of your two-cent theory."

"You in charge, the government, it won't work," Stewart said, laying on the street dialogue thick now. "Never in a million years. You guys like that company went bust, Enron. You all over the place instead of taking care of what you got. You spreading yourself too thin, too fast. You acting all excited and shit, but you in over your head."

"You through?"

Stewart popped another olive into his mouth and smiled. "You see who's on Letterman tonight?"

"Fuck you," Morris said. He opened the front door to get out.

"That country girl, Faith Hill," Stewart said. "Those long-ass legs she got. She fine."

"Asshole," said Morris. "Make sure you're at the hotel later." He stepped outside, then slammed the door shut.

"I wonder she for real blonde, though," Stewart said.

## Chapter 26

When Dale tried to hook up with Don Ekroth, he learned his friend had rushed home because of an emergency. Ekroth's mother-in-law had suffered another stroke. Dale was hoping Ekroth would accompany him to meet with the New York detective staying at the Lawrence Welk. He was on his way there when Marsha Nordstrom called.

Marsha was just leaving work. She told him that the black man with the face mask was back and that he was sitting with a few men she had never seen before. Dale thanked his former girlfriend for the tip and continued on his way to the hotel.

He spotted the man Marsha had described as soon as he entered the lounge. Afraid someone might recognize him, Dale sat at the hook of the bar so he could watch the black man and the two younger white men he was with.

He tried his best to act inconspicuous. He ordered a beer and drank from the bottle. He read the local college newspaper cover to cover twice, then used a plastic swizzle stick to clean his fingernails.

When he noticed the man with the face mask heading toward the bar, Dale started to read the college newspaper a third time.

"Another round," the black man told the bartender. "One Heineken and two clubs with lime."

Dale kept his head buried in the newspaper. He read for a second time how the Minot University Beavers basketball team had won their last two road games.

"Where'd that lovely thing was working here run off to?" the black man asked.

"Miss North Dakota?" the bartender said. "Her shift ended twenty minutes ago."

"That what she was, a Miss North Dakota?"

"Was," the bartender said. "Her name is Marsha." He set the tray with the drinks on the bar. "Marsha Nordstrom. Look up above the bar. We advertise her. I forget what year she won. A couple dozen years ago, I guess. Something like that."

The black man stepped away from the bar and read the banner above it. "Ain't that something?" he said. "Well, she got my vote."

"And she has a kid," the bartender said. "You'd never know it, that woman was actually pregnant at one time. Belly out to here, you can believe it." He held his hands out away from his stomach.

The black man set a ten on the bar and winked. "Not in a million years," he said.

"Change?" the bartender asked.

"Keep it," the black man said.

"Well, thank you very much, sir," said the bartender, all smiles.

Dale looked up as the black man was turning to leave. He noticed the decline in the man's face where the mask ended, as if a part of his cheek were missing.

□ □ □

"Club and club, fellas," Stewart said to the two men in khaki pants and polo shirts. "Sorry, but I forget who is who."

"I'm Josh," the tall, curly-haired man said.

"Todd," the one with the short hair said. He half raised his right hand.

"Todd or Ted?" asked Stewart, a moment before waving his question off. "Don't take offense."

They were having their drinks in the lounge of the Lawrence Welk Hotel. Special Agent in Charge Morris was in the lobby giving them some time alone. He had already handled the introductions.

Stewart was enjoying himself. The investment bankers were still nervous from their bust a few days ago. He could tell they didn't know what to expect.

"State bird a Western meadowlark," he said. "The flower, a wild prairie rose. North Dakota is approximately seventy thousand square miles and was issued statehood on November second, eighteen-eighty-nine. Got two big lakes here, Sakakawea, the big one, the one Lewis and Clark traveled on, and Devil's Lake, what white settlers called the Bad Spirit Lake. State nickname is Peace Garden State, what you see on the license plates, but it's better known as Rough Rider Country. Speaking of license plates, the state industry, what they have the cons inside the joint here make, that's called Rough Rider Industries. Make furniture, road signs, things of that nature. You familiar with the Spanish-American War and Teddy Roosevelt charging up San Juan Hill, that's where the Rough Rider thing comes from. Big national park in his name too, southwest of here closer to Dickinson and Montana. This here is the Lawrence Welk Hotel. Lawrence some big time band leader back in the day. He from here, North Dakota. Little town called Strasburg. Blink while you're passing through and you missed it."

He stopped to sip his beer. He suppressed a belch and said, "That's one half the story, the white man's tale. There's another side, of course. The Native American. Indians to you, probably. Those people been fucked worse than niggers. Some trying to reestablish their nation now, petitioning the government and whatnot. I doubt they get anywhere with it, but that's because they going about it the wrong way. Trying the Ghandi route, all peaceful and shit. Ask me, they should repopulate themselves like the crazy Hasidim back in Brooklyn, have the women reproduce like jackrabbits before anyone notices. They'll have numbers to make some noise then."

Josh said, "I guess you have a lot of time to read, huh?"

"When I was in prison, I did, sure," Stewart said. "Then they came up with a new game plan, our federal stepmothers and I got to live the experience. You got any other questions, fire away."

"Can you maneuver?" Josh said.

Stewart smiled. There it was, an educated white boy, probably spoiled all his life, worried now about following the rules, already looking for a way out.

"You the brains, huh?" Stewart asked him.

"How close do they watch you?" Josh asked. "Can you operate?"

Stewart took a drag from his cigarette. "There's wiggle room," he said. "You know what you're doing."

"Do they protect you?" Todd asked. "For real, I mean."

Stewart took his time lighting a fresh cigarette, then sipped at his beer. "They relocate you," he finally said. "Give you a new name, a place to live. Sometimes they get you a job, but you two don't want that. It's usually something dumb and too boring to show up to every day. But don't kid yourselves, you start to fuck up, the first thing they hang over your head is giving you up. They not your friends. That's the first thing to remember. They not your friends."

Josh sipped at his club soda. "How long?" he asked. "How long have you been in?"

"I hope I don't look that stupid," Stewart said. He sipped his beer again. "You in the program, you're giving somebody up. You'd give me up just the same."

"Drugs?" Todd asked.

Stewart frowned. "You the labor, huh?"

"He won't tell us specifics," Josh explained to Todd.

"No offense," Stewart said.

The two bankers looked at each other. Josh turned to Stewart and said, "They want us to work for them. Long-term. After we testify."

"They want more than they already got," Stewart said. "That's to be expected."

"I'm not sure it's safer that way," Josh said.

Stewart sucked on his cigarette and waited for more.

"What do you think?" Todd asked.

Josh added, "They told us that's what you're doing. You really have more liberty that way."

"You can always get out the program once you do what they want," Stewart said. "Unless you fuck up, get into trouble before you're out. Then they got you all over again. You get out, though, finish what they want, then they leave you on the side of the road someplace, make no mistake. You go out with the clothes on your back, unless you Sammy the Bull, somebody big like that, although all he did was get himself put back inside."

He stopped to crush out the cigarette. "You call living under their thumb liberty, yeah, I guess so," Stewart added. "They're not breathing down your neck, but they around. The man, Morris is."

"I can't do the time," Todd said. "Not in Pelican Bay."

"No shit," Stewart said.

"That's what they're threatening us with, Pelican Bay," Josh said.

"He's right, neither of you can do it there," Stewart said.

"I'm not ready to be somebody's girlfriend," Todd said.

"You'd do good to be somebody's girlfriend in Pelican Bay," Stewart said. He wasn't really sure about Pelican Bay, but he thought he had seen it on a late-night documentary on one of the cable channels.

"I can't go away," Todd repeated. "I'll never make it in jail."

Josh put a reassuring hand on Todd's knee, but spoke to Stewart. "They want to use us," he said, "to go after the guys who put up the money."

Stewart said, "They hard guys, you best stay in the program. They not connected, you could take your chances. You know who you giving up, you need to make a choice."

Todd said, "They're definitely connected."

Josh kicked Todd under the table.

"What?" Todd said.

"He playing it safe," Stewart told Todd. "So should you."

"They're probably connected," Josh said. "What he meant to say."

"Then you know what you need to do," Stewart said. "You take enough money, hard guys gonna want it back."

Josh nodded.

"I believe I need another one," Stewart said, then downed the rest of his beer.

□ □ □

This time when the man with the face mask went to the bar, he didn't say anything. He ordered a beer, lit up a cigarette, and took his time smoking it. He seemed to be watching the two men at the table behind him in the bar mirror.

Dale caught another glimpse of the man's face and saw that his cheekbone under the mask was flat. He had seen similar wounds in the Gulf

War, disfigured faces from bullet wounds and shrapnel.

The black man finished his cigarette, paid the bill, and headed back to the table. Both the white men were whispering to one another.

Dale ordered another beer and was surprised when another black man joined the crowd. He couldn't be sure, but the new addition to the party looked official. Federal, Dale was thinking. Don Ekroth had said the New York detective had mentioned the FBI, something about them protecting someone in the witness protection program. Dale wished he had met with the detective before he'd come to the lounge.

He sat there another half hour waiting for them to leave. He was curious about the second black man who had joined the table. Then the man with the face mask stayed behind when the other three left the hotel together. Dale followed them. He was surprised when they all got into the same car, one with a Hertz license plate. The official-looking black man got behind the wheel.

Dale stayed back as he followed them south on Broadway to Highway 83. He noted the rental plate and the model car. When they passed the junction at Highway 52, Dale turned around and headed back to the police station. As soon as he was settled, he called Sergeant Ekroth at his home.

"How's she doing?" he asked about Ekroth's mother-in-law.

"She's at Trinity. I'm on my way in a few minutes."

"Oh, okay," Dale said. "Give me a call when you get a chance. I got a confession from the Ljunndgren woman and I think I just spotted a fed at the Welk."

"Ljunndgren name Ahearn?"

"Yeah, she did, but she was sky-high when she did it."

"Damn."

"At least we know what happened. Ahearn was pissed about his wife making eyes at the Barron kid and stuck him with a second fix, had to be the one that killed him."

"You say you saw a fed?" Ekroth asked.

"I'm pretty sure. Looked like one."

"Then it probably was. They can't help themselves."

"Do we know of anything going on up here?"

"Not officially. Just what that New York feller said. Could be coincidence."

"So could Ahearn having Becker for an attorney the other night," Dale said. "And Tyrone Williams getting shot in the head three times. And some kid never used before dying of a heroin overdose. And now the feds are in town. It's all too coincidental."

"Not to mention that New York guy," Ekroth said. "Maybe we should catch up later. We'll go see him together."

"I was heading over there when this happened in the lounge. I wished I had met with him first."

"Well, let's go together. Go home and put your wife to bed while I head over to the hospital. I'll call you from there when I'm done."

Dale suddenly remembered what had started their conversation. "Jesus, I'm sorry, Don, go ahead," he said. "I'll wait for your call."

"Soon as I'm free," Ekroth said.

Dale turned toward home instead of heading back to the Lawrence Welk.

## Chapter 27
## U.S. 83 South/Minot, North Dakota

"It's so fucking cold up here," said Todd, rubbing his legs.

"Get used to it," Morris said. "Because unless you decide to brave it out, your drug charges, this'll be your new home. This state."

"Great," Josh said. He was looking back at the truck stop they had passed a few minutes ago. In the distance, with all the vast open space surrounding the area, the lights could be Las Vegas, he was thinking.

"And what about this guy tonight," Todd asked. "Isn't it possible that he could tip somebody off about us?"

"Especially if you relocate him against his will," Joshua added. "Maybe he likes it here."

"He'll be gone before we move you in," Morris said. "For now, you'll stay in Bismarck."

"Can we ask why we're moving up here?" Joshua asked. "Aside from the anonymity?"

"Not really, no," Morris replied. "You shouldn't ask, but I'll tell you anyway. He's run his course is the reason. He's got things going on we knew he couldn't resist. He's served his purpose and now we don't need him anymore. Not here."

Todd asked, "Will you protect him?"

"We don't have to," Morris said. "Now that he's breaking the rules all over again, we don't have to do anything. But, yeah, we will. Probably. He's pretty good at what we need him for. He can sell it. We'll probably move him someplace else."

"We're nervous," Todd said. "How are we supposed to take over that guy's trade up here? We're bankers, not drug dealers. Not the kind on the street, like him."

"We'll stick out like sore thumbs up here," Joshua said.

"So maybe you're thinking we could put you in South Beach?" Morris said. "That it?"

"No, but not here," Joshua said. "We're from California. We're lost up here."

"You're down here checking out some real estate, the both of you," Morris said. "There's anybody looking, they'll get a fix on you here and we'll be waiting on them."

"What, like bait?" Todd asked. "That's what we're here for, to make ourselves targets?"

"Don't piss your pants so fast, sonny," Morris said. "That's a worst case scenario. I'm saying if, but we'll be holding your hands. Nobody'll get close enough to do anything."

"I'm not sure that makes me feel better," Joshua said.

"Your alternative sucks," Morris reminded them. "Look, you're a pair of dudes now, real-to-life cowboys."

Todd turned to Joshua. "This is fucked up," he said.

"Or you can fight the case," Morris said.

"Maybe we should," Joshua said.

Todd leaned forward and rubbed his forehead with both hands. "I can't do the time."

Morris laughed. "You want I should let down one of the windows, get you used to the weather?"

"That isn't funny," Joshua said.

▢ ▢ ▢

He had thought they put something in his soda until he realized he was still thirsty. They had offered him a Coke but Pavlik had refused the drink. They had let his left arm free and he'd eaten a few potato chips before asking for a cup of water, but he didn't remember drinking it. He had become groggy before he sipped the water.

He knew he was still conscious because he could see the agents sitting in front of the television. He heard the telephone ringing, but wasn't sure if they had answered it.

Aelish would be calling. So might Dexter Greene.

Eddie Senta came to mind. He remembered how the man had come out of the bedroom of his house with his hands behind his head and the stare down they'd had on the stairway before the FBI guy, Morris, yelled for an ambulance.

Now Pavlik was sure he'd overheard part of a phone conversation in the motel room. He did his best to make out what was said between the two agents, but couldn't tell their voices apart. When he tried to find them, he was blinded by the light from one of the night table lamps. It had been repositioned alongside the bed with the shade removed.

"What happened?" he heard one of them ask.

"I told him he tried to push us," the other said. "SAC said he used to be a boxer before he was a cop. He earned a gold shield nailing a serial killer, but was forced out. SAC also said he has quick hands. He ruined some mob investigation slapping a guy the bureau flipped."

"What about the phone?"

"He had them jam the lines in New York."

"How much longer?"

"Soon's we clean up."

"This one is gonna make a complaint."

"Probably, why we're sticking around a couple more days."

"Shit, this place is too cold to sit surveillance."

"Why they had us bring our winter coats. Come on, let's get our shit together. Don't forget to dump those chips."

"Where we staying? Not one of those small dumps across the road, I hope."

A toilet flushed before the conversation became mumbled. Pavlik heard the sound of a door closing and could swear his arms were free again. He tried to sit up, but his body seemed to float instead. It felt as if he were slipping in slow motion into unconsciousness.

□  □  □

When Stewart left the Lawrence Welk Hotel, it was to pick up a bottle of rum from a local liquor store. By the time he returned to his room, he found two telephone messages without a voice recording.

He poured himself a tall glass of rum and Coke and turned on the television. He listened to the local news and learned about a young woman found frozen to death near Lake Sakakawea.

"Should've dressed for the weather," he said.

He lit a cigarette and relaxed on the bed. When the telephone rang, he smiled at the voice on the other end.

"Where they headed, baby?" he asked.

"Looks like Bismarck," Lynette said. She was chewing on something. "At least that's the direction they're headed, south."

"Makes sense. You trailing far enough behind?"

"Two cars."

"Good girl."

"You coming down?"

"That's why you're there, baby. For when they call me, make sure I'm still here."

"Oh," Lynette said. "Okay."

"Take a room," Stewart told her. "Let them get settled first and get yourself some sleep."

"Will I see you tomorrow?"

"I don't know yet. Guess who I met tonight? Well, almost met?"

"Who?"

"Miss North Dakota."

"Really?"

"Almost really," he said as he sipped his drink. "She a bartender at the Lawrence Welk."

"And?"

"And nothing. She fine is all. Blonde, just like you."

"If you're trying to make me jealous, it's working."

"I'm just fucking with you."

"Wash?"

"Yeah, baby."

"I miss you."

"I miss you, too."

Lynette kissed him through the phone.

## Chapter 28

Dale spent some time with Emily before meeting up with Donald Ekroth and the Minot chief of police, Mike Ottmaire, at his home on North Hill. It was a few minutes past midnight. Ottmaire led the men into his living room and put on a fresh pot of coffee.

Dale was anxious. He wiped sweat from his brow and spoke without sitting down.

"I got a witness on the Nathan Barron overdose," he said. "We can make a case for murder, but it could probably be pled down to manslaughter. The problem is the witness is a junkie and she was high when she told me what happened."

Ottmaire was a large, bulky man with a full head of gray hair. He was wearing a heavy blue robe. He looked to Ekroth. "Will she tell the same story when she's off the junk?"

"She didn't," Dale said. "I've talked to her before. She was involved with the Barron kid. She knows the players, though. She named the guy who gave Barron the lethal injection. The kid was already cranked from an injection shortly before the second one. The guy, John Ahearn, was jealous of him. His wife was flirting with Barron."

Ottmaire rubbed his forehead. "And she wouldn't admit this when she was straight? Why the hell not?"

"He's an intimidator," Ekroth said. He pulled the plastic coffee stirrer from between his teeth. "Ahearn has been through the department a few times. I had to calm him down once myself. He's a bad dude, Mike."

"I also think Ahearn is calling my house making threats," Dale said. "Just a hunch, but I think it's him."

"Threats?" Ottmaire said.

"He said something to Emily, but it was from a blocked call so...."

"What about the woman, your witness? She getting clean now?"

"She's at Trinity, but who knows how long they'll hold her," Dale said.

Ottmaire looked at Ekroth. "What do you think?"

Ekroth said, "She didn't budge the last time."

"She's terrified of the guy," Dale said, finally taking a seat. "He gives her black eyes when he's in a good mood. Which is why I'd like to go after him first. If we can get him in here, maybe provoke him into using his hands, we can bust him and hold him for a few days, maybe then she'll feel safe enough to talk when she's clean."

"I can get to him," Ekroth said.

Ottmaire frowned. "You talking about entrapment, Don?"

Ekroth winked. "Just the kind where I get him to take a swing at me. Don't ask me why, but he doesn't like me very much."

Ottmaire leaned forward on his elbows. "You going to approach this guy on your own?"

"I'm not that old, Mike."

"You're not that young, either."

"I can go with him," Dale said.

"No," Ekroth said. "He already knows how to push your buttons."

"And what if he decks you?" Ottmaire asked. "If he gets the jump on you, then what?"

Ekroth pointed at Dale. "That's where this young feller comes in," he said. "We stay in close contact, a few minutes apart."

"Very close contact," Ottmaire said.

Ekroth and Dale nodded.

"And keep everybody up to speed on it," Ottmaire told Ekroth. "At the station, I mean. Make sure we know where you are and what's going on. The guy is a junkie, you don't know what he might do."

Ottmaire turned to Dale. "What else do you have?"

Dale sat forward on his chair. "If you go back two months, we can see a definite pattern of heroin showing in or immediately around town," he said. "A bust in Harvey. Two in Velva, same person. Two in Minot. One in Bulleah. One at the college, the student suspended. One at the Air Force base, although it was like pulling teeth to get them to turn anything over. Then Nathan Barron turns up dead from an overdose.

"I arrest a Tyrone Williams on possession, an Air Force Private, and suddenly Henry Becker shows up to represent him. A couple days later somebody takes Williams out, three in the head, and sticks him in a drainage pipe outside of town, closer to Velva.

"Now a woman is found frozen near Sakakawea and is determined to have been a regular user. A guy everyone suspects is involved in dealing drugs, this Ahearn creep, is picked up with seven hundred dollars in small bills. Ahearn's wife was flying on heroin and again Becker showed up to back us down. Ahearn lives in Velva.

"The Air Force said Williams was AWOL at the time he was killed. I lean on a few people surrounding Ahearn and Emily gets a couple of nasty phone calls at the house. And I have to tell you that I believe something federal is going on here in Minot. I know I spotted an agent at the Welk tonight. I'm positive I did."

Ottmaire looked to Ekroth. "What do you think?"

"There is a pattern," Ekroth said. "There's also that thing up in Mohall last week, the woman found murdered in the trailer."

"From what I understand, it's nothing to do with drugs," Ottmaire said. "Jim Salinger up there said it's not right. Whatever happened, whoever killed her, it wasn't something random. That's the theory because of computer records they found belonging to an account she had with some dating service thing. Jim thinks there's more to it."

"The husband?" Ottmaire said.

"According to Jim, yeah, looks like. She didn't take much care to conceal her extramarital activity and the husband claims he didn't have any suspicions. They have the name of the guy the wife was in contact with, but they assume it's fictitious. They can't find him."

"Can't trace the computer records back to someone?"

"A name is all they have. Supposed to be a black feller but that could be a spoiler, something thrown in to have people look in the wrong direction."

"The husband has an alibi, I assume."

"And it's rock solid. Salinger isn't convinced what they have is real. He's trying to get some federal support, for the technology, I guess."

"Maybe I should take a ride up there," Dale said.

Ekroth said, "There's also a feller in town from New York, a retired detective. He stopped at the station today looking for Dale. He says the feds are hiding someone in the witness protection program right here in Minot. Guy with one eye, the other one shot out back in New York."

"He black, the guy he said was shot in the eye?" Dale asked.

Ekroth nodded. "According to the New York guy, this Pavlik feller, he is."

"Damn," Dale said. "I might've seen this guy tonight. He stayed behind at the Welk after the other guys left."

"At the Welk? That's where Pavlik is staying."

"Something isn't right," Ottmaire said.

"I can't believe I was in that lounge with him," Dale said.

"Maybe we should head over there now, to the hotel," Ekroth said.

"If the feds are up there protecting somebody, you won't get through," Ottmaire said. "I'm not sure I want you to. I don't need the aggravation they can cause."

"Except if this feller from New York has any validity, something is going on here we should know about," Ekroth said.

"If he has any validity," Ottmaire said. "You check him out?"

"Just a little, to make sure he was a former detective like he said. He gave me a file to copy and I did. That was genuine enough. I didn't double-check everything in it, but what else would he be doing here, except for what he said?"

Ottmaire huffed. "He's staying at the same hotel this guy Dale saw?"

"That is weird, I suppose," Ekroth said.

"Well, it's too late anyway to head up the hotel now," Ottmaire said. "Let's give it until tomorrow, do some double-checking if we have to. I don't want to find out after it's too late this retired detective is working a freelance hit for some drug cartel back East."

Dale said, "Why don't we take a run over there in the morning and see if we can't learn something? You said this Pavlik was concerned about tipping off the feds, right? We don't want to let too much time slip by."

Ekroth turned to Ottmaire, "Pavlik did say if the feds thought we were close to the guy he's after, they'd move him out of town."

"I'm not sure that's such a bad thing," Ottmaire said.

Dale said, "I can't believe I was right there tonight. At the bar, six feet from the guy."

Ekroth said, "Well, I still think it's kind of unusual how this started, all this death of late, maybe with that murder up in Mohall. Maybe you should head up there, Dale."

"Or it could have nothing to do with that," Ottmaire said. "And Dale would be that much further away from Velva and you, if you intend to try and provoke that other miscreant."

"Ahearn," Ekroth said. "I'll wait for Dale to get back."

"You better," Ottmaire said.

The three men nodded at one another.

Ottmaire motioned at Dale. "What about those phone calls? Is Emily alright?"

"Shaken up," Dale said. "Like I said, I have a feeling I know who that is. Em is being extra careful. She knows how to handle this kind of thing. I have a car going by every so often checking up."

"I can look into the federal thing but you'll have to be prepared to back off if you're right," Ottmaire said. "They'll give me all the nonsense about being exposed in the middle of an investigation and all the crud that goes with it, but my hands will be tied, Dale. If it is federal, I mean."

"Then don't ask them," Dale said. "Let me and Don work the case a few more days and see if we can make something happen."

## Chapter 29

Once Morris called him from Bismarck, Stewart left the hotel through the back door and drove up to the airport to book a room at an Econo Lodge. He made a single call from a disposable cell phone and then watched television. The local news was giving high school basketball results. Stewart closed his eyes. Half an hour later, his cell phone woke him.

"I'm in the lobby," Joe Mayo said.

"Come on up," Stewart said through a yawn. "Second floor, room two-ten."

"You sure?"

"They called less than an hour ago," Stewart said. "From Bismarck."

"Okay."

Stewart had first met Joe Mayo's gangster father while visiting Helena, Montana, less than three months ago. Lynette had found a woman on the Internet personals she thought Stewart might like. They had arranged to meet in Helena during the high school wrestling tournament being held there.

When they stopped for lunch at a diner, Stewart spotted an older stocky man playing a form of horseshoes with two men he guessed were United States marshals. Stewart watched the game until he recognized it as bocce, a game the old world Italians used to play back in New York. When the stocky man removed his hat to scratch his head, Stewart was pretty sure he recognized the cauliflower ears as those belonging to Nick "Ears" Mayo, a big-time East Coast mobster who had cut his own deal with the federal government.

Stewart spent the next hour at a local library using the Internet to find information about the New York mobster turned government witness. When he learned enough of what he needed to know, he went looking for Nick Mayo at the university where a wrestling tournament was being held. The old man had once been a competitive wrestler before quitting high school and had remained a fan of the sport. He hated the freak show brand of wrestling on television and had often attended high school and college matches during his street days. So it was part luck and part research how Stewart spotted the old man a second time. The marshals were eating snacks and shooting the shit at a food wagon about fifty yards away. Mayo was eating peanuts.

Stewart walked up behind the stocky man. He said, "You in the program, same as me, huh?"

Nick Mayo half turned around, just enough to glance at Stewart.

Stewart said, "I'm one state over, in North Dakota."

"What the fuck you want, pal?" Mayo finally said. His voice was hoarse, his accent definitely New York.

"Make friends," Stewart said. "Seeing we're both in the same boat, a pair of cons made a deal. Maybe we can do something together."

Mayo turned and dead-eyed Stewart. "You looking for trouble?"

"Easy, pops," Stewart said. "I saw you playing bocce this afternoon. On my way into town. You in the program, you need to forget that ethnic shit. 'Specially with those Martian ears of yours."

Mayo took a step up closer to Stewart.

"No disrespect," Stewart said. "I'm looking to help."

"Who the fuck are you?"

"A friend. Consider me that for now."

Mayo waited for more.

"It's a long drive from where I am," Stewart said, "even though it's next door, North Dakota. You hit the highway, once you pass the mountains going back, all you'll see is sky."

Mayo had glanced back at the marshals and saw they were talking between themselves.

"They catching up," Stewart said.

"The fuck you want, Moe?"

"Buddy, pal, Moe, I like that," Stewart said. "Makes me feel like I'm home." He offered Mayo a piece of gum.

Mayo tossed his peanuts in a trash can and accepted the gum.

"You got anybody I can contact?" Stewart asked. "I might have something you be interested in when you're out. You gonna need start-up money. Unless you intend to spend the rest of your life out here."

Mayo chewed his gum without expression. "How do I know you're not an agent testing me?"

"You don't," Stewart said. "I contact your people, if you got somebody, and you let them check me out."

Mayo chewed his gum some more before telling Stewart a telephone number. "Ask for Joe," he said after giving the number.

"How much time you got left?" Stewart asked.

"Call the number and ask for Joe."

Stewart nodded, then said, "Remember, no more bocce."

□ □ □

Now Stewart hid a Glock under his jacket on the table while he waited for Nick "Ears" Mayo's only son.

Joseph Mayo was thirty-three years old and had been a Los Angeles restaurant owner who'd been chased out of town after his father's induction into the witness protection program. The younger Mayo had lived in hiding the last several years, but he'd been involved in drug deals wherever and whenever the opportunities arose. His father was scheduled for release from witness protection in a few days.

He had just driven to Minot from Montana.

"How long you in a car?" Stewart asked.

"Ten hours," Mayo said. "Staying anywhere close to the speed limit is torture on these highways. Not to mention it's freezing outside."

Stewart poured two rum and Cokes, handed one to Mayo, and sat at the table close to the jacket hiding the Glock. Mayo sat on the chair across the table.

"You found a place to make delivery?" Stewart asked.

"We still talking about bulk, right? The extra stuff you mentioned, too."

"Packed and waiting to go."

Mayo sipped his drink. "I'd do a lot better with a hot chocolate," he said.

Stewart waited.

"We have a place," Mayo said. "You don't really need to know where it is."

"I'm making delivery, I do."

Mayo sipped his drink.

Stewart said, "Unless you want to pick it up yourself. It's not far from here, where it is. You got the money with you, that's fine with me, too."

"You already know where the money is," Mayo said.

"But I don't know where the stuff is going and I need to."

Mayo lit a cigarette. "You'll show yours first."

"Of course."

Mayo dug a piece of paper from inside his wallet. He glanced at it before handing it over to Stewart. "There," he said. "It's not too far from here, either, near that small town in Devil's Lake. Once I see yours, you'll see mine, and we'll both be on our way."

"Man's got to have start-up money," Stewart said.

"We still have to move our stuff before we see dime one of start-up cash."

"You'll do fine," Stewart repeated. "Your old man knows his business. You, too, I suspect."

Stewart toasted Mayo with his drink. Mayo drank from his glass.

"How's your daddy doing?" Stewart asked.

"Honestly? The man's a ball-breaker. A relentless ball-breaker. He's nervous about watching his back. He's paranoid they'll find him. Some guy from New York he testified against, his people moved to Vegas. My old man sees this guy in his dreams now."

"They a big network, the mob. Have some long-ass arms."

"The way I figure it, the people in Vegas will get turned by the feds just like everybody else gets turned these days."

"Probably," Stewart said. "Unless they find a way out."

"You mean a miracle."

"Maybe."

"Well, God bless them. Me, I have my own set of plans. My old man can be tough to be around. He gets out of control I'm not sticking around for the excess abuse."

Stewart said, "He's probably just looking out for you, don't realize you a man yourself."

"He's a ball-breaker," Mayo said. "Always was and always will be."

"Maybe you can be a miracle worker, make your own moves. Let the old man do his own thing, like you said."

"You know something I don't?"

"Living with the feds, little birds fly in my ear all the time."

Mayo said, "That's a scary thought."

"All you need is friends," Stewart said. "Like the man in Vegas, for one."

"My old man cost him too much. I don't think he'd be my friend."

"Wanna make him one?"

## Chapter 30

Pavlik was seeing Timothy Waller.

He was back in Far Rockaway, Queens, on a dark and damp night. He saw light inside the basement windows of an abandoned house and dropped down on all fours for a closer look. The man he had tracked through the New York public school records was putting out cigarettes on the back of a young boy. Pavlik clenched his teeth until one chipped.

He saw camera equipment arranged around the basement and could hear the loud music pumping through at least three speakers he could see. The boy appeared to be in shock.

It was an anxiety dream during which Pavlik couldn't get down to the basement in time to save the boy. Eventually, the dream ended the way it always did, with Pavlik screaming until he collapsed outside the basement window.

It wasn't what had happened. Pavlik had found his way inside the house and saved the boy. Then Pavlik had used his fists on Waller. It took a team of FBI agents to stop Pavlik from beating Waller to death. Waller, with several video cameras filming, had lured the off-duty detective into a near murderous assault.

In the dream, however, the boy was found decapitated.

He was sure the nightmare was over until he saw James Singleton standing side by side with Timothy Waller across a wheat field, the two of them sharing a laugh at Pavlik as he stood over the headless boy.

□  □  □

Mary Beth Wilson lit a fresh cigarette and curled her legs on the front seat while Joe Mayo counted off forty-two dollars to pay the gas station attendant. It was bitter cold outside. Mary Beth pulled up the fur collar of her lambskin coat.

"Check your oil, sir?" the attendant asked.

Mayo handed the attendant the money. "Too cold, pal," he said as he brought the window back up. "Thanks anyway."

The attendant counted the money and tapped on the window. Mayo let it down a crack.

"It's forty-fifty, sir," the attendant said. "You gave me too much."

Mayo waved it off. "Keep it," he said as he brought the window back up. He winked at Mary Beth and pulled away from the gas pumps.

"My husband like to kill himself before he tipped somebody," she said.

"Why you left him, honey," Mayo said.

"He used to call men who didn't pump their own gas fairies."

"You think I'm a fairy?"

Mary Beth giggled. "No way."

She was an attractive woman at twenty-nine; petite with short blonde hair, big breasts and a perfect cherry ass, exactly the way Joe Mayo liked them. She had been married at twenty to a pig farmer fifteen years her senior; an abusive alcoholic with quirky sexual habits that neglected his wife's natural desires, what she had told Mayo over the Internet when they first met.

When he was back on the highway again, Mayo set the cruise control at seventy-five miles per hour. "Think your husband called home yet?" he teased.

"About a hundred times," Mary Beth said.

"Good. I hope we give him a good case of *agita*."

"What's that?"

"Like stomach cramps. Only it starts up here." He tapped his head.

Mayo had responded to an ad Mary Beth had posted through a dating service. She had grown tired of life with her husband. When Mayo visited his father in Montana a few months later, he met with Mary Beth and the two became lovers.

Now they were running away together. They were on their way to Grand Forks to meet up with his father, Nick "Ears" Mayo. From there they would drive to Lakota to pick up a shipment of heroin. Then, heading further east, they'd make stops in Cleveland, Boston, and finally New York.

After that, Nick "Ears" Mayo had told his son, he planned to move down to Mexico someplace "where the United States dollar hadn't turned to shit yet."

Joe Mayo wasn't sure where he wanted to live.

"I can't wait to see New York," Mary Beth said.

"It's been a while for me, too," Mayo said.

"I want to visit the Empire State Building," she said. "I want to see where the towers were. I still can't believe that happened."

Mayo couldn't help but remember September 11, 2001. It was the same day he was run out of Los Angeles.

"Is your cousin from New York, too?" she asked.

"Yeah, from Brooklyn. But he's not as refined as I am. Frank's a little rough around the edges."

Mary Beth giggled again.

"He was a thug before he was let go," Mayo continued. "Once my father cut a deal, anybody associated with our family was blackballed. Frank wasn't too happy about that when it happened, but he wasn't going anywhere anyway. They kept telling him they closed the books in New York, but they just didn't want him. Frank was always trying prove himself doing stupid shit. Drew too much attention."

"Closed the books?" Mary Beth said. "What's that mean?"

Mayo smiled as he reached across the console and grabbed her breasts through the lambskin coat. "It's like when a Lodge or the VFW isn't taking new members," he said.

Mary Beth giggled once more.

"I love that laugh," Mayo said.

"So your cousin is close with you and your father?"

"More or less. The old man isn't too crazy about him, but I think Frank's okay. Besides, I got an ace in the hole I'm playing my old man doesn't know about."

"What's that?"

"A couple guys down in Bismarck."

"What about them?"

"They're negotiable."

"Huh?"

"It's a long story," he said before he reached across the console and grabbed at her again.

Mary Beth giggled on cue.

□  □  □

Colonel Robert Schmidt sat with Washington Stewart at a back table of a truck stop diner off the junction of Highways 52 and 83. At a few minutes past one in the morning the diner was mostly empty. On a laptop Stewart was searching the *New York Daily News* online for a possible story about a man being murdered in a Long Island hospital.

Schmidt sipped at a black coffee and glanced around the diner. He leaned forward and said, "Am I still following the hick from Velva?"

"Name's John Ahearn," Stewart said. "And the answer is yes." He glanced at his watch. "You should probably leave in the next ten minutes. Lakota's a good three hours from here."

Schmidt ignored the advice. "And the diversions?" he asked. "You have those in place?"

Stewart paused to read something on the screen before answering. "Yeah, I do."

"And if he takes off in the wrong direction once he's paid?"

Stewart was typing now. "I'd hope you shoot him," he said. "In case that makes you nervous just stay with him and give me a call. Then I'll shoot him."

Schmidt reached across the table and pushed the laptop's power button.

The screen blinked once and turned black.

"Now what the fuck you wanna do that for?" Stewart said.

"Because I want your attention," Schmidt said. "Do I have it?"

Stewart dead-eyed the doctor.

"I flew over Mohall the other day and saw my wife's car was still parked outside the trailer park. It hadn't been moved."

"So, that's a good thing, no?"

"Maybe. There's a cop up there who doesn't buy my story about Michelle. He knows I'm full of shit."

"Don't crack now, my man. We too close to out of here."

"I have an idea about how to handle him."

"The cop?"

Schmidt nodded. "But I'm also thinking maybe an anonymous call to the law before we leave might be a good idea."

"Anonymous call about what?"

"A bomb, especially since you intend to use one or two in Minot, right?"

"You wanna set one off in Mohall?"

"I didn't say that."

"No, you said something about an anonymous call. So, make it."

"I'm thinking it should come from you."

"And why's that?"

"To your FBI sponsor."

"Huh?"

Schmidt frowned.

Stewart suddenly understood. "Oh, okay. Send what's left of the troops up north. Terrorism type thing. Good idea, except I have other plans for my sponsor. Maybe I'll call the Minot police."

"Whatever," Schmidt said. He sipped his coffee, set it down and said, "See what happens when you pay attention?"

"I was multi-tasking. A man can—"

Schmidt put a hand up. "I don't care," he said.

## Chapter 31
## Lakota/Minot/Mohall, North Dakota

It was four o'clock in the morning when John Ahearn filled the pick-up's tank with gas outside Lakota before crossing the train tracks into town. He was there to exchange Washington Stewart's cuckoo clock for money. He'd be killed, he'd been warned, if the total amount wasn't delivered back to Minot.

Ahearn had an address and a telephone number. Stewart had been cryptic but deliberate. He was to deliver the clock he had altered to accommodate the heroin. He was to receive money for the clock after the heroin was tested. He was to drive back to Minot with the cash in less than three hours and ten minutes.

Ahearn assumed Stewart would have somebody sitting on him but so far he hadn't spotted anyone. He found the house on G Avenue West, a run-down one-family with an abandoned home alongside it.

A scruffy man answered the door and led Ahearn inside. Once Ahearn unboxed the clock, the scruffy man was rough with it. Ahearn had been hoping to salvage the unit and maybe resell it, but the scruffy man used a hammer and screwdriver to break the clock apart.

Ahearn was thinking it was the Mafia or some other kind of organized crime behind the deal Stewart was making and that he was the dumb courier they usually killed or the cops locked up for the rest of his life. He was anxious to make the exchange and get going.

The scruffy man took his time testing the product. He sat at the kitchen table and tested samples from each of the six bags Ahearn had managed to staple inside the clock. When he was finally through, the scruffy man took even more time counting the stacks of hundred dollar bills. The total came to four hundred, fifty thousand dollars. Ahearn started to sweat. He was nervous and lost his place during the recount.

When the scruffy man sealed the FedEx box with tape, he explained how it wasn't to be opened again before it was delivered.

"You rip the tape, it shows," he said. "Then you gotta answer to whoever you gotta answer to. I'm supposed to tell you that you're being watched from the moment you leave this place so don't be stupid. Personally, I was the gofer on this deal, I'd make for the Mexican border I was hauling that much cash. I'd take my fuckin' chances."

"I won't open it," Ahearn said.

He was handed the address in Minot where he was to deliver the package, then the scruffy man answered a phone call during which he laughed out loud a few times.

Ahearn was thinking about breaking the scruffy man's face when the loudmouth finally turned off his cell phone.

"What?" Ahearn asked.

"Nothing," the scruffy man said. "You can go now, we're done."

□ □ □

He had forgotten where he was until he sat up and saw it was light outside. He turned to the digital clock on the night table and pushed himself off the bed. Twenty minutes later Pavlik was dressed and on his way down to the lobby to call his former partner in New York on one of the pay phones.

"The bastards used a stun gun on me and kept me locked up through the night," Pavlik told Dexter Greene.

"Jesus Christ," Greene said.

"I get ahold of those two, I'll knock their teeth out."

"Easy does it, cowboy. What the hell happened?"

"The guy had to be here last night," Pavlik ranted. "In the same hotel, probably. Somewhere close. Why they gave me babysitters."

Greene said, "Alex, slow down."

"It's Singleton, Dex. James Singleton. He's here."

"You're sure?"

"Positive. The feds had two agents hold me hostage through the night. You believe it?"

"You're in over your head on this one."

"In over my head?" Pavlik said. "That fuck Morris doesn't know what he's got coming."

"Is the guy still there, the one you're looking for?"

"I don't know. Probably not. They slipped me something to put me to sleep. When I woke up, my babysitters were gone. I have to assume so is Singleton."

"But he can't be far."

"Unless they put him on a plane. He could be on his way to Tokyo."

"Or back to where he was safe in North Dakota. You're upset, you're not thinking."

"I'm upset. You're right about that. This prick Morris. First he pays some hick to take a swing at me and now this."

"Alex, calm down."

"I am calm!"

"Right, you're as calm as a crooner."

"What?"

"Just listen to me a minute. You need to go to the local police up there. You need to have somebody watching your back."

A thought crossed Pavlik's mind. "Dex, you need to check on Eddie Senta."

"Huh?"

"My client's husband, the guy shot Singleton in the eye. If Singleton is still running around, Senta can't be safe."

"Jesus Christ, Alex, I have a job, remember?"

"Then send somebody to the hospital to watch him."

"I'm not the fuckin' mayor. I send anyone there, it'll be me, and I already have a job."

"His wife will pay, Dex. Moonlight if you have to. I'm telling you Senta isn't safe so long as this animal is still being protected."

"I'll see what I can do."

"Please, Dex. The woman trusted me on this, Senta's wife."

"I'll take a ride there in the morning. Where?"

"Long Island Jewish, out near where they lived."

"I have to be on the job in the afternoon."

"He's not done with Eddie Senta. He's gonna try again so long as they're protecting him. Not him, but he'll send somebody."

"I'll stop in, see what's what, but I can't spend the day."

"Get somebody to stay if you can't, Dex. I'll authorize it for my client. She'll be happy there's somebody watching her husband."

"Let me see what I can do."

"Three hundred a shift, if it helps, but Eddie Senta can't be left alone."

"All right, I said. I'll be there."

"And be prepared. I'm telling you this guy is not gonna rest until he gets Senta."

"What about yourself? You gonna talk to the cops there?"

"I already did. I've been waiting on them to get back to me, but nobody seems to be in a rush."

"Because they don't know what they're dealing with, probably."

"Whatever, but I'm telling you that prick is here and I'm going to nail him."

"You're not a cop anymore, Alex. You kill the man, you'll go away for it."

"I didn't say I'd kill him."

"Well, you can't beat the shit out of him, either."

"Says you," Pavlik said.

□ □ □

Jim Salinger was the same age as Don Ekroth. The two had grown up in Bowman and served two years in the Army together before returning home and marrying their high school sweethearts. Ekroth and his wife had moved to Minot within six months of his discharge. Salinger had moved to Mohall and became a policeman there the same year Ekroth joined the Minot police department.

Dale had never met Salinger before, although the two had once planned on ice fishing with Ekroth the weekend a blizzard precluded travel of any kind for four days. The two men met at the Paragon Café on Main Street West. It was just after what passed for a morning rush had ended.

"Don gave me a heads-up," said Salinger after the two men had introduced themselves and were seated at a table with fresh cups of coffee.

"We don't know if there's any connection, but it all seems to have started with your murder up here," Dale said. "And this thing with the feds makes it all the more mysterious. It could be they're hiding some guy from back East in the witness protection program."

"Not to mention the good doctor is an Air Force colonel?"

"That, too, I suppose. The base could have something to do with it, although our chief isn't convinced they're one and the same. I just don't know. I'm curious about what you think. Don said you didn't buy what appeared to have happened to the woman."

Salinger was a tall, thin man with a thick mustache and curly gray hair. "Too clean," he said. "Everything about it is too clean. No loose ends, not really."

"And a hunch?"

"Yeah, but I think the hunch comes from the thing being so concise. The doctor's wife was waiting on somebody for sure. She was dressed for action, so I don't doubt she was having an affair, and the fact the name is a phony, the guy, I mean, suggests it's a past affair, or that she's well versed in cheating. It wasn't random, somebody she just picked up, we're pretty sure about that, but with all the convenient circumstances surrounding this thing, that's exactly what the Internet correspondence suggests, that it was a blind date. They were gonna meet and have sex, spend the weekend looks like. Her husband was in Montana scouting real estate in her hometown. He even picked out some presents at her high school to give her when he returned."

Dale used a paper napkin to wipe coffee he had spilled in the saucer.

"And even if it was something coincidental," Salinger continued, "what about the timing? What she tell her husband? I'm going to see my sister, but don't call me. The sister didn't know anything about it. Would she take those kinds of risks?"

"Maybe it was an open marriage?" Dale said. "There are people who live that way."

"Except he acted upset at us when we first mentioned the situation, as if he had no clue what she was up to. I didn't buy that, either, his distress. And then I nudged him a little more. He didn't like that much, either."

"Nudged him how?"

"Called his place and left a message. I was parked about two hundred yards from his office. I asked him to call back, which he didn't, then I stopped him for speeding on his way home about an hour later. I did that and then followed up with another phone call to his home. It was harassment, pure and simple, but it got to him. I know it did."

Dale nodded.

"More important," Salinger said, "what bothers me more, anyway, is the fact the guy is a neat freak. Schmidt I'm talking about now. When we went to his office and the house in Minot, everything was in its place, nothing out of order. Not a thing, except for what his wife was doing the past two, three years? All that order in his life and he couldn't figure out she was cheating on him?"

"Could you trace her extramarital activity?"

"At least two years," Salinger said. "There are signs, Dale, when people are doing things they shouldn't. A spouse goes astray, I find it hard to believe it takes a murder three years down the road to a supposedly blind date in a trailer a good fifty plus miles from where you live. And the husband is what, four hundred fifty miles away at the time? He's that conveniently out of touch?"

"It does stink, doesn't it?"

"I made a call to the FBI office in Fargo to see what they thought," Salinger said. "They agreed to take a look-see at her PC hard drive, but she had a laptop we know of and that's missing. And let's face it, her PC won't be a priority to the FBI, not these days."

"You know anything else about the husband?"

"We're a three-man operation up here. I did some Internet searching and so on, but there's nothing unusual. He's a guy looking at a quiet retirement."

"Money?"

"He'll do well."

"Life insurance on the old lady?"

"No motive there. No insurance on her. One on him, though. Couple hundred grand. She would've done fine off his assets, anyway, what they had in the bank."

"You still have the evidence here?"

"Sure."

"Can I take a look-see?"

Salinger waved to the waitress for the check. Dale reached for his wallet and Salinger stopped him.

"I got this," he said before winking. "You can buy the pie later."

Dale smiled. "Fair enough," he said, then his cell phone rang.

□ □ □

Afraid the two agents had planted bugs in the hotel room phone and his cell phone, Pavlik continued to use the hotel lobby telephones. He called the number the sergeant had given him the day before, but Donald Ekroth didn't pick up. Pavlik left an emergency voice message describing what had happened the night before. When he hung up, he realized how crazy it would sound and called back. He left a somewhat calmer second message and pleaded for the sergeant to return the call to the hotel's front desk as soon as possible.

His next call was home to Aelish. He told her what had happened.

"Is it okay to talk?" she wanted to know.

"Probably not on your end, but I don't care anymore," Pavlik told her. "These FBI pricks pissed me off."

"FBI?" she said. "Maybe you shouldn't stay. I don't like hearing the FBI is involved already."

"It's no different than what they pulled ten years ago on Long Island."

"Except they used a stun gun on you, Alex. That's dangerous."

"Then they held me in my room. Fucking kidnapping."

"Why not come home, love?"

"Too late now. They pissed me off."

"You can't fight the FBI, Alex."

"Only because they're cowards. I'd kick their asses they give me the chance."

"This isn't a pissing match."

"Assholes."

"I think you should come home. Tell Diane Senta what's going on and maybe she can do something about it with the press, but it isn't safe anymore. I don't like it."

Pavlik craned his neck to look out a lobby window for the agents.

"Besides, if the FBI knows you're there, they've probably moved the one you're after anyway," Aelish added.

"Except maybe they didn't. I have a feeling he was here in this hotel last night. That means he's close. Maybe I fucked up their plans a little. Maybe they can't move him yet."

"Please come home."

"Not yet."

"When?"

"When I'm satisfied I can't find them."

"Then I'll come out there and join you."

"That's crazy. No way."

"Alex, I'm coming out there if you don't come home."

"I can't come home. Not now. And you can't come out here."

"Don't tell me what I can do."

"I have to go now. I'll call you again later."

"Alex!"

☐ ☐ ☐

It was a few minutes before eleven in the morning. He wasn't sure if Miss North Dakota was working today or what time she started, but he needed to get in touch with her Minot detective friend and fast.

He found Dale Hehn's home telephone number in the telephone book and told his wife it was an emergency and that her husband should please call back to leave a message at the hotel as soon as possible.

Next Pavlik found Miss North Dakota's last name on one of the flyers in the lobby and used the telephone book to call her at home. She was surprised to hear from him.

"I'm trying to get hold of Dale Hehn," he told her. "I just left a message with his wife, but I really need to see your friend. I'm positive the guy I'm looking for was at the hotel last night."

"He was," Marsha Nordstrom told him. "I called Dale. I'm pretty sure he went to the lounge. I was off before I saw him, but he said he would go."

"Damn it," Pavlik said.

"What is it?"

"I was held in my room by two FBI agents all night."

"What?"

"It's a long story that'll sound crazy but that's what happened. It has to do with something that happened back in New York ten years ago. The FBI knows I'm here and they're protecting a murderer again."

There was a pause on the line.

"I know it sounds crazy," he said.

"It sounds surreal."

"But it's the truth. You were right about me, I was a cop. Sorry I lied, but right now I need to see your friend. Is there any way of getting him? I'm afraid to meet at the hotel. I don't know if they're watching me or not. Is there someplace else we could go?"

Another pause frustrated Pavlik. "Please," he said.

"Let me get back to you," she said.

## Chapter 32
## Interstate 80, New Jersey; Minot/Bismarck, North Dakota

"Seventeen hundred and twenty miles and we almost there already,"
Roger Daltry told Ox.

The big man was taking his turn at sleeping. He had been snoring so
loud Daltry had cracked the window open to drown out the noise. Ox
woke up after a while. Daltry figured the beast had finally felt a chill.

"Where are we?" Ox asked.

"About to cross the Hudson River."

"Where's that?"

"Separates Jersey and New York."

"How much longer?"

"Hour or so, except I need to take a dump and get something inside my
belly. What about you?"

"I'm hungry, too."

"What about the bathroom?"

Ox reached down to feel his pants. "Must've pissed myself while I
slept," he said.

Daltry's eyebrows furrowed. "You kidding me?"

Ox shook his head no. "I was sleeping."

"Well, hold on until we find an exit the other side of the bridge. Don't
even think about shitting yourself."

Ox yawned loud.

Daltry looked to Ox and saw the big man was about to pick his nose.
Ox must've felt the stare. "What?" he said.

Daltry decided there and then that Ox had to die.

□ □ □

Pavlik was at the university library looking over past Minot daily news-
papers when Marsha Nordstrom called him back. She told him that Dale
Hehn would be out of town until later in the afternoon. Pavlik thanked
her and told her he'd meet her at the lounge in an hour or so.

He spent the next forty-five minutes searching for something that
might reveal how long James Singleton had been in Minot. He was frustrated for his efforts. There had been some drug arrests over the last few
weeks. Some had involved heroin and cocaine, but there was nothing solid
except for the murder of the private from the Air Force base who had pre-
viously been arrested for heroin possession.

When Pavlik returned to the hotel lounge, he could tell Marsha Nordstrom was a little apprehensive. "You look okay," she said.

"I know what I told you sounds crazy," Pavlik said, "but it's true. I had issues with an agent I think is running things here ten years ago in New York. He's probably the handler for the guy I'm looking for."

"Handler?"

"What the FBI calls their babysitters."

Marsha wasn't getting it. She set a coffee down in front of Pavlik.

"Can you make a Bloody Mary?" he asked.

"Spicy or mild?"

"Spicy."

She started to mix the drink.

Pavlik said, "When they make these witness protection deals they have a vested interest in keeping their snitches out of trouble as well as alive. The guy I'm looking for was a drug dealer who gave up a few people back in New York. They had him working the street. He decided to try something on his own and wound up killing three people in the process. The FBI protected him from the murder charges, but he was shot through the eye. My guess is they relocated him out here and now he's working for them all over again."

"They actually do stuff like that, the FBI?" Marsha said.

"They do a lot worse than that," Pavlik said. "Sammy Gravano, the New York wiseguy, he walked away from nineteen murders, nineteen he admitted to, and wound up dealing drugs a few years later in Arizona someplace. Taxpayers treated him to plastic surgery before the government gave him a new life."

"I knew about that one, but didn't he bring down a lot of the New York mob?"

"A lot less than they'd like the rest of the world to believe, but he did bring down John Gotti, which was all they really wanted. They didn't really need Gravano to do that. Gotti had buried himself with his own words they'd recorded with bugs. The FBI didn't need to let the second in command walk away from nineteen murders. That was a combination of politics and sending a message, the deal they gave that guy. They had tapes and a slew of underlings they'd already flipped. That was the feds taking the easy way out."

"Flipped?"

"Sorry," Pavlik said. "I'm talking a different language here. Flipped means they made a deal."

He could see she was still confused. "Turned rat," he said.

"And what's the message?"

"They don't have to do time. Give up the guy above them and they can skip the justice their victims' families expect."

"That's horrible."

"It's how the feds do things, except if the guy they're protecting is important enough, they turn their backs on all the other crimes their informant might commit, including rapes and murders."

"And you think the guy with the mask is in the witness protection program?"

"I'm positive," Pavlik said. "He's not only in it, he's actively working with the feds, which gives him even more clout. I'll guarantee you he's behind some of these murders here."

"That's horrible."

"It's the way the feds operate. They stop cops from doing their jobs all the time. They make deals with murderers, pedophiles, rapists, serial killers, and then they hide behind the Justice Department."

Marsha poured his drink in a pint glass with a stalk of celery. "Well, I hope Dale can meet with you later," she said. "He said he would try."

Pavlik set a twenty on the bar and took a long sip of the drink through the straw.

"I hope so, too," he said. "Because other than him, I'm pretty much on my own right now."

□ □ □

The investment bankers were in their room on the second floor of a Bismarck motel a few blocks from the state penitentiary. They each had a cup of coffee. Todd was looking out from behind the blinds. Joshua sat on the bed flipping through television channels with the remote.

"I can't believe he left us alone," Todd said.

"That's because we aren't alone," Joshua said. "Look out at the parking lot. That other guy that was with him before is still there. He's our babysitter. Besides, we have no place to go, we want to run away. It's zero fucking degrees outside. All we have are light clothes."

"I don't like the way this is going," Todd said.

"Yeah, right," Joshua said. "You have a better idea?"

"I don't trust that guy last night."

"Which guy?"

"The one with the mask. I don't trust him."

"Well, he's a rat, just like we are, so I guess we shouldn't trust him."

"What's to stop him from making a phone call, Josh?"

"A phone call where? To whom?"

"Duh, hello? Las Vegas."

"To whom, Todd. Think about it?"

"I am thinking about it. It wouldn't be that hard to figure out who to call there. What's to stop him from finding out?"

"The same thing keeping us in this shit-hole motel instead of taking a flight to South America. The agents outside."

"Except they aren't watching him the same way."

Joshua rolled his eyes. "Todd, I'm not in the mood for this now, okay? You didn't sleep all night. Why don't you try again now?"

"You hear that wind out there?" Todd asked. "Just listening to it makes me cold."

"So get away from the window."

"I hate this place."

"It beats Pelican Bay. I'm sure of that much."

"Maybe Pelican Bay is safer."

"You must be losing your mind."

"I'm serious. Maybe it is."

"It isn't," Joshua said. "Trust me, I know. I can tell from the lock-up shows on cable. I have no intention of going to Pelican Bay or any other prison."

"Morris doesn't like us," Todd said. "That's the only thing I believe that guy with the eye patch said. Morris isn't our friend."

"And neither are we his friend," Joshua said.

Todd finally turned away from the window. "He's setting us up," he said.

"What?"

"He's setting us up."

"Who is? Morris? What the fuck for? We're his case."

"No, the other guy," Todd said.

"How the fuck is he doing that? He's in the same boat as us."

"He is, I can tell."

"You're paranoid, my friend. Take a pill or something."

"I don't have one."

"Then count sheep."

## Chapter 33
## Mohall, North Dakota

He had followed John Ahearn from Velva to Lakota and back to Minot with one delay that Schmidt was sure was the big man stealing some of the money. Now the doctor had plans of his own.

The Mohall policeman that had made himself a nuisance, Salinger his name was, had a surprise coming. Once the cop had set the speed trap, he had sealed his fate. Schmidt was about to set his own trap.

It had started when the cop didn't believe the alibi or that Schmidt was unaware of his wife's infidelity. The doctor could tell by yet another phone conversation when Salinger had said something like, "I don't know, Doc, your house seems in pretty good order to me. I don't see how you could miss her having affairs over a two-year period. Just doesn't seem right."

The doctor had lost his temper and told the cop he didn't care what he believed.

"Okay, Doc, I'll be talking to you," the cop had said.

Schmidt had felt the same kind of rage he used to experience with Michelle whenever she lied to his face about where she had been or what she had been doing. The Mohall cop was also smug. Schmidt was eager to teach him a lesson.

He drove up to Mohall in an old Jeep Cherokee he'd bartered a few years back when one of his patients couldn't pay for Schmidt's medical services. It was an unregistered vehicle with license tags he'd lifted from an abandoned car. So long as he wasn't stopped while driving the Jeep, he'd be fine. He'd ditch it as soon as he was finished.

He was in a hurry to return for one o'clock office hours. With a little luck, he could get it done and be home with a few minutes to spare.

Schmidt drove a few miles over the speed limit until he was sure it was safe. Then he drove a little faster.

□ □ □

The calls from his wife, Marsha Nordstrom and then Don Ekroth were all about the private investigator from New York. Dale didn't have time to talk to the New York guy, but he told Marsha to arrange for them to meet later in the afternoon or at night.

He examined the Mohall crime scene evidence, but found nothing that even hinted at drugs or anything else that might help with his investigation back in Minot. He told Jim Salinger what he thought might be going on in Minot and asked him not to discuss it with the FBI until they knew more.

"What about Schmidt getting involved in drugs and maybe trading off his wife in a deal?" Salinger said.

"As in Schmidt pushing drugs?"

"It's not unheard of, doctors running their own side business. And he does have access to the Air Force base. He likes to log fly time. Sometimes he flies out of Minot International, but lately he's logging time on choppers. He took a quick trip up here a few days ago, what we got from an Air Force flight log. He didn't land or anything, but he flew over the crime scene."

Dale smiled. "You really are trying," he said. "An Air Force flight log?"

"It was like pulling teeth, but I can feel this one," Salinger said. "The colonel is dirty."

"And we're positive the heroin is coming from the base," Dale said. "Either it's being distributed from there or it's flyboys doing the dealing. I caught one myself and he was killed the next day."

"The one in the drainage pipe outside Velva, I heard," Salinger said.

"Anything on Schmidt pushing drugs?"

"No such luck."

"Although it wouldn't be too hard to cover up from his office," Dale said. "Who's to say one's a patient and another is a drug courier?"

"If I had the manpower, which I don't, I could sit people on him. I pushed it the day I drove down to Minot to harass him. We'd still need something substantial to even ask for any kind of help here in Mohall. And it'd all be useless without a wire on his phones and so on."

Dale shook his head. "We'd need a lot more than what we have to get court orders like that."

"I don't buy it that this was some kind of open marriage he's suddenly embarrassed about or that the wife was able to outsmart this guy," Salinger said. "No way."

Dale said, "It might or might not have something to do with what's going on in Minot, but I'm not sure we'll figure it out without some kind of break on this doctor. You check for malpractice suits? Maybe one of his former patients holding a grudge might know something."

"I asked, but haven't heard anything from the medical board yet," Salinger said. "They're not anxious to divulge information either. I tried the insurance company and they were even less inclined to help."

Dale nodded. "Well, I should probably get back," he said. "I appreciate your taking the time to show me around, Jim."

Salinger winked. "You're a friend of Don's, you're all right by me."

They shook hands.

A few minutes later Dale was inside his cruiser. He made a quick U-turn on Main Street before heading south back to Minot. He was thinking about the New York guy when a dusty Jeep Cherokee doing at least twenty miles over the speed limit whizzed by. He thought about calling it in to Jim Salinger but decided to let it go. The guy was busy enough without having to worry about speeders a few miles outside his town.

□ □ □

Schmidt discovered the heroin at the base by pure accident, and he had his wife to thank for it. Earlier in the day he had taped a conversation she'd had with another woman about a swingers party they planned to attend in Minot the same night. Until then, he hadn't been aware that Michelle might've engaged in swingers parties so close to home.

When he confronted her about it, Michelle called his bluff.

"Why don't you come along?"

"Excuse me?" Schmidt replied.

"Why not? You obviously get off on what you're doing. Maybe you should go all the way and watch me one night. You might like it."

"You think that, huh?"

"Or why haven't you divorced me yet?" Michelle said.

Schmidt had wanted to kill her right there and then. Suppressing his rage at that moment had required his best efforts.

"You know I'm out there, Robert," she continued. "You know I've been with other men. You don't put a stop to it and you don't sleep with me anymore. All you do is snoop around like some voyeur. You won't divorce me. What else am I supposed to think, except you enjoy it somehow? It isn't all that uncommon. There are plenty of men who get off knowing their wives are with other men."

He'd clenched his fists behind his back while trying to act as indifferent as possible.

"Well, if you're going to use the car tonight, at least drop me off," she said. "And you're welcome to come in if you change your mind."

He decided she had to die. It was one thing to let his wife's affairs excite him, it was another that she'd become so confident as to call him on it.

When he dropped her off later that night, he parked a few blocks from the house and then circled around on foot to the backyard. With binoculars he spied through the windows in the back and was surprised to see a number of black men among the crowd. There was nothing sexual going on while he watched, but a few couples had already paired off and were kissing one another. Schmidt preferred imagining to seeing. He headed back to his car.

When he arrived at the base, late by half an hour, he noticed someone dropping duffel bags from one of the choppers. There was no guard at the gate to the chopper area. When Schmidt turned on a flood light to illuminate the area, the men handling the duffel bags near the chopper scampered away. A minute later a car pulled out of a restricted area and sped away. Schmidt discovered the heroin in the duffel bags.

Intending to hand them over if he was stopped, he'd brought the bags inside the hangar until he was sure it was safe to move them to his car. Schmidt figured his being late had walked him into a powdered gold mine, and it was his wife who had caused the delay.

Now he watched Jim Salinger the Mohall cop making his rounds from a safe distance. When he saw the cop cross the street to step inside a diner, Schmidt pulled out onto the street and positioned the Cherokee so it was facing the same way as the police cruiser.

The cop was inside just over five minutes. When he stepped outside, he was sipping something hot from a container. Schmidt wondered whether the cop was a hot chocolate or a coffee guy.

The cop set the container on a window ledge and lit a cigarette. He took his time smoking and then sipping and never once jammed his hands inside his pockets to warm them.

Schmidt was impressed.

Five more minutes passed before the cop finally tossed his container into a trash pail and dropped his cigarette into the gutter. He waited for one car to pass before starting across the street toward his cruiser.

It was then Schmidt gave the Cherokee gas.

It happened much faster than he'd expected. Suddenly he was on top of the cop and it was too late to veer one way or the other. The thud of the impact was loud. Salinger flew clear across the hood of the police cruiser parked at the curb. Schmidt could see the cop's body crumpling in front of the cruiser a moment before he had to turn to head south again.

He wasn't sure if he had killed the cop, but he knew he had done serious damage. He remembered Jim Salinger's smugness as he drove out of Mohall. If Salinger survived, maybe Schmidt would mail him the speeding ticket the cop had given him.

## Chapter 34
## New Hyde Park, New York

They had gone over the plan at least half a dozen times. Daltry would use a fire extinguisher at one end of the hall to create a distraction while Ox would cross the hallway and break Eddie Senta's neck.

Or stab him.

The big man had bought a serrated-edged hunting knife at a sporting goods store on Long Island and was anxious to use it. It scared Daltry, the way the big man talked about gutting Eddie Senta like a fish after cutting his throat.

Daltry planned on shooting the beast first chance he had. If Ox made it back to the car, he'd die on the drive to the airport. If the beast didn't make it back out of the hospital, Daltry was taking off without looking back. He was giving Ox no more than three minutes to get the job done.

"Ready?" he asked the big man.

Ox tapped the knife in its sheath and nodded.

"Just make sure you kill the dude," Daltry said.

"I'll kill him."

"Good. Let's go."

□ □ □

Dexter Greene had been with the New York Police Department going on twenty-three years. Today he was sitting guard for Eddie Senta for the sake of a few extra dollars and to do his former partner a favor. Alex Pavlik had explained there might be someone looking to take a second crack at the man in the bed.

The job would pay three hundred dollars cash for a twelve hour shift. Greene had already hired another detective to sit late afternoon into the night. Greene planned on returning after a few hours sleep.

He was looking through a *Time* magazine when he heard a commotion in the hallway outside the room. Greene heard the first scream and immediately set the magazine to one side. He pulled his Glock 9mm when he heard the second scream.

Something crashed in the hallway a moment before the door banged opened. A huge man wearing a hospital gown stepped inside. Greene stood up from the chair and aimed the gun at the big man's chest. Then he spotted the knife the big man was holding.

"Drop it," Greene said.

The big man stopped in his tracks but still held the knife.

Greene said, "I'll ask you one more time."

The big man raised the knife up over his right shoulder and growled a moment before he started to throw.

Greene shot him through the heart.

□ □ □

Daltry had kept his face hidden when he took the elevator with Ox to the floor where Eddie Senta was recovering. Then he pulled a wool face mask over his head when he spotted the fire extinguisher on a hallway wall. Daltry grabbed the extinguisher and motioned at Ox to go ahead. The big man nodded before heading down the hall to room 326.

Daltry ripped the safety cord from the extinguisher and started spraying white foam up the hallway close to the nurses' station. A woman getting off another elevator screamed when the doors opened. Daltry turned the extinguisher on her and she screamed a second time. When he saw two nurses step out from their station, he heaved the extinguisher down the length of the hallway and headed for a stairwell.

By the time he reached the lobby level, Daltry had no intentions of waiting for the big man. He sprinted around the corner to where he had parked the car instead. He was halfway through a U-turn on his way for an exit when he heard the first siren.

Daltry hoped it was because Ox had killed Eddie Senta, but there was no way he was sticking around to find out. There were two airports he could use to catch connecting flights that would get him back to North Dakota. The Long Island Expressway was less than half a mile from the hospital. Daltry followed the signs leading back to the city. He remembered Stewart had told him to drive back to North Dakota, but Daltry was already too nervous to drive. He wanted distance between himself and whatever the fuck had happened at the hospital. Daltry figured he'd head to Canada if Ox had been caught.

He studied the map as he waited in the slow-moving traffic heading toward Manhattan. When he finally saw a sign for LaGuardia Airport and Citi Field, he turned off the expressway onto the Grand Central Parkway. He checked the time and wondered once again whether Eddie Senta had been killed.

Daltry felt a rush of panic when he imagined Ox being arrested. Knowing he'd been abandoned, the monster would give him up in a heartbeat. Then Daltry thought about Stewart and what he'd have to face when he returned to North Dakota if Ox hadn't killed Senta.

Daltry decided he needed a game plan of his own.

## Chapter 35
## Minot/Velva, North Dakota

Pavlik was sure the FBI wasn't finished with him yet. After leaving Marsha Nordstrom in the lounge, he tried his best to remember the conversation he had overheard in his room while he was handcuffed to the bed. When he couldn't remember what had been said, he decided to take a ride to try and flush the agents out.

He spotted the tail on his way downtown. He was heading to the bar where the guy who'd tried to assault him said he first met Morris. Pavlik guessed they were agents following him in the red Pontiac Grand Am. One wore sunglasses and the other a baseball cap, pulled down low on his forehead.

It was a cloudy day, but the temperature had risen to a few degrees above zero. Pavlik decided to try and split them up by parking in a lot one block from Trinity Hospital. The bar he was looking for was a few blocks north of the lot.

He took his time walking until he was sure one of the agents was also on foot. Then Pavlik stepped inside and took a quick look around the room. It was empty except for the bald man behind the bar.

Pavlik ordered a beer and set a ten-dollar bill on the bar. He took two sips before excusing himself to use the men's room. There were two bathrooms and a third door that led to a parking lot out back. Pavlik knew one agent would remain in the car while the other looked inside the bar. He stepped inside the men's room and took a seat on one of two toilets. He looked at his watch and timed the action.

It was exactly ten minutes when he heard the back door open. Pavlik stepped outside the stall, stood alongside the bathroom door and waited for it to open. He could see it was the taller agent's face in the mirror over the sinks as the door slowly opened. He was about to kick the door closed with his right foot when there was a loud thud and the agent dropped to the floor inside the bathroom. A short man wearing an MSU sweatshirt stood in the doorway. He was wearing a black sap glove on his right hand.

"I'm a friend of Tom's," the short man said.

Pavlik was confused.

"Odakota," the short man said. "The other one is in the car out back."

"How'd you know?" Pavlik said.

"Tom's been calling your room," the short man said. "He figured something was up when you didn't answer. Then he called me. I made it to the

Welk a little while ago when you were leaving. I spotted this guy and his partner in the lot. They were waiting on you to leave."

"You saw them too, huh?"

The short man shrugged. "They're not hard to spot, agents."

"I guess I owe you guys," Pavlik said.

"Huh?" the short man said.

"I'll take care of it," Pavlik said. "Tell Tom. I promise."

"The thing is I have to bow out now," the short man said. "I'm on a leash myself. Parole. I give them any reason, I'm back inside."

Pavlik stuck out his right hand. "I appreciate it," he said. "I'll show it."

"You probably have about five minutes before the one in the car looks for this one."

"Probably less than that."

"Alright then. You take care."

"I'll do my best."

The street out front was clear. Pavlik got out of there.

□ □ □

When Dale called Marsha back, Alex Pavlik had gone up to his room. She asked him when he'd get to the hotel and Dale explained that he'd just intercepted an emergency call back in Mohall. A cop he'd visited earlier had been struck by a car.

"I can't believe it," Dale said. "I was just with the guy. The emergency call sounded pretty serious. Nobody saw anything, although it happened outside a diner. At least there were people on the scene to call for help."

"Jesus."

"He's Don Ekroth's friend. They grew up together."

"My God, Dale, that's terrible."

"I'm on my way back now," Dale said. "I have to go see him."

"Jesus, I hope he's okay."

"I can't believe what's going on, kiddo. It's crazy already."

Marsha felt an emotional tug. Dale had called her kiddo back when they dated.

"I'm headed back to Mohall now," he said. "I'll be there in two minutes. Then I'll probably follow wherever they take him. My guess is the Air Force base. I'll meet up with you guys later. Just let me know where."

"Sure, Dale, I'll call you," Marsha told him.

She hung up the phone and dialed Alex Pavlik's room. No one picked up.

□ □ □

James Sikes was a twenty-seven-year-old cowboy with a traveling rodeo. He was average height, thin, with long dark hair and a gold nose ring. He lived with his sister and her husband whenever he was on break from the rodeo or when he was injured, which was way too often for his brother-in-law, John Ahearn.

Today he was in North Dakota visiting Kelly and her husband two weeks after breaking his left arm in a fall off a horse. It was the fourth consecutive year his cowboy work had been cut short by an injury.

Sikes sucked hard on a joint while his sister prepared a vodka punch in the kitchen of the Ahearn house. It was a little past three o'clock in the afternoon. John Ahearn had returned home a few hours ago and was working in the basement.

"He throwing a party?" Sikes asked his sister. He pointed toward the cellar door.

Kelly Ahearn was a tall, thin woman with lots of freckles, stringy red hair and bright blue eyes. She had been a junkie the last eight years and her worn look made her appear much older than thirty.

Now she was high from the same joint her brother was smoking. She reached for it as she answered his question.

"He's doing something big," she said before taking a hit.

"John's always doing something big," Sikes said. "Except it never pans out."

Kelly held the smoke in her lungs another few seconds before speaking. "This one really is," she said.

"Bullshit," Sikes said.

Kelly exhaled hard. She lost her breath and coughed a few times. She took a sip from the can of fruit punch and held up a finger. "He scored," she said. "I saw it. And he came home with money. He gave me this." She pulled a folded one-hundred-dollar bill from the pocket of her housedress.

Sikes's eyes opened wide. "Fuck me," he said. "John's got coin?"

Kelly raised the bill higher.

"Be right back," her brother said.

□ □ □

By the time he had reached the town of Rugby on his drive back to Minot, John Ahearn was sure he wasn't being followed. He had stopped twice along the way to see if any cars that might be trailing him would pass. When they did after the second time he stopped, Ahearn could no longer resist the urge to open the box with all that money packed inside. He stopped at a FedEx office in Rugby and purchased an identical box. Then he stopped at a hardware store and bought two rolls of duct and electrical tape.

He parked alongside an abandoned building on his way out of Rugby and opened the box holding the money. He pulled the tape from one end of the box and pulled out four stacks of hundred-dollar bills, twenty thousand dollars. He resealed the box as best he could and was on his way again.

Now he was in his basement counting the money. He heard his brother-in-law's boots on the stairs and quickly hid the stacks of cash under a workbench.

"Kelly tells me you're in the money," Sikes said.

"Kelly's got a big mouth," Ahearn said.

He didn't like his brother-in-law. It went back to when Kelly's parents had died in a car accident a few years back and James emptied their parents' bank account without offering Kelly any of the five thousand dollars.

Ahearn put up with Sikes because of the dope the cowboy moved for him with the rodeo.

"She said you scored, too," Sikes added. "Heroin?"

"You'll have something to bring back to Mexico," Ahearn said. "If you can pay for it."

Sikes held up his broken arm. "How'm I gonna pay for anything with this?"

"You out of work again, Jimmy?" Ahearn said. "Geez, that's too fucking bad."

"I can use the help, if you're offering," Sikes said. He held out what was left of his joint.

"No, thanks," Ahearn said. "That stuff'll make you go soft."

Sikes winked. "I wouldn't know about that, going soft."

Ahearn didn't flinch as he smirked at his deadbeat brother-in-law.

"What?" Sikes said.

"I'm just thinking of a way you can earn some of the money you want to borrow and never pay back," Ahearn said.

Sikes took a seat on an empty milk crate.

"I got a cop breaking my balls," Ahearn continued. "Local guy back in Minot. He carries a gun, so I wouldn't ask you to take him on, 'specially with your injury and all, but he's got a wife works up at the college. A professor or some shit. You might be able to handle her."

Sikes smiled. "Fuckin'-A," he said. "She a cute one?"

"From what I hear she is."

"She's a wife, she's no virgin."

"I wouldn't think so."

"You got a name?"

"I sure do. I'll get you the address and the telephone number, too, while I'm at it."

Sikes took a last hit from the joint. He sucked the smoke into his lungs, squinted hard and spoke without breathing. "Cool," he said. "I can use me a honey."

## Chapter 36
## Minot, North Dakota

Dale told Emily what had happened in Mohall in her office at the university. She was horrified. She insisted he spend the rest of the night at home. His cell phone rang before he could argue with her.

It was Don Ekroth. Dale had called the sergeant shortly after Jim Salinger was taken to the Air Force base by helicopter. Ekroth was on his way to the hospital there. Dale asked his friend to let him know how Salinger was doing as soon as he heard.

When Dale ended the call, his wife shook a finger at him.

"You shouldn't go. Not tonight."

"I have something else tonight," Dale said.

"What?"

"I have to meet that guy from New York, the one called you here."

"Where?"

"I don't know yet."

"Can't you put it off?"

"He's been trying to get me for two days."

"What's it about?"

"The heroin maybe. He definitely knew something federal was going on here and he was right. I'm not sure what good it'll do now, but I have to meet with him."

"Darn it, Dale. After what you went through this morning, I really think you should come home and relax for one night."

"I'll make it quick."

Emily frowned.

"Don't make me feel guilty," he said. "I'm already feeling it today."

"There was nothing you could do about what happened."

"I know, but I can still see him lying there waiting to be flown away. The guy was broken up bad. His hip was completely smashed."

Emily stroked his face. "That's what I'm talking about. Why don't you put off this thing tonight and stay home?"

Dale put his arms around her. She kissed his neck and he clutched her tight against him. She could feel the tension in his body. When she looked up, Emily saw one of her students waiting at the office door. She waved her away.

□ □ □

He returned to the Lawrence Welk hotel and spent most of his time in the restaurant there waiting to see if the federal agents would come to arrest him. After an hour had passed, he knew they wouldn't. He requested a new room and had a bellboy return to his old room to move his things.

He spent nearly half an hour on the phone with Marsha Nordstrom again and confirmed the meeting with Dale Hehn over dinner. He didn't mention his trip downtown.

Marsha would be there at the dinner as well, although she warned Pavlik that the Minot detective had had a bad day. It had been a frustrating couple of days, but he was sure that James Singleton was still close enough to keep the FBI nervous. Now he needed local police support he wasn't sure he could count on. He had thought he connected with the sergeant at the police station two days ago, except the guy still hadn't returned his last calls.

Pavlik was in the middle of changing his clothes when his cell phone rang. He recognized Dexter Greene's number and answered after the first ring.

An adrenalin surge quickly turned to rage at what had gone down back in New York. Pavlik felt guilty having asked Greene to take on the moonlighting job.

"Jesus, I'm sorry," he said.

"Yeah, well, it's a fuckin' mess," Greene said. "I told the locals I was stepping in as a favor for a friend. I didn't mention anything about—"

"You don't have to say it, I understand," Pavlik said. "And I appreciate the favor."

"The guy stopped in his tracks and I thought that was it. Then he went to throw the knife he was holding. I had to shoot."

"I'm sure you did."

"There were two of them," Greene said. "There was another one out in the hall the nurses said made a commotion with a fire extinguisher. They have both of them on tape going in, but the one got away was wearing a mask. The cameras there didn't get a good shot."

"Probably the same one that got away last time," Pavlik said. "At least the cops there know it's for real now."

"I'm waiting on the Port Washington PD," Greene said. "I guess the locals here contacted them when I explained what I was doing here. Why I was doing you the favor."

"They know where the guy you shot was from?"

"He had Canadian paperwork on him," Greene said. "Regina, Saskatchawan. Somewhere in Canada, I guess."

"Any word from NYPD?"

"On what?"

"You."

"No. Not yet. Although I'm sure I'll catch it tomorrow. There aren't many in the department gonna believe I was here by a coincidental favor, Alex."

"I'm really sorry, Dex. I mean it."

"Yeah, well. No more favors like this. Not anymore."

Both men shared an uncomfortable chuckle.

Pavlik said, "And Senta is okay, right?"

"He wasn't touched."

"Does his wife know?"

"I'm sure by now, yeah."

"Okay, I'll call her later."

"I'll be here."

"I guess I owe you, huh?"

"Yeah, you do," Greene said. "See you when you're back."

Pavlik looked at himself in the mirror and frowned. Dexter Greene had been his best friend since the two were teamed up as partners more than twenty-five years ago. Now his best friend would have to go through a shit storm of bad publicity and innuendo that would affect the rest of his career. Pavlik could only hope it wouldn't wreck their friendship.

◻ ◻ ◻

Dale picked up Marsha at her house at the top of North Hill. She was dressed for a date. He whistled when she sat in his car.

"You must like this guy," he said.

"Behave yourself," Marsha said. She was blushing and hid her face. She turned away as she smoothed her skirt.

Dale pointed to the hem. "That's a little short for my taste," he said. He leaned over and pointed at her shoes. "That what they call pumps?"

Marsha play-slapped his hand. "How do I look?" she asked. "Be honest."

"Beautiful. Never better."

"Thank you," she said. "Liar face."

Dale pulled away from the curb and headed down the big hill.

"Got a babysitter?"

"My neighbor."

"And I'm the chaperone. You do pretty good for an ex-beauty queen."

"No, you're not a chaperone. He's been trying to meet you for two days now. How is the officer in Mohall?"

Dale shook his head. "He's recovering, but they aren't sure there's not spinal damage. Hit-and-run, it turns out. Nobody saw it happen, and nobody bothered to stop after hitting him. Somebody up the road said they saw a Jeep Cherokee speeding out of town. I saw one speeding toward Mohall earlier, but who knows. The poor guy was banged up pretty bad."

"I'm sorry, Dale."

He nodded, then asked, "Is this New Yorker really looking for that guy with the mask?"

"The way he described him, yeah, I think so. Alex said he's a dangerous killer."

"Alex? You on a first name basis already?"

Marsha ignored his teasing. "He was a detective in New York," she said. "Highly decorated, apparently."

"He tell you that?"

"I'll ignore that. He also mentioned that he was forced to resign from the police force there. Politics, he said. I told him where to meet us now. He said he'd be waiting for us."

"He okay this guy? You really think he was held hostage last night?"

"I want to believe him," Marsha said, "except he said it was FBI agents holding him."

"He might be right."

"What?"

"I'm not sure yet. Just the way things are going on around here. What else?"

"He seemed pretty upset the last time he called. He wanted to talk to you pretty bad."

Dale paused a moment, then said, "He nuts?"

"I think he's okay," Marsha said. "Really."

Dale turned onto Broadway and headed up toward the airport. "I found an eyewitness to Nathan Barron's overdose yesterday."

"That's great, Dale."

"Except she was sky-high stoned on heroin when she told me," he said. "And she'd denied knowing anything about it before that. I can't even use it for a simple search warrant."

"Who gave him the drugs? Do I know them?"

Dale turned to Marsha to see if she'd recognize the name. "That mean guy, apparently," he said. "Ahearn. Him and one of those two I think you saw at the hotel. Short black guy named Daltry. Roger Daltry."

"Roger Daltry?" she asked. "Like *The Who*?"

Dale shrugged.

Marsha smoothed her skirt again. "Well, I can ask around at the hotel. If he was selling up there, somebody might know who Daltry is."

"Ahearn lives in Velva. He's married but has a posse of junkies he fools around with. The eyewitness was one of them."

"What's her name?"

"Kathy Ljunndgren."

Marsha squinted as she shook her head. "I don't know the name."

A few minutes later they were pulling into the Field and Stream Restaurant parking lot. Marsha used the visor mirror to check her makeup.

"You look great," Dale said. "Trust me."

Marsha was excited. She leaned over and kissed him on the cheek. "Thank you," she said. "I'm a nervous wreck."

☐ ☐ ☐

Inside the restaurant they ordered cocktails while Pavlik explained the history of James Singleton and what he believed were the killer's most recent attempts at murder back in New York. He handed Dale the folder on Singleton. Then he went over what had happened the night before.

"I know it sounds crazy," Pavlik said. "Like something out of a Bond movie, but that is how this shit goes down sometimes."

"The guy is protected," Dale said, "that's what you're telling me."

"Totally, yeah, he is," Pavlik said. "I'm afraid they might've moved him again."

"Except you're not here in an official capacity," Dale said. "You can't even arrest him."

"I can help," Pavlik said, looking from Hehn to Marsha and back. "I can help you. Obviously the FBI won't let me near James Singleton. And they'll probably put the brakes on any attempt you make to find him. You said you were close to him last night, right? I'm surprised they didn't spot you. If they did, he'd be gone for sure by now. And you'd have been officially backed off."

"And you're sure our guy is your guy?" Dale asked.

"Has to be, or why would the FBI bother with me? It has to be Singleton. If I'd have taken a room someplace else in town, they probably wouldn't have gone near me, except to make sure I didn't walk in the lounge at the hotel. I can identify him. I would've if they didn't sit on me last night."

"Did he really send those guys to New York to kill somebody?" Marsha asked.

She had been listening quietly until she asked the question. Pavlik apologized for ignoring her.

"Please, I find this intriguing," she said. "This is North Dakota, Alex. It doesn't get very exciting around here otherwise."

"She's an incredible source for me," Dale said. "Guys stop in the hotel bar and try to smooth-talk her wind up spilling all kinds of dirt."

Pavlik said to Marsha, "Yes, it was Singleton who sent those guys. Like I said, they made another attempt on Eddie Senta's life earlier today, this time at the hospital where he's recovering. Some guy from Canada was killed. He was toting a hunting knife he'd bought a few hours earlier. That's all I know, except one of them got away again.

"I'm here because of Kincaid. The police in New York were able to trace his record back here to North Dakota."

Pavlik turned to Dale. "Kincaid's been in and out of your penal system his entire adult life. And there was another guy, a black guy. He got away. Probably the same one got away today."

"Well, I brought something to my chief last night that smells of federal," Dale said. "After what I witnessed in the lounge. The guy with the mask and the other two, yuppie types they looked like, and then the guy I'm sure was a fed, a stocky black guy."

"Morris," Pavlik said. "How I'd like to get my hands on him right now."

"Easy, partner," Dale said. "I can't be around if you do anything crazy."

"It's between me and him."

"But not around me."

Pavlik had thought he might tell Dale about what happened at the downtown bar at some point during their conversation. Not anymore.

"Did your chief go to the feds yet?" he asked.

Dale shook his head. "I asked him not to. Because of exactly what you're worried about, they'll call us off."

"That they will," Pavlik said. "They did it to me and my partner ten years ago. They also forced me to retire the year after that, the feds."

"Aside from identifying this guy, how can you help?" Dale asked.

"I know what he's about," Pavlik said. "I know the types of people he's used to dealing with. I know the level of ruthlessness he can reach. It's low and it's dangerous. The man is a classic sociopath. He's street smart enough to have survived this long and he's probably picked up a few dozen things since he's in the program."

Dale took a deep breath. "Maybe we can work something out tomorrow morning. I need to go see the officer was hit by a car in the morning. Then there's another guy we have to check on, me and Don Ekroth. Maybe we can pick you up when we're on our way."

"What's up with your friend?" Pavlik asked. "He made copies of my file, but then didn't return any of my calls."

"He's going through it, too, right now," Dale said. "His mother-in-law had a stroke and the officer hit by the car up in Mohall today was a close friend of Don's."

"Sorry," Pavlik said. "I'll be ready tomorrow. I look forward to it."

Dale said, "This other guy we're looking into tomorrow is another piece of work, but he might have something to do with this Singleton. Maybe you can learn something from him."

"Where do you want me?" Pavlik asked.

"I'll call you soon as I know," Dale said. "We'll either swing by the hotel and pick you up or you can come meet us. That okay?"

"Fair enough."

They exchanged handshakes. Dale said, "And now I'll leave you two to dinner. Alex. Miss North Dakota."

Marsha tossed her swizzle stick at Dale.

"You might want to cut her off," Dale said to Alex.

"Go away," Marsha told him.

□ □ □

"Field and Stream?" Emily asked Dale.

"I just had a beer," he said. "The guy from New York is here looking for a killer in the witness protection program."

Emily raised her eyebrows. "Excuse me?"

Dale told her about Alex Pavlik and the mysterious man with the face mask. He opened the file Pavlik had given him and they took turns examining the information and history of James Singleton.

"Jesus, this is scary," Emily said. She was reading about the triple homicide Singleton had committed in New York. "I thought he sounded frantic when that New Yorker called. Now I know why."

"It's scarier if the government is protecting this Singleton character," Dale said. "This guy, Pavlik, he knows he can't do anything if he finds Singleton. Except to help us. Help me. If it's the same guy, but it sure looks like it might be."

"And the government knows about this guy, the one they're protecting?"

"According to Pavlik they're sponsoring him. He claims a couple of agents kept him handcuffed in his room last night while I was watching the masked guy."

"My God. You believe him?"

"He was pretty convincing."

"That's crazy."

"Thing is, I might not be able to do anything about it either," said Dale, closing the folder. "Not if the federal government stops me."

Emily held herself. "And I was frightened by a few telephone calls," she said.

"There were more calls?" Dale asked.

Emily waved it off. "A few. I'm letting the machine pick up. We had two hang-ups since I did that."

"That's the other thing," Dale said. "I think I know who's behind those calls. The same person that killed Nathan Barron, I think. I can't do much about that, not yet, but I'm going to try one more time tomorrow."

He stood up from the table and headed inside the bedroom. He came back with a Berretta and held it up.

Emily saw the gun and waved her hands. "No," she said. "No way."

"I want you to keep this where you can get to it," Dale said. "Somewhere accessible."

"I hate those things," Emily said. "I can take care of myself. I know what to do."

"Yes, I know," Dale said. "But sometimes knowing what to do isn't enough. Sometimes these are necessary."

"Dale, no. I'd rather not."

He stood staring at her. She set her hands on her hips defiantly. He stepped inside the kitchen and glanced at the cabinets. He chose one close to the refrigerator. He opened it and spotted two large cans of crushed tomatoes. He racked the slide, put the safety on, and set the gun behind the crushed tomatoes.

"It's there," he said. "It's loaded and I put one in the chamber. You know what to do. Just like at the range."

Emily closed her eyes tight.

Dale said, "Aim at the chest, hold your breath, and squeeze."

## Chapter 37
## St. Louis, Missouri/Lake Sakakawea /Minot, North Dakota

Morris tried Washington Stewart's cell phone several times before he gave up in frustration. He also called the number on the boat a few times but hung up each time the answering machine clicked on. He sent two messages to Stewart's e-mail address, then tried the boat number one last time. When the machine picked up, Morris left a message through clenched teeth.

"I'm stuck in St. Louis until tomorrow," he said. "We need to meet pronto. I just got a call from New York. You got some fucking explaining to do. As of now, you can expect me at the Minot Airport tomorrow morning. I'll leave another message when I know for sure. Be there to pick me up. And answer your phones."

Morris slammed the telephone down when he was finished. He checked his watch and noted the time.

"Rough day?" one of his colleagues asked.

"This fucker up in Minot," Morris said. "We knew he was doing a little side business with the junk, but now he's gone too far."

"What he do?"

"You wouldn't believe it if I told you."

"Try me."

Morris shook his head. "It'll only piss me off more than I already am, I do that."

□ □ □

Stewart and Lynette both smiled at the sound of Special Agent in Charge Eugene Morris's voice. They had moved from the RV to the boat once the power was restored. The portable heaters on the boat were turned up high.

"That sucker's got a problem," Lynette said. She was checking profiles on Yahoo's personal ads. The laptop was set on a short plastic table. She leaned forward on the galley bench as she worked on the computer.

"Man give himself a heart attack he don't let up," Stewart said. He was in the recliner off the galley. He opened a bottle of Beck's and drank deep.

"You gonna meet him?" Lynette asked.

"Maybe," Stewart said.

"You want, I can go."

"You're not supposed to know who he is."

"Oh, right."

Stewart watched her work the keyboard with two fingers. "You pretty fast," he said.

"I should be a secretary," she said.

"You are. You my secretary."

Lynette sat up. "I'm answering an ad from Fargo," she said.

"Blonde?"

"Dirty-blonde."

Stewart made a face. "That means she brown where it counts," he said.

"Really?"

"I think so. Ones I knew were."

"She's young and she can't spell. Her introduction is all fucked up."

Stewart waved it off. "Skip her," he said.

"Okay," Lynette said. She leaned forward and hit the ESCAPE key, then leaned back and grabbed her beer.

Stewart pointed to the computer. "Why don't you check and see if Miss North Dakota posted an ad on that thing?"

"Uh-oh."

"What's uh-oh?"

"That's the second time you're baiting me with that one, Miss North Dakota."

"She a blonde."

"So are most of the women in this state. Did she come on to you?"

Stewart chuckled. "No, baby, she didn't come on to me."

Lynette frowned. "Okay," she said. "I forgive you."

"You do, huh?"

Lynette smiled at Stewart, then said, "Hey, where's Roger been? I haven't seen him since the doctor's office."

Stewart shook his head. "No clue."

"I thought he'd be hanging around more since he made his little score for you."

"Maybe he's getting some."

Lynette made a face. "Not with that Indian, he's not."

Stewart hadn't mentioned anything about what Daltry was doing for him, nor had he told Lynette about what had happened to Daltry's friend, Joseph Kincaid. He was surprised when she brought the man up.

He said, "You know him, the Indian?"

"Joe Kincaid? Shit, yeah," Lynette said. She rolled up her T-shirt and exposed the symmetrical scars on her stomach. "This was Kincaid," she explained. "It's some kind of Indian symbol. For pregnancy, I think. Being fertile or something like that. He did this one the last time before he went away in Bismarck."

Stewart set his beer down. "He famous or some shit? How you know him?"

"Not off the reservation he's not. Ahearn knows him, too. They had a brawl once at a party. Kincaid cut Ahearn's stomach pretty bad, but then John knocked him out with a brick. It was a pretty vicious fight until then."

"What the Indian do to get famous on the reservation?"

Lynette sipped her beer. "He's just another convict," she said. "He's anything but famous."

Stewart sat up straight in the recliner. "How'd you meet him?"

"About five years ago," Lynette said as she lit a cigarette. "I lived with him and some other Natives in a trailer park near Dickinson. Those were my real wild days. Lots of crank, booze and acid. I was a mess. We all were. Half of them are dead now, that I know of."

"And how long Roger know this Kincaid?" Stewart asked.

"Least a couple years," Lynette said. "Ahearn introduced them, but I know they were doing stuff together before I met you."

"Motherfuck me," Singleton said.

"What?"

"Nothing," he said, waving it off.

She pointed at her facial scars. "I got this when I was living in Dickinson," she said.

Stewart stared at her. "I like your face."

Lynette turned away from him. "You don't have to say that. I know what I look like. I'm no Miss North Dakota."

"You my Miss North Dakota."

Lynette frowned.

Stewart shook his finger at her. "Don't tell me what I like," he said. "Besides, I got something a lot worse than that, baby."

Lynette wet her lips before sipping her beer.

Stewart slowly removed his face mask. Lynette wasn't watching him. He said, "Hey."

Her eyes opened wide. "Wow," she said, awestruck and unable to stop staring at him. The scar was long and thick. She leaned over and traced his scar with a finger.

"What do you think?" he asked.

"I think it's beautiful," she said.

□ □ □

When they were finished with dinner, Marsha invited Pavlik home for coffee. It was a short drive back to her house, but he was nervous being alone with her. He did his best not to take his eyes from the road when she spoke.

She put on a fresh pot of coffee before giving him a quick tour of the detached two-story home. When they ended up back in the kitchen, she couldn't help but notice how nervous he was.

"Don't be so frightened," she told him. "I'm not going to maul you, Alex."

Pavlik blushed. "That obvious, huh?"

"It's flattering, don't get me wrong," Marsha told him. "But you're okay, I promise. It's nice just to talk to someone interesting again."

The coffee finished brewing. She poured two cups and suggested they sit in the living room where it was more comfortable. She waited for him to choose a spot on the couch and then sat alongside him.

Pavlik could feel his heart starting to race. When she told him her daughter was staying with a neighbor and that he was welcome to spend the night if he was afraid the FBI had bugged his room back at the hotel, he surprised himself and said it was an offer he couldn't refuse.

"Except I'll stay here on the couch," he added.

"That's fine," Marsha said, "but you're free to use my daughter's bed."

"I insist," Pavlik said.

"The couch it is."

A long moment of silence ensued. Finally Marsha said, "I have to tell you, Alex, when you first told me you were kidnapped by FBI agents, I thought you may have been crazy."

"I can imagine," he said. "People don't believe this kind of stuff until it happens to them. There were a couple of documentaries about it. *Dateline* or *Sixty Minutes*, I forget which, but it happens a lot more than people think. The FBI has its own agenda. So do the federal prosecutors they work for. Often times it's contrary to the communities they operate in, never mind the general public."

Marsha noticed his right leg was bouncing. "I hope that isn't me making you nervous like that."

"I'm sure you have something to do with it," he said.

"It's okay," she said, "I swear I won't bite."

He was getting more uncomfortable in the former beauty queen's house. They were alone, the lights were low, she had already said her daughter would be sleeping over at a friend's house and he had committed to sleeping on her couch.

And he'd had a few drinks.

Not to mention she was beautiful.

She rubbed his back with one hand. He flinched at first, but then allowed himself to relax as she continued to rub small circles on his back.

"You told me you live with someone," she said. "I know the boundaries."

He couldn't speak. He sipped his coffee instead.

"And I'm enjoying your company," she said. "You're an interesting man. And I won't attack you because I find you attractive."

He nearly choked. "You find me attractive?"

"Very much so."

"Uh-oh."

"Well, you are. You're handsome."

He reached for his cigarettes. He stopped before pulling one out. "Is it okay if I smoke?"

"Of course."

Marsha moved closer. This time she used both hands to rub his back. Pavlik fumbled with his cigarette.

"You okay?" she asked through a chuckle.

"I'm torturing myself," he said.

"Over me?"

He spoke without looking at her. "You're beautiful, Marsha. You're probably the most beautiful woman I've ever... I don't know."

"I guess that's a compliment."

"No, it is. Really, it is."

"But?"

He lit the cigarette. "Can I be frank here?"

"Of course."

"Half of me wants to run for the door and the other half wants to stay."

Marsha smiled. "That could be a compliment, too."

He crushed out his cigarette and rubbed his forehead. "Jesus Christ," he said.

Marsha pulled him back on the couch. He closed his eyes as she stroked his face with her fingers.

"Oh, God," he whispered.

She leaned into him. "I don't want to marry you, Alex," she whispered.

He bit his lower lip and hoped she wouldn't kiss him. Then he could feel her breath on his lips just before they touched.

"Oh, Jesus," he thought to himself a moment before she slid her tongue deep inside his mouth.

## Part IV

### Chapter 38
### Minot/Bismarck, North Dakota

Colonel Robert Schmidt was waiting in the parking lot above the university football field. The sun had yet to come up. The temperature was just above zero. Washington Stewart pulled into the lot from the far end and parked alongside the colonel. The two men walked to the edge of the gate overlooking the football stadium. Schmidt was carrying the FedEx box. He tapped it a few times before handing it off to Stewart.

Stewart said, "Light by how much?"

"Fifty thousand. Either they shorted him or he shorted us, but he's the one who stopped at a FedEx office in Devil's Lake, so my guess is it was Mr. Ahearn."

"Or it was you," Stewart said.

Schmidt smiled. "Or it was me, right."

Stewart said, "I don't suppose you'd want to drive over to Velva and whack Mr. Ahearn, would you?"

"No, I wouldn't," Schmidt said. "And the truth of the matter is we probably don't have time for it anyway. We still have product and a lot of money. We're too close to go settling scores now."

"Man robbed us," Stewart said.

"Put it in perspective. So what? We're almost out of here."

Stewart said, "I have to drive back to Sakakawea after this. My FBI pals were out of town last night, but they'll be back this morning." He stopped to glance at his watch.

Schmidt said, "Will I be cued on the diversions?"

"No need," Stewart said, "although there's one about to happen in Bismarck, it didn't happen already."

"I suppose I'll hear about it sooner or later."

Stewart cupped his hands as he turned his back to the wind to light a cigarette.

"The cold is finally breaking," Schmidt said. "It's supposed to stay above freezing the next few days."

"Figures, last day it gets warm again."

"It'll be a lot warmer in Mexico."

"Life's a trip sometimes. Spend the morning in Antarctic weather and the evening wearing shorts."

"If we make it out of here," Schmidt said.

"No reason we shouldn't."

"The best laid plans of mice and men."

"Who that, Shakespeare?"

"Close enough."

Stewart held up a finger. "I've been thinking about one more diversion," he said. "A safety valve, more or less."

"What's that?"

"A hostage."

"Not to take with us, I hope."

Stewart shook his head. "For my woman, Lynette."

Schmidt smirked. "Are you serious?"

"In case I need to draw people away after I handle Ahearn."

"Or you could forget Ahearn and not need a hostage or Lynette."

Stewart said, "I'll take care of it."

"With the FBI around?"

"I'll take care of them, too."

"How?"

"Chloroform," Stewart said. "Why I'm lucky you a doctor."

□ □ □

After picking up any equipment they might need, Heinrich and Jan Müller had been rushed to McCarran International Airport in Las Vegas where a Lear 25 jet was waiting for them. They were given phony passports and driver's licenses for the ground transportation they would need when they arrived in Bismarck. Fifteen minutes later, they were airborne.

They had been sent by the boss of the Las Vegas mob after he received a tip about a pair of investment bankers that had been arrested in a federal sting operation. They were told the investment bankers had already made a deal with the government and had entered the witness protection program.

The German-born brothers had spent most of the night in the van that awaited them at the Bismarck airport. The investment bankers were being guarded in a motel just north of Interstate 94 at exit 159.

This morning they planned to strike as soon as the marshal guarding the motel room stepped away from his car. If he didn't do it before sunrise, Heinrich would kill the marshal while Jan took care of the investment bankers. They would kill as many marshals as they needed to get the job done.

The brothers wore black clothes and black ski masks. They each worked with Uzi submachine guns equipped with sound suppressors. As they

approached the hotel parking lot, it was a pleasant surprise when Heinrich noticed only one marshal sitting in the car.

"*Nur ein,*" he whispered to his brother.

"*Wo ist das andere?*" Jan asked.

Heinrich motioned at the hotel with his weapon and joked in broken
English, "Take a shit."

They crouched down low behind a pickup and waited.

At 5:10, the marshal left the car and crossed the parking lot. At 5:13 he
stepped inside a Denny's restaurant. At 5:15 Jan Müller kicked his way
inside the motel room. Heinrich double-checked the parking lot and followed his brother inside.

They both fired at the bodies covered with blankets on twin beds. Blood
spotted the sheets as the government witnesses rolled off the bed onto the
floor.

At 5:17 they were back inside the van and on their way out of the parking lot. It was 5:22 before the marshal left Denny's. The brothers drove
west on the avenue to a minivan that was waiting for them. The van made
a quick turn and headed south. It was 5:40 before the first police sirens
could be heard in the distance.

□  □  □

Emily was uneasy when Dale sat up at five-thirty.

"I was hoping you wouldn't run out of here today," she said.

"I wanted to drive up to the hospital at the base," Dale said, "but I'm not
sure if Don is still there. I still need to talk to Kathy Ljunndgren and that
guy I think is calling here."

"They might've moved him already," Emily said. "You should check
before you go."

"I will, but I doubt they moved him already. He was pretty tore up."

"Call and see how he's doing first. Maybe you don't have to leave so
early."

Dale held her hands. "I know what you're trying to do, Em. There's no
need. I'm not that fragile. I had a rough couple of days. I'm not going to fall
apart."

"You almost did yesterday."

"If that's what you want to call it."

"That's exactly what I call it. You need to let go, Dale. You probably need
a good cry, but you won't let yourself do it. It's about time."

"I don't have time to cry," he told her. "I'll be fine, but I need to get on
the road. There are a few people I need to check on today, especially if this
New York guy is right about what's going on. One of them, I'm pretty sure,
is the asshole calling here."

"I'd feel a lot better if you stayed home. At least through the morning."
Dale kissed her on the forehead and hopped out of bed.

"What if I put on my garters?" Emily said.

"Trust me, I'll keep that image in my head," Dale said before he stepped
inside the bathroom.

## Chapter 39
## Minot/Fargo/Lakota, North Dakota

Marsha brought Pavlik a fresh cup of coffee at exactly five-thirty in the morning. He was sitting up on the couch. He turned away when he saw the short terry-cloth robe she was wearing was untied.

"I know I should feel guilty, but I don't," Marsha said as she handed him the coffee.

Pavlik immediately sipped from the cup. "I do," he said. He motioned at her robe. "Can you close that, please?"

"All we did was kiss, Alex," she said. "I wanted to go further, but you obviously didn't and I wasn't about to rape you." She tied the robe.

"I'm feeling guilty enough about the kiss," Pavlik said.

"I could tell you were awake most the night," she said. "And I saw you holding that silly cell phone like you wanted to call and confess and that's when I wanted to die."

"You saw that?"

She sat alongside him. "It was just a kiss," she said. "We didn't kill anybody."

"I might as well have if she ever finds out."

"Don't tell her. It's true what they say, Alex. What she doesn't know can't hurt her."

"Yeah, but I know. And now it hurts me."

"Then I guess I feel guilty, too, but I'm not sorry. I just hope you don't hate me now. I especially hope you don't hate yourself."

"I don't get it." Pavlik turned to her. "You're beautiful. What the hell are you doing living alone?"

Marsha stood up. "Not settling, for one thing." She grabbed her own cup of coffee. "I've had offers. Working at a bar, you get a few dozen a night, but I have a kid and there's more involved because of her."

"Her father stay in touch?"

"No."

"That's a shame."

"They taught me how to walk as if I had a fifty-cent piece up my ass for the Miss America pageant. I did all the right things for all the wrong reasons. I left school for the wrong reasons. I moved away for the wrong reasons. I got married for the wrong reasons. I like to think I've learned something."

Pavlik took one of her hands. "If I lived out here and didn't have Aelish, I'd find a way into your kid's heart."

"I'll bet you would," Marsha said.

He got up off the couch. Marsha finished her coffee and set the cup on an envelope on the coffee table.

Pavlik said, "I shouldn't bring home any presents, right? I heard buying roses after a guy cheats is a dead giveaway."

"Cheating would require sex of some kind," Marsha said, "but you seem determined to torture yourself anyway. I think it depends on the woman, but I also think you should get cheating off your brain. At least out of your vocabulary the next few weeks."

"I'll never be able to look her in the eyes again."

"Oh, you'd better do that. Never avoid a woman's eyes, detective."

He was shaking his head. "I'm such a dumb fuck."

"Do you love her, Alex?"

"Of course."

"Then give yourself a break. You kissed another woman who was anxious to kiss you. Big deal. Call it a mistake if it makes you feel better. Whatever you do, don't tell her, because it won't make her feel better. No matter how much you feel you need to confess, don't, for her sake. No matter what Dr. Phil might say, not everything needs to be out in the open between people in a relationship."

"I don't like playing a semantics game," he said. "I shouldn't have been here last night."

"Fair enough."

"You must think I'm a big dope."

Marsha grinned.

Pavlik sipped his coffee.

"The thing about the roses is true," Marsha added. "She'll know if it's from guilt. Get her something else. Something from up here, North Dakota. Boots are always nice. Cowgirl boots."

Pavlik nodded. "Maybe. Sure."

Marsha put a hand against his cheek. "You're extremely cute when you're guilty."

"I feel extremely shitty."

Marsha chuckled. "Drink your coffee," she said. "I don't think I can handle much more of it and I have to be at work early today to set up."

"Are you throwing me out?"

"Yes, Alex. Miss North Dakota is officially giving you the hook."

□ □ □

Nick "Ears" Mayo was chain-smoking in the Fargo International Airport lounge when his son and the blonde finally showed. He was cordial

while being introduced to the woman, but as soon as she used the bathroom the old man was in his son's face.

"Took you long enough," he said. "The plane landed almost two hours
ago."

"I was outside watching," Joe Mayo told his father. "Checking for
agents."

Nick motioned toward the bathroom. "You getting married?"

"I didn't have a choice," Joe said. "Lighten up, she's good company. I
actually like her."

"Your cousin still around?"

"Your nephew? Yeah, last I checked."

"I don't trust the cocksucker."

"He's alright. He wasn't getting anywhere in New York. He'll be grateful for the opportunity."

Nick smirked. "That shine came through, huh?"

"Apparently."

"Kills me, paying that spook."

"He could drop a dime, we didn't pay him."

"He can still drop a dime."

"Not without us doing the same thing. Then everybody loses. It was a
good plan you two came up with. We'll be alright."

Nick lit a cigarette. "Unless your cousin gets ambitious, he didn't
already."

Mary Beth was back from the bathroom. She put her arm around Joe's
waist and smiled at the old man.

"You're a pretty girl," Nick told her.

"Thank you," she said. "And I see where Joe gets his good looks from,
too."

Nick looked at his son. "Good-looking and smart," he said. "You done
good for yourself with this one."

Mary Beth giggled.

□  □  □

Frank Mayo was still flying from chasing the dragon. He had used the
tin foil wrapping from a fried egg sandwich to heat the heroin, then used
a straw to inhale the smoke.

Cousin Joe had brought him the money for the exchange the day
before. Frank had been grateful to test the heroin. It had helped him maintain his cool. He wasn't sure when his uncle and cousin would return, but
the dope he was holding was more than enough to start his own drug cartel.

He had considered taking off a few minutes after his cousin had left the day before, but he'd been afraid it was a test. His uncle and cousin might've been waiting around the corner. Had he tried to take off and they were testing him, he'd be a dead man.

Or maybe it was the guy bringing the product who unnerved Frank. He couldn't be sure. His nerves had started to fray waiting for the goober who'd showed up. It was while he was waiting when he decided to get high on his own stash.

He had even fucked with the farmer's head when his cousin called to make sure the guy had showed. Frank had stayed on the line after his cousin had hung up and laughed to unsettle the hick. He'd even offered the farmer some free advice, to take the money and run, something he might've done himself if his drug habit hadn't made him so paranoid of late.

When he started to think about taking off with the product, Frank knew enough to test the new stuff the same way he'd smoked his own stash earlier. The heroin immediately calmed his nerves. He relaxed on the couch in the living room of the furnished house his cousin had rented. He closed his eyes and imagined having his cousin's blonde girlfriend. He liked her look; the big tits and cherry ass. He even liked the way she giggled all the time.

## Chapter 40
## Lake Sakakawea/Minot, North Dakota; St. Louis, Missouri

When Roger Daltry finally called Washington Stewart, it was from a parking lot at the marina in Lake Sakakawea. Daltry had taken a late night flight from New York to Minneapolis where he made a connecting flight to Sioux Falls, South Dakota. Then the puddle jumper from Sioux Falls left him in Bismarck.

In Bismarck Daltry had picked up a small tape recorder at a Walmart, boosted a car in the parking lot, and driven north to the lake while recording everything that had happened over the last two weeks.

His stomach had been in knots since he'd left New York. Washington Stewart had warned him more than once about getting the job done and now that he'd failed a second time to kill Eddie Senta, the recording was his only protection; just in case Stewart really was thinking about killing him.

He talked for fifty-five minutes and used up most of one side of the tape. It was a jumbled explanation of what had happened and how he became involved with Stewart, but it was something tangible the police might use in the event he was killed.

He was a bit calmer when he finished the tape. He stored it in the glove compartment and used a disposable cell phone to call Stewart. He was nervous all over again when he heard the man's voice.

"Roger?" Stewart asked.

"Yeah, Wash, it's me."

"You okay?"

"Yeah, but I fucked up again. The guy I brought, I mean. I'm sorry."

"Forget it. I'm glad you're back."

Daltry was confused. "I fucked up," he repeated. "The guy I brought with me is dead."

"I heard," Stewart said.

"You did? That was fast."

"Not about the guy you brought dying. I called the hospital to check on Eddie Senta. They said he's recovering, I didn't need to ask anything else."

"There was a bodyguard in the room," Daltry said. "Some off-duty cop or some shit. It was all over the radio back in New York."

"And CNN here. It's a national story now. Probably because it's the second time and all. Anyway, you okay?"

"Huh?"

"Are you okay?"

"I'm fine, yeah. Little shaken is all."

"You coming in? We got business in town."

Now it was time to show his cards. Daltry said, "Ah, yeah, sure, but I gotta tell you something first."

"Tell me when you see me."

"No, no, I can't. I gotta tell you now." There was a slight pause. "Wash?" Daltry said.

"I'm listening."

"I made a tape."

"You made a tape."

"To protect myself."

"I was gonna ask you what kind of tape. Now I know. Fine, you made a tape. What else?"

"In case you do something," Daltry said. "Because I know you wanted me to take care of this thing and it didn't happen again. I'm sorry about that, I am, but I had to protect myself."

"You give the tape to the law? That what you telling me?"

"No, no, nothing like that. I put it someplace. In case something happens to me."

"You afraid of me is what you're saying."

"It's just business, Wash. I have to protect myself."

"Well, it's the smart thing to do, I'll give you that."

"I felt I didn't have a choice."

"So long's you didn't give it to the law, I can understand."

"For real?"

"What I just say?"

Daltry waited for more.

"You sure you didn't do that, give it to the law?" Stewart asked.

"Swear on my mother's eyes," Daltry said. Then he almost said he had it with him, but stopped himself.

"Okay," Stewart said. "I'm not giddy about it, your tape, but I can understand."

"So, we cool?"

"It make sense for me not to be cool?"

Daltry didn't respond.

"Hello?" Stewart said. "You still there?"

"You at the boat?" Daltry said.

"Yeah, with Lynette. The weather is finally breaking. Probably be on the boat from here in unless it gets arctic again."

"Okay, I'll be right there."

□  □  □

Lynette was packing the last of Stewart's duffel bag when Roger Daltry pulled up near the boat. She waved to him before he got out of the car.

"Hey, Lynette!" Roger yelled. "Where's Wash?"

Lynette thumbed over her shoulder. "Inside," she said. Daltry started for the boat. Lynette said, "Bring me back a beer?"

"Sure," Daltry said.

He got to the top of the ladder leading to the deck and Stewart shot him three times in the chest. Daltry's body flew off the ladder. It landed on the cold hard ground a few feet from Lynette.

"Shit," Stewart said from the deck.

Lynette was looking up at him. "What, honey?"

Stewart pointed to Daltry. "Now we gotta carry him back up here."

Twenty minutes later, after Roger Daltry's body had been placed in the recliner on the boat, Stewart told Lynette, "Say good-bye to this place, baby. Couple more hours, that boat'll be nothing but splinters and ash."

He had just set one half of the C-4 explosive Schmidt had given him earlier in the week. Stewart was guessing he had less than twelve hours before he and the good doctor would be on their way to Mexico.

Lynette was teary-eyed.

"I'm gonna miss that boat," she said when they were in Stewart's pickup.

"It just a boat, baby," he told her. "Couple weeks from now, things go right, we'll have a new one. I'll even name it after you."

Lynette leaned into him for a kiss. "Really?"

"Promise," he said.

□ □ □

Ten years ago, Special Agent in Charge Eugene Morris benefited from the botched undercover operation aimed at a member of the Russian mob in New York. When all was said and done, after James Singleton eventually testified against a Brooklyn drug dealer, the dominoes fell in the right order and several federal RICO laws bagged a big-time cocaine dealer from South Beach in Miami.

Ten years later, project Buffalo Chips, a North Dakota sting operation, was working well until Morris heard the news about the attempted murder of Eddie and Diane Senta back in New York a week ago. Then there was a second attempt the day before.

Morris was furious. Singleton, this time as Washington Stewart, had violated the terms of his government deal one more time. Morris was determined to have him locked up at Marion penitentiary for the rest of his natural life.

He had been maintaining control of his rage until he received a call from federal agents in Bismarck. Now he was being told that his witnesses in Bismarck had been killed earlier in the morning. Morris was midflight on his way to Minot.

"What do you mean, the marshal was getting coffee?" he asked. "Who were they?"

"We don't know," another marshal said. "We're checking to see if there are any cameras in the area. A bank or something."

"Jesus Christ."

"We're trying to seal the highways but these guys were definitely pros."

Morris thought back to the night he had left the two yuppies with Stewart at the lounge in the Minot hotel. He said, "I want people sent to Sakakawea. I want that done yesterday."

"To the boat?" the marshal asked.

"At Sakakawea, yeah."

"We're kind of strapped here for manpower, sir."

"Find some, goddamn it!" Morris yelled.

□ □ □

There were a few reasons Alex Pavlik didn't want Aelish to fly out to North Dakota, not the least of which was his guilt for straying from their relationship. When he couldn't reach her at home, he called her brother's cell phone and learned that Aelish was taking a morning flight to Minneapolis for a connecting flight into Minot.

Pavlik called Aelish's cell phone from his new room several times before she finally answered.

"You can't come out here," he told her.

"I already am," she said. "I have a ten-thirty flight into Minneapolis. There's an hour layover before I fly to Fargo and then Minot. Can you meet me?"

"Of course, but I don't want you here."

"Why not, I hear the weather is finally breaking there. According to the news this morning it is."

"It's nothing to joke about," Pavlik told her. "This might get dangerous and I don't want you around in case it does."

"It already is dangerous as far as I'm concerned," Aelish said. "After what you told me yesterday? Besides, I already booked a room. I'll stay out of your way if you need privacy, but I'm on my way and that's the end of it."

"Aelish, I really wish you'd turn around. Please."

There was a pause on the line.

Pavlik said, "You there?"

"I'm worried about you," Aelish said. "I'm coming out there to bring you back in one piece. What happened at the hospital with Eddie Senta scared me. That man you're after had enough clout to try and kill a man across the country twice now. I want you home, but you're not going to do that unless I come there first."

Now Pavlik remained silent.

"Unless there's another reason you're not telling me," Aelish said.

Pavlik nearly choked. "No, nothing," he said. "You're on your way, then fine. Come. It's a big waste of time and money, but fine."

"I'm not strapped for cash, Alex."

"I know that."

"Then why mention it?"

Pavlik panicked. He was blowing it, talking instead of keeping his mouth shut. He told her to be careful and that he loved her. Then he kissed her through the phone.

Another uncomfortable pause followed before Aelish said, "Alex, what's going on?"

## Chapter 41
## Velva/Minot, North Dakota

Sergeant Don Ekroth had spent part of the night at the Minot Air Force Base hospital waiting for word on his friend. When he was told Jim Salinger was stable and that he would recover, albeit over a long period of time, Ekroth said a private prayer of thanks and headed back to Minot. He'd caught a few hours sleep at the Minot police station when Dale called to say he would be delayed a few hours before he could follow Ekroth out to John Ahearn's place in Velva.

Ekroth was too anxious to wait for Dale. The sergeant's wife was home after visiting with her sick mother. The couple had been looking forward to spending their first full weekend together in a few months. Contrary to what the chief had told him about keeping someone close, Ekroth left a message for Dale, then drove out to Velva on his own.

As he pulled up in front of Ahearn's house, Ekroth noticed a pickup leaving the driveway with two people inside the cab. He recognized Ahearn's junkie wife behind the wheel, but he didn't know who the man was. Ekroth buttoned his jacket and pulled on his gloves before stepping out of his station wagon into the cold. The last temperature reading he had heard over the radio was six degrees, a relative heat wave, he thought.

He knocked on the front door several minutes before Ahearn finally answered. The big man was disheveled and seemed to have been sleeping. "The hell do you want?" he asked from his doorway. He was wearing a thermal long-sleeved top and green sweatpants.

Ekroth removed the plastic coffee stirrer from his mouth. "We need to talk," he said. "About Nathan Barron, the kid that died from the overdose at the college."

"I already told you people about that," Ahearn said. "I don't know anything."

"Somebody else says you do," Ekroth said.

"Somebody else who?"

Ekroth pointed inside. "Let me in and we'll talk."

"Why should I let you in?"

Ekroth held up a plastic bag filled with oregano with his free hand. "Because I have some dope I can plant on your property if you don't," he said. "And I'm pretty darn tired of driving back and forth out here. You give me some real information and I'll go away. Maybe for good, but I want some names I can work with."

Ahearn took a deep breath, looked out the door to check for the other cop, then stepped back inside when he didn't see him.

"Yeah, well, come in and let's get it over with," he told Ekroth. "I got a busy fucking day ahead."

Ekroth put a hand on his service weapon as he entered the house. He let go when he sat on the end of a long worn couch. He set the plastic stirrer back in his mouth and took out his notepad and pen. Ahearn stood in the middle of the living room with his hands buried deep inside the front of his sweatpants as he scratched at his crotch.

"Talk to me," Ekroth said.

Ahearn removed one hand from his sweatpants and held up two fingers. "Roger and Tyrone," he said.

Ekroth feigned ignorance. "Roger and Tyrone?"

"Roger Daltry and Tyrone Williams."

"Excuse me?"

Ahearn laughed. "The fuckers from the base, man. One of 'em bought it, I guess. Tyrone. You already know somebody plugged him. It's been on the radio."

"What about the other one?"

Ahearn took a seat in his recliner. "They were the ones who killed that kid," he said. "More or less. They're dealers. They sold to my wife, too."

"You saw this happen?"

"Fuckin'-A right, I did."

"You'll testify?"

"If it covers my ass, I will."

"What did you have to do with it?"

"Nothing," Ahearn said. "Not a goddamned thing. I was busy watching my old lady, making sure she didn't overdose herself."

Ekroth moved the plastic stirrer with his tongue and smiled as he looked up from his notepad. "There's a woman in town who claims she saw you give Nathan Barron the lethal overdose of heroin."

"Bullshit," Ahearn said.

"We have her statement."

"What's her name?"

Ekroth bit his lower lip as he played dumb. "Ljunndgren, that sound right? Ljunndgren or was it Lundquist?"

"Fuck you and fuck her," Ahearn said.

"And she mentioned something about your wife flirting with Nathan Barron," Ekroth continued. "That's why you did it, she claims. You were jealous. And that goes to motive, John. A handsome young stud putting the moves on your old lady, a jury might believe that goes to motive."

Ahearn said, "I think you need to leave now."

"Unless you have another name you can give me?" Ekroth said.

"Excuse me?"

Ekroth pointed to his eye. "Some feller missing an eye or something," he said. "A tall black feller?"

Ahearn glanced at his watch as if he just remembered something. "Come on, get out of here," he said. "I'm not saying another word without my attorney. You already know who that is. Becker, in case you forgot."

Ekroth stood. "John, it's important you cooperate. Becker can't help you now. Not with a statement from a witness. This won't go away."

Ahearn pointed to the door. "Get the fuck out," he said.

Ekroth scratched at his head. He put his notepad away when he stood up. He glanced at Ahearn and frowned.

"I thought even you were smarter than this," he said.

"Good-bye."

Ekroth crossed the room. He stopped a few feet from the door, pulled out the bag of oregano and dropped it. "What's this?" he said. He squatted down to the floor to examine the bag. "This what I think it is? Looks like marijuana."

Ahearn's jaw tightened.

"John?" Ekroth said. He started to turn when Ahearn charged and slammed an elbow into the sergeant's left temple. The policeman staggered a few feet before he dropped to the floor unconscious.

□ □ □

Washington Stewart, as James Singleton, had been a pretty good athlete growing up. He had played high school basketball and football at DeWitt Clinton High School in the Bronx. He was a legitimate All-City candidate in football until his junior year, when he ruined his knee making a tackle on a kickoff.

Until his injury Singleton was also a pretty good student. Living in a depressed area of the South Bronx, he had learned street politics at a young age. When his father left home and never returned, young James had become the man of the house by default. After his alcoholic mother lost her job and the family had to struggle to survive, Singleton began a life of crime he would never stray from. Mostly it involved petty thefts and burglaries, but eventually the attraction of fast drug money lured him to a survivalist street life; fast money, women, drugs and murder. Then came the witness protection program.

He had tried to escape it once and it had almost cost him his life. Today he was determined to make it happen. He had a plan and money and a few key people to help him. First, though, he had to get rid of Special Agent in Charge Eugene Morris.

Stewart had expected Morris would come to scold him for the second attempted murder of Eddie and Diane Senta back in New York, but thanks to the agent's phone messages, he knew Morris was blaming him for what had happened in Bismarck. Stewart knew Morris was there to take him off the street.

He'd been waiting in the Dodge Ram in the airport parking lot, the engine running in case Morris had brought help. Stewart beeped his horn and Morris headed his way. Stewart was relieved when he saw the Special Agent in Charge was alone. He unlocked the doors and leaned across the console to push open the passenger door. He saw Morris wasn't holding a weapon and waited until the special agent in charge closed the door before jabbing a morphine syrette into his left thigh.

Morris jumped from the pinch, but Stewart used a rag soaked with chloroform to subdue the big man. Once unconscious, Stewart cuffed Morris's hands to an ankle restraint. Morris had slumped over with his head resting on the console.

"Man shot my eyes out," Stewart said. "The fuck you think I was going to do?"

Twenty minutes later, once Morris was able to speak again, Stewart repeated what he'd said earlier.

"The man shot my eye out."

"Should've killed you," Morris said.

"Then you'd be mowing the grass down in Quantico," Stewart said. "But you not. You here. Special agent in charge, too. You did alright by me. I lost an eye. I look like a monster."

"The investment bankers in Bismarck," Morris said.

"Hey, you're the one brought them to me," Stewart said.

"You gonna kill me too now, Jimmy?"

"The name is Stewart. And no, why the fuck would I?"

Stewart pulled into an abandoned lot and stopped to pour chloroform onto a rag. "You were replacing me up here with those LA boys anyway," he said, "so now you'll find somebody else. That's the way it works, right?"

"The fuck you doing?" Morris said.

Stewart pressed the rag against Morris's face again and held it there while the agent struggled. Stewart maintained the pressure and Morris's body eventually slumped as he returned to unconsciousness.

◻ ◻ ◻

There were two bruisers standing together in the lobby when Pavlik went down to see if Marsha had arrived for work. He saw one goon look across the lobby and followed the big man's eyes. It was then he spotted the man from the parking lot a few days earlier. He was in a wheelchair today, his injured leg was in a cast up to the knee. Pavlik crossed the lobby to confront him.

"You tore it?" he asked the man in the cast.

"Had to get surgery," the man said.

Pavlik noticed the two goons were standing to his right now.

"And you're here why?"

"He needs your name," one of the goons said. "You were a witness."

"Who's he?" Alex asked the man in the wheelchair.

"My brother."

Pavlik motioned to the other man. "He your brother, too?"

"Just a friend."

"What makes you think I'd be your witness? You tried to hit me and twisted your knee."

"And all I got was fifty bucks."

"Not from me. Go find the guy gave it to you."

"I don't know where he is. It was easier finding you. Didn't have your name, but the description was easy enough. You're a big man."

Pavlik smirked. "You've got a pair of stones, I'll give you that."

"I talked to another friend and he said I have a case against the hotel, slipping on the ice like that."

"It helps if he has a witness," the goon that did the talking said.

"You didn't report it?" Pavlik asked the man in the wheelchair.

"'Course, I did. At the hospital."

"So?"

"He needs a witness for the lawyer," the goon said. "He needs you to verify his story."

"He can forget me. I'm not doing him any favors."

"Maybe you want to think about that," the goon said.

Pavlik turned to the two big men. "You're talking about extortion. You sure you wanna go that route?"

"We're talking about satisfaction," the goon said.

"So, what, if I don't agree to be a witness, you'll break one of my legs? That's extortion."

"I'm not walking away from this with a bad knee," the man in the wheelchair said.

"You use my name with anyone?"

"I don't know your name."

"Then why me? Use one of these two geniuses. You slipped on ice that hadn't been cleared. You were here meeting a friend at the lounge and went down."

"You're a real smartass, aren't you?" the goon said.

Pavlik spoke to the man in the wheelchair. "I won't be your witness, but there's nobody to say these two morons weren't there when it happened."

"How much you think they'll give me?"

"I have no idea," Pavlik said. "But I'm busy now and it's all the free legal advice you're getting."

"You're a pussy lawyer, huh?" the goon said. "That figures."

Pavlik shook his head before turning to the man in the wheelchair again. "Do yourself a favor and let the other one do the talking. This one'll blow your case."

"You're pretty sure of yourself, huh?" the speaking goon said.

Pavlik looked him up and down. "Positive," he said.

"Come on, fellers," the man in the wheelchair said. "He's right. Wheel me out of here."

Pavlik watched them leave through the lobby front doors and wondered how the hell people that stupid survived puberty.

□ □ □

When they were teenagers, James Sikes could get his sister to do pretty much anything he wanted because he had witnessed their father's molestation of Kelly the day after her twelfth birthday.

Sikes spent the next few years bullying his sister into submitting to his own incestuous lust by threatening to tell their mother, an abusive woman when she was drunk. The threat of her mother's wrath was enough to keep Kelly in check. For four years, until she was sixteen, Kelly was her brother's personal sex slave. It wasn't until Kelly ran away that his sexual blackmail finally ended.

A few weeks after Kelly left home Sikes became the victim of their father's pedophilia. It lasted until Sikes also ran away. Several years would pass before the siblings met up again.

Sikes and Kelly never discussed what had happened in their past. Drugs seemed to have diluted Kelly's memory and Sikes had become consumed with the day-to-day opportunities a hustler needed to survive.

Beating down a detective's wife for his brother-in-law had become one such opportunity. The fact he'd get some tail while he was at it would be an extra bonus.

He was wondering what the woman looked like as he peered over the top of the Red & Green, the university newspaper, outside the home where Emily and Dale Hehn lived. Sikes had switched positions with his sister and was now seated behind the wheel of the pickup.

When she saw the man leaving the house in a rush, Kelly said, "That's him! That's the cop who arrested me."

Sikes sat low behind the wheel as the man got inside the car parked in the driveway. A few seconds later the car bucked into reverse and backed out of the driveway.

"We'll give him ten minutes," Sikes told his sister. "In case he forgot something. Then I'll go in and you wait here in case he comes back after that. You lean on the horn if he does."

"He'll recognize me," Kelly said. "If he comes back and I beep the horn. He knows who I am."

"So you duck down to the floor."

He waited five minutes before he had had enough. The sun was bright and the weather report insisted the temperature was above freezing, but it was still cold inside the pickup without it running. Kelly had fallen asleep and was lightly snoring. In another half hour or so people might notice them.

He nudged his sister.

"What?" she asked.

He pointed at his watch.

"I don't want to be out here by myself," she said.

"Then give me five minutes and come inside," he told her. "But you best put on a mask before you get out the car if you do."

Sikes handed his sister a ski mask. "I'll use this," he said as he pulled a similar ski mask from under the seat.

"We have to be careful," she said.

Sikes stared at his sister a long moment. "No shit?" he said.

□ □ □

When Dale emerged from his shower, he had been pleasantly surprised to find Emily spread out naked on their bed. He was glad she had convinced him to spend some extra time making love. He was even more grateful for the two-hour nap it had led to.

When he woke up from the nap, he was panicked about keeping the schedule he had worked out with Don Ekroth the night before. He hustled out to the car and sped off to meet with Kathy Ljunndgren at Trinity Hospital. He was close to the hospital when he realized he had forgotten his cell phone.

"Shit," he said.

He glanced at the time and realized he needed to catch Kathy before she was released. He could always head back to the house to pick up the phone later. Or maybe Emily would drop it off at the station.

Dale left the car parked at the curb in front of the hospital and raced up to Kathy's room. He found her busy gathering the personal items her mother had brought her. He stood in the doorway until she felt his presence. She wouldn't acknowledge him.

"Good morning," Dale eventually said.

Kathy continued packing her things.

"I'm hoping you remember our discussion two days ago," Dale said.

"I don't," Kathy said.

"It was important information you gave me."

"I was high," she said.

"Maybe, but I think you told me the truth. I think you wanted to tell me the truth all along."

"I don't know what I told you."

"If I repeated it, would you at least confirm or deny it?"

"I'd rather go home."

"Me, too. It's supposed to be my day off."

Kathy finished packing. She leaned against the bed and waited until Dale stepped further inside the room. When they were facing each other, he folded his arms across his chest.

"Look, John Ahearn is a mean guy," Kathy said. "If he knew that I said something, he'd do something to me. If not him, he'd get somebody else to do it. He's a crazy fuck and I don't need him after me."

"We'll be out to his house this afternoon," Dale said. "We're going to press him hard, Kathy. We know he was involved with Nathan Barron's overdose. We knew it before you told me."

"I'm not going there," she said. "Forget it."

"I really don't want to lean on you," Dale said. "But I will if you force me. I'll be all over you legally until I can arrest you. And I will put you in jail if I have to. John Ahearn is a bad guy. I need your help to put him away."

Kathy didn't hesitate. "I'll take my chances," she said. "I don't know anything."

## Chapter 42
## Minot/Lakota, North Dakota

Stewart had purchased a used Winnebago RV a few months earlier and kept it in the garage of an elderly woman he had met through local newspaper classified ads. The old lady was living on Social Security and was anxious to rent the garage. Stewart had prepaid her three months in advance and told her he wouldn't be using it for at least two months.

The woman wasn't home when he moved the tied and gagged special agent from the pickup into the RV. Stewart met up with Lynette at the McDonald's on Broadway. They grabbed a late breakfast before he drove the RV to a parking lot bordering the university.

They had some time to make love. Stewart rolled Morris off the bed onto the floor to make room. The agent was groggy from a dose of heroin. He moaned through the gag.

Lynette stripped naked and lay on her back. Stewart kissed the patterns of scars on her stomach, then climbed on top of her and they had sex. Lynette cried from her orgasm. Stewart used a tissue to dry her eyes.

"We heading to Mexico, baby," he said once they were dressed again.

They sat on the bed smoking cigarettes. Lynette's eyes were still wet.

"When this is over with, we going to Mexico, you and me," Stewart repeated. "Live under the sun for a change. Some warm weather. Beaches."

"I haven't been to a beach once in my life," Lynette said.

"We get you a nice thong bikini," Stewart said. "Let your hair grow out. Down to your ass."

"It'll be a new world for me," she said.

"Yes, it will," Stewart said. He reached a hand out and held one of Lynette's hands. "I hope you don't get homesick on me."

Lynette kissed him. "Never," she said. "I love you."

When they were ready to roll again, Stewart put on a green and white sweatshirt that read "Fighting Sioux." He posed for Lynette with his hands out.

"What do you think?" he asked her.

"Didn't they just retire that name?"

"Because they too political," Stewart said. "Same people call Obama a black man forget he half white. Forget he a millionaire too. I call a spade a spade."

"I think it looks great," Lynette said.

"I'll have to burn it soon as we safe, but I thought it be good luck in the meantime."

He sat behind the wheel. Lynette sat up on the console alongside him. He took her hand as he pulled out of the parking lot. She had just nibbled on an Egg McMuffin sandwich and had smeared sauce around her mouth. Stewart pointed to the white spot at the corner of her mouth. Lynette wiped it away with the back of her wrist.

"Use a napkin, baby," he said.

"Sorry," she said.

Stewart glanced at his watch. "We need to make a couple extra stops this morning," he said. "John Ahearn for one."

"Ahearn? What do we need to see him for?"

"Man took something of mine," Stewart said.

Lynette was surprised. "John stole from you? I never would have thought it. You're the only person I know that guy to be afraid of."

"Apparently he wasn't."

"I can't believe he even tried."

"Fifty grand he took."

"Wow."

Stewart turned on his seat to face Lynette. "Man's an ape. Should be an exhibit in a museum. How he knows when to wipe his ass is what I'd like to know?" he said. "He gonna rob me? I don't think so."

Lynette checked the time. "That bomb is about to go off," she said. "We have time for Ahearn? What if he's not home? We're on a tight schedule, Wash."

"I left the pickup in a driveway up the block from McKinley Elementary. Kids are inside the school so it should be safe. That goes up it'll keep most of the cops busy. We should have time, but I didn't plan on stopping in Velva. It's on our way."

"Can we do without it, the money? It might be safer if we do."

"It's the principle of the thing," Stewart said. "Man that stupid doesn't deserve to live."

Lynette licked egg from her fingers. "What if his wife is there?"

Stewart rubbed the bridge of his nose. "I see what you saying. Maybe we need another hostage, for before we get to Velva, somebody to hold on to until you in Jamestown, besides Morris, I mean. He's law enforcement anyway. They might not negotiate over his black ass."

Lynette smiled.

"What?" Stewart asked. "You got somebody in mind?"

"Uh-huh."

Stewart was intrigued. "What you thinking, baby? This must be good."

"It is."

"Who?"

"She's pretty."

"She is?"

"You already said so."

Stewart squinted trying to think of who it could be. He smiled when he thought he knew. "She serve drinks?"

"Apparently," Lynette said.

"She would make a good hostage. In case we need her after we deal with Ahearn."

"And I'd like to see what she looks like," Lynette said. "After all the fuss you made."

"I was just playing with you."

"Uh-huh, we'll see."

Stewart leaned forward to look in Lynette's eyes. "You sure?" he asked. "We talking about the state beauty queen, right? The one at the Lawrence Welk?"

"I really want to see her, Wash."

"You not getting jealous, are you?"

Lynette shrugged again.

"Okay, then, that's what we do. First, though, we need an angle. Something to get her out that hotel."

"Like what?"

"According to a bartender there, she has a kid. That'd work."

"Boy or girl?"

"I don't know. Why don't you go online and see you can find out. Her name is Nordstrom. Marsha Nordstrom. Then we'll head up to see Mr. Ahearn."

Lynette leaned across the console to kiss Stewart on the mouth. "Is he gonna be surprised to see you," she said before booting her laptop.

"If he's still there," Stewart said. "Man's probably got a plan of his own since he took that money. Something dumb, no doubt, but he's not staying home watching television, not for long."

"What if he's not home?"

"Then it's his lucky day."

"Will you kill him at his house?"

Stewart nudged her with an elbow and said, "Unless you want to."

□  □  □

Dale was on his way home to retrieve his cell phone when he heard the explosion. He made a quick right off Broadway at Eighth Avenue Northwest, then backtracked to where he could see the smoke. His heart began to race when he realized it was close to an elementary school.

When he saw a body lying on the sidewalk across from the fire, he parked at the curb and attended to the woman. She seemed to be dazed, but there were no visible wounds. He positioned himself between the fire and her body a moment before a second, smaller explosion erupted.

A minute later he could hear sirens as children were being filed out the front of the school further up the block. Dale waved at the first police cruiser to arrive on the scene. The blare of fire engine horns could be heard in the near distance.

"What the hell was it?" a man standing on a nearby porch asked.

"I don't know," Dale said, "but get back inside your house, sir. I don't know if the gas tank blew yet."

"Something blew."

"Please get back inside your house."

Dale let the officer on the scene tend to the woman before he jogged toward the fire.

□ □ □

Nick Mayo lit a fresh cigarette while his nephew Frank opened a cold bottle of beer. Several empty bottles littered the kitchen table and cabinets. The sight of them annoyed Nick.

"You having a party or something?" he asked his nephew.

Frank Mayo scratched at his beard stubble. "It was on sale," he said.

Nick looked through the kitchen window and saw his son and the blonde standing in the yard talking. The woman was holding on to Joe's arm.

Frank looked over his uncle's shoulder and pointed. "She's not bad," he said.

"You pay the guy?" Nick asked.

"Huh? Oh, yeah, sure. Every dime. I counted it out, packed it, and sealed the box."

"Four hundred fifty grand?"

Frank was watching his cousin and the woman embrace in the yard. "Yes, sir," he said. "Joe's got himself some nice snatch there, huh?"

"He picked her up in Montana," Nick said. "We're gonna use her car from here."

Frank scraped a kitchen chair out from under the table and sat. "You get a piece?"

"Huh?" Nick said, annoyed at the question. "I got better things to worry about."

"You look good," Frank told his uncle. "You took off a few."

Nick leaned against a kitchen cabinet and ignored the snow job. "You test the product?" he asked.

Frank chuckled. "It's good stuff."

"I hope you're not using that shit. I don't want that once we leave here."

"Just a few tastes," Frank said. He guzzled most of his beer, then belched. "Excuse," he said as he watched his cousin grab the woman's ass through her jeans.

"Joe tell you to pay the guy?" Nick asked.

Frank was scratching his crotch. "Huh?"

Nick slapped the cabinet with his hand. "Oh, over here," he said. "The four fifty. My son tell you to pay him?"

Frank turned to his uncle. "Yeah," he said. "And I did. Why?"

"I'm surprised."

"What do you mean?"

"The guy from up here?"

"What do you mean?" Frank asked again.

"The guy you gave the money. The one you paid, he's from up here, North Dakota, Minnesota, wherever the fuck we are?"

"Yeah, I guess," Frank said. He finished his beer and immediately opened another. "He had a pickup. He wore the boots and the overalls. You know, the suspenders thing. And he had one of those baseball caps without a team logo."

"And you paid this hick cocksucker four-hundred fifty grand?"

Frank held his hands up. "Hey, Uncle Nick, what's going on here? Joe tells me to pay the guy and now you're pissed I did it?"

Nick waved it off. "I'm not pissed," he said. "I'm surprised is all. It's a different time, I guess. You're a sharp kid. I figured you might keep a few bucks for us. I didn't bring Joe up for this life, but your father was grooming you. It almost don't make sense, you know what I mean? A sharp kid like yourself feeding some farmer all that money. Four hundred fifty large."

Frank remained silent.

"I mean, I wouldn't be upset you saved a few bucks," Nick said. "So long as you whacked it up, of course."

Frank guzzled from the bottle again.

"That's a lot of gelt, four hundred fifty large," Nick continued. "To give to some hillbilly pro'bly fucks his sister, I mean."

Frank slowly smiled.

"What?" Nick asked. He crushed out one cigarette and lit another.

Frank shrugged.

"What?" Nick asked again.

"I gave him four twenty," Frank said.

Nick started to smirk. He thought better and smiled instead. "Four twenty?"

"Four twenty," Frank said.

"So we get to keep ten each."

"That was the idea," Frank said.

Nick stared at his nephew long enough to scare him. "Good boy," he finally said. "Where is it?"

"Huh?"

"The extra thirty grand, where is it?"

"Oh, in my duffel bags in the car," said Frank, a bit more nervous now. He pointed toward the kitchen window. "Out there. I split it, fifteen in each bag."

"In the car?" Nick asked.

"Yeah, I buried it before the guy got here. Just in case."

"Just in case of what?"

Frank shuffled. "You know, the guy came with reinforcements, he came here to rob us."

Nick took another moment, then tapped his head. "Good thinking," he said. "Like I said, you're sharp. Just like your old man. My brother'd be proud."

"I was hoping you'd appreciate it," Frank said.

"I do," said Nick, winking at his nephew now. "Of course, I do."

□ □ □

Mary Beth Wilson was anxious to start her new life with Joe Mayo. She didn't understand some of what he talked about, especially the gangster stuff, but she knew enough from the news and movies to accept the fact that Joe's father, Nick, was a member of the Italian Mafia.

The old man had unnerved Mary Beth during the drive from the airport. Nick Mayo had seemed annoyed at her presence. He'd also showed little gratitude for the running-around his son had done to meet the old man.

Mary Beth was hoping that once they were finished helping Nick get across the country, she and Joe could go off by themselves. It was what Joe had promised her more than once.

She wasn't comfortable around the cousin, either, but Joe had told her that Frank would stay with Nick in Cleveland once they got there. Frank Mayo had leered at Mary Beth a few times since they'd arrived at the house. At one point, she had caught him staring directly at her crotch.

Now she was taking garbage from the floor of the car, empty coffee containers and crumpled paper bags, to the trash can alongside the back wall of the house. She was walking past the kitchen window when she saw Nick shoot his nephew in the back of the head.

Mary Beth stopped in her tracks. There was no noise from the gun. She recognized the long tube at the end of the barrel as a sound suppressor. She saw Frank lunge forward and fall to the floor. She saw a blood splatter on the wall across the kitchen. Then she saw the old man stand over the body and shoot two more times.

Mary Beth dropped the trash she was carrying and flattened her back against the wall of the house. She glanced at the garage and could see Joe was still inside. She looked to her car and remembered she had the extra set of keys. She felt the keys through her pocket and carefully, quietly made her way across the driveway.

## Chapter 43
## Minot, North Dakota

It had been some of the best lovemaking Emily could remember and she was grateful for the extra rest it had provided when Dale fell asleep afterward. Then he was up again and anxious to get to the hospital.

Emily stepped under the shower and let the water run hot. It was her favorite way to relax. She stood with her back to the spray and tilted her head until the water reached her forehead. She stood still a long while, until she heard the cell phone ringing.

She knew it was Dale's cell phone because hers was programmed with Bizet's "*Habanera*" as a ring tone. Dale must have forgotten his phone when he rushed out.

Emily was running across the hallway when she sensed something was wrong. She stopped outside her bedroom and focused on the quiet inside the apartment. Then she smelled something.

Cigarette smoke, except Dale didn't smoke.

▢ ▢ ▢

James Sikes was comfortable in the brown leather recliner. It was awkward cleaning his fingernails with the tip of his Bowie knife because of his broken left arm. The cast restricted his movement. He set the knife on his lap to take a hit from his cigarette with his free hand. He flicked the ashes onto the rug, then set the cigarette back on the arm of the recliner and picked up the knife again. It was then the woman called out.

"Dale?" she said. "Is Don with you?"

Suddenly she was there standing in the hallway near the kitchen. She was wearing a robe. It was open enough so he caught a glimpse of her blonde bush. Sikes smiled when she covered herself.

"Your husband forgot the deadbolt," he said.

▢ ▢ ▢

He had grown anxious wondering if Dale Hehn would show, then he heard the explosion. It was loud and rattled the windows. Pavlik thought it might be a plane crash. He went down to the lobby and saw people gathering outside. He asked the bellboys what had happened, but nobody knew. They said they heard an explosion but weren't sure what it was about. They were all watching the television for a news update.

Pavlik decided to call the detective's home. It was then he realized he had forgotten his cell phone at Marsha Nordstrom's house. He used one of the pay phones. He let Dale Hehn's home phone ring half a dozen times before he gave up.

He remembered Marsha had said she needed to be at work early and headed for the lounge to look for her. When he didn't see her, he asked for her at the front desk and learned she had called in late.

He did a quick check around the lobby and then outside for the agents. When he was satisfied they weren't there, he decided to wait upstairs in his room in case Hehn finally called him back.

Pavlik didn't like feeling hopeless. He didn't like waiting around, either. He checked the time and saw it was a few minutes after eleven. He was giving the Minot detective another hour or two before he drove down to the police station. If the local police weren't interested in what he had to say, he would assume James Singleton was gone and he'd report being held hostage by two agents of the FBI.

The thing Pavlik wouldn't do was let the FBI protect James Singleton with immunity one more time. This time, if the killer escaped again, Pavlik would bring it to the media's attention.

☐ ☐ ☐

Marsha was still tired from her long night with Alex Pavlik. She hadn't stopped thinking about him while she prepared herself for work. When she found his cell phone under one of the couch pillows, she nearly called the hotel to let him know she had it. She decided to bring it to work later and leave it at the front desk. She wasn't sure he would want to talk to her after he had more alone time. The man had been wracked with guilt when he left.

She remembered a prescription she had to pick up and called work from her car. She was on the road within five minutes after stopping at the drugstore and would only be a few minutes late to work. She drove in a trance as she continued to feel guilty about the night before. She pulled into the parking lot hoping to see Alex Pavlik one more time, at least to say good-bye.

Once inside the lobby, she forgot about his cell phone and headed for the bar. She was uncomfortable when she saw a scarred woman sitting there. She guessed the woman was somewhere in her thirties but the facial scars and worn look added years to her appearance.

After getting settled, Marsha wiped down the bar from one end and stopped when she reached the scarred woman.

"Beer," the woman said.

Marsha pointed to the clock above the bar. "Not for another hour, sorry."

"It's after eight o'clock, hon. State law says the sale of beer on premises is legal from eight o'clock in the morning until two in the morning."

"And the hotel policy is I don't sell until there's security in the lounge and our security doesn't start for another hour."

"Soda then," the woman said. "And give me some pretzels or fish or whatever else you got. I'm hungry."

Marsha finished pouring a Coke and set it on a coaster in front of the woman. She dipped an empty plastic bowl into a box of cheese goldfish crackers and set it on the bar.

"Thanks," the woman said.

"Sure," Marsha said.

The woman lit a cigarette. After a few drags, she asked, "You really a Miss North Dakota?"

"A long time ago," Marsha said without making eye contact.

"My man thinks you're still hot."

Marsha stopped wiping the bar. "Excuse me?"

"My man thinks you're hot," the woman repeated. "He'd like you to join us one night. A threesome. What do you say?"

Marsha squinted at the woman. "Not interested," she said, no longer trying to be polite.

"He'll pay you, if you want money."

Marsha went back to wiping the bar. "No, thanks."

"You should think about it. My man's got a big one. Could put out fires with his hose."

Marsha returned to where the woman was sitting and leaned both hands on the bar. "I think you should finish your soda and leave," she said.

The scarred woman took a long drag on her cigarette and winked. "Or what, hon?"

"Or I'll call the police."

"Was I rude or something?"

"Very."

The scarred woman finished her soda and got up off the stool. She set two dollars on the bar and said, "Keep the change, beautiful."

Marsha watched the woman leave through the lounge and head toward the front lobby. When the woman was out of view, Marsha finished wiping the bar.

## Chapter 44
## Lakota, North Dakota

"Where's the broad?" Nick Mayo asked his son from the rear door of the house. "Where'd she go?"

Joe Mayo was checking the oil on his cousin's car. He had just pulled the dipstick and was wiping it to read when his father called.

"Where the hell she go?" Nick asked again.

Joe looked up at his father before he noticed Mary Beth's car was missing. "Oh, shit," he said. "I didn't see. Why?"

"I think she saw something."

"Saw what?"

Nick waved his son toward the house.

"What?" Joe repeated.

The old man glanced around the area, then said, "Your cousin. I think he hurt himself."

Joe looked confused until his father made a gun of his hand and held it against his head.

"Oh," Joe said. "Oh!"

□ □ □

Joe Mayo wasn't sure what Mary Beth would do once she was on the highway, but he was positive that she'd witnessed his cousin's murder. He finished packing his cousin's car and pulled out of the driveway. He beeped a few times until his father appeared on the front porch.

"I knew bringing that cunt was a mistake," Nick Mayo told his son as soon as he was inside the car.

Here we go, Joe was thinking. "You didn't have to kill Frank. Not in front of her."

Nick ignored his son. "What she got in her car, this hick twat of yours?"

"One of my bags. Dirty laundry, I think. I had the stuff in the garage with me."

"Thank fucking God you did something right."

"You're welcome."

"You tipped off those guys in Vegas, right?" Nick asked.

"Yeah, I told you."

"Then they owe you."

"That's what they said."

"Good," Nick said. "Now let's get out of here."

Joe turned onto an avenue that led to State Highway One. He shook his head as he looked around the road.

"I hope she doesn't go to the cops," he said.

"She's probably shitting her pants someplace," Nick said. "We'll ditch this car at the first exit we find on the Interstate. It'll be April before somebody smells your cousin in the trunk. Then we'll boost a car from wherever we stop, take a hostage, and head south a couple states."

"A hostage? Great. Now you can kill somebody else."

"Try not to wet your pants."

They drove in silence until Joe spotted the sign for the highway. "I just hope you're right," he said. "This new game plan."

"I am," Nick said. "I was a skipper. I'm always right."

□ □ □

Mary Beth was crying hysterically by the time she turned the corner. She could no longer see the house, but her body was shaking from adrenaline as she drove through two stop signs and a red light. When she spotted signs for U.S. Route 2, Mary Beth wasn't sure whether she should head back west to Montana or search for a local police cruiser. Then she saw flashing lights along the entrance ramp of the Interstate. An officer had just pulled someone over.

Mary Beth was leaning on her horn when she pulled up behind the police cruiser. The Minnesota State patrol trooper was approaching the driver of the car he had stopped when the incessant blaring of the horn caught his attention.

□ □ □

Nick Mayo was giving it to his son as soon as they pulled away from the house. More than forty years in the rackets, seven of them behind bars, and all he had left was a kid with little more street sense than the average hillbilly. Nothing had rubbed off; the kid was his mother's son.

Twenty-five minutes had passed since they discovered the woman and her car were gone. He was yelling at his son again for bringing her along in the first place.

"What, for a blow job?" the old man asked. "Because she wet your noodle? You know how long it's been since I knocked off a piece?"

Joe Mayo was doing his best to remain quiet. He'd already heard more than enough.

"Fuckin' twat," Nick said. "You're lucky she didn't grab the product. You're lucky she didn't get these, your cousin's bags." He pointed to two small duffel bags filled with the money his nephew had shorted from the drug deal. "He stiffed that farmer thirty grand, by the way, your cousin. He was a lot sharper than you."

"That why you killed him?" Joe asked, unable to restrain himself anymore. "Because he did something you approve of?"

"You're so fuckin' smart," Nick said. "Why you think I put you in the restaurant business, you fuckin' clown?" He grabbed at his own crotch. "Because you don't have the balls," he said. "You don't have what it takes."

It had been a long haul since he first became involved in helping his father. It was bad enough having to live on the lam the last few years, but now it had become as dangerous as it was insulting. He was thinking he should have taken the money his old man had stashed before going away and then running off with it. Half a million was more than start-up money. He could be in Mexico living like a king right now instead of listening to this bullshit.

If the bullshit wasn't enough, he was now an accomplice to a murder.

"You're a real jerkoff sometimes," his father said.

It was the last insult he was willing to take. Fuck loyalty. He saw a bus stopping at a corner near a red light and pulled to the curb. He grabbed one of his cousin's two duffel bags and opened his door.

"Go fuck yourself," Joe told his father a moment before getting out of the car.

The old man's eyes opened wide. "What the fuck!" he yelled. "Get back in here! Joe! Joey!"

Joe Mayo flipped his father the bird as he jogged to make the bus before it pulled away from the curb.

□ □ □

Ten minutes after his son had left him sitting in the car alone, Nick Mayo accepted he was on his own. He was doing fine making his way through the streets until he turned onto the Interstate. Then he saw the flashing lights of the roadblock around the first curve and pulled the car up onto the grass. He grabbed the duffel bag and left the keys behind as he walked as fast as he could back toward the entrance ramp. He was less than fifty yards from the abandoned car when two State Police cruisers turned onto the ramp.

"Shit," Nick said.

The police pulled onto the grass and blocked Nick's path. The old man could see the blonde in the rear seat of one of the cars. She was pointing at him.

Nick did a quick about face and started back toward the car.

"Turn around with your hands up!" one of the patrol troopers yelled.

Nick ignored the command. He jumped when he heard the shot, then stopped and turned around. Two Minnesota State Troopers had drawn their weapons.

"Drop the bag and hands up!" one of them yelled.

Nick dropped the bag.

"Hands up!" the trooper yelled again. "Now!"

"Fuck you," whispered Nick as he raised his hands. "Hick cocksucker."

## Chapter 45
## Minot, North Dakota

Stewart injected the federal agent with a second mild dose of heroin once Lynette left to meet with Miss North Dakota inside the Lawrence Welk Hotel. Morris was tied and gagged on the floor at the foot of the bed inside the Winnebago's small bedroom. Stewart nudged him with a foot.

"Just for the record, which one bled the most?" he asked. "Josh or Ted? Or was it Todd?"

Morris moaned something unintelligible. He tried to see where he was but was barely able to focus.

Stewart pointed to the plastic cuffs on Morris's wrists. "Those too tight?"

"What… you doing?" Morris said.

"Rough riding," Stewart said. "Just like Teddy. This RV my horse. I'm gonna charge up the hill, too. Up and out and gone for good."

"'Immy?"

Stewart smiled. "Change of attitude now, huh? The name is Stewart, motherfucka."

"What… doing?"

"Sorry," Stewart said as he took a long drag on his cigarette. "Can't tell you, my brother, or then I have to kill you."

☐  ☐  ☐

"How'd it go?" Stewart asked Lynette once she was back inside the RV.

"She's a priss," Lynette said. "That woman's never had a hard day in her life."

"You can tell all that from just a few minutes, huh?"

Lynette was hurt. "She's perfect-looking, Wash. She don't need you to defend her."

"I'm not defending her, baby."

"It sounded like it."

"Well, I wasn't."

"Okay."

"Yeah, okay. It's good, too, she a priss."

"What's good about it?"

"Turning her," Stewart said. "Making her humble. If we get to spend any extra time with her, it might be fun."

□ □ □

Marsha was about to call Alex Pavlik's room when the bar telephone rang. She picked it up hoping it was him.

"Lawrence Welk lounge," she answered. "Marsha speaking."

"Miss North Dakota?" a woman's voice asked.

"Speaking," Marsha said.

"This is the girl who was rude to you," the woman said. "The one you threw out."

"What do you want?"

"I'm going to give you some instructions," the woman said. "You need to listen to them very carefully."

Marsha made a face. "What the hell is this?"

"Just listen," the woman said. "I want—"

"Good-bye," Marsha said. She hung up.

She looked through the lounge to see if she could spot the woman. When she didn't see her, she reached for the phone to dial Alex's room number. It rang again before she picked up the receiver.

"Lawrence Welk lounge," she answered.

"We have your daughter," a man's voice said.

Marsha gasped. "What?"

"This time don't hang up," he said. "You come outside soon as I hang up with you. You'll have exactly thirty seconds to be outside the lobby. If you're not there in thirty seconds, if you stop to call the police or anybody else, you stop to powder your nose, you'll never see your little girl again. Understand?"

Marsha gasped again. "Yes," she said. "Yes, I do."

"Okay," the man said. "I'll wave to you when you're outside. You come to me and get inside my RV. It's a good-sized Winnebago. You can't miss it. Now, you have thirty seconds."

Marsha heard the line click dead and dropped the phone. She ran as fast as she could.

□ □ □

Pavlik had been standing at the window looking at the smoke that continued to billow from the fire in the valley. He had turned on the news and learned it was a car fire from an unexplained explosion and that all volunteer firemen were reporting to an address on Fifth Street Northwest.

He was distracted when a Winnebago pulled into the lot. He saw a blonde-haired woman get out from the passenger side and head inside the hotel. He assumed there was someone inside the RV because the engine was still running. Pavlik could see the exhaust from the tailpipe.

It seemed strange to him that a Winnebago would park in a hotel lot, but he reminded himself that he was in a place where lots of people traveled by RV.

Or maybe they were just waiting on someone.

Then he saw the blonde woman running out to the Winnebago again. She stepped back inside, but Pavlik couldn't see her sitting up front. He glanced from his watch to the telephone and felt a rush of panic. What if Aelish called his cell number and Marsha answered it?

He hoped Marsha had arrived at work and was about to call downstairs to find out when he saw her run out to the Winnebago in her uniform. Then she stepped up inside and he wondered what it was about.

When the RV made the wide U-turn, Pavlik saw that a black man wearing a face mask was driving. He raced out of the room.

## Chapter 46
## Minot, North Dakota

Emily had run to the bedroom and locked the door. When she grabbed the telephone from its cradle, she found the line was dead. She had started for the window when the door was kicked open.

"Don't touch me," she'd warned the intruder with a threatening finger. The man held up his knife and giggled.

"I swear it," Emily said, "don't you touch me."

□ □ □

Sikes had stopped himself from attacking the bitch because she had started issuing threats. He wondered if she knew karate or kung fu or some other form of martial arts.

She looked good, especially with her hair still wet from her shower. He liked that, having a woman with wet hair.

He pointed the knife at her and gave her free advice.

"This can go down easy or hard," he said. "That's up to you. But it will go down, lady, make no mistake."

"I'm warning you," she said, still pointing her finger.

Sikes grabbed a pillow and ripped it open with the knife. "And now I'm warning you," he said. "That pillow will be your face you don't play nice."

□ □ □

Kelly Ahearn had been too uncomfortable waiting in the pickup. She forgot the ski mask and grabbed her handbag instead. Then she crossed the street to the house. She rang the bell a few times, but it was a full minute before she tried the doorknob and found it was unlocked.

Kelly found her brother and the Hehn woman in a bedroom standing across the bed from each other. Kelly was scared when she saw her brother holding the knife.

Sikes motioned at her to open her handbag. Kelly took out the hypodermic and the bag of dope.

The Hehn woman pointed to it. "What's that?" she asked.

Sikes smiled. "Lunch," he said.

"Me first," Kelly said.

"Jesus Christ," the woman said.

"Jesus don't do drugs," Sikes said, "but you can right after my sister. Then I'll do you, darlin'."

□ □ □

Emily was a fighter. She had always been a fighter. The only child of a widowed sheriff, Emily Leland had learned from necessity early on. The night she met Dale she had been the victim of a brutal mugging. A transient railroad worker had followed her into a desolate parking lot in the small town of Palermo, North Dakota. The man had used a two-by-four to assault her.

Emily had required thirty-two stitches behind her left ear after the beating. Her face was badly bruised and both eyes were blackened. Still, when the opportunity presented itself, after the mugger had assaulted her, Emily killed him with a rusty nail file she had found in the dirt during the assault.

Now she was being held captive in her own home. It had already gone on more than half an hour. The sister was high and had passed out on the floor. Emily wasn't sure if the woman had overdosed or if it was a normal reaction to the drug she'd injected into a vein in one of her arms. She assumed the drug was heroin and that it had everything to do with what Dale was investigating.

The brother had positioned himself in front of the bedroom door. He nudged his sister from time to time with a foot, but all the woman did was mumble something inaudible. Emily figured he was waiting for her to come around again before he tried whatever he was intending.

The gun Dale had left was in the kitchen cabinet. Emily would have to neutralize the man and his knife before she could get to it. She glanced at her dresser and tried to find something she could use to defend herself. A large pin was in the second drawer of her jewelry box. There was spray cologne she could use to try and blind him. Then she saw the body powder in the white plastic canister.

Emily warned him again. "If you leave now, I'll give you ten minutes before I call the police."

The man looked at her incredulously. "Say what?"

"That's the deal," Emily said. "Take it or leave it."

□ □ □

The balls on the bitch forced him to stop and think. James Sikes looked to his sister.

"What do you think?" he asked.

Kelly Ahearn was just coming around from her high. "I think we should go," she said.

Then the bitch said, "She's right. You should get out of here before you can't."

Sikes raised his knife menacingly. "You shut the fuck up!" he yelled. He was unnerved when the bitch didn't flinch.

## Chapter 47
## Minot/Velva, North Dakota

She was already terrified from the image of her daughter being kidnapped. When she saw who was holding the gun, Marsha couldn't breathe. It was the black man with the face mask, the same one she had told Dale about earlier in the week, the same one she had learned was a murderer the night before; he was holding the gun.

"Where's my daughter?" she asked, her voice barely above a whisper.

"Home probably," said the scarred woman, after slamming the door shut.

"Unless she's in school," the black man said.

Marsha was sitting between them. She looked from one to the other. "What do you want?"

"Shhhhh," the man said.

Then a cloth soaked in ether covered her face and everything went dark.

□ □ □

Morris couldn't tell how much time had passed but when he came to again, there was a woman tied up alongside him. He recognized the uniform the woman was wearing but the heroin left him disoriented.

He tried to listen to the conversations up front. His mind couldn't process the information. He heard the word "helicopter." He heard the phrase "beauty queen." He heard the name "Ahearn." He also heard a few dollar amounts.

Then a blonde woman with scars on her face was in the same room with him and the woman and he could hear clothes tearing.

□ □ □

Pavlik was out in the parking lot looking for the RV. When he saw the Winnebago turn south on Broadway, he sprinted to his rental. Driving like a madman through the parking lot and then onto South Broadway, he only slowed down again when he spotted the RV about half a mile ahead.

He had no phone and no way to stop for help without losing Singleton. He maintained a safe distance behind and searched for a police cruiser. He knew most of the police were focused on the fire in the Valley, but hoped he might see a stray cruiser somewhere along the main drag that was Broadway.

Desperate for communication, Pavlik considered pulling to the side of the road to ask for help, but then they were at the highway junction for 52 and he panicked when the Winnebago made the light up ahead. He had hoped it would have to stop. He thought about running the light himself when an eighteen-wheeler blocked his path.

□ □ □

Sikes couldn't believe his ears. He was holding a towel against his shoulder to stop the blood from where he had accidentally stabbed himself. The bitch had thrown perfumed powder in his face and blinded him. Then when he'd tried to cover his face he'd plunged the knife deep into his shoulder. It had been a sharp pain he felt when the blade struck bone.

Now he was still covered with the powder. He sneezed for the fifth time from the fragrance. And there the bitch was, holding a gun with one hand and holding up her cell phone with the other.

"You think I could wash my face?" he asked.

"Think about it," she said without looking at him.

Sikes turned and tapped the bathroom door with his foot. His sister had locked herself inside.

"You can come out now," he said.

"No way," she yelled.

"Great," Sikes said. "That's great."

□ □ □

When Don Ekroth regained consciousness, he was tied and gagged on a folding chair in a basement. He could see John Ahearn gathering clothes from the dryer and stashing them inside a suitcase. Ekroth also saw small stacks of cash and what appeared to be a plastic bag filled with white powder.

Ekroth was dizzy. His head throbbed. He closed his eyes to avoid the brightness of a naked bulb hanging from a wire directly overhead. He was jostled by a sudden shove.

"I'm gonna borrow your car," John Ahearn said. He was standing over Ekroth. He dangled a set of car keys from an index finger.

"My wife and brother-in-law will be here soon enough," Ahearn continued. "You tell them I said good-bye, okay?"

Ekroth closed his eyes again. He heard Ahearn taking the basement stairs. A few seconds later he heard the front door slam. He tried to relax in the chair, but his head continued to pound.

□ □ □

"There he is," Stewart said.

He was pointing at John Ahearn as the big man crossed the front yard. Ahearn was wearing a heavy coat that was still open. He walked quickly with his head down. He carried a suitcase in each hand.

Lynette stepped out of view. She checked on the two hostages in the rear bedroom and felt a measure of sympathy for the topless beauty queen. She closed the shutter doors, then grabbed the Beretta 9mm from the cabinet above the microwave and stood alongside the side door as the Winnebago slowed to a stop.

Stewart let the passenger window down. "Need a lift?" he said.

Ahearn was about to get inside the station wagon. He turned to Stewart and was surprised. "Hey, what are you doing out here?"

Stewart opened his hands as if presenting a picture. "What do you think?"

Ahearn said, "I didn't think you were the camping type."

Stewart heard the side door open. Ahearn was still holding the suitcases. "Hey, Lynette," Ahearn said.

Stewart reached under the seat for the Glock he had hidden there earlier. He lifted himself off the seat to better see out the passenger side window and was holding the gun in his left hand when he saw Ahearn reacting to Lynette and her gun.

"What's that for?" the big man said.

Stewart heard the first shot a moment before he saw Ahearn slam into the station wagon's open door. Ahearn's neck snapped back from the impact. He started to fall forward when Lynette fired another three shots. The impacts kept him standing a few seconds before his body dropped to the street.

Lynette grabbed both suitcases and was back inside the Winnebago. She hid the Beretta in a compartment in the console as she sat on the front seat. She looked to Stewart and smiled.

Stewart winked at his girlfriend and then pointed to the seatbelt harness.

"Oh," she said, then buckled in.

## Chapter 48
### Velva/Balfour, North Dakota

Pavlik followed the Winnebago east on Highway 52. Twenty minutes later the Winnebago pulled into the town of Velva. Pavlik drove past the town, then made a U-turn to head back. He used Main Street and drove across train tracks into the town itself. He saw the Winnebago had turned west onto Third Avenue. He drove up to Fourth Avenue, then drove around the block until he saw the Winnebago parked alongside a white station wagon. Pavlik drove past and caught a brief glimpse of the black man behind the wheel. He drove into a driveway further up the block and slumped down low in his seat.

Half a block ahead he saw a big man carrying two suitcases across a front yard. The big man walked around the front of the station wagon and opened the front door before he turned toward the Winnebago.

Pavlik watched as the man talked to someone inside the camper. Then the blonde woman appeared out of the side door and Pavlik sat up straight. She was hiding a handgun. She stepped toward the big man and pulled the gun. The big man jumped from the first shot. Then there were three more shots and Pavlik ducked as the woman turned around. When he looked again, he saw the woman carrying the two suitcases inside the camper. It was pulling away when he sat up straight again.

□ □ □

The last time he had tried to flee the country and the witness protection program he had made the mistake of involving people he couldn't control. The Russian gangster had ruined it for him by doing stupid shit at the last moment. Singleton/Stewart had become trapped in a bad situation when things became chaotic and a bullet took out his eye, half his cheek and had nearly killed him.

The fiasco back in New York had left a bitter taste in his mouth.

Now he was playing the game with a home-field advantage he never could have imagined ten years ago. Thanks to the United States Federal Government he had a new identity, four kilos of heroin, and four hundred thousand dollars in cash.

And this time he'd made his own game plan.

"What time you got?" Lynette asked.

Stewart glanced at the digital clock in the dashboard. "Two minutes to outa here," he said. "It's just over the hill there."

Lynette leaned across the console and held Stewart's right hand. He felt for her. Somehow he knew she could sense they wouldn't be together, that he was using her to help him get away. It was another con, but in Lynette's case he didn't enjoy running it. He'd hoped taking the beauty queen out of her usual spotlight might make Lynette feel better. The only attention Lynette had received until he came along were the stares from strangers because of her scars.

It was Lynette's feelings that had kept him from raping Miss North Dakota half an hour ago. Once he had torn the blouse off the beauty queen and exposed one of her breasts, Stewart saw the look on Lynette's face and stopped.

"They probably fake," he had said, but it was too late.

Lynette had pulled her sweatshirt up to examine her own breasts and Stewart had seen her frown.

Lynette had fallen in love with him. As much as he cared for her, this was about his survival and he couldn't let his feelings interfere. Morris had once called him a fucking sociopath for the way he'd treated another blonde he'd once used before he killed her. At least this time, he thought, he wouldn't have to kill Lynette. Not physically anyway.

"It's okay," he told her. "We close to Balfour now. You take this road to Jamestown. Give them both a dose each and catch that afternoon flight to Sioux Falls. We meet up tomorrow in Nebraska."

"What about the money?" Lynette said.

"You sure there's only twenty there?"

"Not even. Nineteen and change. He must've spent a few hundred."

"You sure?"

"I counted it twice."

"You take something for yourself. For the trip to Jamestown. Just in case."

"How much?"

"A few hundred. Put the rest in my bag."

"Will he be there, the colonel?" Lynette asked as she did what he'd asked. "I hate to leave you there and we don't know."

Stewart checked his side view mirror. He spotted a car off in the distance. "He'll be here," he said. "Man wants out of here just as bad as me."

"I can drive you in, just in case."

"No good. You keep going straight to Jamestown. Just in case anybody following. I can't see it now, but there was a car pulled in a driveway back in Velva. They had to see what happened to Ahearn. Anyway, you get pulled over, remember what I said, you tell them it was a guy named Jimmy Singleton killed Ahearn. Jimmy Singleton."

"I'm afraid for you," Lynette said.

They creased the top of the hill and Stewart could see the abandoned farmhouse, the barn with the collapsed roof and several small shacks about a quarter mile off to the right. He rode the brake down the hill as he slowed enough to stop at a dirt road.

"There it is," he said.

"I don't see a helicopter," Lynette said.

Stewart looked off beyond the barn and could see it flying low over a wheat field. He pointed to it. "There," he said. "Now, come here and kiss me good-bye."

He pulled her into his lap. They embraced. He kissed her long and hard on the mouth. She sobbed. He kissed her again before guiding her off his lap.

"Okay," he said. "You be strong. I'll be fine but you might run into something. This not over yet."

He gathered his bags and opened the side door. Lynette ran into his arms and they hugged one more time. Then Stewart stepped out of the Winnebago and jogged along the dirt road leading to the farm.

□ □ □

It was the hardest moment of her life, watching Washington Stewart leave. She had come to love the man. He had protected her from the first moment they met. Now she wanted to protect him.

As she watched Stewart heading toward the barn, Lynette sensed they would never be together again. Until the final moment when he left she had hoped that he would change his mind and take her with him.

Or he could've gone with her. They could have driven to Jamestown together or taken the Winnebago to Canada to start over up there. She'd wanted a second chance at life and she'd wanted it with Washington Stewart.

It had been wishful thinking, she realized. The best time of her life had just ended. There was nothing to go back to. She had one chance for happiness again. If she could make it to Jamestown in time for the flight to Sioux Falls, then the connecting flight to Omaha, Nebraska, they might be together again. If it was where Stewart was actually heading. She couldn't be sure.

She waited until a small car raced past the Winnebago. She watched Stewart once more as he neared the end of the dirt road. He stopped behind a small shack and turned to her. He set his bags down and waved at her to keep going. She sobbed one more time before she eased her foot off the brake.

She drove along the side of the road until she gained enough speed to veer onto the highway. She kept her foot on the gas as she tried to put distance between herself and the barn. She turned the radio on to hear if her murder of John Ahearn had made the news, remembered the helicopter and looked for it in her side view mirror. A bend in the road removed everything from her view and Lynette choked down another sob.

She was driving less than five minutes when she spotted the flashing lights up ahead. When she saw the ambulance, she thought it was okay and that she would just have to wait to pass the accident. It looked as though the patrol troopers on the scene were taking the drivers' information.

Then she saw the car that had raced past her a few minutes earlier. A tall man was talking to one of the troopers. He was pointing directly at the Winnebago.

▢ ▢ ▢

Pavlik was surprised to see the Winnebago stopped along the road when he first crested the hill. It was parked at the end of a dirt road that led to a farm off the highway. He maintained a steady speed as he passed, then checked his side and rearview mirrors until he spotted Singleton running toward the farmhouse.

He picked up speed to put distance between himself and the Winnebago. What he planned was to turn around as soon as the camper was out of his rearview mirror. Then he would double back to the barn and hope to hell that a state trooper would see him speeding and give chase.

Pavlik knew his luck was finally changing when he spotted the accident directly ahead. Two police cruisers and an ambulance were parked alongside the wreck. Pavlik drove off the highway and leaned on the horn as he pulled up behind the ambulance.

## Chapter 49
## Minot/Balfour/Velva, North Dakota

Colonel Robert Schmidt had prepared for this day since he first contracted for the murder of his wife. Escaping the Air Force base with a helicopter was easy enough. The tough part would come once they were in Mexico. So far Schmidt had been able to trust his partner. Things might change once they were alone with all that money and heroin.

Schmidt and Stewart had first met through an airman first class from the Minot Air Force base the doctor sometimes peddled prescription drugs to. There had been instant chemistry. It started when Schmidt inquired about Stewart's facial injuries and the killer told him about being shot in the face while working a sting for the government.

"Why would you tell me something like that?" Schmidt had asked. "Why would I believe it?"

"Because I can sense you're a man in need himself," Stewart had told him. "You moving product, you either need money or you planning something. Then there's your wife. Roger tells me she's out there banging half the base. Claims she's developed a particular taste for dark meat."

"And?"

"She's hiding it from you, trying to anyway, it means she's eyeing the pot."

"Can you help me?" Schmidt had asked.

They worked out the details and made an agreement to help one another. Stewart would kill Mrs. Schmidt. Schmidt would fly Stewart out of the country. They would be partners in their escape and with the Afghanistan heroin that had fallen into Schmidt's lap before he met Stewart. When they reached Mexico, they would decide what to do next.

Schmidt had already cleaned out the savings he'd been transferring to a safe deposit box the last few months. He was flush with cash no matter what happened. He knew he couldn't trust Stewart for long and he'd brought along a two shot derringer just in case.

For now he was delivering on his end of the agreement. He brought the chopper in close alongside the barn. He looked for Stewart but saw a car instead. The car stopped about twenty-five yards from the barn. There were two men inside. Neither man moved to get out.

Schmidt checked his watch. He was exactly on time. If Stewart made it within the next ten minutes, Schmidt figured he could land the chopper outside of Bismarck within the next hour.

He set a stopwatch for twenty minutes, the maximum time they had both agreed he would wait before taking off by himself.

□ □ □

Pavlik had told the highway patrolmen what was going on, then one of them got in the rental. The other patrolman used his radio to try and locate Detective Hehn as Pavlik raced west back toward the barn alongside the highway. Pavlik could see the blonde-haired woman behind the wheel of the Winnebago as they sped past.

They were on the highway less than three minutes when Pavlik's eyes opened wide as he spotted the helicopter approaching the barn and pointed to it as he drove across the highway. He headed for the farmhouse driveway and parked no more than fifty feet from an abandoned barn. The chopper hovered directly above the barn.

□ □ □

Dale was fortunate he wasn't burned when the second explosion sent flames shooting in all directions. He'd been knocked to the ground from the blast. When he rolled over he could see the roof of the garage adjacent to the driveway had caught fire. Then two of Minot's firemen helped him to his feet and walked him back out to the street.

He was toweling some of the soot from his face when one of Minot's police officers ran up to him with a message about shots fired in the town of Velva. Suddenly panicked, Dale used the officer's radio to call the Velva police. He asked about Don Ekroth and was relieved to learn his friend was okay. Ekroth had been assaulted and was probably suffering the aftereffects of a concussion, but Dale was assured his friend would be brought to Trinity Hospital in another few minutes.

"Who was it was shot?" Dale asked.

"Our town pain in the ass," the Velva officer said.

"Ahearn?" Dale said.

"Bingo."

"Anybody see who did it?"

"Nobody's volunteering anything. Not yet. My guess is they want to wait until Ahearn is in the ground."

Dale frowned on his end of the call. "Can I speak with Don?" he asked.

"Right now he's got a good size lump on the side of his head that's being treated by EMS, so I doubt they'll let him talk, but we just got a call for an all points further east on 52. I'd go there myself if it wasn't for the mess I have here."

"What's that about, the all points?"

"Hostage situation, apparently. Something to do with a former Miss North Dakota."

Dale was back in his car and on his way. He used his siren to bypass the lights on Broadway and was on Highway 52 heading east within minutes. When he saw the military helicopter off to the right a few miles after Velva, Dale assumed it was providing surveillance for the situation up ahead. He passed a car speeding back the other way and continued driving until he pulled up behind a Winnebago.

A woman inside the camper had a handgun and was holding two hostages. One of the troopers had crawled underneath and placed a cell phone on the steps inside the side door. Dale spoke with the woman from another phone.

"What's your name, ma'am?" he asked.

"Lynette," the woman said through a giggle. "What's yours, hon?"

"Detective Dale Hehn," he said. "Who do you have inside the camper?"

"Some FBI guy," she said. Her voice seemed impaired. "And a former Miss North Dakota," she added.

Dale felt his heart sink. "Can you release them, please?"

"No way," the woman said. "Not yet."

"What about the woman?" Dale asked. "Can you let her go?"

"Not yet."

Dale said, "Can I speak to the woman?"

"N-no."

"Can I speak to the man, the agent?"

"No."

"Then how do I know they're not harmed?"

"You don't."

"That won't work, ma'am. I need to know they're okay."

"Too bad."

"Ma'am?"

"Don't bother me now," she said. "I need a fix and I'm getting really fucking cranky."

She killed the call. Dale tried calling back but she didn't answer.

□  □  □

Lynette was sweating from anxiety. Leaving Stewart had shaken her. She had swallowed three Halcion pills and washed them down with a beer.

Now she was irritable from the drowsiness. She wanted a fix. She wanted to lie down and sleep. She wanted to hold Stewart again.

They had left a cell phone on the steps. She used it to talk with first one cop and then another. Her job was to delay and distract the police if she ran into trouble. She was doing her best.

When she glanced out the windshield, she saw it was over. There were police cars everywhere. She thought about driving through the roadblock, but the scene she imagined in her mind's eye frightened her: She would run the gauntlet of cars until they shot out the tires and the Winnebago broke down.

She sat on the kitchen bench and set the gun on the table. The detective was calling on the cell phone again. She ignored it until it became annoying. Then she turned the phone off.

Then there was a knock on the side door of the Winnebago. Lynette frowned at the sound before reaching for the gun.

□ □ □

Stewart waited in the shed where he had parked a motorcycle earlier in the week in case the chopper didn't show. His alternate plan, if need be, was to use the tinted helmet and cycle to drive straight west through Minot and the rest of the state into Montana.

He wasn't sure if Lynette would make it to Jamestown. Killing Ahearn had been a wild card Stewart hadn't counted on.

He heard the helicopter at the same time he spotted the light blue car heading toward the barn from the highway.

"Shit," Stewart said.

He racked the slide on his Glock and peeked out from behind the shed door. The helicopter was close. The whirring sound of the blades was distinct in the quiet countryside.

The car crossed the yard and headed straight toward the barn. Stewart stepped out of the shed and ran along the back side of the barn. He stepped through a hole in the back wall and was inside. The darkness was calming.

He used the few streaks of sunlight provided by holes in the roof to navigate his way across the barn. He could hear the blades of the helicopter as he passed through the front doors. He looked up and saw the car was a few yards ahead.

□ □ □

He made his way around the camper to the side door. He held his Smith & Wesson .380 tight against his chest. The bulletproof vest was heavy and uncomfortable. He adjusted it by shifting his shoulders.

Dale knocked a second time before he turned the doorknob to the camper and pushed the door slightly ajar. He tried to use the rearview mirror to see where the woman was inside the RV, but couldn't locate her. He took two careful steps and peeked around the door.

The woman stood next to the galley table. A 9mm was set on the edge of the table. The woman was short and badly scarred in the face. Dale noticed her hand was poised over the handgun. He asked her to please step away from the table.

"What's the point?" she asked.

"Please, ma'am," Dale said. He had turned his body on the stairs. All he need do was step out and shoot. He had her whenever he was ready.

"James Singleton killed John Ahearn," she said.

"Excuse me?" Dale said. "What's that, ma'am?"

It was a good sign. So long as she talked, it was good, he thought.

"There are hostages in the back," she added. "They're both okay. The woman was topless for a few minutes. I gave her one of my shirts."

"Please step away, ma'am."

"The agent had a few hits of heroin."

"Ma'am, please."

"The woman is fine, though."

"Ma'am?"

Dale swallowed hard when he heard the sound of the rack sliding. He called again, louder this time.

"Ma'am!"

The gunshot startled him. He dropped to the floor of the camper and aimed his weapon up where the woman had been, except now she wasn't there. He looked straight across the floor and saw her leg twitching. He crawled across the floor and saw she had shot herself. He cradled her bleeding head as the last of her life ebbed. Just a few seconds passed before her leg went still along with her heart.

## Chapter 50
## Balfour, North Dakota

Pavlik didn't see Singleton but he knew the chopper was there for the killer. He assumed it was another government operation that had gone bad and that they were taking their prize witness out of harm's way one more time in his criminal life.

The trooper pulled up to within fifty yards of where the helicopter was hovering. Nearly ten minutes had passed before it finally touched ground. Pavlik and the trooper stepped out of the car. The trooper showed his weapon and the pilot waved.

Pavlik realized the pilot wasn't waving at them and looked to his right. James Singleton, his face half covered with a mask, was holding a gun less than ten yards away. There were two luggage bags on the ground at Singleton's sides. The killer pointed his gun directly at the trooper.

"Drop it," he said.

The trooper glanced at Pavlik.

"I won't ask you again," Singleton said.

The trooper let go of his weapon.

"What did you do with the woman, Jimmy?" Pavlik asked.

Singleton looked from the trooper to Pavlik. "I know you?"

It was the first time Pavlik had ever heard the man speak. "What you do to her?" he asked again.

"You the New York cop?"

Pavlik remained silent.

"I see," Singleton said. "Miss North Dakota fine."

"I was there the first time you tried to kill Eddie and Diane Senta," Pavlik said.

Singleton smiled as he turned the gun on Pavlik. "And now you come all the way out here to die? That a damn shame."

"You gonna shoot me, too?" Pavlik asked. "The FBI let you do that, shoot cops?"

Singleton fired his gun. Pavlik felt the kick in his left shoulder and turned from the force of the impact.

Singleton shrugged as he aimed the gun back at the trooper.

□  □  □

Dale had picked up the radio message about the helicopter and instructed a trooper to notify the state air patrol and the Air Force. Then he got into his car and headed back to the barn. Speeding the entire way, Dale covered the distance in just a few minutes.

The chopper was already on the ground. Dale crossed the highway and stopped about four hundred yards from the farmhouse. He popped the trunk of his car and pulled out his hunting rifle and an old blanket. He rolled the blanket up and placed it on the hood of the car as a rest for his Winchester 70. He estimated the range to be about 400 yards. He remembered making longer shots back in the Sandbox, but his 7mm magnum would be maxing out at this range. The air was still, so he had no worries about wind drift, but the light 140 grain bullet would be dropping almost a foot and a half at this distance. He steadied himself and placed the crosshairs a few inches above the man with the gun's head.

He could see Alex Pavlik and a trooper standing defenseless between the chopper and the masked man holding the handgun. The gun seemed to be aimed at Pavlik. Dale was about to fire when the masked man fired first and Pavlik spun to his left.

Dale pulled the trigger and the rifle barked. He cranked in a fresh round, but it wouldn't be necessary. The masked man was on his back. Dale sighted him anyway, just in case. Dale watched through the scope until he was satisfied the masked man was dead.

The helicopter took off to the right and headed south. Dale turned his attention to Alex Pavlik. The trooper was already attending to him. Dale used the scope of the rifle to see that Pavlik was conscious. He moved his scope to the right and could tell it was a shoulder wound.

Dale waited until he saw Pavlik was talking again before he could let his body relax. He took a deep breath before getting in the car and calling for ambulances.

## Part V

## Chapter 51
## Minot, North Dakota

Emily had just signed the complaint against James Sikes and Kelly Ahearn at the Minot Police Station when Dale called. She had heard some of what was going on at the front desk and was relieved to hear the word-of-mouth reports were correct; Alex Pavlik had been wounded in the shoulder but was okay. Dale was safe.

He explained what had happened to Don Ekroth and how a woman "had killed herself not ten feet from where I was on the steps inside in the Winnebago."

"Jesus, Dale."

"It was horrible. She was with the guy Pavlik was looking for. She helped kidnap Marsha Nordstrom from the lounge."

Emily hesitated. "Is Marsha okay?"

"She is now, yeah. They kidnapped her and might've taken some liberties, except she said they didn't. They also had some FBI big shot tied in the RV, believe it or not. We have to assume they were taken as hostages."

"Did you shoot him?" Emily asked. "The man with the mask."

Dale coughed on his end of the line.

"Dale?"

"Yeah, honey, I did."

"Are you okay?"

"I'm okay, yeah."

"Where are you?"

"Trinity. Pavlik is being treated for the shoulder wound and his girl-friend is here from New York."

"And Marsha is okay?"

"Yeah. She's down in emergency. She was shook up pretty good. Something to do with her daughter, how they got her to get inside the RV. The woman who killed herself and the guy Pavlik was after told Marsha they'd kidnapped her daughter."

"Oh, my God."

"The kid was in school, but it got her inside the RV. The FBI guy was given a dose or two of heroin. He was the handler, Pavlik said. The same guy he had a run-in with back in New York a few years ago."

"Is Pavlik going to do anything about the FBI holding him in his room?"

"I don't know. I didn't ask. I'm not sure. The FBI guy will be here in the hospital another day. At least until his system is clean."

"They shot him with heroin?"

"What it looks like, yeah. I don't know any more than that, though, except the place is packed with agents. I don't think I've ever seen so many, not even in the movies. Pavlik was right about this."

"There was some word on Jim Salinger up in Mohall," Emily told him. "I overheard it at the front desk. He's going to be okay, Dale. He'll have to retire and go through a lot of therapy, but he'll be okay. They're replacing both his hips."

"Christ. I'll make sure and pass it along to Don."

"When can I see you?"

"You're finished at the station?"

"Yes."

"Everything okay there?"

Emily wasn't about to go into what had happened in their bedroom now. She was too anxious to hold him.

"Everything is fine," she said.

"Great," Dale said. "Why don't you come over to Trinity?"

"I'm on my way."

□   □   □

When Marsha Nordstrom first learned that her daughter had been in school all day, she broke down sobbing. She hadn't been able to tell if her kidnappers were lying or not about abducting her daughter, but when she finally learned her daughter had been safe all along she couldn't restrain her emotions. An hour later she was exhausted and wanted to go home. The emergency room physician had asked her to stay a little while longer until the sedatives she had been given wore off.

She reluctantly agreed. A few minutes later a blonde woman with heavy freckles and an Irish accent rushed into the emergency room and frantically asked for Alex Pavlik. She was an attractive woman, probably in her early forties, Marsha thought. She had fair skin and bright green eyes.

Marsha guessed it was his girlfriend and felt a pang of jealousy. When she heard the concern in the woman's voice, her jealousy turned to guilt.

The woman was talking with the attending physician. A few minutes later she was led out by a security guard. When the physician returned to see how Marsha was doing, she asked him who the woman with the accent was.

"Her boyfriend is one of our patients upstairs," the physician said. "The guy on the news before. He was shot in the shoulder. He'll be okay, but I'm not so sure about his girlfriend. She's a wreck. Apparently she learned what happened from one of the televisions at the airport after she landed. Imagine?"

"That's horrible," Marsha said.

"I think her accent was Irish. She certainly had enough freckles."

"She's pretty."

"Very, especially if you like freckles," he said. "I'll bet North Dakota seems like Mars to her, though. At least it's warming up."

"Is her boyfriend out of surgery?"

"He's already in recovery. It wasn't complicated. Clean wound. He'll have pain the next few weeks, but he'll be fine. One of our guys from here saved him, you know. Killed the guy with a deer rifle or something."

"Dale Hehn," Marsha said.

"That's it, yeah. He's one our guys here in Minot. Makes one proud, huh?"

"He's a war hero."

"It doesn't surprise me. He's probably that woman's hero too right now."

Marsha smiled at the irony and decided to change the subject.

"Can someone call me a car to get home?" she asked.

◻ ◻ ◻

Special Agent Gregory Feller showed Alex Pavlik half a dozen still photographs of him having dinner with Marsha Nordstrom. He showed another half dozen of Pavlik driving with the former Miss North Dakota in his rental, getting out at her house and of the two of them going inside.

Pavlik's shoulder had already been cleaned and bandaged. He handed the pictures back to the special agent.

"So I don't talk," he said. "Nice."

"We could've had you arrested for assaulting a federal agent," Feller said.

"Except then there'd've been a record," Pavlik said. He stared into Feller's eyes until the agent shrugged. "Besides, it wasn't me."

"We know that now. We know you had help."

"Was a miracle. Sort of like the loaves and fishes, but where were you two geniuses when your boss was getting his ass stabbed with heroin needles?"

"There was a bomb went off near a school in town. We're trained to respond in case of terrorism."

Pavlik chuckled.

"Just doing our jobs," Feller said.

"Yeah, I remember. Your boss okay?"

"He's recovering."

"How'd Singleton get the jump on him so easy?"

"Morphine."

Pavlik smirked. "The Effa-bee-eye," he said.

"Could've happened to anyone," Feller said.

"Yeah, sure," Pavlik said. "And now I have to eat being kidnapped by you clowns because you losers had nothing better to do than follow me around Minot."

"What do I tell my superiors, sir?"

"Tell them they have a deal," Pavlik said. "Then to go fuck themselves."

Feller half smiled as he gathered the pictures and jammed them inside an envelope.

Pavlik said, "That's a real shit job you have there, sonny. I hope you know that."

Feller left Pavlik without saying another word. A few minutes later Pavlik spotted Aelish. Her eyes were red from crying.

"Jesus!" he gasped.

She rushed to his side and leaned over to kiss him. She sobbed hard when he leaned into her.

"I told you not to come," he whispered. A surge of guilt overwhelmed him. "Now your eyes are all bloodshot," he added.

"I couldn't sleep," she said. "Last night or on the plane out here. I was worried sick."

"I hope you brought your mittens."

"They said the weather is breaking. I never felt cold like this before."

"You should've been here the last few days."

She lightly slapped the side of his bed. "I was sure you'd get yourself in trouble and I was right."

"He's dead, though," Pavlik said. "This time at least Singleton is dead."

"Bollocks. And so almost were you. Do you have any idea how scared I was?"

"All a waste of energy."

"Maybe, but a woman can get stupid sometimes. Maybe think she loves a lummox like you and then she gets stung for it."

Pavlik remembered what Marsha had told him about keeping things to himself. He swallowed hard now to bury it.

"What?" Aelish asked.

Pavlik shook his head. He briefly imagined what would have happened had Aelish walked in the room a few minutes earlier when a special agent of the FBI was flashing pictures of him with another woman.

"You happen to bring a checkbook?" he said.

"No, but I have credit cards. So do you. Why?"

"A donation."

Aelish's eyebrows furrowed. "I can make a withdrawal off a card and get a bank check. What's it for?"

"The Republic of Lakotah."

"Excuse me?"

"I'll explain it later, but you'll be happy I did it, trust me. It'll be a big donation."

Aelish's eyebrows remained furrowed. "Fine," she said. "Is it over now? Can we go home?"

"Yeah, we can go home first thing in the morning, unless they need me for something else. I assume they won't."

"The news says it was one of the local police killed him. Did you know him?"

"Yeah, I just met him the night before. Dale Hehn his name is. He nailed Singleton from a good distance with a rifle. He saved my ass with that shot."

"I guess I owe him, huh?"

"Only if you still want me around."

"Like I said, sometimes a woman can be stupid that way."

## Mandan, North Dakota

Colonel Robert Schmidt was forced to land on a farm outside of Mandan, North Dakota. He frowned when he realized how close he was to the small town of Lincoln, where the second leg of the trip to Mexico was to begin. The two F-15 Fighting Falcons sent from the Grand Forks Air Force Base had buzzed the helicopter twice before one of the pilots made direct communication. With no way to escape, Schmidt set the chopper down in a large flat field.

By the time he was out of the helicopter a string of police cruisers could be seen headed his way in the distance. Schmidt saw he could make it to the farmhouse first. He pulled the two shot derringer he had brought along and was surprised when he saw an old man standing on a porch holding a shotgun.

"You can put that away," Schmidt told the old timer. "There's some kind of mix-up. I'm a colonel in the Air Force."

The old man didn't budge. He raised the shotgun up so it was pointed at Schmidt's chest instead.

"Hey, no need for that," Schmidt said, this time slowing down to stop at the front gate. He figured there was a good ten yards between them. He would need to get closer before he could jump the old bastard.

"I'm a doctor," Schmidt added. "And a colonel."

"And some kind of a criminal, too," the old man said. "I'm just listening to it on the television."

"It's all a mistake," Schmidt said. "Really."

"Why don't you drop your gun just for the hell of it then?" the old man said. "I don't have the reflexes I used to. Gun might go off accidental, I get nervous."

Schmidt could see the police cruisers were maybe half a mile away. There was no escaping unless he grabbed the old man hostage. Even then, he knew he couldn't get away, but Schmidt wasn't about to go down without a fight.

And there was no way he'd let this old bastard stop him.

"Easy, feller," the old man said. "You get too close and I'll shoot."

Schmidt was through the gate and slowly making his way closer. "Come on, gramps," he said. "I'm your friend here."

"Don't take another step, son," the old man said.

Schmidt stopped but didn't drop the derringer.

"Let go the gun," the old man said.

Schmidt glanced back over his shoulder and saw the string of police cruisers had closed the gap by half. He dropped down to a firing crouch and began to aim the derringer when the shotgun blast hit him full in the face.

THE END

# More books from Stark House Press

1-933586-26-5 **Benjamin Appel** Sweet Money Girl / Life and Death of a Tough Guy $21.95

0-9749438-7-8 **Algernon Blackwood** Julian LeVallon / The Bright Messenger $21.95

1-933586-03-6 **Malcolm Braly** Shake Him Till He Rattles / It's Cold Out There $19.95

1-933586-10-9 **Gil Brewer** Wild to Possess / A Taste for Sin $19.95

1-933586-20-6 **Gil Brewer** A Devil for O'Shaugnessy / The Three-Way Split $14.95

1-933586-24-9 **W. R. Burnett** It's Always Four O'Clock / Iron Man $19.95

1-933586-38-9 **James Hadley Chase** Come Easy--Go Easy / In a Vain Shadow $19.95

1-933586-30-3 **Jada M. Davis** One for Hell $19.95

1-933586-34-6 **Don Elliott** Gang Girl / Sex Bum $19.95

1-933586-12-5 **A. S. Fleischman** Look Behind You Lady / The Venetian Blonde $19.95

1-933568-28-1 **A. S. Fleischman** Danger in Paradise / Malay Woman $19.95

1-933586-35-4 **Orrie Hitt** The Cheaters / Dial "M" for Man $19.95

0-9667848-7-1 **Elisabeth Sanxay Holding** Lady Killer / Miasma $19.95

0-9667848-9-8 **Elisabeth Sanxay Holding** The Death Wish / Net of Cobwebs $19.95

0-9749438-5-1 **Elisabeth Sanxay Holding** Strange Crime in Bermuda / Too Many Bottles $19.95

1-933586-16-8 **Elisabeth Sanxay Holding** The Old Battle Ax / Dark Power $19.95

1-933586-17-6 **Russell James** Underground / Collected Stories $14.95

0-9749438-8-6 **Day Keene** Framed in Guilt / My Flesh is Sweet $19.95

1-933586-33-8 **Day Keene** Dead Dolls Don't Talk / Hunt the Killer / Too Hot to Hold $23.95

1-933586-21-4 **Mercedes Lambert** Dogtown / Soultown $14.95

1-933586-14-1 **Dan Marlowe/Fletcher Flora/Charles Runyon** Trio of Gold Medals $15.95

1-933586-07-9 **Ed by McCarthy & Gorman** Invasion of the Body Snatchers: A Tribute $19.95

1-933586-09-5 **Margaret Millar** An Air That Kills / Do Evil in Return $19.95

1-933586-23-0 **Wade Miller** The Killer / Devil on Two Sticks $17.95

0-9749438-3-5 **Vin Packer** Something in the Shadows / Intimate Victims $19.95

1-933586-05-2 **Vin Packer** Whisper His Sin / The Evil Friendship $19.95

1-933586-18-4 **Richard Powell** A Shot in the Dark / Shell Game $14.95

1-933586-19-2 **Bill Pronzini** Snowbound / Games $14.95

0-9667848-8-x **Peter Rabe** The Box / Journey Into Terror $21.95

0-9749438-4-3 **Peter Rabe** Murder Me for Nickels / Benny Muscles In $19.95

1-933586-00-1 **Peter Rabe** Blood on the Desert / A House in Naples $21.95

1-933586-11-7 **Peter Rabe** My Lovely Executioner / Agreement to Kill $19.95

1-933586-22-2 **Peter Rabe** Anatomy of a Killer / A Shroud for Jesso $14.95

1-933586-32-x **Peter Rabe** The Silent Wall / The Return of Marvin Palaver $19.95

0-9749438-2-7 **Douglas Sanderson** Pure Sweet Hell / Catch a Fallen Starlet $19.95

1-933586-06-0 **Douglas Sanderson** The Deadly Dames / A Dum-Dum for the President $19.95

1-933586-29-X **Charlie Stella** Johnny Porno $15.95

1-933586-08-7 **Harry Whittington** A Night for Screaming / Any Woman He Wanted $19.95

1-933586-25-7 **Harry Whittington** To Find Cora / Like Mink Like Murder / Body and Passion $23.95

1-933586-36-2 **Harry Whittington** Rapture Alley / Winter Girl / Strictly for the Boys $23.95

**Stark House Press**
**4720 Herron Road, Eureka, CA 95503**
**707-498-3135**
**www.StarkHousePress.com**